By Right of Blood

Lorrieann Russell

By Right of Blood

Edin Road Press

This book is a work of fiction. Although certain real locations, events and public figures are mentioned, all names, characters, places and events described herein are the product of the author's imagination or are used fictitiously. Any resemblance to actual events, places or persons (living or dead) is purely coincidental.

On the Web:
www.facebook.com/lorrieannrussell

Jacket art and Interior book design by the author

Dedication

To my husband, Toby, for his love and for showing me the way to the summit.

Prologue

Fylbrigge Manor, Aberdoir Scotland

29 May 1588

"ONE MORE, DEAR; one more," the midwife urged. Lady Cyslie Fylbrigge, exhausted and near the end of her labors to deliver the child, twisted the linen straps at the sides of the bed in her weakening grip, crying out, "Sweet Brighid, I cannot!"

"It is almost over, m' lady," the midwife said quietly. "Rebecca, is the knife ready?"

"Yes, Mehgrit," Rebecca presented the blade on a piece of hot linen.

"Push, m' lady!"

"I cannot," Cyslie moaned. "So... tired."

"She's failing, Mehgrit," Rebecca whispered, reaching for a cool cloth for Cyslie's forehead.

Mehgrit nodded her agreement. "The child is near, I see the head. One more, please, m' lady. We cannot lose you both," she added, almost silently.

Rebecca caught her breath, stifling the urge to cry, and continued to mop her mistress' brow with the cool cloth. "Please, Blessed Mother, grant that we lose neither." Cyslie's hand went limp. "No... m' lady, the bairn will need his mother. Please, one more," she pleaded, and forced an encouraging smile though her heart was breaking. Her own loins ached in empathy with Cyslie's struggles as she was only two weeks out of child bed—her own child lost to her at his birth.

Mehgrit, mindful of Rebecca's heartache, suggested allowing Cyslie's daughter-in-law, Bryndah, attend the lady in her place. Rebecca bristled at the mere thought of allowing 'that woman' come anywhere near the birth room. and Rebecca assured Mehgrit that she truly wanted to be with her mistress when the child arrived, just as Cyslie had sat vigil during her own labors. Cyslie had held her hand and mopped her brow, uttering her encouragements as she struggled to deliver her son. But the child was small and failed to thrive. He died at her breast only an hour after his birth. Cyslie had been her strength then and Rebecca was determined to be strong for her lady now. "Please," she said again, tears staining her false smile. "Please. One more push, m' lady."

Cyslie turned her head, fixing her fading eyes on Rebecca. "Child, I am too old. Was a foolish dream."

"No, m' lady. You're a strong woman, you'll see. This is the child you have longed for and he shall be your joy." She took Cyslie's hand in her own and squeezed.

Cyslie squeezed back, a faint smile coming to her face. "One more." Her face twisted into a mask of pain, as she gave her last bit of strength to push her child from her womb to the waiting hands of the midwife. Her grip tightened painfully around Rebecca's fingers and she cried out as the child passed from her loins.

"'Tis a boy child!" Mehgrit exclaimed, as the child's birth-cries mingled with the cries of his mother as the midwife bound and cut the birth tether, fully separating him from his mother. "M' lady, you have a son!"

Rebecca felt her mistress' hand slip from her own. Cyslie's breath grew shallow, her eyes half closed.

"M' lady?" Rebecca looked to Mehgrit to see the aged midwife shake her head. "Let me hold him close to her." She reached out to take the child from Mehgrit and placed him on his mother's bosom, folding Cyslie's arm around him. "Your son, m' lady."

Cyslie's head turned slightly toward the mewling child, her eyes blinking slowly. The babe quieted for a moment, looking up at his mother with his languid newborn eyes. She smiled and slowly drew up her hand to stroke his tiny cheek. "William," she said in a whisper, then let her hand fall away.

Rebecca caught the child, William, before he rolled away and clutched him up to her own bereft bosom, as she would her own babe. "Poor lamb. There, there little one... I'll take care o' you... Shh."

In his salon on the opposite end of Fylbrigge Manor, Lord Henry Fylbrigge, the current earl of Aberdoir, sat by his window staring out at the green hills of his estate. The goblet he held had been empty for the better part of an hour, though he was barely conscious of it dangling from his hand. His thoughts were only on his wife and the child she was laboring to deliver; Cyslie's time had come earlier than expected.

The last month had been especially difficult for Cyslie, and Henry had staunchly resisted being away from the manor for more than a few hours at any time. Most matters of the estate were put on hold, however, certain business promises could not be left undone. Lord Edward Stonehaven, his good friend and the duke that he served, was expecting the delivery of a pair of thoroughbred hunters to him at his home at Drumoak Castle in Stonehaven, a day's journey north of Aberdoir. The horses were to be a gift to the king on the occasion of His Majesty's first and only visit to Stonehaven. Certainly, that could not be put off. Henry had reluctantly sent for his son, Thomas, to fulfill the obligation. Thomas was more than willing— eager, in fact— to be of help to his father. Thomas never impressed Henry as possessing much of a business mind; he'd always seemed more interested in less important pursuits such as jousts and hunts. Henry was, therefore, pleasantly surprised when Thomas had handled the delivery so efficiently, even negotiating the sale of another horse for Lady Anne, Lord Edward's wife. In fact, Thomas had proven himself an invaluable asset and had impressed Lord Edward enough that the duke granted Thomas his daughter Bryndah's hand in marriage, a union that pleased Henry greatly. Henry felt a wave of relief knowing his eldest son was showing an interest in the well being of the Fylbrigge family... especially now, as Henry suspected he was dying.

The cough had been barely noticeable a month ago, no more than a slight annoyance he had attributed it to the unusually cold April weather. With each passing week, though, the cough lingered; his breath became more labored and painful, and the handkerchief he carried bore the constant tell-tale crimson stain of consumption. The nostrums and broths Bryndah prepared for him would ease the symptoms temporarily but always, the cough would return. Henry ordered the household staff to withhold the news of his failing health from his wife, fearful that it would affect the child she carried and though it pained him to do so, he had found excuses to seclude himself from her.

He sat waiting for word from the birthing chamber, musing about the son or daughter that was coming into the world. A miracle, he thought, as Cyslie was nearing forty and he forty-four. Neither had dreamed they'd ever be blessed with another child; Thomas was nearly twenty-one and their only surviving child until now. In the years since Thomas' birth, Cyslie suffered three miscarriages, one stillborn daughter, and the loss of another son who had lived but three months. Henry did not allow himself to become optimistic that this child would be born and survive but now, sitting and waiting for the midwife, he prayed with all his heart that this little one would survive to someday join his brother in the furthering of the Fylbrigge family.

"Father?"

Henry turned, allowing the goblet to fall to the floor. "Is there word?"

"We came to ask that of you," Thomas replied, as he stood aside to allow his wife to enter the room before him. "We've only just heard that Mother is in her lying in."

Bryndah rushed to Henry and took his hand in her own. "Why did you not call for me? Surely Lady Cyslie is expecting me. After all she was with me when our Richard, was born, and I promised I would be there—"

"Forgive me, my dear," Henry interrupted, squeezing her hand. "It all began in the small hours and my mind is not thinking clearly. If you wish, you may go in... but I'm sure Mehgrit has everything well in hand."

Bryndah gave his hand a squeeze in return, then beamed a charming smile toward him. "I'm sure she has. But, for my own peace of mind, I think I shall go and see for myself how my lady does. I'm sure it will ease your mind as well."

"And mine," Thomas added. "Mother has been so frail. I fear for her."

"Your mother has never been frail, Thomas," Henry said, rubbing his eyes. "She's merely weary with her burden."

"Of course," Bryndah interjected, "but she is not a young woman to be in child bed."

Henry shook his head, finding no argument to offer. "Aye, well, she's been stout of heart through all the others. God be willing, she is fine and the child is strong." He smiled at the thought of the child. "Another Fylbrigge, Thomas, at long last. You shall not be left to deal with this place by yourself in your old age after all. Perhaps, in years to come, the whole of Scotland will come to the Fylbrigge brothers for the best horses in the highlands and beyond. Or, if it be a lass, then she will be wed to a proud clan and the family will prosper even more. Won't that be lovely?" He looked up to see Thomas and Bryndah exchanging an odd look. "Do you disagree?"

"Oh," Thomas began, smiling, taking his father's hand. "Of course not, Father. It shall be... simply wonderful. I've always wanted a... brother to share in the family business."

"He'll be a wonderful companion to our little Richard, Thomas," Bryndah cooed sweetly, with a note of quiet caution, "if he survives."

Thomas nodded, sympathetically. "Ah, yes. Father you must prepare yourself for the eventuality that the child will not thrive."

"Aye, it is best to prepare for such," Bryndah agreed.

Henry opened his mouth to retort when a fresh spate of coughing seized him. Bryndah hurried to him, taking his arm and leading him to his chair. "Please Father, you mustn't allow yourself to worry. You see how it brings on the cough."

When the spell passed, Henry managed a half-hearted smile

of gratitude. "You do care for me, don't you, my dear." Another small cough and he turned to his son. "Aye, Thomas, *I know* there is the possibility the child will whither and it is more than likely he'll go the way of the others. And I am mindful that you have a fine and strong son of your own to share in the family fortune. But if you please, allow me my moment of hope and happy daydreams. I am awaiting a birth after all, not planning a funeral... just yet."

Thomas patted his father on the shoulder. "Of course."

The chamber door swung open quietly and Mehgrit slipped in.

"Well?" Thomas and Bryndah said, together.

Mehgrit looked from one face to the next, then ignoring both went directly to Lord Henry. "My lord... I'm sorry."

Henry drew a long, staggered breath, drawing his hand to his face as another round of coughing seized him.

"Easy, Father. Bryndah, some wine for him, if you please," Thomas said quietly.

"My lord," Mehgrit began, taking a step forward.

"You've delivered your news, now leave us," Bryndah snapped, then turned a soothing look to Henry, holding a goblet of red wine. "There, there, Father, drink this. It will quiet your lungs."

"But, my lord... you don't understand. Your son—"

"I said, leave!" Bryndah repeated.

Henry raised his hand to Bryndah, giving a hopeful look to Mehgrit.

Bryndah demurred with an apologetic smile. "Forgive me, Mehgrit. Please, go on," she said, resuming her sweet tone.

Mehgrit pursed her lips and took a tentative step forward, the lines in her face deepening. "My lord, you have a son. He is small for coming early, but he seems to be well and strong. She called him William, m' lord."

"A son. William?" Henry repeated the words silently, his eyes welling with tears. "Called? Mehgrit? Tell me... the rest," he said, though in his heart he knew what she would tell him.

"She worked so hard, m' lord. The child would not turn and took so long a time... I did all I could to deliver her, but in the end... " she sniffed into her apron before finishing, "... she named the child with her last breath."

"She's dead?" Bryndah blurted loudly, an odd chuckle in her voice. Thomas nudged her with his elbow and she silenced herself.

"Yes, m' lady," Mehgrit replied, with a non-apologetic glare toward Brynda.

Henry looked toward Bryndah in time to catch the hint of excitement in his daughter-in-law's eye, a look that sent a shudder of sudden revulsion like a blow to his stomach. He pulled away from her and the look vanished from her face. Thomas stood beside her, his head lowered, a hand shading his eyes as he drew a sorrowful breath. "My poor dear mother," he said in what sounded to Henry to be an exaggerated display of grief. "May God rest her soul in peace. 'Tis nearly certain the child shall fail to thrive and follow her to the grave."

"The child *is* thriving, sir," Mehgrit reminded him firmly, an angry challenge in her voice. "And may God grant him a long and happy life!"

Thomas' eyes flared at her, showing no trace of the sorrow he'd proclaimed for his mother a moment before. He raised an authoritarian hand, as if to strike Mehgrit for her tone, but Bryndah nudged his arm and warned him with a quick gesture toward Henry. Thomas steeled his jaw but lowered his hand, giving half a glance toward his father.

"Of course. I did not intend to imply that the child, too, had succumbed. Forgive me, Father, for my thoughtlessness. Indeed, it is in God's hands if he should live or die. But given the frailties that come with an early birth, his future, if any, does appear rather bleak. Though of course I pray that God shall be merciful—"

"Hold your false prayers for your brother, Thomas," Henry interrupted, angrily, noting how Thomas flinched at the word 'brother'. "It would serve you better to pray in earnest for his well being." A sudden, violent round of coughing seized Henry. He held his handkerchief to his mouth and spat out the glob that had lodged in his throat. He took a moment to recover, then turned again to his eldest son. Thomas was eyeing the blood-soiled handkerchief, a slight curl forming on his lip. *The bastard is only biding his time... I'm not dead yet!* "Pray for your brother, Thomas," Henry said, then turned to Mehgrit, dismissing his son and daughter-in-law from his attention. "Where is... my son? Where is William?"

"With Rebecca, m' lord; she's asked to be wet nurse, if you have no objection."

Henry forced down a wave of emotion, remembering how Cyslie had always protested the services of a wet nurse, arguing that it was a mother's right and joy to suckle her own child. But he believed that she would be well pleased to know that Rebecca— whom she was always fond of— would nurse her son. "I would ask for no other, Mehgrit. Thank you. Now, if you please, take me to my son."

15 July 1588

"Lord Stonehaven, thank goodness." Quentin Chase, Lord Henry's trusted chamberlain bowed deeply in greeting, as Lord Edward Stonehaven crossed the foyer into Fylbrigge Manor. "I'm so glad you've arrived. I do so hope you'll forgive me. I confess I took the liberty myself to send the page to Drumoak for you to come, sir. I'm sure I've overstepped my role, but the circumstances did seem dire."

Edward tapped the chamberlain lightly on the back. "Rest easy, Chase. Of course you've done right."

Quentin rose and smiled gratefully. Of all of Henry's companions, he always was most fond of Lord Edward.

"Tell me, how is my old friend, truly? My heart has been heavy for him since the loss of Lady Cyslie. He seemed so troubled and weak of spirit at her funeral, but I assumed the weariness he wore was purely of grief. I had hoped his young son would eventually lift his spirit and bring him around. But your letter tells me otherwise."

"Alas, the physicians have been with him continually night to day, but he has not rallied to any of their ministrations."

"Is he truly dying, then?"

Quentin nodded. "I'm afraid it won't be long now, God help us, before there is a new master of this manor."

Edward grasped Quentin's arm gently for a moment before asking, "How does the child?"

"He does well," Quentin replied, brightening slightly. "At least for the moment," he added, tightening his jaw.

"How do you mean?" Edward asked. "Is he weak? Ill?"

Quentin looked up sharply. "Oh, no, my lord, he is quite

strong and thriving well in my daughter Rebecca's, care." He had been waiting for this opportunity to voice his concern for the welfare of the newborn Fylbrigge boy but it was far from his place to speak out, especially to the duke his master served— especially against his master's own son and heir. He hesitated only a moment, gauging Edward's concern, then leaned forward and began explaining in a quick and hushed tone, "I fear for him, my lord. I beg of you, please consider taking the child with you back to Drumoak—"

"Chase!"

Quentin looked up, startled to see a scowling Lord Thomas standing on the grand staircase. "Aye, m' lord?" he replied, cautiously, straightening up.

Thomas' eyes flared. Quentin held his breath, anticipating a cross rebuke for speaking out of turn. In the days of Henry's illness, Thomas had ingratiated himself into his father's role, standing in for him in business negotiations, acting as his proxy in diplomatic matters. No one was really certain that Lord Henry had asked Thomas to assume these duties but no one dared challenge him. Every member of the household staff, it seemed, had received a stern scolding and a threat of dismissal for this trivial infraction or that. To Quentin's own mind, the staff had done nothing that Lord Henry would have ever called out.

Thomas narrowed his eyes, scrutinizing Quentin from head to foot, his mouth drawn into a hard, lipless line, before turning his gaze toward Lord Edward. Instantly, his expression transfigured from stern master to welcoming host.

"Why was I not told of Lord Edward's arrival?" Thomas asked as he descended the stairs, crossing the floor with an outstretched hand. "My lord, a pleasant surprise. I was not aware you were planning a visit. Chase, please show the duke to the drawing chamber and provide him with some refreshment."

"That won't be necessary, Quentin," Edward replied, raising a hand to the chamberlain. He nodded at Thomas' hand, still extended in greeting but lowered his own, folding it under his cloak. "Why was I not told of Henry's ill health?" he asked. "I am to understand he is near death. I should like to see him immediately."

Thomas' faux smile vanished, his hand lowering slowly. "And who has told you this?" he asked calmly, his eyes shifting toward Quentin.

Quentin swallowed but took his courage from Edward's presence and said quietly, "I thought it wise, m' lord, to send the page." He saw the crimson rise near Thomas' ruffled collar but continued as defiantly as he dared. "Lord Henry has been asking for him."

Again, Thomas' face made the smooth transition from threatening to concern. "Yes, he has indeed. I do hope you've not alarmed Lord Edward too severely, Chase. I assure you, my lord, my father is merely recovering from a bout of bilious distress and there is surely no cause— where are you going, my lord?"

Edward ignored Thomas, heading up the grand staircase on his own. Thomas skittered up behind him but Edward kept to his path, neither turning nor acknowledging his son-in-law.

Quentin watched until Edward's shadow vanished from the top of the landing, then slipped quietly from the foyer, all the while willing the tremble in his stomach to settle. *Blessed Mother, please grant Edward the sense to take the child back to Stonehaven, far away from that bastard.*

Part I

1600

Chapter 1

Drumoak Castle, Stonehaven

2 August 1600

"**B**ACK, YOU BLACKGUARD!" The young combatant whirled, elegantly deflecting the blow from his opponent's blade with a two-handed strike of his own. The battle had gone on for nearly a quarter of an hour and his muscles ached under the weight of the broadsword he wielded. Strike after strike, he met and answered, his vision blurring with the perspiration that stung his eyes. His shoulder and thigh muscles screamed at the strain with each jarring clash of metal but he ignored the pain, pushing himself beyond his own limits—this was not a challenge Sean Wilbrun could afford to lose.

His opponent faltered on some loose gravel and Sean stole his moment to lunge. But the older man feinted to the left, then jagged suddenly to the right, twisted his blade around Sean's, and wrested it from his grip, sending it clattering to the gravel. Stunned, Sean made the mistake of turning his head and in the blink of an eye, found himself in the one position he'd never been able to recover from— flat on his back, his opponent's foot pinning his wrist to the ground. He stared up at the long, gleaming blade that was held to his throat, then to the toothy grin of the man who wielded it.

"Arrogant whelp! Prepare yeself!"

The blade was raised two-fisted then brought down quickly, the point planted neatly in the gravel less than a hand-span from the top of Sean's head.

Sean winced, allowing his free arm to fall to the ground by his side. "Damn." He shook his head, discouraged, as his opponent held out a hand to help him off the ground. "I thought I had you that time, Galan."

"And so you nearly did." Galan smiled, brushing the dirt off Sean's back. "But you made a fatal mistake." He turned Sean to face him, resting a hand on each shoulder. "And you know what it is too, don't you, Seany."

Sean grimaced at the name "Seany"; he was fourteen, after all. He'd outgrown the name by the time Lord Edward had chosen him to be trained for a future post in his personal guard. He would never consider correcting the man who was assigned to train him— Sir Galan Berra, the captain of the guard at Castle Drumoak. It was a rare honor for any page to be trained by Galan personally; an even rarer honor for Galan to consent to train the son of common servants. Sean had been astounded when his father had told him that Lord Edward himself had come to him with the request that Sean be allowed to train for the guard. He would be the first of his family to break out of the servant's class should he succeed in his training; the weight of family pride rested heavily on his shoulders.

"Aye, Galan. I know my mistake. I took my eyes off you." He frowned and shook his head. "And with Lord Edward and my father watching, too. I'll never earn a post in the guard now."

Galan grinned and gave him a pat on the cheek. "You're certain, are you? Look there, lad. I think you be mistaken."

From the far side of the ring, Lord Edward clapped his hands as he approached. Sean's father, Arthur Wilbrun, stayed back, leaning against the fence.

"Well done, lad! Very well done, indeed!" Edward extended a hand toward Sean, who took it with a tenuous smile. "Galan, I see you did not exaggerate about the lad's talent. Excellent."

"Thank you, m' lord, but... " Sean shook his head. "I lost."

"Aye, so you did." Edward laughed. "But you lasted far longer against Galan than I expected. In fact, I was beginning to think you would best him; in which case, I'd have to send him off to retire." He gave Galan a grin.

"You mean... I was supposed to lose?"

Galan burst into laughter, clapping Sean on the back. "Of course! You're good, lad, but not that good. And you winnae be getting any better if you force me into retirement, now, will you?"

"No, I suppose not," Sean conceded, grinning.

Edward turned and gestured for Arthur to join them. The elder Wilbrun nodded and proceeded slowly. Sean noticed him favoring his left leg a little more than usual but his face was full of pride as he approached his son. It was unusual for Arthur to take time away from tending the stables to watch him train— even more unusual for Edward to come watch— and a sudden excitement and hope welled up inside Sean as it occurred to him what may be about to happen. He smiled back to his father, not daring to speak, lest he be wrong and jinx the moment.

When Arthur had joined them, Edward turned to Galan. "Well, now. I believe we're ready."

"Not quite," Galan replied. He jogged over to where Sean's sword lay in the gravel. He picked it up and dusted the blade with his glove before presenting it to Edward. "You'll be needing this, m' lord."

"Quite right," Edward said, taking the sword from Galan. He turned to Sean, smiling. "Now we are ready."

Sean's heart began to race and he could not keep the smile from finding his face.

"If you would, lad... " Edward tapped the tip of the sword to the gravel and gestured for Sean to kneel.

Sean cast a quick glance to his father, then slowly lowered himself to one knee, as was the proper custom.

Edward raised the sword and touched it lightly to each shoulder, saying, "It is my privilege and desire to name you as a guard to the house of Stonehaven. Do you accept this honor and all responsibilities that lie therein?"

Sean drew a breath and placing his right fist over his heart, spoke the required response proudly. "I do, my lord, and swear my fealty, as is my honor, to uphold and defend your tenants. Under pain of death do I break this oath."

"Then from this time thus, you shall be known unto all as Sir Sean Wilbrun. Please rise, Sir Sean."

Sean could barely contain his pride as he stood to face the duke. Edward presented his sword to him in the proper knightly fashion— hilt first over his bent left arm. Sean took it reverently and slid it into the scabbard on his hip. He looked to his father and grinned. Arthur nodded, smiling broadly, his eyes bright with the threat of proud tears. He seemed to be standing a little taller than he was moments ago.

"Now, lad," Edward began, drawing Sean's attention, "you must understand your title is genuine. However, until you complete your training, it will be mostly honorary. Come midsummer, there will be a formal ceremony in the great hall for all the newly appointed guard. You will receive your badge then. In the meantime, Galan will see to it you have a proper uniform and armor, and find you quarters in the castle barracks with the rest of the guard. Congratulations. Now, are you ready for your first official assignment?"

"Thank you, m' lord," Sean replied. "I am eager to begin my duties. What do you ask of me?"

A ghost of a shadow crossed Edward's face and his smile faded. "I don't want you to misunderstand me, Sean. This may sound a bit odd, considering the oath you've just taken. You see, I need you to be... a boy for just a while longer."

Sean wrinkled his brow, confused and slightly offended. "Sir? Are you unsure of my—?"

"Oh, no. Not at all," Edward assured him. "In fact, I can think of no one I am more sure of than you for this particular assignment. I'd like you to consider it more of a personal favor, actually."

Galan had taken a step back, and was standing beside Arthur. Both watched quietly as Edward put an arm on Sean's shoulder and led him away slightly. It was to be a private request, Sean reasoned, and he felt the pride return to him as Edward confided in him.

"You know that I have fostered many a nobleman's son over the years here at Drumoak."

Sean nodded and Edward continued.

"And you've seen many of those men grow to train and learn the skills of nobility – swordsmanship, jousting, and what not."

"Aye, sir," Sean replied. He was careful to keep his dislike for most of the noble fosters from his voice. They were an arrogant lot for the most part, who never seemed to regard Sean as more than a peasant to be ordered about.

"A carriage arrived from Aberdoir this morning." Edward paused, the grimness returning to his eyes. "One I have eagerly awaited for a long time. When the groomsman came to me this morning to tell me he'd finally arrived, I was overjoyed... "

Sean waited for Edward to continue, but when the man remained quiet, he asked, "My lord? Who has arrived? Another fosterling?"

Edward nodded and called back his smile. "Aye. A very special fosterling. A lad I've been waiting to join me for twelve years. He's actually more than a month late in his arrival but, be that as it may, he's finally here. You see, since his infancy, he's been in the care of Lord Thomas of Aberdoir and my daughter, Lady Bryndah, so I suppose he could nearly be called my grandson in a manner of speaking. His father was Henry Fylbrigge; you've heard me speak of him?"

"Oh, aye, sir. Many times," Sean answered, then looked up curiously. "'Tis his boy who has come? I didn't realize Lord Henry had another son, other than that lout... " Sean closed his mouth quickly, realizing he was about to insult the duke's own son-in-law, who every servant at Drumoak regarded as a pompous ass. His gut rumbled involuntarily at the thought that the new fosterling, being a Fylbrigge, would likely be the worst of the lot of fosters who had come before him. "Forgive me. I meant no disrespect—"

Edward chuckled congenially, patting Sean on the shoulder. "You were right the first time, lad. Thomas is a lout and, if I only suspected it before, then I am convinced about it today. This is why I need you."

"Sir?"

"You'll find the lad in the barn," Edward said, looking to the sky. "I've yet to see him for myself but your father tells me he is a sight to see. He would not respond to me when I called to him nor would he even answer to Arthur, who is the most gentle-spoken man in my employ."

"Who?" Sean asked, concerned with the look on Edward's face. He'd never seen the duke seem so distressed. "Do you mean the new foster is hiding in the barn?"

Edward turned to face Sean, placing his hands squarely on the young man's shoulders, as Galan had done. "Sean, listen closely. I'm counting on you. He is terrified and shaken. He refuses to come out of the barn, crying out about demons and monsters he seems to believe inhabit the castle. I am at my wits' end as to how to reach him. That is why I need you. You're close to his own age, Sean. Please... talk to him. Gain his confidence. Coax him out. Will you do that for me? You realize that I could order it of you but I'd prefer you do it... as a favor."

Sean straightened his back, filled with pride that Edward would ask him such an important favor. "Aye, m' lord. I shall do my best to dispel his fears." He shook his head. "Though I fail to imagine how he could believe Drumoak be possessed of demons. 'Tis the grandest castle in Scotland to be living in. Everyone knows that."

Edward laughed. "Thank you, my boy. I think so too. And I have every confidence in you. Perhaps the two of you shall even become friends."

Sean raised a skeptical brow. He'd never been the least bit interested in friendship with any of the other fosters, and this one was no exception. Especially if he was as demented as

Edward described. But he would do his duty, and do his best. "Aye, sir. Uh... m' lord?"

"Hmm?"

"How should I call him by? Should I address him formally?"

Edward shook his head. "I don't believe he'd respond to formality at all. His name is William. I believe that will do."

"Aye, sir. William it is."

With that, Sean returned to Galan and Arthur, and relayed the gist of the assignment to the pair. Sean never would have imagined his first assignment as a guard to the house of Stonehaven would be so simple.

Sean and Arthur walked toward the barn together, Arthur explaining what he'd seen of the lad who was now cowering in a hay bin. Sean kept his usual long stride, his mind reeling through what had just occurred and how he would approach Edward's new foster son. He slowed, then stopped and waited when he realized Arthur was having trouble keeping up.

"Papa, are you well today?"

Arthur looked up smiling, his eyes shining while he caught his breath. "Aye, son. I am. This day is quickly becoming a diamond among the stones." He reached for his son, giving his arm a squeeze. "I am beyond proud of you, Seany. Or must I now be callin' you Sir Sean?"

Sean stood taller. "I'm just Sean, Papa." He patted his father's arm, beaming, then stood back a moment.

Arthur turned away slightly, looking toward the barn setting his sight on the little cottage beside the stable that Edward had provided for the Wilbrun family. Arthur served the duke as his lead groomsman and stable master. Sean's mother, Agnes, worked in the castle as one of the maids. Sean watched his father's eyes grow misty as the old man looked at the cottage and realized what might be troubling him.

"Papa, I really don't need to move into the castle barracks right away. I'm sure Galan won't mind if I stay with you and Mum."

Arthur chuckled and shook his head. "Well, now. That presents a wee bit of a problem for me, son. We'll be needing a bigger cottage if you stay."

"How's that?" Sean asked, taken aback.

"I told you this was a grand day for the Wilbruns," Arthur began, a mischievous twinkle in his eye. "I can't imagine there be a happier man alive than I be right this very minute."

"Papa?"

"She told me this morn, lad. Ye'll have a wee brother... or sister."

Sean's eyes went wide and he pulled his father close for a hug in the middle of the stable yard, giving no thought to who may see them, he was that happy. Arthur and Agnes had long awaited another child and he knew what this news meant to them.

"That's grand! Papa, I'm so glad; is Mum well? When will the bairn come?"

"Aye, son. She is quite well. She tells me it will be near Christmas." Arthur stood back, his smile fading as he leaned on Sean to catch his breath.

"Papa?"

"Is jus' m' age bedevilin' me, lad. I'm a fair few years older than ye mum. I only pray that God grants me the years to see this bairn grow to be at least half your age."

"Papa, don't talk that way. You'll see him and his bairn age far older than I am. Lord Edward pays a handsome wage, and I'll see to it you an' mum and my brother are well provided. You'll not be workin' so hard—"

Arthur shook his head and glanced back to the barn. He cleared his throat as if to change the subject. "Don't you be worryin' on ye Papa jus' now, aye? You've got a nettle of a task ahead of you, son. I think you need a kennin' o' what 'tis you be up against." Arthur gave Sean's shoulder a squeeze, then turned and headed toward the barn. "The lad is hiding in the empty stable at the south end."

Sean fell in step, keeping his pace slower this time. "What is he afraid of?"

"Not sure, really. The driver that brung him from Aberdoir would nae say. Said only that I should be gentle and not judge the lad too harshly for his cowerin'. But then, when I seen him step out of the carriage looking like a starved whelp— all eyes and bones— an' the driver told me who it were, I dinnae believe him. No son of Henry Fylbrigge would be in such sorry shape as that."

"What do you mean?"

"Henry was a good man, lad. Provided well for his sons at his death— uh, the elder one at least. You know who I mean."

"Oh, him." Sean sniffed. "Aye, I ken who you mean. The bastard has the best stables in the country but treats his grooms like animals. You've told me oft' enough."

"Aye, him. Lord Thomas Fylbrigge of Aberdoir, hisself."

"And this lad is truly his brother?"

"Aye, young William. Edward told me a few months back to come to him immediately upon the lad's arrival. Apparently

Henry left orders in his will that William be fostered here upon his twelfth year. I didn't even know he existed until I got the order. To tell you true, son, I've not been looking forward to any kin of Thomas Fylbrigge coming here but Edward certainly seemed eager for the lad to arrive. But I be well certain he never expected this."

"Is William feeble minded?" Sean asked.

Arthur shrugged. "Could be, I suppose. Shame if he be, too. This life can be terrible cruel to the feeble minded. But, my heart says... no, he's no more feeble in the mind than you or me. His eyes are quick and wide, and he be alert to everything around him." Arthur stopped and rested on the bench outside the barn door, catching his breath. "Go on in. Be gentle, Seany."

Sean nodded, and headed into the barn. *Gentle? Be he a lad or a rabbit?*

"Hello?"

No reply came other than the nickering of the horses and the startled flutter of a barn swallow as it flew from the rafters. He walked casually toward the far stall, humming to himself but still listening. The stall seemed completely empty, the hay freshly scattered, showing no sign that anyone had been there. Maybe Papa meant the other end—

"Sean?"

"Ah!" He jumped and wheeled, startled at the tap on his shoulder.

"Ah!" The young lass, equally startled, jumped back and stumbled into a pile of hay. "I thought you heard me!"

He caught his breath and laughed, extending a hand to help her stand. "Sweet Minerva's ghost! Laurel, you're lucky my sword was sheathed. Don't ever sneak up on me again, you hear?" He gave her a stern glare, but grinned.

"Yes, m' lord!" She bowed, mocking him laughing. "What are you doing out here? I thought you were with Galan, learning how to slash and maim."

"I'm done with that for today." He straightened up. "I've news to tell you, but it will have to wait."

"Why? Is it secret? Have you found pirate gold on the beach?" She giggled.

Sean half-smiled, then turned serious. "Not now, Laurel. Truly, I need to be about my business here."

She sighed and plucked a basket off a hook on the wall. "Fine. I've got m' own chores t' tend, you know. Elinor is clamorin' for turnips and she's waitin' on me."

A soft rustle sounded from the stall and Sean glanced that way. *So he is in there.* Laurel must have heard it as well, as she gave Sean a curious look.

"Shh," he hushed her quietly, then whispered, "Go on, lass, I'll come see you as soon as I'm done here." As inspiration, he added, "Go ask m' father what be his news. He'll be glad t' tell you, aye?"

She scowled with a nod, and answered in a whisper of her own, "Ye nae be fun anymore." She winked, and trotted out of the barn.

He watched her go. Laurel May McCary, at thirteen, was a year younger than Sean, and worked in the castle with Elinor, the lead housekeeper for castle Drumoak. Elinor ran a tight household, keeping everything in perfect order— though keeping Laurel in order was akin to keeping the wind in a bottle. He wondered if Elinor would ever see her turnips that night. Silly as she was, Laurel was also a good friend who could be trusted to keep a confidence and for a moment, he wished she'd stayed with him. *She and Elinor are good with the bairns... no, best not embarrass the lad by calling out the women to coddle him... yet.* He leaned against the stall, scooping up a piece of hay to chew on, noticing a slight movement near the wall. He dropped down, sitting cross-legged with his back to the pile.

"Must have been some ride you had. I know the Causey Mounth road from Aberdoir can be quite a fright along the cliffs," he said casually and paused to listen. The rustling stopped. "The ruts are so close to the edge, if the horse makes one bad step, och! 'Tis fearsome. Is that what's frightened you, lad? The road?" He risked a glance over his shoulder. "I wouldn't blame you if it did. I surely don't like riding Causey Mounth – especially after it's rained like it has."

Still no reply.

Frustrated, Sean idly scanned the barn until he spied a basket of early apples not far from where he was sitting. "You don't mind if I do m' chores? I need t' feed the horses, you see." He stood and scooped up a couple of apples and headed to the first stall occupied by an animal. "This is Hawk. He's a yearling. Not quite broken yet but he'll be a fine mount one day." He pulled a sharp dirk from his belt and sliced one apple in half, holding one half flat-palmed for the horse. "I'm hoping he'll be mine. He suits me." Another glance over his shoulder and he caught sight of a pair of wide green eyes peeking through the straw. *There you are. Papa's right, you do have big eyes.* He moved to the next stall.

"This one is Ceres. No one has ridden him yet. He's full of fire, this one." He stroked the horse's nose, then offered the other half of the apple. "Do you like horses?"

The straw moved slightly and Sean could see an entire face now. Small and staring, the boy looked no more than eight years old. *I thought Edward said he was twelve?*

Sean gave him a smile in greeting, then turned his attention back to the horse. "There're more to feed; would you like to help?"

The boy did not answer but Sean saw him peek out a litte more, looking toward the other stalls. He sliced another apple and moved down. "Hello, Gallant, are you hungry? Aye, I see you are. There's plenty... there you are."

A moment later, Sean felt someone standing close behind him. He did not turn but kept to his task of feeding the horses. When he'd run out of apples with two horses left to feed, he turned to reach into the basket for more. Instead, he found the lad holding out an apple with one hand. Sean smiled and took it from him, slicing it in half. "Thank you."

The boy nodded, then stood back, half concealing himself behind a post. Sean fed one half of the apple to the horse in the stall, then held out the other half toward William. "Star may like this one."

William stared at the apple, then up to Sean, then back to the apple.

"Go on, she won't hurt you. Just hold it like this, with your palm flat."

William took it and held it to the filly in the stall he stood next to. She nickered and chomped it down, shaking her mane in gratitude. Sean saw William's eyes widen and the trace of a smile cross his face. He also noticed something else— ghastly purple marks encircling his fragile looking wrists. He quickly averted his sight, so as not to startle the lad. *He's been bound!*

Good God. What am I dealing with here?

"She likes it," William whispered.

Sean forced a smile, somewhat shaken by the dark hollows under William's eyes when the lad turned to look at him. "Would you like to give her another one?" he asked, making an effort to keep his tone as gentle as possible.

Just as William was about to answer, there came voices from outside. It was Laurel speaking to Arthur. William spun on his heel and, without warning, dove back into the hay.

"Lad... wait, there's nothing to... " Sean stopped and gasped at the sight before him. He hadn't seen the boy's back before now and he stopped, astonished. The shirt was flayed open in crimson-stained shreds, the flesh beneath caked in dried blood. He stood for a moment, not finding anything to say to the boy but knowing something needed to be done. Sean turned and headed toward the door. He'd have to let Edward know what he'd seen, and to let him know that he'd have to wait a while longer to meet his new foster son.

Edward stroked his beard thoughtfully, pacing the floor of his suite after Sean finished describing his brief encounter with young William Fylbrigge. A deep crease formed between the duke's brows at Sean's assessment of the child's appearance.

"This is deeply distressing," Edward said, rubbing his eyes between his forefinger and thumb. "I should have never allowed... ." He shook his head and turned toward the open window, leaning on the sill, looking out toward the stable yard as he spoke. "You said he seems small?"

"Aye, m' lord," Sean replied. "M' lord? Are you certain this is the right... " Edward turned to look at Sean, a brow raised. Sean took a breath. He had not meant to challenge the duke, but he could not help but wonder. He steeled his nerve and continued, "That is... you said he was twelve. This lad cannae be more than eight. Nine at best. He barely stands t' my elbow, m' lord. Could he be the wrong lad?"

Edward grumbled under his breath, and turned away again. "Believe me, the thought did cross my mind that Thomas would send an imposter, just to defy me. I've been waiting since the end of May for William's arrival. I sent two dispatches to Thomas reminding him of his obligation to deliver the lad to me. I should have just sent a carriage straight away on the proper day to collect him myself, I suppose."

He grumbled again and without warning, cleared the papers from his writing table, sending the ink crashing to the floor. "By God! Thomas shall not find satisfaction in deceiving me." He slammed his hand loudly against the table. Sean straightened up, startled, as Edward suddenly turned on his heel, tossing a chair to wall.

"Twelve years! For twelve years I have respected Henry's wishes and allowed the lad to be raised at Aberdoir, foolishly trusting, believing the glowing reports Thomas has sent of his progress; how well he's grown, how bright he is, how witty, how he is the joy of their household! Page after page stained with fawning gratitude for me that I allowed William to remain... *cared for* by the lord and lady of Aberdoir. And now we see his true progress. Is there any wonder why the boy fears me so? I am the one who... allowed his mistreatment! Have I not so much as visited Aberdoir myself in several years? I've not seen the lad with my own eyes since he was six or so. Even then I ignored my own doubts."

Another chair met the fate of its table mate, crashing against the stone hearth, shattering to splinters. When the echoes subsided, he stood leaning against the table, forcing his composure before he looked up again. What have I done?"

Sean waited for the scarlet to fade from the duke's face before he spoke, quietly, "My lord, forgive me... but what has passed, has passed. The lad is here, now. He'll come to know that his fears of you and this place are unfounded. I'll see to it myself."

Edward smiled wearily. "I appreciate that, my boy. Thank you. I don't mind evoking fear in the hearts of my rivals but I certainly do not wish to be feared by my children." He looked toward the remains of the shattered chair and sighed. "This is certainly no way to start. I trust you'll keep my little display of anger to yourself."

"Aye, sir."

"Go on back to the barn, then. Take all the time you feel is necessary to draw him out. I'll leave it to you, lad."

"Aye, sir."

Before going back to the barn, Sean stopped in the kitchen, hoping his mother might be there helping Elinor prepare the evening meal. He was pleased to hear the cheers of congratulations before he even pushed the door open. He entered to an enthusiastic welcome as Agnes quickly crossed the kitchen to him with her arms held wide.

"There you are, Sir Sean!" She flung her arms around him, embracing him. "Your father just told me. I'm so proud!"

Sean blushed but squeezed back. "Thank you, Mum."

She stood back, still holding him at arm's length, happy tears beginning to shine on her lashes. "'Tis a glorious day, indeed."

He nodded, laughing. "It is at that. Mum, I'm so happy. I hear I'm to have a wee brother." He looked up quickly, noticing Elinor dashing across the room toward them, a wide grin spreading across her face. "Didn't she tell you, Elinor? There's to be another Wilbrun underfoot. He'll be as much of a nuisance in your kitchen as I am, I'm sure."

Elinor laughed, swatting at him with a dish rag. "I don't think that is possible, Sean. No one is a bigger nuisance near my stew pot." She turned to Agnes. "I was right! I thought there was something about you. 'Tis wonderful news, it is!"

The two women embraced for a moment. Sean stood back patiently until they took notice of him again. "As glad as I am with all the news of the day, I'm afraid I need to hurry along." He straightened up, proudly assuming an important expression. "I've my first mission for Lord Edward to see to."

Agnes grinned, impressed. "So soon?"

"Aye," Sean replied. "Lord Edward's new foster son—" he began, then stopped suddenly, uncertain if he should divulge too many details to the ladies about the lad in the barn "—will be arriving soon."

"Another noble whelp is coming for fostering?" Elinor sighed. "I suppose he'll be expecting a welcome dinner fit for the king himself. I swear the young nobles are worse than their fathers for giving orders, sometimes. Where is this one coming from? Do you know?"

Sean laughed lightly. "Aberdoir. 'Tis Thomas Fylbrigge's young brother. William be his name, I'm told."

Elinor wrinkled her nose, affecting a haughty air. "Oh, a Fylbrigge is it? I shall have to practice my curtsey." She bowed deeply.

"A Fylbrigge?" A voice chimed in from the doorway. "There goes my stomach." Laurel pushed the door open with her backside, lugging the basket laden with turnips. Sean hurried to her, taking it and setting it on the work table. "Thank you, Sean. What's this about a Fylbrigge? Here? Och, that will foul the very air and water, I'm sure. If he's at all like Lord Lout, there'll be no rest for us poor working folk."

Sean's smile faded. He had no idea what to tell them about the boy just yet but he was fairly certain Laurel's assessment was far off the mark. "Well, we'll see," was all he said, then turned back to Elinor and Agnes. "I'm not sure how long I'll be. I may be late for dinner, Mum."

"Sean Wilbrun late for dinner?" Laurel scoffed, before Agnes could reply. "Don't tell me that little lord is already pulling your reins." She waggled a finger in Sean's face. "You're in the guard now, Sean, don't you be letting his nibs Fylbrigge be orderin' you about like some common lackey. You got rank now." She lowered her hand, a teasing grin on her face. "Sir!"

"So you heard of that, have you?" Sean said, allowing his pride to show in his smile.

"Aye," Laurel answered. "News like that spreads fast, you know that. Lord Edward naming you to his personal guard right there in the ring. I even heard you come close to besting Galan." She leaned forward, placing a hand to the side of her mouth, as if to tell a secret. "I'll bet you let him win, didn't you?"

Sean shook his head, but could not help but laugh. Laurel looked so serious. "Nay Laurel, he won fair. But I put up a noble fight." He leaned forward, mocking her secretive tone. "But thank you for the confidence, lass," he said, then offered a knightly bow toward Agnes and Elinor. "Good day, ladies." He turned and walked out the door.

He almost managed to make it half-way from the kitchen to the stable, keeping a brisk pace as he walked, before he realized Laurel was scurrying from behind to join him.

"Sean, wait!"

He stopped abruptly and turned around, causing her to nearly stumble into him. "Laurel, please. I really don't have time," he said, speaking more harshly than he intended, eager to get back to the barn and anxious about Laurel knowing the condition the boy was in.

"I... I'm sorry. I just wondered if we were still going to the seawall later."

He sighed, shaking his head. He'd forgotten that he had promised her that they would go exploring the caves below the cliffs that day, but that was before he'd been promoted and given the charge of coaxing young William out of the barn. He glanced toward the barn then down to Laurel, her large brown eyes looking back hopefully. "Was that today?" he asked, feigning forgetfulness.

The look in her eye told him she was not convinced.

"You know it was." Her shoulders drooped as hope turned to disappointment. It would be the third time that week he'd cancelled their plans. "If you don't want to go, just tell me."

He glanced back to the barn one more time, then turned back to her, hesitating with a moment of indecision. *Surely he wouldn't be afraid of Laurel... but then, what if she spouts out about Lord Thomas and he hears? That could set him to hiding again. And what of those marks on his back? That could frighten Laurel! No reason to upset her with those... But Edward is waiting...*

she'll keep following...

"All right. A quick trip to the seawall, then." Laurel's face brightened but he raised a hand before she could reply, saying, "I suppose I can spare a half hour. But no more than that, aye? You don't want me to anger Edward on my first mission do you?"

"Aye, right. Only a half hour. Won't be much more than that afore the tide floods the caves anyway." She reached for his hand, eagerly pulling him along, launching into a babbling dialog as they walked. "I heard McLander lost another goat from his herd over the cliff. You know he leads them too close to the edge and then the dogs get them to running and the poor beasts just fall right over. Why, it's so that anyone walking on the path below could be hit with a falling goat!" Sean pulled back, extracting his hand. "What now?" she signed.

"Just give me a moment. I want to let my father know I won't be long." He turned back toward the barn, then looked over his shoulder holding up one hand. "Stay right there, I'll be right back."

Laurel huffed, crossing her arms across her chest. "One moment, then I'm comin' to fetch you."

"I'm sure you will," he muttered under his breath. He hurried to the barn, making an effort to keep his expression as friendly as possible, should William be watching for him. A subtle rustle in the hay at the far end confirmed that the boy was still huddling in that end. Arthur was busy grooming one of the stallions with the curry brush. He nodded to Sean in welcome, then tipped his head toward William's hay pile with a wink. It was all Sean needed to know that his father had seen the lad and understood the need for delicacy. Sean was relieved that

Arthur was there; his easy manner would surely show William that there was naught to be fearing at Drumoak— at least in the stable. Sean acknowledged Arthur's signal with a grin as he jogged toward him.

Arthur set the brush on the rail, leaving the horse stall. He motioned to the apple barrel that stood against a beam aside the stall where William was hiding. "Ah, Seany. Jus' in time. I could use a nip o' help wi' this barrel if you dinnae mind. This beastie has a mind t' stick his nose o'er the gate to help himself to the whole lot." Another nod and a wink toward William, Arthur pantomimed reaching into the barrel.

Sean smiled, understanding what Arthur was suggesting. Move the barrel, and he'll have to come out of the hay eventually to eat... "Aye," Sean said, gripping the rim of the barrel.

"Good lot, this batch. These beauties should be in Elinor's kitchen bein' baked into pies, not in the horse barn." Arthur chuckled. "But if these be what Edward ordered for the horses, I'd wager what is in the kitchen be even better, aye?"

"Oh, no doubt about that," Sean agreed, giving Arthur a grateful smile— he'd been given an angle to use. "The baking is glorious, already. Lord Edward has ordered up a fine welcome dinner for his new fosterling." He paused, glancing to the hay. No movement but Sean spied one wide green eye peeking out at him. *That's it lad, listen close.*

"Did he?" Arthur replied, warmly. "That be jus' like the duke. An' a fine welcome it should be. He's been eager for this one."

"Oh, aye. Do you know the lad is to have the east turret suite? The one with the grand balcony. And I heard Lord Edward sent word to have Geoffrey come and play his lute for the welcome." Sean was embellishing; he didn't know for certain that William would be given the east turret suite or if the court musician had been called, but it seemed like something Lord Edward would do. Sean tipped the barrel slightly, rolling it on its edge toward the door as he spoke. "Has he told you which horse is to be Master William's, then?"

A quiet gasp came from the hay.

Arthur and Sean exchanged looks and Arthur whispered, "That got his attention." In a louder voice, he answered Sean's question. "I have a fair suspicion it will be the black filly with the white on her forehead."

"Star?" Sean asked, sounding impressed for William's benefit. "She's the finest filly in the lot!"

Another rustle from the hay and Sean saw the hand reach around the gate post, then half of William's face. Sean tipped his head slightly with a smile in William's direction and the boy shrunk back behind the gate. Sean leaned toward Arthur, speaking softly, "Did you see his wrists and his back?"

Arthur placed his arm on Sean's shoulder and led him out of the barn before answering. "Aye, I did." He shook his head. "Damned sin to mark a child that way. And knowin' where he come from, 'tis fair to believe he took that lashin' for naught. Least, that's what the driver what brung 'im told me."

"Sean, are you comin?" Laurel called impatiently, still standing in the spot where Sean had told her to wait. "The tide will beat us!"

Arthur gave Laurel a wave and a smile, then patted Sean's shoulder. "You headin' for the caves?"

"Aye. I told her we'd go." Sean waved to Laurel, then turned his back to her for a moment. "Lord Edward is trusting me to use my judgment to coax him out. I think it best that... has anyone else seen him?"

Arthur shook his head. "Nary a soul, son. And I think it should stay that way for now. Give the lad his dignity until Lord Edward can sort him out."

Sean relaxed, knowing Arthur felt the same as he did. "I think it best for him to see and hear for himself that Drumoak is fair and safe. You see? Lure him out slowly on his own. Perhaps even have Edward come and just talk like we've been doing. Then, perhaps, he'll not be so frightened."

Arthur waved again to Laurel, then said quietly, "You go on wi' Laurel, son. I'll have a word wi' Lord Edward to tell him what we're about."

"Thank you, Papa." Sean smiled, then headed toward Laurel.

"You mind those caves, lad. Dinnae be there when the tide comes in!" Arthur called, raising his finger in the air.

"Yes, sir, and I'll be sure to mind the falling goats!" Sean replied, scooping up Laurel's hand, and running toward the path to the sea.

Chapter 2

CROUCHING ON HIS haunches, half concealed under a shroud of sweet-grass hay, William Mastin Fylbrigge peered between the slats of the horse stall, watching the two men conversing over the barrel of apples. He'd been waiting for the older of the two to leave or to at least turn his back, allowing the opportunity to snatch an apple from the barrel. He could not remember the last thing he'd eaten. His stomach was aching for something to fill it and the apples looked delicious. Twice he'd come close to nicking one but the man had turned in time to spy his hand reaching toward the barrel. He pulled back, fearful of being caught and called a thief. The last thing he wanted was to be hauled before Lord Edward of Stonehaven as a common thief as he was sure he would be thrown into the blackest pit of the Drumoak dungeon to be forgotten and left to die— after all, that was what Lady Bryndah had always told him happened to thieves in Stonehaven— even petty apple thieves.

His stomach growled as he watched the horse in the stall beside him chomp down half of an apple that the old man had tossed into the trough. Two more halves remained and, for a moment, William considered reaching into the trough to grab one before the horse could eat it. But the thought of the dungeon and the echoes of his brother's many threats prevented it.

"The horses are sacred and valuable," his brother, Lord Thomas, had told him, over and over. "The horses bring me fame and wealth, and earn their keep!"

Thomas demanded the stables be kept clean, the horses

groomed and exercised daily, and that they be fed first, before the groomsman and stable hands. The horses were given the first of the grains and the best of the fruits. Their water was drawn from a special well, dug solely for them. Thomas was fond of his power and his temper was legendary when crossed; William had seen, too often, an unwary stable hand suffer under a heavy handed lashing for the simple crime of drinking from the horse well. William made the mistake one day, when he was no more than seven, of offering a carrot that was meant for Thomas' mount, to a young lad who had just come to work in the stables. William saw Lord Thomas approaching the barn and quickly took the carrot away from the lad but Thomas had seen him. Both William and the stable hand were punished for stealing from the horses. The stable hand had been dismissed after receiving a single blow from Thomas' riding crop, but William had been taken into the house for a more private lesson.

"You ungrateful thief! Do I not feed you enough that you take what is not yours?" Thomas held William's arm tightly, dragging him into the storage room behind the kitchen, deep within the center of the manor house— where sounds would not carry to the outer rooms. The pantry shelves were lined with crocks of pickles and preserves, cheeses encased in wax shells, dried meats, and bins of vegetables. William was tossed to the floor, the door slammed tight and the beam dropped, locking him in the darkness of the pantry. Thomas bellowed his warning through the door, "I am aware of everything that is in there with you! Touch one morsel and I shall know of it, thief." William had spent two days hungering in a room full of food. That was the last time he dared take anything that belonged to a horse.

He shrank back against the stall, watching the horse chomp down the last bit of apple in the trough. *So much for that.* His stomach groaned again and he slipped back into the hay. He was exhausted but wary of falling asleep, lest the groomsman come and carry him out of the barn. *Best to wait until dark... when no one will stop me from running away.* He stifled a yawn and shook his head, keeping his eyes on the door. *Stay awake! It won't be long, now.*

He gripped the post, keeping his vigil on the door. The voices carried and he listened carefully for any sign that the two conversing over the barrel were plotting to deceive him. The black filly across from him nickered, shaking her mane impatiently at a fly that had landed on her forehead.

"Shh," he whispered, placing his finger to his mouth. He creased his brow, trying to reconcile the gentle smile the young man had offered him and the way the old man tended the horses with the tales of the demons and devils of Drumoak he'd been told over and over by Lord Thomas and Lady Bryndah. Unbidden images filled his head— Lord Edward decorating the halls of his castle with the decaying corpses of his rivals, of fiendish feasts of raw meat and blood wine served while still-living victims dangled by their wrists from iron chains above the very table where the bloody duke and his minions reveled in the gore below. Bryndah took a perverse joy in threatening to send him there to become one of Edward's wall decorations should he misbehave.

He remembered Bryndah's eyes; their queer hazel flickering in the candle light when she leered at him, the curl of her grin and the lift of her brow, the hideous satisfaction in her eyes when she knew she had frightened him. Mostly, he remembered her chilling laughter when she told him the day would come when she and Thomas would at last be free of the burden of him and joyfully deliver him to the demon who was waiting to devour him at Drumoak castle.

"'Tis Drumoak for you tomorrow if you run from me again! Do you want that, William? Do you want Lord Edward to strip the skin from your body and hang you in the hall as a trophy? Do you?"

"No! That can't be true! Stop it!"

"You call me a liar? Is he not my own father, William? Do you think I do not know of these things first hand?"

William shuddered, hugging his knees, trying desperately to force his foster-mother's voice and the image of her eyes from his mind. He'd always only half-believed the monster tales but it was the half that he did believe that was keeping him cowering in the barn. He leaned back against the stall for a moment, wincing as his back made contact with the rough-hewn post. He could only imagine what his back looked like but, judging from the itching, he reasoned that the bleeding had ended and the gashes were crusted over by now— it had been two days since the lashing. His right hand found its way to his left wrist and he massaged the ring of bruises around it. His shoulders twinged as if not wanting to be forgotten amongst the pangs of hunger and the pain in his wrists and his back. He dropped his forehead onto his knees for a moment, grinding his teeth. *It's over, you're free. The stories were lies... you know that...* He glanced up, the younger of the men was smiling, the older chuckling at something the other had said. *They're not demons. They can't be. Look at them... he said I was to have a horse... a horse? Me? No, it's a trick... a lure. They took the apples... No. Don't do it, it's a lure...*

With this self argument continuing in his head, William drifted off to sleep.

"Will, come on. No one's looking. Now's our chance."

William looked up, surprised to see a young boy standing before him, haloed by the sunlight that was at his back. He squinted, holding his hand against the glare, trying to better see the boy's face. "Who are you?" he asked, his own voice seemed foreign to his ears, as though it were coming from outside of his head.

The boy extended his hand and leaned forward. "What are you waiting for? There's no better chance than now. Trust me."

William slowly reached for the offered hand, looking up again to the boy, who smiled and winked. William skittered back away when he realized who was standing in front of him— his nephew Richard, Thomas and Bryndah's son. "Go away! Go back to your mother and leave me alone!"

Richard straightened up, placing his hands on his hips. Again the sun shown around him from behind, obliterating his features as he stood shaking his head. "Is that any way to talk to your friend? After what I did for you?"

"You're no friend." William pushed himself backwards with his heels and his palms until he felt something at his back and he could go no further. "You led them right to me! You betrayed me!"

"Believe what you will." Richard shrugged, then turned his back and walked away. He paused in the doorway and turned, setting his sight behind William. He slowly nodded once as if to send a signal before he melted into the sunlight.

"Heathen!" A voice growled from above. William whirled to

his knees to look up at the being who had spoken, and he froze at the sight. A huge figure dressed in the brown woolen robes of a cleric, its face hidden beneath the folds of the voluminous hood it wore, bent as if to look at him. Within the shadow of the hood, William could see the eyes, red and blazing, peering down at him. He wanted to turn away but found himself transfixed by some unseen weight that held him fast, forcing him to watch as the hideous face emerged from beneath the hood. Its mouth stretched slowly into a salivary grin, the lips baring a row of sharp, bloody teeth, with two curled tusks protruding from its piggish snout. The boar-beast loomed over him, raising one enormous hand toward William's face and pointing a massive, calloused finger. The other hand reached into the folds of its robe then withdrew, producing a scourge of nine flails, each tipped with an iron hook. The pointing hand came down upon William's shoulder as the other raised the flail.

"No!" William screamed, pushing with all his strength away from the hands that held his shoulders. "Go away!"

"Easy, lad. 'Tis only me."

William blinked and drew in a halted breath, as he took a look at the face before him. It was the young man who'd been in to feed the horses earlier. He was looking at him closely with a deep furrow in his brow and what seemed to be a genuine expression of concern in his eyes. William looked closely into those eyes, that were as deep and green as his brother Thomas' and for a moment, he allowed the panic to come over him again. "Go! You're... go away!" He pulled himself free, and dashed to the far end of the barn.

"Master William, please," the young man called, though he

made no attempt to follow.

William stopped short of charging out into the barnyard, instead heading for a nearby bale to duck behind. "Just... stay away from me."

The young man stood slowly, brushing the hay from his knees. "I'll stay as far as you like," he said, calmly. "I was just worried you were hurt. I heard you cry out." He took a cautious step forward, not taking his eyes off William. "You're nae hurt are you?"

William shook his head, watching him carefully, looking for any sign of the scourge he'd seen the cleric-beast in his dream wielding. *Fool, that was a dream. And it wasn't him... it was... it wasn't him.* William crept out from behind the bale slowly. *Thomas is back in Aberdoir, not here.* "What's your name?" he asked, quietly.

The young man grinned, and bowed with a flourish. "I am Sean... *Sir* Sean Wilbrun. At your service, m' lord."

"Sir? You be a knight then?" William stepped carefully to the front of the bale. "Where be yer armor? And yer sword?"

Sean chuckled. "I'm still in training, no armor yet. The title is purely honorary for now. But one day, I shall be a sentry in Lord Edward's personal guard. As for my sword," he said, gesturing to the wall by the door, "it be hanging there. Well out of harm's way."

William glanced over his shoulder; the sword hung in a worn scabbard right where Sean said it was, on a hook next to the door.

"'Tis a beauty, isn't it?" Sean went on, proudly. "Of course it could use a touch of polish and the hilt needs some repair."

William took a closer look at the weapon that Sean seemed

so proud of. It was fairly plain to his eye, not like any he'd seen the sentry's in Aberdoir carry. Their swords were all specially crafted with elaborate hilts, the scabbards encrusted with gems and gold gilding, the blades meticulously polished to a mirror-like sheen— as was Lord Thomas' orders. This sword had a modest, iron hilt, smooth at the grip, and unencumbered with any sort of filigree or gems. The blade looked functional to be sure, straight and sharp, but quite dull in its finish. It certainly did not look like the type of sword any sentry to the personal guard would dare carry in Aberdoir. William turned a skeptical eye toward Sean, scrutinizing his garments, which were also far from knightly in their appearance. His leggings were worn at the knees, and the tunic sewn out of the simple flaxen cloth favored by the country folk. Sean's face flushed slightly, and William worried he'd offended him by staring.

"All right, so it isn't Excalibur; but it is mine and I've a right to be proud of it. Lord Edward give it to me, himself, you know. Besides, it's only for training now, isn't it?"

"'Tis a fine blade," William replied quietly. *Lord Edward gave it?*

Sean chuckled as his smile returned. "It's a piece of rubbish that the smithy hammered out of scrap," he admitted with a shrug. "But I'll have a fine polished blade one day. Lord Edward told me that himself."

"You talk about him a lot." William said, as he stepped backward to the bale and sat down. "Are you nae afeared to be in service to him?"

"Of Lord Edward?" Sean blurted with a laugh. "I respect him well enough and would nae want to cross his temper, but I certainly dinnae fear him. He's a fair minded... ."

He paused, and took a step forward. William instinctively pushed himself back further onto the bale and Sean stopped.

"Master William—?"

"Why do you call me that?"

"Is only out of respect. You be my lord's foster son, after all—"

"Nae! I am nothing like that." William pulled his knees up and forced himself to calm down. *Don't make him angry.* "If you please, I am just William."

"Forgive me; William it is. I dinnae mean to upset you. It isn't m' habit to be familiar with the wards." He pointed toward another bale, not far from the one William occupied. "Would you mind terribly if I sat down?"

"'Tis fine."

"Thank you." Sean hopped onto the bale. "Been on my feet all day. This be the first chance I've had – say, do you like caves?"

"Caves?" William asked confounded, finding himself unexpectedly amused with Sean's easy manner.

"Aye, caves. We've a fair number down by the seawall. They're great fun to explore. Laurel is convinced there be pirates lurking in them. But they seem fairly empty to me."

"Laurel?"

"Oh that's right, I dinnae introduce her, did I?" Sean slapped his forehead, and laughed. "She was in here earlier. You may have seen her, the young lass with big eyes. Bit of a monkey, that one. She lives here at Drumoak, as well. She tends to Lady Mehlyndia— you must know who Lady Mehlyndia is."

William thought for a moment. He had heard Bryndah speak of her, alternating from fond to angry tones, and always upon her return from visits to Drumoak. William could never tell if this Mehlyndia was someone Bryndah cared for or despised. "I have only heard the name. I do not know who she is."

Sean shook his head with an incredulous sigh. "Did they not tell you anything useful about Drumoak? She's Lord Edward's younger daughter—"

"You mean he has another?" William blurted, alarmed at the thought that Bryndah would have a sister.

"What's wrong? She's a lovely girl," Sean assured him. "Even Laurel likes her and frankly, Laurel is a hard nut to please. I bet she will like you, though. Silly as she is, Laurel's a right good judge of character. After all she picked me for a friend too." Sean allowed himself a chuckle.

William relaxed slightly at Sean's easy way and the memory of the silly girl who had come by looking for a basket for her turnips. "I saw her. She works here too? But you had time to go explore... forgive me but I was watching earlier. You took her to the sea?"

"Aye. I'll give you a word of advice." Sean leaned forward with a sly grin, "Never promise to do anything with Laurel unless you can do it straight away. She'll hound you ragged otherwise." He sat back laughing. "Not that I dinnae enjoy the caves as much as she does."

"Does Lord Edward know?"

"Know what?"

"That you... slipped away that way? Both of you? Away from your chores? Are you nae worried he'll... are you nae afeared of bein' caught?"

Sean smiled and his voice softened. "Lad, he is nae an ogre."

William's face flushed and he pulled his knees up tighter. "That's not what I've been told."

"So I see."

A voice from outside the barn took their attention. Sean hopped off the bale and walked toward the door and looked out, then waved toward William. "Come here a moment."

William cautiously climbed off his bale and slowly joined Sean, being mindful to stay in the shadow of the door. Sean pointed toward the middle of the stable yard, where the elderly man was conversing with another man dressed simply in leggings and a tunic, not terribly unlike the clothes Sean was wearing. The elderly man was speaking in a cheerful animated way, his whole face seeming to burst with the grin he wore. The other man seemed to share the cheerful mood and suddenly drew the old man to him in a hearty embrace, then held him back at arm's length.

"Who are they?" William asked, quietly, smiling at the sight in spite of his trepidation of being seen. "They seem very glad about something."

"The one facing us is my father, Arthur Wilbrun. He's the lead groomsman here at Drumoak. He has good reason to be glad." Sean stood a little taller, his chest rising. "He's had a grand day, lad. His eldest son— that's me— has just been promoted by the duke, and he's just learned that there's another son— or a daughter I suppose— on the way." Sean's smile seemed to encompass his whole body as he watched his father. "I'm to have a wee brother or a sister."

"Congratulations," William replied. He suddenly realized why Sean seemed slightly defensive about his sword earlier. If he truly was the son of the groomsman, that would explain his garments but it would also explain the look of utter pride on his father's face. *He's a servant... but he's been promoted. No servant was ever elevated like that in Aberdoir.* "Who is the other? Another servant?"

"That, lad," Sean began and carefully placed a hand on William's shoulder, "is Lord Edward of Drumoak, the Duke of Stonehaven."

William's eyes opened wide and he backed away slightly, thinking Sean was mistaken. This man could not possibly be Edward. Dressed like a commoner? Embracing a servant man? Laughing? Where were the hooks and flails he supposedly always wore at his belt? Where were the spiked gloves and the boots tanned from the flesh of his rivals? Where were his fangs, his claws? *Where is your mind, Fylbrigge. He's just... a man.*

"Are you ready to meet him, William?" Sean asked, gently.

William shook his head, slipping back into the shadow. His back brushed against the wall and he gasped.

Sean frowned and shook his head. "You need to have your back tended. Elinor, the lead housekeeper, is a healer as well. She'll fix it right proper for you."

"My back... is fine. It's healing well on its own."

"Will, whatever it is you be fearin', I can assure you, you winnae find it here."

William stepped away from the wall. "You called me Will."

"Forgive me—"

"No! Please. I like it. It's a name for a friend, aye? Will you be my friend then... Sir Sean?"

Sean grinned and extended his hand. "Sean. Just Sean."

"Sean." William shook Sean's hand, then turned back to watch Lord Edward and Arthur. Despite his growing trust for Sean, he was having a difficult time putting the monster tales behind him. His face flushed unintentionally and he turned away, saying in a nearly inaudible whisper, "I cannae go out there. Not yet."

Sean sighed and gave William a gentle pat on the shoulder. "In your own time, then." He started to walk away.

"Where are you going?"

Sean looked over his shoulder. "Mum's waiting supper on me. You can come if you like."

William shook his head, and shrunk back into the shadow of the doorway.

"Suit yourself. I'll be back." Sean waved and jogged off toward Arthur and Edward.

William's stomach groaned as he watched Sean greet the two men. Edward smiled and shook Sean's hand, saying something in a cheerful voice, but he was too far away for William to hear it clearly. A moment later Sean and Arthur headed in one direction, while Edward strolled in the other. Probably going in to eat his supper, too. Again his stomach ached, and growled as if scolding him for his foolish paranoia. *You could have had a real meal, you foolish twit.* He wandered back to the bale and climbed up to wait for Sean to come back. *Maybe he'll bring me something...* He yawned once and shook his head in a vain attempt to stay awake.

"I've got two apples here. Pity to waste this one. But I'm just not feeling hungry today. Sean, would you like it?"

William started when he heard the voices coming from just beyond the barn door. He blinked, rubbing his eyes. He'd fallen asleep again after all. *Sean's there? Who is that...?* He crept quietly to the door, and peeked around. *Oh God, it's him.* The familiar knot of hunger twisted his stomach, mixing with the instinctual fear of Lord Edward. *Sean's with him – Bryndah lied to me. Believe your own eyes, fool. They all lied!*

"No thank you, sir. Just had my supper," Sean answered and glanced over his shoulder toward the barn, then nodding a greeting toward William.

"Well, maybe one of the horses would like this one." Edward set the apple down aside him on the bench.

William eyed the apple, hungrily. It was big and round and the grandest looking apple he'd ever seen. Then he realized, that Edward had just offered it to Sean. *They're not just for the horses?* He looked up again to Sean, who nodded again, then to Edward, who remained with his back turned, simply looking up toward the sky. William allowed his hunger to lead him and before he realized what he was doing, he had crept up behind the bench and was reaching for that glorious looking apple when he heard the duke speak.

"Son, there is a warm bed and a hot meal inside waiting for you."

William froze, his hand in mid-reach, then withdrew slightly.

"We've been prepared for a long time to welcome you to your new home." Edward did not turn but spoke casually to the sky. His voice was calm and William could barely believe what he said next. "The horse in the far stall is named Star. She's very gentle. I thought she would suit you as a first mount. Of course, she needs a gentle rider as well."

William looked back to Sean, who nodded a third time, smiling. He took a breath then replied, quietly, staying behind the bench, "I've never ridden. I am not allowed."

"She's yours, son. You're allowed."

Edward slowly turned to face William and he got his first

close look at the man he had always believed to be the devil incarnate. His eyes were bright blue and lined at the sides, but they seemed to twinkle in the light. His smile was kind, hidden within a grand silver beard. There was nothing sinister nor demonic about him. His voice was soft and inviting as he extended a hand toward William, saying, "This is your home now. I'd very much like to meet you. You can trust me, lad. I'll take care of you. I won't let anything happen to you ever again, I promise."

Promise? No one ever promised to take care of me.

William stood staring at the outstretched hand and the sparkling eyes creased at the corners by a gentle smile. He made a quick look to Sean in a silent plea for reassurance and was answered with a wink and a half-nod of encouragement. As he turned back to Edward, meeting his gaze eye to eye, he slowly accepted his new foster father's hand. Whether it was Edward's words, or his manner, or the hunger in his own belly that moved him, he would never be quite certain, but the moment he felt the touch of Edward's hand, it was as if he had drawn his first breath. For the first time in his life, William Fylbrigge felt welcome.

Chapter 3

"**O**NE MORE SPLASH, then 'twill all be done."

William closed his eyes and braced himself for the last dousing of hot water to be poured over his head from Elinor's ewer. This one was not nearly as hot as the first but still warm enough to be comfortable. The last of the soap slipped off his shoulders and into the oak tub with a satisfying splash. With the last rinse finished he opened his eyes, blinking away the droplets that clung to his lashes. Elinor stood grinning at him, her cheeks rosy above a dimply smile as she held up a sheet of soft lamb's wool.

William had given up any notion of guarding his modesty when Edward had left him in Elinor's care, though he still blushed at the thought of standing up without the cover of soapsuds to hide him. Elinor seemed aware and obliged him by turning her head while he stepped over the rim of the tub and into the sheet. He winced at the touch of the lamb's wool as it brush against the lash wounds on his back.

"I'm sorry, did I hurt you?" Elinor asked, quickly drawing her hands away from his back.

"No ma'am," he said shyly, the first words he'd spoken to the gentle housekeeper. His back did sting him a little but it was nothing he felt he should complain about, lest he hurt the lady's feelings. It had only been an hour since Edward had led him quietly to his new chamber and introduced him to the kindly head of the household staff, yet he already felt a growing fondness for her. "It does nae hurt so much now, thank you."

Elinor sighed, though her smile remained. "Aye, well, I'll be sure to be careful just the same."

He nodded, offering the slightest smile. "Thank you, ma'am."

"Oh now, there be no need to be so formal wi' the likes of me, Master William," she chuckled. "I'm simply Elinor. Call me that, aye?"

His smile crept up on him. "Aye... Elinor. And I am just William, if you please. You call me that, aye?"

"As you wish, William." She reached for a smaller cloth and draped it over his head, gently swabbing his hair dry. "My goodness, but you have a lot o' hair, lad. When was the last time it were groomed proper?" Elinor gently stroked the hair at the side of his face. "Well, we'll fix that, then. Come sit down here by the fire and I'll trim it right proper. Let the world see how handsome ye be, aye?"

William glanced to the bench near the fireplace, noticing for the first time the array of tools Elinor had lain on a small table next to it. There were combs and brushes, vials of colored liquids and yards of folded linen strips. On the floor, a wooden case lay open, containing more vials and pouches. But it was the sight of the shining steel blade and the leather strap that sent him wheeling, backing away from her until he came up against the post of the massive four-poster bed, his eyes never leaving the mysterious contents of the wooden box. "What do you mean to do... with that?"

Elinor made no attempt to approach him but moved toward the tools, lifting the blade. "This? 'Tis only for trimming your hair, lad. Oh, I know that you be fearin' it's not sharp and it will pull your hair. I suppose Sean told you that I pulled his hair but one time when he were six and I'd not honed the edge proper.

He's had hundreds of haircuts since with no troubles 'tall, but he'll ne'er let me forget that one time." She chuckled. "Well now, don't worry on that. I made sure it be good and sharp." She pulled an errant curl from under her caul and held it taut while drawing the blade, neatly cutting the ends. "You see? 'Tis good and sharp. 'Twon't be pullin'—"

"Not that." William nodded toward the strap. "That."

"What? This?" She asked, placing the blade down and reaching for the strap. "What d'ye think it be for? 'Tis for honing— Lamb, what is it?"

William pressed himself close to the bed post. Beneath the sheet, his left hand had found its way to his right wrist, where he began messaging the ring of bruises around it. He stared at the strap in Elinor's hand but suddenly it was not Elinor who he was seeing— it was the boar-beast in cleric's robes and the strap, his flail. He stood there, oddly unaware of his surroundings, fighting back the childish tears he felt welling in his eyes, yet helpless to stop them, as every horror story ever told to him about Drumoak and its inhabitants came rushing back. His knees began to fail and he groped for the bed post but it too had changed, taking the form of the hitching post he'd been bound to, and the floor beneath his bare feet became the gravel of the stable yard.

"Master William!" He heard someone yell, as the world turned on its edge and he sank to the floor, tangled in the sheet.

The darkness felt thick, and suffocating. William strained his eyes searching for any trace of light until he saw a faint glimmer of yellow-orange flickering far above him. He went to reach out toward it but his arms felt leaden and weighted, held fast to his sides. He kept his eyes on the glimmer, willing himself closer to it.

"Little one!"

William turned his head toward the sound of the voice, hopeful to have been found and to be rescued from this strange dark place. The light followed his line of vision. "Where are you?" he called, his voice sounding small and frail in his head. The voice did not respond. "Don't leave me!"

"Do not fear, little one." The glimmer grew brighter, closer, until he could see clearly the flame dancing on the wick of the candle.

He watched, drawing in his breath slowly, as the small circle of candle light grew to illuminate the form of the hand that held it until the smiling familiar face of the one person in the world he had ever loved shown amid the darkness.

"Mum?"

"I'm here."

"I cannae move."

She smiled and set the candle a float in mid-air. "All is well, little one. You're free."

The unseen weight lifted from his arms and he reached up quickly toward her. Her arms opened wide, welcoming him in their ethereal embrace.

"It is time for me to go, little one."

He clung to her, sobbing, "No, you can't leave me. Not now. Not here, in this place!"

"You do not need me any longer."

"I do!"

"No." She pushed him back and wiped his face with her hand. "You are free. You are safe."

"Mum?"

"Remember me, William. And may the Blessed Mother be with you."

She smiled one last time before stepping backward into the darkness, leaving him alone once more.

"He's comin' 'round, Elinor."

William blinked, and slowly opened his eyes. A young lass with large brown eyes was leaning over him, removing a cloth from his forehead. "Laurel?"

She flashed a wide, toothy smile. "Aye, that's m' name, Laurel May McCary. Sean must have told you, aye?"

William nodded and sat up, looking about the room and trying to get his bearings. In the far corner near the fireplace, he saw Elinor standing near a table, scanning the pages of a huge, leather bound tome and rummaging through her wooden box. The blade and strap were conspicuously missing. She looked up and smiled, but did not come forward.

"Ah, lad, you be awake. Are you feeling better?" She asked pleasantly, though William could sense a hesitation in her voice.

"Aye. I'm well, thank you." He squinted into the dim corner realizing the sun had set. He wondered how long he'd slept and if there was something wrong with him for all the sleeping he'd done. Then he remembered what had brought about this latest little nap and his face warmed with the thought. *Git, you frightened yourself into a fit.*

"I... I'm sorry for... I guess I was right tired. Uh, baths do that for me. Make me, uh, tired. I just drop off... "

Laurel let out a little trill of giggles. "I'd say you must have been exhausted. You dropped off right there on the floor."

"Laurel, dear," Elinor interrupted, "go on down to the kitchen and bring up a tray, would you? There is a fresh stew in the kettle, and honey and sweet cream for the bread."

"Aye, Elinor," Laurel replied, still giggling, then turned to the door, chattering merrily the whole time. "You'll like it, Master William. The stew, I mean. 'Tis right tasty. Not too salty like it was last week, and the broth is nae thin as wash water—"

Elinor raised a brow and scowled.

"Well it was, Elinor, you must admit when even Sean won't finish— I'm going, I'm going. Won't be a moment."

Elinor quietly closed the door when Laurel had cleared the corridor. She picked up a mug of water and small pouch from her box and giving another glance to the page of the large book, she closed the cover and came to him slowly. "This is just something to help the aches."

"What is it?" he asked, eyeing the powder that Elinor was emptying into the water.

"Oh, just a wee bit of crushed yarrow root and barley," she explained, swirling the concoction around with her finger. She added a dash more powder, swirled it some more, then added even more until the mug was full of a thick grey paste. William grimaced at the thought of drinking the mix. Elinor gave it one more swirl and drew her finger out. A glop of evil looking grayish goo plopped off the end, landing with a splut back into the mug.

"There, perfect!" she proclaimed holding up the mug.

"I'm not going to drink that!" William protested, covering his mouth with his hand and drawing his knees up under the sheet.

Elinor chuckled. "Well, I should hope not! 'Twould be a foul tastin' thing if you did." She pulled a piece of linen from her pocket and dabbed an end into the mug. "Lean forward, lad. It goes on ye back, you see. Into the wounds here."

"Not for drinking?"

"No."

William leaned forward, hugging his knees. "Does it sting?"

"No, lamb. I promise," Elinor replied. "'Tis just to draw out the foulness that be in there and help heal the wounds. 'Tis what yarrow and barley be for, you see."

He felt the cold mixture ooze into his damaged flesh. Elinor's touch was gentle as she expertly applied strips of linen over the paste. To William's relief, it did not sting at all, just as she promised, and even better, the itching had nearly stopped completely.

"There now, all finished."

"Thank you, ma'am... Elinor." He offered his first true smile. "That does feel better."

"Well, look at that," she said, beaming. "You do know how to smile. And a handsome smile it is."

Although he blushed at that, he kept smiling. "Where did you learn how to do that?"

"Do what? Oh, the yarrow? Well, I suppose was m' mum. She was right talented in the craft you see, and was she who taught me about the herbs and the healing lore. She was the one gi' me my book."

"That big book there?" William asked, his nervousness giving way to an odd fascination with the book. He'd never seen such a thick book, its pages yellowed and well worn, bound in a richly tooled leather binding.

Elinor nodded. "Aye, that's the one."

"That big book is just full of healing?"

Elinor hesitated a moment. "Well, there are some other things too but, aye, all my healing recipes are there."

"What else?" he asked, eagerly. "Stories?"

"Oh, no," she chuckled. "Just things a lad would have no interest in. Trifles and foolishness. But it be my own."

"Your own. Just yours and no one else's. Yours alone." William sighed wistfully, staring at the book and suddenly aware of an odd lump in his throat.

"Do you nae have anything to call your own?" she asked, as though she'd reached into his thoughts.

He shook his head, not trusting his voice to be steady. He'd arrived with only the tattered clothes on his back, looking more like a beggar's bastard than the brother of one of the wealthiest earls in Lord Edward's duchy. Nothing at Aberdoir had truly belonged to him. His clothes and shoes were cast offs from his nephew, Richard. Whatever toys he'd ever played with were Richard's as well, though there had been precious few times he'd ever actually played with them. Richard had a trunk in his chamber that was filled with brightly painted, carved figures of soldiers and horses that they liked to set up on the floor in neat rows. They would play whenever Richard's parents were away from Aberdoir, relishing the freedom to just be children while Thomas and Bryndah were gone. But the games had stopped abruptly when William was six, the day Bryndah had found him in Richard's room alone, lost in his imagination playing with the painted horses.

"Richard said I could play with them," he'd explained tearfully, as Bryndah gathered the figures and locked them away, calling him a thief and telling him for the thousandth time he was nothing more than a burden to Aberdoir and he would be punished.

"I don't own anything. I'm not anyone," he said quietly, then looked away from the book.

After an awkward moment, Elinor stood and went to her book. "You own far more than you think, lad."

He looked up, confused.

"'Tis all up here, you see," she explained, with a tap to her temple. "What is in your mind, no one can give you and no one can take away. And what is in here," she tapped her breast, above her heart, "is what makes you who you truly be."

"My heart and mind?"

"Aye. They be what make you, you. What makes you special."

"I'm not special."

"Oh, sweet Blessed Mother, guide me for what I'm about – you are, lad. I can see you are." She looked toward the door, nervously, then closed the drapes on the window. She flitted about muttering to herself, "Aye, aye, I know 'tis a risk! You've not led me wrong before... but he be just a lad... "

"Who are you talking to?"

"Hmm? Oh, uh... ne'er mind me," she said with a chuckle. Even in the candle light, she had a blush in her cheeks. She picked up her great book, clutching it to her bosom, then returned and seated herself on the bed. "William, you must una'stand what I'm 'bout t' tell you cannae ever leave this room. Must be kept between you and me. Do you promise?"

William looked at her, stunned, and nodded. "You wish to share a secret? With me? Why?"

She heaved a sigh, and looked skyward. "Daft if I know why, lad, but it seems to be what is expected of me. And I'm not one to question Mother."

"Mother?"

"Aye, the Blessed Mother." She gave him a wary look. "Do you know who I be speaking of?"

William hugged his knees tighter, nodding slowly. He knew, all right. But it had been many years since he'd heard anyone mention the Blessed Mother aloud. Not since he was six, just after the incident with the toys, when Rebecca had tried to prevent Bryndah from punishing him. Rebecca had taught him secretly about the old religion; the one the peasants followed in secret since it had been deemed a crime by the king. The one that got people burned alive— like Rebecca. He looked closely at Elinor, her eyes wide, looking back as she clutched her book closer to herself. She looked into him, again as though pulling his thoughts from his own mind, as if she knew what he'd kept to himself since the first beating he'd ever endured in the name of God, and he answered, quietly. "The Mother. Brighid."

When he spoke the name, she relaxed and smiled. "Aye, lad. You do know."

"Rebecca taught me when I was very young. I've never told anyone; it hurts people to tell."

"Aye, lad. Sadly, that be the way of the world we be in. But in here–" She tapped her heart again. "–is just faith. And this book is my way of keeping that faith. I write in it every night. It is everything that I am. But you see, it serves no purpose unless there is someone to pass on the craft to. Someone to teach. Like you, lad."

William sat up straight suddenly understanding what the secret he was to keep was. "You wish to teach me to be a witch?"

"Stuff and nonsense!" she spouted indignantly. "That's the

king's word, not mine!"

He shrank back against the pillows. "Forgive me, I meant no disrespect. But that is what it be called."

"Shh, lad, I know. I know you've seen some terrible things in your young life, what with the hunters and burnings everywhere. And I don't blame you for being afraid. And to be true, that be the name hung on us who cling to the old ways. But 'tis not evil that I'm wishing to teach you. 'Tis just... the ways."

"The ways? But I've been schooled at the abbey and what the priests teach—"

"Aye, they've taught you t' hate," she sighed, shaking her head. "I guess I were wrong t' offer. I didn't realize you'd been indoctrinated already."

"No, I dinnae hate anyone just for that."

William's head began to reel. His first day at Drumoak had certainly not been what he'd expected. The demons were non-existent, everyone had been kind to him, especially Elinor. But how was he to accept what she had just told him? Had he not been painstakingly lectured for years on end in the abbey, on the Scriptures and the virtues of the king's religion? Had he not had the verses beaten into him, time and time again, so that they were carved forever in his mind— and on his back? Had he not been taught to pray to the one true God of all things? And had he not witnessed the consequences of divergence from those teachings when he was forced to watch the death fire that stole Rebecca from his life— the only one who had loved him as a mother loves a son. He looked up to Elinor's kind, sad eyes and his heart began to pound at the thought that she too could share Rebecca's fate should he ever slip and tell her secret.

"I shall never tell a soul, Elinor. I swear on my life."

"Taking oaths?" Laurel asked cheerfully, balancing the tray on one arm as she closed the door.

Both Elinor and William looked up startled— neither had heard her open the door.

"Laurel, child. You really must learn to make more noise!" Elinor chided with a wink. "One would think you be part mouse." She took the tray from Laurel and brought it to the bed.

"So, what's all this swearing of lives I'm hearing?" Laurel asked, plunking herself down on the foot of the bed. "She's not cajoled you into a life time of kitchen work already, has she?" She laughed.

William gave Elinor a wary side-glance. "No, Laurel, 'tis naught. We just be talking."

Elinor placed her hand on his shoulder and leaned down. "It's well, lad. Laurel is safe."

"Am I? Safe from what?" Laurel chirped, snatching a handful of bread off William's dinner tray.

"She is?" William asked, passing the honey pot toward Laurel without a thought. "So she is also a... a um... like you?"

"Aye, lad— Laurel dear, save some for William," Elinor said. "You've had your supper, lass, leave him to his."

Laurel wrinkled her nose, then winked and put the bread back. "So how is it I'm supposed to be like her? Old and wrinkly you mean?" she asked mischievously.

Elinor tried to look stern, but her eyes betrayed her and she began to laugh. William found himself laughing as well, watching the easy banter between the two. How easily they jested. Laurel's merry giggle sounded like a songbird and Elinor shook as she laughed. Whatever fear he had felt quickly vanished in the joy he felt in simply laughing with the women.

When the laughter had waned, he caught his breath and answered Laurel. "No, lass, I meant, you're like Elinor. She's teaching you... " He hesitated for just a moment, catching Elinor's eye to be certain. She nodded with a grin. "She's teaching you the ways."

Laurel's eyes grew wide and she clasped her hand to her mouth. William startled, thinking he'd already betrayed his new friend's confidence. But then, Laurel's eyes brightened and he could see she was laughing behind her hand. After a moment, she reached out and took his left hand in hers, a far more serious expression on her face.

"Yes, Master William. And if you know that, then it must be that she's going to teach you, too. I know she'd not have told you otherwise. Is this well for you?"

William felt an odd leaping in his stomach at the touch of her hand that was not altogether unpleasant. She seemed suddenly older looking back at him this way. He gave her hand a shy squeeze, and said, "Aye, she has. It is well." A thought crossed his mind that since Drumoak was such a complete surprise to him, everyone there must be of the same mind. "Do you teach Sean as well?" he asked, fully expecting an affirmation.

Both ladies answered together, nearly shouting, "No!"

"And, please, please dinnae tell him!" Laurel added, her eyes going wide. "'Twould be disastrous!"

William flinched, startled at the ladies reaction, wondering suddenly if he had placed his trust too easily in Sean. "Disastrous? Why? Is he not your friend?"

"Aye, he is! My best friend! Is why we cannae tell him," Laurel explained in a ramble. "Would do no good to tell him and besides, he doesn't really believe in any of it and he'll only think your head were muddled or you were dropped out the window or something terrible— oh please, Master William, please don't tell him!"

"Laurel," Elinor said sternly, placing her hand on Laurel's shoulder. "You're babbling."

Laurel's face flushed and she shrunk back on the corner of the bed.

Elinor gave her a congenial wink, then turned to William. "We keep to ourselves, lad. Surely you can una'stand. 'Tis only Laurel I've been teaching and there be no reason to tell anyone about it."

"I won't tell, I swear it," William said. "I can certainly understand why you keep it to yourselves. But Sean seems like a decent fellow and you say he's your friend. So, why do you fear he'd turn you in?"

"I do not!" Laurel huffed. "Sean Wilbrun is a decent fellow! He'd never turn us in. That's not what I meant at all."

"I'm sorry. I didn't—"

"Sean be the salt o' the earth, he is! The idea he'd turn on us is ridiculous."

"I meant no offence, Laurel."

"Turn us in? Pah!" Laurel crossed her arms across her chest and sat back against bed post. "Why would you even think such a thing?"

William looked to Elinor, pleading for help with his eyes. Laurel truly was a confounding lass. Cheery one moment, angry the next.

Elinor seemed to understand his silent plea for help and explained quietly, "'Tis not for our protection we've not told him, but for *his*." The smile faded from Elinor's face. "Sean's family is devout with the king's church, ye ken?"

"Oh," William said, nodding his understanding. "Because people get hurt..."

Laurel's youthful glee and cheery mischief, by now, had completely vanished. Even the flare of anger drained away, replaced with a far more serious expression. She looked older again and William noticed that she was quite pretty, though her sudden somberness was somehow disconcerting.

"Aye, Master William. Because people get hurt," she said, simply. "Even people devout in the king's church. 'Tis the way it is. 'Tis the way it will always be. Now, if you be done with this, I'll take the tray back to the kitchen."

William sat back against the pillow and allowed Laurel to take up the tray. He hadn't even realized that he'd eaten all of the cheese and bread while they were talking. "Laurel?" he called, just as she was about to leave the room.

"Aye?"

"You can trust me."

A half-smile returned to her face. She nodded once and was gone, leaving him and Elinor alone again.

"The child means well, Mother bless her." Elinor sighed.

"Elinor?"

"Aye, lad?"

"You can trust me, too. I promise. I'll never tell a soul. No matter what."

"I know, lad," she said, then pointed skyward with her eyes. "And I have that on good authority."

William followed her gaze, half expecting to see some ethereal specter hovering in the corner. Nothing was there for him to see but he had no doubt that Elinor believed there was something guiding her. He was not sure if he believed it was the Blessed Mother or not; but he certainly believed that Elinor believed and it brought him an undeniable feeling of comfort. He watched her silently as she went about gathering the bath linens in a bundle, closing up her marvelous wooden kit. He rested his chin on his tented knees, listening to her hum a cheery madrigal to herself as she busied herself about the room, filling the water goblet, checking the candles. When she pushed aside the heavy window drapery, a warm summer breeze washed over him and his eyes began to close.

And thus, William slept peacefully, his dreams free of dragons and demons, as he spent his first night in the castle he'd feared his entire life— and he knew he had truly come home.

Chapter 4

THE WEEKS OF that first summer were a blur of lessons that William had never imagined he would be learning. The first tutor Lord Edward introduced him to, much to William's initial dismay, was a young monk still in his novice robes by the name of John.

"We will meet promptly every day at nine in the morning, for no less than two hours," John announced, briskly. "We shall study primarily from the book of *Psalms* and then, *Proverbs*. I assume you can read some Latin?"

William only nodded, his heart sinking with the thought of two hour lessons with a monk every day.

"Good, and have you been taught the canon? The commandments—"

"I know them!" William nearly shouted, then looked down in horror at the tone he'd used. He braced himself for the clap on the ear he feared was coming.

John only chuckled and placed a gentle hand on his shoulder. "Good. Then there is that much less to study." The monk went on outlining his lesson plan, in a businesslike but friendly manner. "Lord Edward would like your education to be well rounded and broad. Of course, I am only qualified to see to your ecclesiastical studies, so you shall have different tutors for mathematics and astronomy. Your music and artistic training shall be with Geoffrey McGuiness."

William looked up astonished. "Music and art? Truly?"

John grinned. "I've yet to know the gentleman who is not well schooled in many disciplines. You shall study music, painting, and the usual social essentials should you be fortunate enough to be sent to the king's court one day."

The thought of court life had never entered William's mind but he found himself amused at the thought of being called to court one day. It was an honor that his brother Thomas had sought after for years, yet had always eluded him.

"I had no idea there were lessons to be taught on being haughty," William said to himself, then blushed when he realized John had heard and was laughing.

"Well, I'm not certain that lessons in haughty are quite necessary— that seems to be a natural born talent with most. But you shall learn a proper procession and pavane, and even how to dress."

William heaved a sigh. "I am glad of the music lessons. But the rest still seems... haughty."

John's brow went up as if he meant to argue. "No, no," he began, then a smile caught his lips as he thought. "You're absolutely right."

It was the first time William had ever laughed with a monk. He settled easily into his lessons with John thereafter and even excelled at some. He found that with a gentle teacher, the tedious task of memorizing was not so painful. He was even surprised to discover that much of the Scripture was not devoted to pain and retribution and the wrath of God— as he had been led to believe by his former teacher, the ogreous Brother Joseph in Aberdoir. He was certain the notion of 'love thy neighbor' was one that Brother Joseph obviously never subscribed to.

After a month or so with John, William was becoming so comfortable in the company of his new tutor that he did something he would have never dreamed of doing with Joseph— he questioned something in his lesson.

"Are you certain the word is 'witch'?" he asked, one hand skimming an ancient piece of parchment with the Scriptures written in an even more ancient language, as he compared it with the lines in a newly published version that had been translated for King James. "It seems this translation is... incorrect, Brother John."

"We must not dwell upon the old, William. It was translated for the king by many, many more learned men than you and I."

"But the word here, if I make it out correctly, should more rightly be translated as 'poisoner'—"

"Then the old one must be wrong!" It was the only time John was ever short with William. John then called an abrupt ending to the lesson that day as he nervously went about gathering his lesson books.

William did not press the issue, though he was certain he was correct. He learned quickly when to stand and when to bow. Given the way John had reacted, he felt this was a time better left to bow, though he was certain he would bring it up with Elinor later.

"You were right to let it go, lamb," Elinor said as she lead William up the winding back stairway to her chamber for the special lessons he shared with Laurel. "It does us no good to call attention to those sorts of things."

"I hope you had the sense not to argue," Laurel chimed in. "It would not take much to get you into trouble."

"But it is clearly wrong, Laurel. Surely someone should point it out. Maybe the king doesn't even know it's wrong and that's why he's so hard on folks that practice the witch-ways," he said, then catching Elinor's scowl, rephrased, "that is... the Olde Ways."

"'Twould be a blessin' lad, but I am quite certain King James more than kens the proper translation. As far as he is concerned, if it is not *his* way, it be the wrong way." She pulled the ring of keys from her apron and unlocked the door to her chamber. "There now, you two go on over to the bench there. Laurel, child, where is your basket? Did I not tell you we were going to be making a brew today?"

Laurel sighed, slapping her head. "I left it in the kitchen."

"Well, go and fetch it. Quickly, I have nae time to spare." Elinor chided, but Laurel had already vanished from the room. She chuckled gently, turning her attention back to William. "Did you get a chance to pluck the yarrow from the herb garden, dear?"

"Uh, mostly."

"What do you mean?"

He pulled a small bundle of weeds from a leather pouch and placed it on the table. "I'm not certain if this is yarrow... it could be thistle."

Elinor picked up the little bundle and raised a brow.

"Foxglove?" William guessed.

She shook her head.

"Lavender?"

"Lunk! It's sage." Laurel piped in, making him jump, as she dropped her basket onto the work table.

"Why do I never hear you coming!" William scolded with a chuckle. It had become somewhat of a game with Laurel to sneak up as quietly as a mouse and startle him. "So, how do you know what it is? It's all dried up and looks like any other bunch of leaves."

"I'm smarter than you are, that's how," Laurel told him, crossing her arms across her chest.

"That will do, Laurel." Elinor guided Laurel to her seat at the far end of the bench. "Now, sit and listen. If, that is, you think there may still be a thing or two you can still learn from me."

William sniffed at the leaves. "Is this sage, Elinor?"

"It is," she said, opening the grand leather bound book. "Very useful but not what I was hoping to discuss today. Now then— Laurel, what are you doing now, child?"

Laurel peeked up from under the table. "Nothing." She reached down clearly trying to hide something in her hands.

Elinor tapped her foot and held out her hand. Laurel rolled her eyes, surrendering a little gray mouse she had cupped in the palm of one hand, and the small bit of cheese she had in the other.

Elinor sighed with a smile as she carried the little creature to a box near the window. "Come on then, Lucy. Your dinner will be taken in your box here."

William leaned close to Laurel, keeping an eye on Elinor as she tended the wee mouse. "Is that how you walk about so quietly? You carry a mouse? Is it a spell?"

Laurel gave him a sly wink, but did not answer.

"Will you teach it to me?"

Elinor dropped a hand on his shoulder, making him jump again. "No spells today, I'm sorry to tell you."

"If I carry a mouse to be quiet, then Elinor must carry a mule with giant ears in her pocket, the way she always hears everything," Laurel whispered.

"I heard that."

"You see?"

The lesson itself was far less entertaining or mystical than Laurel and her mouse had been. But William enjoyed it just the same. He watched fascinated as Elinor ground up seemingly random herbs and leaves, and transformed them with water and oils into gloppy messes that dripped from her pestle. She explained patiently what each mixture would be used for— this one for pains in the knee, this one for elbows— and how important it was to pluck the herbs at just the right time and prepare them just so. To William's eye, it seemed that nothing Elinor did was remotely close to magical or mystical but simply logical. But as he watched, it became clear that the simple mixing of herbs and stirring within the cauldron were not what would bring trouble upon her, but the frequent pauses she took and the mutterings to her Blessed Mother made over her boiling brew. But even with this, odd as it may appear, it did not seem any different to him than a priest who chanted a prayer while he prepared a Eucharist for the Communion.

"There," Elinor announced, drawing in a long sniff of the aroma rising from her pot. "It's done."

"What will it do?" William asked, giving the pot a sniff of his own.

"Laurel? You tell him."

She grinned. "Pure magic!"

William's eyes went wide. "Really?"

"Ahem." Elinor tapped her foot.

"Really." Laurel laughed. "It makes a nobleman quit bellowing for wine and bread after we've retired for the night."

"I don't understand."

"It's for sleeping, lunk!" Laurel rolled her eyes. "Dinnae you pay attention? Belladonna, valerian, and a wee bit of crushed poppy seed; and the sot will sleep all night."

Elinor smiled. "Very good, dear; yes, that is exactly right."

"But... sleeping isn't magic," William protested. "Is it?"

"Oh, you may think so one day, lamb, when the demands of the world keep you up at night. Look at the sun. That is all for today." Elinor closed her big book and began gathering her tools.

William started toward the door, then turned and asked, "Am I doing well?"

"Aye, lad." Elinor answered with a twinkly smile. "If I were to be reporting to the duke, I would tell him you're making high marks."

"I wish I could tell him," he said, then added quickly, "but I swear I won't."

Edward was pleased with William's progress in all the areas he was aware of and required weekly reports on all of his lessons. With each glowing report, he beamed and congratulated his foster son. William soaked in the praise like rain on parched earth.

At the end of summer, the lessons he had anticipated more than any finally began. "William, this is Geoffrey McGuiness; he will see to your music lessons."

Geoffrey McGuiness seemed an unlikely tutor, small and wiry, and, to William's eye, quite old. His back hunched and his hands were more grizzled than what William expected a musician's hands to be.

"I am pleased to meet you," William bowed and extended

his hand.

To his surprise, Geoffrey's hand did not feel at all fragile, belying its weathered appearance. Instead, the grip was firm, and the fingers flexible and strong. "And I am pleased to know you as well."

The old man kept hold of William's hand, and examined it as a jeweler examines a precious stone. He examined each finger, turning the hand over and back, measuring the length of William's palm and width of his wrist, pushing up the lace cuff of his sleeve to do so. William was suddenly self conscious of the scars but Geoffrey made no indication he had even noticed them.

"Very, good; very good indeed. A natural player." Geoffrey proclaimed with a grin, releasing William's hand.

"You can tell that from simply looking?" Edward marveled.

"Oh yes, I have an eye for these things." Geoffrey affirmed with great seriousness. "Have you played before, lad?"

"No, sir," William replied. "But I have watched... and have always hoped to learn one day."

"And so you shall." Geoffrey chuckled. "We shall take our lessons daily, promptly at two. Just after the Lady Mehlyndia. Or perhaps, it might be good if you share lessons with her to start. My lord, will that suit?"

"I think that is a splendid idea, Geoffrey. And it will give you a chance to be better acquainted with Mehlyndia, lad. What say you?"

He had not spent very much time with the duke's daughter and it had not been entirely an accident. Upon his first introduction to Mehlyndia, the first thing that struck William was her deep resemblance to her sister. Mehlyndia was fair haired where Bryndah was dark - however, the curve of her face and the slope of her nose were near perfect matches to her sister - only in a younger version. She had been pleasant upon their first meeting and cordial ever since but still, the family resemblance had put him off and he'd found many a excuse to avoid her company.

"The lad is overcome with joy, my lord." Geoffrey laughed, when William offered no answer to the duke. "I'm sure they shall make a fine musical duet for your fine dinners."

Edward grinned, clapping Geoffrey on the back, nearly sending the elderly man off his feet. "And so they shall. Perhaps by the Christmas ball, they shall honor us with a tune."

"Christmas?" Geoffrey's brow raised. "Well I shall do my best. Perhaps the lad here will be ready but I'm not certain I can guarantee the lady shall be. We are still working on... her warble."

"Oh, yes." Edward placed a thoughtful hand to his chin. "So you believe that perhaps singing is the answer?"

"It could well be, my lord. She has the voice of..." Geoffrey paused, clearly seeking a kind word, "a bird. Yes, quite. She sings like a bird."

Edward was not fooled, though he allowed a grin to find him. "Geoffrey, perhaps you are misplaced within my employ. I do believe I should use you as diplomat rather than a musician. I agree my Mehlyndia has a birdlike singing voice - but how long can one listen to a jay?"

William stifled a chuckle, not quite certain if agreeing with Edward's assessment would be polite. "I cannot believe she would sound as bad as that," he said instead, slightly surprised with himself.

"Ah, a diplomat as well," Geoffrey said, smiling.

"Indeed," Edward agreed.

When Geoffrey had left them, Edward placed a hand on William's shoulder as the two walked. "You've been here for a few months now. How are you liking Drumoak?"

"I like it well, sir," William replied, honestly.

"Good, I am pleased to hear that. Do you think you would like to stay then?"

William stopped walking and turned to the duke. "Stay? I... assumed I... was home."

A look crossed Edward's face that William could only believe was relief. "You are, son." They continued their walk. "And home, it shall remain."

"Will?" Sean called from the far end of the stable, waving as William made his way from the Abbey after his morning lessons with Brother John.

William stopped and waved, and jogged to the fence to meet his friend. "I've wondered if you were still alive. Where've you been, Sean?"

"Off with Galan on a secret mission," Sean said, grinning.

"How secret could it be if you're telling me." William laughed. "And what is this fine piece of jewelry that I see on your shoulder?"

Sean beamed, polishing the silver disk with his sleeve. "Second place. Not the best, but I held my own. After all, Ogham's man was nearly twice my age and three times my size. I supposed if I had to come in second— what is it?"

"The games!" William sighed. "I forgot all about them. I've

been so buried in lessons that— so tell me about your victory!"

"Second place." Sean corrected. "You really didn't miss much, Will. It was just the guards and a lot of local blokes. Just us commoners on this one. You'll see the next one that comes in October. That's the one all the lace and velvet class comes to."

William felt a sting. He'd never considered himself 'lace and velvet' and he certainly never thought Sean considered him that way. "I still would have liked to see you compete. Was it swords or lances you won for? Quintain? Joust?"

"Joust?" Sean laughed. "I told you, this was commoner games. Cabers and stones, lad. I tossed a river stone."

"Oh."

"See, hardly impressive now." Sean vaulted over the fence, landing lightly on his feet. "So, what have you been studying? More Latin?"

William nodded. "So much I am beginning to dream in Latin. Do you mind if we walk? I've another lesson soon. Lute and verse. Hardly impressive."

"Why do you say that?" Sean asked. "I would very much like to learn to play."

"And I would very much like to toss river rocks and cabers but I suppose it would only ruin all this lace and velvet." There was more anger in his voice than he intended but once it began, there was little he could do to pull it back. "Do you think I enjoy spending all of my time learning to bow and fawn, and spout out Latin for show? I would much rather spend my time learning something useful, like how to handle a sword. Just once, I would like to have a lesson that would get me dirty!"

"Wards dinnae get dirty, lad," Sean said quietly.

William stopped, spun on his heel. "I thought you were my friend!"

It was Sean's turn to look stung. "I thought so as well, Will; why do you say other?"

"I... " William shook his head, lost for an answer. "I meant naught. I suppose I am still not used to my place. In Aberdoir, I was nothing as far as my brother was concerned. It was the common folk, as you put it, who were the ones I was close to. It was the servants who took care of me, so I never felt part of the lace and velvet. I still don't."

Sean was quiet for a moment while they walked. When they reached the castle door, Sean took the satchel of quills and tablets William was carrying from him. "You know, I've been promising Laurel a trip to the caves."

William took back his satchel. "Have a good time. I've a lesson to go to."

Sean snatched it back. "Yes you do and it has naught to do with Latin."

"Music."

"That either." Sean held the satchel high, out of William's reach. William leapt to get it, Sean moved it out of reach. "Today, you will learn something useful and possibly get very dirty."

"Sean," William leapt again but Sean kept the satchel away. "Sot! Geoffrey is waiting; he'll be angry!"

"Oh, I think not." A cheerful voice chimed in from the doorway. William spun to see a smiling Geoffrey. "The day is glorious and the weather fair. A bonny day for a musician to seek out inspiration."

"You see?" Sean grinned. "Hello, Geoffrey."

Geoffrey chuckled, clapping William on the back. "You're dismissed, lad. Go. Be a lad. Get dirty."

"How did—?"

"Sean, I believe Laurel has already packed a sack with cheese and bread. She's in the kitchen."

"Thank you, Geoffrey, I'm headed that way now." He tossed the satchel back to an astonished William.

"You had this planned?"

Sean grinned and went into the castle. "Ready, Laurel?" he called as he entered the kitchen.

Laurel stepped out from behind a rack of baskets, her arms akimbo. "I know it is about here someplace."

"What are you looking for?" he asked stepping around the work table.

"My shell basket. I want to take it with us." She stood on the tips of her toes, barely able to peek up onto one of the shelves. "There it is!" She tried to jump but could not reach the basket.

Sean reached up easily and retrieved it for her. "Do you mind if we—"

"You are not canceling again, are you?" She growled, taking the basket from Sean.

He laughed. "Always suspecting the worst of me, are you? No, I am not canceling. I just wondered if you would mind if we took some company along with us today." He gestured toward William. "I've been promising him as well, you see."

William had hung back near the door, still not quite sure if Laurel would mind a tag-a-long on her walk with Sean. He knew how she enjoyed those times and did not want to intrude. He raised his hand in a shy greeting. "I promise not to be any trouble."

Laurel's face lit up in a smile. "Well then, what fun shall you be?"

Sean laughed out loud. "The trouble shall come completely from you and I, Laurel. We'll ease him into it slowly so he can learn how to cause trouble properly later on, aye?"

"I'll be certain to take proper notes." William laughed, tapping his satchel with his hand. "I just need to go put this away. Wait for me please?"

"Aye, we'll wait," Laurel said, gathering her cloak. "It'll be pleasent for a change."

William hurried to his chamber, his heart light in anticipation for his afternoon with his friends. When he reached the corridor where his chamber was, he nearly collided with Mehlyndia, who was walking toward him, startling her into dropping the sketch pad she held in her hand.

"Oh! Forgive me, m'lady," he stammered, quickly bending to retrieve her pad. The book had fallen open and he paused to marvel at the drawings of the horse on the page. "This is incredible," he said, handing the book to her. "It nearly breathes with life, the coat even shines."

Mehlyndia smiled, taking back the book. "A beautiful subject makes it easy to make a beautiful drawing. Were you hurrying for music? Did you know Geoffrey has dismissed us for today?" She looked away, adding coyly, "I should like to practice anyway. I was hoping that perhaps, you could play for me— while I practice."

William blushed at the smile she offered him. "Actually, Sean and Laurel are waiting for me. We're going to explore the caves by the sea." Inspiration struck him and he blurted, "Do you want to come?"

"To the... caves?" A horrified expression crossed her face. "Why on earth should I want to go there? Why on earth do you wish to go there?"

He felt immediately foolish, once again forgetting the gulf of propriety that stood between his place and his friend's. "Because... " He stood straight. "Because they are my friends and it is a lovely afternoon, and Geoffrey has given me the time – and because I want to... m'lady." He braced for a scowl but received only a smile. "I will be glad to play for you when I come back, if you still wish."

"That will be fine, William. Thank you." She gave him a top-to-bottom glance. "If you are going to those dreadful caves, I should suggest you change into more appropriate garments."

He glanced down at the fine clothes Edward had provided. The cambric shirt with lace at the cuffs did seem a ridiculous garment to wear to the sea. But he had nothing less pompous to wear. "This is all I have. Perhaps... you're right. I should stay here."

"Won't Sean and Laurel be disappointed?"

William shook his head.

"Sure we will!"

William turned to see Sean approaching from the far end of the corridor. "Hello m'lady." He made a short bow to Mehlyndia. "I've come to see if he needed anything."

"Hello, Sean." Mehlyndia smiled. "I think he only needs some stout boots. I hear you are taking my foster brother on an adventure. He invited me to come along, I hope you are not offended if I decline."

Sean looked up surprised. "No, m'lady, there is no offense— of course, if you want to come, please do."

"I am afraid I am made of less hardy stock than he is." She grinned. "William can tell me of his adventures when he returns."

"I will bring back some sea shells, if you wish. Perhaps you could draw them?" William offered.

"Thank you." she beamed, then turned toward her room, giving William a parting look over her shoulder and a coy smile.

"So, why do you think you should stay here?" Sean asked, once Mehlyndia had gone.

"Look at me, Sean. I'm all velvet and lace. This won't do at all."

Sean only grinned and produced a bundle from under his arm, which he tossed to William. "Courtesy of Elinor. She's right sharp that one. As soon as you left the kitchen, she came around with this and sent me straight on up. Go change, I'll wait."

William looked at the bundle and his joy returned. He had no idea how Elinor did what she did but she always seemed to know what he needed. "Rough clothes! Thank you! I won't be long."

A quarter hour later, William was eagerly following Laurel along the rocky path that wound around the cliffs behind the castle. Sean followed behind, keeping close and lending a steadying hand when necessary, where the footing became narrow along the shear granite. At one point, along the way, the path was so narrow that William had to turn sideways, his back flat against the cliff wall and the toes of his boots showing over the lip where far below the waves were breaking on a field of boulders. He kept his eyes on Sean, who was moving along, seemingly heedless of the height and the drop. Laurel, too, skipped along the narrow ledge as sure-footed as a billy goat.

"Is this the way you always come?" William asked, craning his neck to peer over the precipice.

"Oh, no," Laurel called back, "but we thought it best not to take you the difficult way on your first time."

William flattened himself against the cliff, as he set yet another small avalanche of scree tumbling into the sea below. "You mean this is not the difficult way?"

"Steady there, Will," Sean said calmly. "You're doing fine."

"Am I?" William laughed nervously as he gingerly prodded the ledge for less volatile footing. "How much farther is it?"

"One more turn and the path will be far more pleasant." Sean assured him. "I supposed it would have been better to take the carriage road on your first trip."

"You mean there's a carriage— what the—!" William gasped as Sean's arm came suddenly across his chest, slamming him back against the granite, just as a shower of gravel and stone rained down from the ledge above. It continued for several moments, accompanied by a chorus of bleats and bells from above.

"McLander!" Sean hollered, looking upward. "Keep your herd away from the bloody edge!"

"I warned you about that. No one ever listens." Laurel sighed.

"Crumbling cliffs, narrow paths, and falling goats?! And you say there is a carriage road?" William shook his head, gathering his breath and his nerves to continue. "I'm wondering if you two are truly daft."

"Daft? Pah!" Laurel scoffed. "This is the safest way down with McLander's goats up there on the carriage road. Unless you fancy being butted over the edge." She skipped along, darting under an overhanging boulder that jutted out at an alarming length far beyond the edge of the cliff.

William crouched as far as he could, still keeping his back to the cliffs as he inched his way under the rock and around a curve. To his great relief, the path opened onto a wide and blissfully flat ledge of granite.

Laurel had already made it across this ledge and was sitting on a flat, table-sized rock, her face turned to the sun. "Isn't this lovely?"

He plopped himself down to sit, waiting for his breath to return. For the first time, he allowed himself to take in the view around him. The sea shimmered gray and wild as it licked against the cliffs. The sun warmed the rocks and the breeze, though steady, was pleasantly soft under a cloudless blue sky. Gulls kited on the breeze, squawking noisily to each other. He listened to sounds of the sea, the gulls and the breeze, and even the distant clanging of bells on McLander's goats and a feeling of complete peace overtook him.

"Drat." Laurel sighed. "The tide has come in."

"How can you tell?" William asked.

"Well, just look!" Laurel said, gesturing to the sea.

William looked and shrugged.

"Now, dinnae tell me you ne'er seen a tide," Laurel said, shaking her head.

William felt a flush come to his face, embarrassed with the feeling he'd just asked something obvious that any other clear thinking lad would know.

"There is a slim strip of beach below us, lad." Sean explained patiently, giving Laurel a warning scowl. "You've never been here, so you wouldn't know what it looks like at low tide."

"But still, the water is so high—" Laurel persisted.

"He's never seen it, Laurel," Sean said, rather sharply.

"I've heard about tides, of course," William said. "I know they come higher when the moon is full— I've been studying about it."

"The moon makes the tides higher?" Sean's brow went up.

William smiled, unsure if Sean was now humoring him to make him feel better or if he truly had never known this bit of knowledge. "It does. It is how the sailors know the best time to cast away, you see."

"Well now, I never knew that. I assumed they simply watched and waited for the waves to be right." Sean leaned back on his arm, taking the sun on his face.

Laurel opened the sack she had packed and drew out some cheese and bread. "I won't be gathering any shells today." she sighed. "I thought we would have been in time."

"How fast does the water come in?" William asked, tearing a hunk of bread and passing the loaf to Sean.

"Oh, right fast," Laurel told him. "You see where this rock goes down on this side?" She pointed toward the water. William looked closely and saw that the rock seemed to descend in steps right into the lapping water. "This goes down right to the sand and right under us is where the cave is."

"It is?" William looked all around, noting the solid cliff faces. "I wondered where the cave was." A wave swelled and smashed into the rock, sending a splash over the lip. "I see why you said you can't be there when the tide comes. A person would drown."

"And people have," Sean said, getting to his feet and going toward the edge. "Come here and take a look. It's safe, I swear."

William followed to the edge and looked over. The waves

swirled around in a spinning pool between swells. He leaned over carefully, holding onto Sean for support. "Oh! I see it!" Fascination overtook his fears of falling and he leaned further to watch the pattern of waves strike against the smooth stones. A wave struck just then, the spray splashing his face, startling him. He stumbled back, his eyes closed tight against the sudden sting of salt water.

Sean laughed loudly, pulling William away from the edge. "Back up, lad. I should not like to explain to Lord Edward how you were swallowed by the sea on your first adventure."

"Oh! Thieves!" Laurel shrieked suddenly.

Sean took to running, his hand going to the hilt of his sword. William turned but did not see Laurel where they had left her.

"Go away!" She cried out again, her voice coming from behind a crop of boulders on the other side of the ledge.

He ran behind Sean, not sure what he was to do but determined to save Laurel from whatever blackguard had attacked her. Sean raised his sword and, to William's astonishment, began making whooping sounds, waving his sword, in circles above his head. It was then William came face to face with Laurel's attackers— two large gulls that hovered about her lunch sack.

"Back, you cads!" Sean chased the last of the rogue gulls clear, then scooped up Laurel's dropped basket and handed it back to her with a regal bow. "My lady, I have dispatched the scoundrels."

Laurel curtseyed, batting her eyes. "You are my hero. Here, a reward for your bravery, kind sir," she said, offering Sean a fist full of seaweed.

He bowed comically, clutching the weeds to his chest. "Such riches; you honor me."

"I know." She peered around Sean, giving William a wink. "And you, sir, what do you have to offer?"

"Me?" William asked, looking around as though someone may be standing behind him.

Sean sheathed his sword, laughing. "I do believe he is empty handed, my lady."

"I'm afraid I am... my lady," William bowed awkwardly. It took him a moment to understand this was some sort of game and he was not exactly certain what his role was supposed to be— the freedom to play still seemed a bit foreign to him.

Laurel approached him, walking with a haughty swagger. "Then you may kiss my—"

William glanced up, startled.

"Basket." Laurel finished, presenting the empty shell basket to him, again batting her eyes playfully.

He grinned and bowed as grandly as courtier, and kissed the hand that held the basket.

Laurel giggled and tapped his shoulder. "Oh, you silly, stand up."

Sean stood with his arms folded over his chest, watching with a slight scowl.

"What is your trouble?" Laurel asked, her hands on her hips.

William stopped laughing, suddenly wary that he'd just offended Sean by being too familiar with Laurel.

"She never offered to let *me* kiss her basket." Sean sniffed, then grinned as he crowned William with the seaweed. "Lunk."

"Sot." William laughed, flinging the seaweed back at his friend.

The afternoon passed quickly as the trio walked the ledges. Sean pointed out the rocks and coves they would be able to explore more fully when the tide retreated. Laurel managed to fill her basket with colored pebbles and some sea grass that they came across. William allowed himself to relax, becoming more comfortable in their company, more easily joining in their little games of make-believe.

He especially enjoyed watching Laurel flit about the rocks, as light as a feather on the wind. She seemed to take delight in everything around her and was quick to incorporate everything she saw into her games. A gull became a dragon, scared off by Sean, her constant knight; a stack of rocks became a mighty fortress from which she required rescuing, again obliged by 'Sean the Good'. William assumed the role of highway man, capturing the damsel and absconding with her treasure, only to be retrieved by the noble knight. Each game led easily to the next as they walked and before William had realized it, they had arrived back at the path into the castle.

"Shall we go again when the tide is down?" William asked. "Tomorrow? Earlier in the day, aye?"

"Don't you have studies to mind?" Sean asked, with a sly smile.

"Tomorrow is Saturday." Laurel reminded him, then sighed. "He may be free but I surely cannae. It's market day."

"I'll go to market with you, if you like." William offered.

"Now there is an offer not to turn down, lass," Sean said, laughing. "It is the rare nobleman who offers an escort to the market."

"I'm not a nobleman," William said. "Please stop playing on that, will you?"

Sean looked at him amused, shaking his head. "Will, there are many ways to be noble that have nothing to do with birth. I was paying a compliment on your manners."

"And I agree, Will." Laurel added. "You are a lot more pleasant company than any of the other wards that have ever stayed here. None of them would ever want to come to the sea with us. Not that we would have wanted them too. Sean, do you remember that one, what was his name? Pomp... Pomf—"

"Ah, him. Pomphrey Woodhall," Sean said, rolling his eyes. "The little popinjay from Kylkannon. Little fop was no more than ten, yet thought he was lord of all he surveyed."

William laughed. "I know who you mean. The son of Lord Ambrose Woodhall. Fancied himself to be the next prince of Wales, as if it were a position he could solicit the king for."

"Aye, that's him, the git," Laurel said, then pinched her nose to make her voice funny. "My father's castle is grander than this— my horse is faster than yours— my my my my."

William laughed at Laurel's dead-on impression and joined the mocking. "My mother is the queen's second cousin's sister's second waiting lady to the bath. You are not fit to even stand in my shadow."

"What ever became of him?" Sean asked. "I half expected he would be back this year. Not that I am not grateful for his absence, you understand."

"Sweats," William said, suddenly turning serious. "I suppose it is not right to jest on him."

"He died?" Laurel's eyes went wide, her hand going to her mouth.

"Last summer, aye. Nasty business that," William said. "His father had business with my brother and was at the manner when a messenger came and told him." William stifled a chuckle. "The sot bawled all over his lace for all of a minute, then scolded the messenger for interrupting his business."

"What a louse." Laurel sniffed.

"I agree. Even Thomas and Bryndah were put out by it. They ordered him out immediately, telling him his place was with his wife at such a time."

"Did he go?" Sean asked, taking Laurel's basket from her, as they walked.

"Not immediately. He was fearing the illness would come on him in Kylkannon, and asked to remain at Aberdoir. But then when my nephew Richard became ill, he left right away."

"I can't really blame him for that," Laurel said. "We were quite lucky here. When the sweats started, Lord Edward closed the gates. The sweats stayed well away. Though it was dull not having the markets come, and the summer players. But Lord Edward said it kept us safe from it and he must have been right since we never—"

"Did your nephew recover?" Sean asked, interrupting Laurel's ramble.

"Aye, he recovered fairly quickly."

"How bad was it at Aberdoir?" Laurel asked. "Worse than Edinburgh? I heard nearly everyone there got it in one fashion or another and it took only a day—"

Sean tapped her lightly on the head. "Laurel, hush! Let him answer!"

William shrugged. "I'm not sure how much worse it was there than anywhere else. I was glad Rich got well like he did. He was the only one in the family who took ill. Chase— he's the chamberlain— was surprised I never came ill. After all, I was with Richard through most of—"

"With him?" Sean said, astounded. "In the room?"

"Why, yes. I was the only one willing to keep him company. Usually I was not allowed to visit. Thomas never let us play much and kept Rich busy with tutors and such. But we were good friends— for a while. Rich thought he was dying and asked Thomas to let me visit. For once, the sot had a heart and told me I could go in."

Sean's brow went up, and shot a glance to Laurel, who shared the same odd expression.

"What? I wanted to be there." William said, looking between them. "I told you, Rich was my friend and I thought it was a fine gesture to allow me to stay with him. It's not like Thomas was always that compassionate and I took the good will where I could."

"Compassionate?" Sean scoffed. "Did he ever go in to see his son?"

"Well, no. And neither did Bryndah but they had the best physicians on call. Though I was not impressed with them. They never actually touched him. If it wasn't for me bringing his tray, I think he would have starved before the fever got him."

"Oh, for the love of Queen Mary's ghost, Will." Laurel sighed. "Did it never cross ye wee brain tha' ye brother were hopin' you would come ill?"

William looked up startled. "I... well, uh. No. I was just... glad to help... what a dolt! I never even considered the danger!"

Sean dropped his arm across William's shoulder and laughed as they walked. "Lad, you are a rare one."

"A rare dolt!" William agreed, allowing himself to laugh, though the reality of what his friends had just made him realize made him even more angry with his older brother. "I wish I had gotten ill, then I would have run to Thomas and given him a great big brotherly hug! The bloody sod."

"That's the stuff!" Laurel laughed. "Brotherly love all around!"

"Aye!" William laughed. "The sort of hug that Cain gave to Abel!" He stopped, clearing his throat. "Or not, it didn't turn out well for either of those two."

"Speak of the devil." Sean sighed, pointing up the lane. "Looks like the duke has a visitor."

William's heart sank he watched the familiar gilded carriage with its ornately painted doors approaching the castle. "Well... it was a lovely day until now."

"Who says it will be other?" Laurel said, taking his hand and pulling him along. "Come on through the kitchen. He doesn't even have to see you."

"Wait, Laurel," Sean said, seizing William's other hand and pulling in the opposite direction. "Why should Will have to slip in through the back. He's every bit a member of the family as that sot. Go right on in through the front, lad."

"Uh... " William looked down at the clothes he wore, the dirt stained knees and scuffed up boots. "I'm not exactly dressed to—"

"And who dressed you?" Sean asked. "Elinor? Hardly. Those clothes came from Edward. I've seen him less well clad than you are right now, many times. If Thomas is offended by good clean dirt, then so be it. If it's good enough for Edward, then it's good enough for you."

Laurel let go of Will's hand. "Sean, you're such a twit." she grumbled.

"What?"

"Cannae you see it is not his clothes he's really thinking

about."

William glared at Laurel. "You think I'm afeared of that fool?"

"Aye. And rightly so," she replied. "I know I am and I've never had the misfortune to ever meet him!"

The carriage had come to a stop on the cobble paved path at the gate. The gateman was opening the latch to allow the carriage through. William looked up to the castle and saw Edward standing on the balcony above the entrance, dressed in the same simple apparel as any townsfolk would wear. Edward saw the three, and waved in greeting. Though it was fairly far, William could see the smile Edward offered and responded with a wave of his own.

"There, you see?" Sean said. "Front door, lad."

"I still think he's better staying clear—" Laurel began.

"Front door!" William agreed. "You're right, Sean. This is my home, now. He's not the lord of me anymore." He brushed his sleeves and straightened his belt and headed toward the gate, just as the carriage passed through. He followed behind until it came to the front door, then hurried around the carriage to stand in the grand doorway, forcing down the urge to run into the castle and up to his chamber. He stood determined to greet his brother with all the grace and manners of a gentleman.

"Master William?" A gentle hand came down on his shoulder. William started, then looked to see the concerned face of Edward's gateman, Roberts. "I think it best you go in, lad."

"Why?" William asked, "I should like to greet my brother."

"All well and good but it is not proper," Roberts said, straightening his back, watching as the footman prepared to open the carriage door. "Greetings take place in the great hall, not on the front stoop."

"What? Then why are you on the stoop, if not to greet?"

Roberts raised a brow shaking his head. "I am not a member of the family." He pushed the door open behind William and motioned him to hurry inside. "And you are not a member of the staff."

William slipped through the door, scolding himself for nearly ruining his moment of defiance. Roberts was right, of course. William would greet his brother, not with the servants but as an equal.

He glanced behind him to the front door, then up the stairs. He still had time to avoid the whole thing and run to his room. He hesitated a moment until he saw Edward coming down the grand stairs.

"Ah, good! You're back. I trust you had an enjoyable adventure?"

William relaxed slightly, greeting the duke with a smile. "Aye. The cliffs are magnificent!"

"Yes, they are; I quite agree. Where are you off to in such a hurry?"

William felt the crimson come to his face and found he did not want to tell the duke he was headed to his chamber because he did not want to see Thomas. He turned slowly trying to keep his expression calm and pleasant. "To wash, m'lord. Uh, I don't wish to be rude to your, uh, your guest by presenting myself this way."

"Mmhmm," Edward raised a skeptical brow, stroking his beard. "You are rather dusty. Perhaps I should freshen as well? I should not like to be rude to my guest."

"Oh! No, m'lord, I did not mean that you – forgive me."

"William, when will you relax?" Edward said with a chuckle.

"I shall not compel you to stay while Thomas is here. But I would like it if you would stay. His visit concerns you."

"Me?" William looked up, startled. "What have I done now?" he asked automatically, then felt immediately foolish.

Edward sighed, laying a hand on William's shoulder. "He has expressed an interest in your progress and well being since you've come here."

William's eyes went wide. "He cares nothing for me."

"I am not a fool, William. He knows he is not in my good grace right now but, as my son-in-law, it is in his best interest to fawn and grovel. I find it rather amusing."

The thought of seeing Thomas grovel brought an unexpected grin to William's face.

"You see, a great deal of his wealth and power, and even his title, are his only at my discretion and pleasure. And he is well aware that he has displeased me greatly where you are concerned, though he does not fully appreciate how displeased I am."

"How displeased are you?"

"There is a banquet to be held next week. A very important event, a convocation of the nobels where we meet and discuss important business, trade, wealth and such. It is very pompous and very dull but it is important. The position at the table is key, it establishes rank and importance, do you understand?"

William nodded, though he was confused why Edward was now speaking about convocations and ranks.

"The seat to my right was once occupied by your father. It has remained empty since his death. Thomas is keenly aware of the vacancy and has long wanted to assume that place. I should like to put his waiting to a rest."

The door clicked open behind him and William could see Roberts' shadow stretching across the floor, next to it, the unmistakable silhouette of the earl of Aberdoir. Before he had the opportunity to consider dashing up the stairs, Edward's hand was on his shoulder. "Stand with me, son. To my right."

William stood straight and took his place at Edward's side as he was told.

"Lord Thomas Fylbrigge, my lord," Roberts announced with a bow, then stepped backward allowing Thomas to enter.

Chapter 5

24 *December 1600*

EDWARD ENTERED THE grand hall, his heart light as he surveyed the preparations for the coming evening's Christmas Ball. It would be the first since Lady Anne, his beloved wife, had died six years earlier. The ball had been her pride and she would spend the whole of the year preparing and planning. The twelve days of festivities, commencing with the ball on Christmas Eve, were the most anticipated by all of Edward's subjects, both noble and common folk. It was Lady Anne who had first opened the doors of Drumoak to the townsfolk for this one evening. Not a few of the earls had scoffed at the notion of sharing a banquet with the lesser born, as they were called, but none dared refuse an invitation if they wished to remain in Edward's graces.

William's arrival at Drumoak had given Edward a reason to reinstate what he had come to regard as 'Anne's Ball'. The idea had come to him the afternoon Thomas had arrived to see William standing with him on the grand stairs at his side.

Though Thomas' appalled expression had amused the duke greatly, it also gave him a keen insight into the William's character. It was all too apparent that he young charge clearly wished to be as far from his brother as possible. Even so, the lad presented himself with all the grace and maturity of a nobleman; greeting his brother cordially, meeting his eye, even smiling. Impressive, indeed.

Thomas had been far less dignified, demanding to know why a peasant whelp had assumed his place— until he recognized who the whelp was. Edward could hardly contain his mirth as Thomas fell all over himself in apology.

"My lord... truly I did not... his garments are rough, after all, and... not unlike yours, my lord, and fine rough clothes they be indeed on you, my lord, but I did not... you're looking quite well, William... taller... more... robust... "

Edward grinned at the memory and an almost childish glee crept over him, imagining how Thomas would react this evening when William would take the coveted seat to his right at the banquet. "Oh, that should be quite a show," he said to the air around him.

"Father?"

Edward spun on his heel, startled by the unexpected tap to his shoulder. Mehlyndia jumped back, then chuckled behind her hand.

"I'm sorry, Father; I thought you heard me come in."

"Quite alright, my dear. Now, let me take a look." He took her hand and turned her around to admire her gown. "I believe I shall have to keep a cudgel at my belt to keep the young swains at bay."

She blushed and offered a demure curtsey. "Please do not keep them all away. After all, I am fourteen and unpromised. People are beginning to talk."

Edward raised a brow. "Hmm, are they? What are they saying? That Lord Stonehaven is saving his jewel for a prince? For the finest of the fine, as she so deserves?"

She blushed, casting her eyes down. "I shall be called the diamond spinster of Stonehaven."

He lifted her chin with a gentle brush of his hand. "I promise you shall never be called a spinster. Please, allow your father to revel in your childhood just a little while longer."

"I'm not a child, I'm fourteen!" She protested. "Bryndah was already wed by my age, and now she's a countess!"

"Ah, so that is what this is? Pairings are important considerations, Mehlyndia, and not to be made lightly. Would you have me arbitrarily choose from the list of eligible sons from my earls? Gerald of Drunbalk has expressed an interest in your hand."

Mehlyndia gasped. "But he's an old man!"

"Thirty-six," Edward said. "Not so very old; he has a title and lands, and would be a smart match. It would certainly forge a prosperous trade alliance with his holdings in Spain. The profits would be enormous!"

"Profits?" The color fell from her cheeks. "Is that all marriage is for?"

Edward chuckled and stroked her chin again. "In many cases, that is true. Kings yearn for sons in which to leave their kingdoms and for daughters for which they can wed into other clans to broaden them." He pulled a silk handkerchief from his sleeve and touched the tear that fell on her cheek. "Now, now; no tears, my dear. You are fortunate that I do not happen to be a king. And my holdings are quite large as it is, so I think I may afford the luxury of allowing my youngest daughter to choose as she will. Now, do you wish me to promise your hand to Gerald of Drunbalk?"

"No, he is far too old—"

"Good," Edward smiled. "I should hate to imagine my grandchildren born with his bulbous nose. Is there anyone that you may already have in mind?"

She glanced toward the top of the stairs with a coy smile. Edward followed her glance to see William standing on the first landing with Sean.

"But I look like a puffed goose!" William was saying as he flattened down the sleeves to the fine doublet he had donned for the ball.

Sean shook his head and re-fluffed the sleeve. "But this is the proper way to wear it."

Mehlyndia cleared her throat loudly. The two stopped arguing and turned toward her. "Melly, tell him!" William called, holding his arms out to display the flattened sleeves as he descended. "This is far better, isn't it?"

"Melly?" Edward said under his breath.

She flushed, again flashing a coy smile as she hurried to the foot of the stair to meet him.

"Please tell this sot I look ridiculous this way," William pleaded, as they met.

"Oh no, William; Sean is quite right. Sleeves are meant to be full and regal. You look very handsome in your new clothes."

Sean stifled a chuckle. "Exactly what I told him, my lady."

"Traitor," William grumbled, as Mehlyndia fussed about his sleeves.

"There. Father? What do you think?"

Edward placed a hand on his chin, looking over the pair. It struck him how grown up the both of them seemed to look—Mehlyndia, radiant and mature in her brocade, could have been Anne reborn standing before him. William, polished and mature in the deep burgundy doublet and trews, bore no resemblance to the terrified child who had crawled from the barn to steal an apple a mere five months earlier. Edward could only look upon them and marvel at how well the pair seemed to go together. "I think you both look splendid."

Sean slapped William on the back. "There! You see? Splendid."

"I don't see you dressed like a holiday goose," William muttered.

"I am not going to the ball." Sean pointed out.

"Oh?" Edward said, looking up. "You may attend with the guards, you know. All are invited."

"No, my lord, I beg your leave this evening," Sean said, turning serious. "My mother is in her lying in, sir. I wish to wait with my father. I should have a young brother by morning."

"Ah! Splendid news. You have leave then, with my blessing. Tell your father I shall come pay my respects in a day or so when your mother is well enough."

"Thank you, my lord, I shall," Sean said with a bow. "I'm sorry I shall miss your music tonight, Will."

"You've heard me practice enough to know I will be a complete disaster."

"You shall not." Mehlyndia protested. "You play like you were born to the lute. Doesn't he, Father?"

"Indeed." Edward agreed, grinning. "Now then, children, let's go see what trouble we can find in Elinor's kitchen." He held a hand to each, then gleefully led them though through the decorated great hall toward the kitchens.

"Still flat, lad; a wee bit more," Geoffrey said kindly, helping William with the tuning of his lute.

"I can not hear it, Geoffrey, are you sure?" He tightened the string more.

"There! Stop. Now, gently, three bars . . . one, two . . . ."
William began the lilt he'd been preparing for the Christmas
ball slowly, too slowly for Geoffrey's liking. "With me, one, two,
three; that's it— Oh, dear."

William winced as the high 'G' string twanged, then snapped
at the bridge. "Oh no! Now I've done it. There is not time to
replace the string and voice it. This is a disaster."

Geoffrey gave him a reassuring pat on the shoulder. "'Tis
well, you may use mine."

William looked up in wonder. Geoffrey never let anyone
touch his prized lute, an instrument he had built himself some
twenty years earlier. William's lute was smaller, more suited to
his size, specially made for him by Geoffrey. Geoffrey had even
taught him the finer points of carving; William, himself, had
carved the simple ivy pattern around the sound hole. He was
quite proud of his lute, though he conceded it did not the have
well seasoned tone that Geoffrey's had. Geoffrey explained the
instrument was like a human singer in that it would improve
with age and 'learn' its voice from its master's playing. William
had been entranced by Geoffrey's playing and put all his heart
and soul into his own, yearning to match the elegance of his
teacher's tones. He had done quite well for a novice; so well that
Geoffrey had assured Edward that William was indeed ready for
his debut at the Christmas ball.

William was thrilled and eager at the prospect but as the
moment came closer, a growing panic was creeping through
him. The hall was full. It seemed that every citizen of Stonehaven
had turned out for the event.

"Geoffrey, I couldn't possibly play yours."

"You can and shall. Here, now, take it gently." He took

William's lute from him and set it down on the bench.

William took Geoffrey's carefully, handling it like a fine fragile treasure. It was the first time he'd ever been allowed to hold it. The wood was smooth as silk beneath his hand from years of use. He brushed his fingers gently across the open strings, and nearly gasped at the tone that came from them.

"Ah! My lord, are you ready for him?"

"I am indeed, Geoffrey, and eager to hear."

William felt himself stand up and follow Geoffrey to the landing overlooking the great hall. He looked down into a sea of faces; some he recognized, most he did not. He scanned the crowd for Laurel but he could not find her readily. One face in the crowd did leap out at him, and he tried in vain not to recognize the all too familiar curl of her grin, and the lift of her brow. Sitting on a tufted bench beside Mehlyndia and bedecked in a garish scarlet gown, Bryndah sat looking up at him, smiling in such a way that he had to tear his gaze from her.

"And now we are in for a special treat," Edward was announcing from the middle of the grand stairs. "As you are all aware, I have a new member to my household. Most of you have already met him in and about town over the past few months, but for some— Lords Drunbalk and Ogham, in particular— this is the first time you shall meet him."

A murmur wormed through the room. William could hear snippets from where he sat.

"A bit grand for a fosterling, isn't it?"

"He's only a boy—"

"Edward is going soft—"

"He'll be gone soon enough; Edward never keeps a ward more than half a year—"

William swallowed hard at the last remark, trying to discern who had said it. He saw Thomas chuckling, standing with Ambrose Woodhall. *I'm not going anywhere. Like it or not!*

Edward quieted the crowd and looked pointedly at Thomas and Ambrose. "Lord Henry Fylbrigge de Aberdoir, God rest his soul, was my dear and good friend. We happily joined our houses with the marriage of my daughter, the Lady Bryndah, to his son, Thomas of Aberdoir." He gestured toward Thomas, who bowed graciously in reply.

William wondered how he could be so courtly with this lot, but attributed it to the duke's diplomatic mastery.

"In his will, Henry entrusted me with the fostering and care of his youngest son, upon his twelfth year. Earlier this year, it was my pleasure to accept him into my family, when Thomas delivered him to me."

Edward spoke so merrily, William could almost forget how angry Edward had been with Thomas.

"Now I have the joy and honor of fulfilling my promise to my old friend. Tonight, with all gathered as witness, I should like to claim him as my son." He turned and looked up to William.

William's jaw dropped, it was the last thing he had expected. A polite chuckle filtered through the crowd, Edward among them.

"Do you accept?"

William nodded, his mouth still agape, eliciting further chuckles - Thomas and Bryndah a notable exception.

Edward turned back to the crowd. "And now the treat. Among his many charms, we have discovered he has a natural talent for music. My customary court musician has graciously provided lessons and has agreed to yield a portion of his concert

this evening, so you may all hear our young William's debut."
He gestured up to Geoffrey, then stepped down from the stairs,
and took a seat right next to Mehlyndia, without so much as a
glance to Thomas and Bryndah.

"Ready?" Geoffrey asked, quietly.

"No," William answered silently.

"Good; now, gently, let the strings do the work, and trust
your fingers, one... two... "

William closed his eyes and let the music calm him as he
played. The tune found itself, ringing effortlessly from the
strings as his fingers found their way. The music echoed through
the hall, amplified by the stone walls around him. He allowed
himself to be lost in the sound; imagining he was sitting on
the wide window seat in his bed chamber, singing alone to the
sunrise, as he had done so many mornings. Eyes still closed,
hearing only the strings, he found his courage and his voice,
and began to sing. Quietly at first but, as he found comfort in
the music, he let his voice lead the way until his song echoed
throughout the hall.

Green grow'th the holly
So doth the ivy;
Though winter blasts blow ne'er so high,
Green grow'th the holly.
Green grow'th the holly,
So doth the ivy;
The God of life can never die,
Hope! saith the holly.

His last note echoed with the last lingering chord from the

lute. When the sound waned, he was startled by the applause, forgetting that he had been singing to a crowded room. He opened his eyes and smiled. Geoffrey prodded him to stand and bow.

Edward stood, applauding and smiling broadly. The others followed his lead, though William noted, some less enthusiastically. Thomas clapped absently, leaning to speak to Bryndah. She nodded about something, and took his hand. The two discreetly left the hall through the back corridor. William counted their departure as a gift.

"Go on down, lad," Geoffrey told him, giving him a light tap on the back.

William reluctantly handed the beautiful lute back to its owner, then turned to meet Edward halfway down the stairs.

"Did I do all right?" he asked.

"You did perfectly, son." Edward replied.

"Am I *truly* your son now?"

"Truly. If you accept, of course."

"I have a choice?"

"Certainly." Edward placed a hand on his shoulder.

William grinned, not knowing what else to do. "I accept... Father."

The two joined the party, mingling and meeting. Geoffrey provided music for dancing thereafter. William danced with Mehlyndia first, as was expected, then with nearly every lass in the room, saving the last dance for Laurel.

When he retired, his sleep came easy.

William of Drumoak had found his place— and his voice.

Part II

1604

Chapter 6

1 September 1604

"**W**ELL, THERE IT is," William said, more to himself than to his companion as he looked down onto Aberdoir from the Causey Mounth road. Star nickered impatiently, stamping her hooves as if in anticipation for the customary race to the stable yard. Sean, astride Hawk, sidled up next to William, doing his best to keep his own mount from charging forward.

"Easy, now," Sean muttered, patting the horse's neck. "We'll run soon enough. Just as soon as Fearless Fylbrigge is ready to lose another race."

"I'm always ready. To race, that is."

Sean hesitated for a moment. "You know, Will, you don't have to go down there. It won't take but a blink for me to deliver Edward's message to the manor house. You could wait here."

"I know," William replied quietly, looking down into Aberdoir; it seemed like any other little cliff-side borough in Scotland.

It was market day, and the high street was lined with the marketers' carts offering all manner of goods; the last of the summer apples, bolts of colorful silks for ladies' gowns, sturdy copper kettles. A typical market in a typical town on a typical sunny, September afternoon. William followed the lanes visually, noting the houses and shops that lined the street ending at the gates of the grand manor at the far end of town. There stood Aberdoir Hall, the Fylbrigge homestead; the former home that he had happily not set eyes on for more than four years.

I must be mad. What am I doing here? he thought, trying to bring to mind his reasoning for accompanying Sean on his mission. Sean would have been pleased enough to handle the simple assignment by himself and had not even mentioned it to William. Had he not seen Sean heading to the stable in the early light and gone out to ask where he was going, he was sure Sean would have just ridden out and returned without a word. In fact, Sean had been reluctant to say where he was going when asked.

At first, William had laughed, accusing his friend of planning a secret rendezvous with one of the rouge-faced tavern dancers Sean had *admired* the night before. He had denied it, comically feigning shock at such a lewd suggestion. He said only that he had something to do for the duke and it would be fiercely dull. He told William that he should not bother himself about it, and he would be back by sunset.

"Well, I've no plans for the day and even fiercely dull is more exciting than nothing at all," William said. "Do you mind some company? It won't take me but a moment to saddle up—"

"No, Will," Sean said, in an odd way, not looking William in the eye. "I've got an... assignment."

William paused. "Oh? A fiercely dull adventure is it? All the better, let me saddle up."

"No, not an adventure, lunk. Lord Edward is simply sending me to deliver a letter."

"A letter?" William laughed scoffing, heading toward the

horse stall. "Come on, I'm not daft, you know. Tell me the truth. Delivering letters? You're not a page anymore, Sean. Isaac Walford has that job now. Why isn't *he* going?"

Sean sighed, impatiently. "Isaac is already on errand to Kylkannen."

"Oh. So, where are you going?"

"To Aberdoir."

William froze in his steps, then turned quickly to face Sean. "Aberdoir?"

"Aye." Sean pulled the letter from his tunic and showed the seal to William. "I'm to deliver it to the earl, personally." He tucked it back into his tunic, and looked up, apologetically. "I didn't tell you because I didn't think you'd want to go... there."

"I see," William said, forcing the crease he felt forming between his eyes to smooth. "Well, do you mind if I go with you anyway? For the ride?"

Without waiting for an answer, he'd hoisted the saddle onto Star's back. Sean hadn't offered further argument, though William could see he was clearly surprised at Will's decision to go back into the dragon's lair, as he had often referred to Aberdoir.

They'd made good time along the cliff road; chatting about this and that, racing on the straights, every so often veering into the forest to jump fallen logs. William took a spot of malicious delight in Sean's startled reaction when he set Star charging at full gallop toward a craggy gorge, intent on jumping over it. As if she and William were of one mind, Star had charged without hesitation and launched toward the edge, gracefully touching down safely on the other side.

"Are you mad?" Sean hollered, leading Hawk to a narrower

part of the gorge. "I'm responsible for you, you know. I truly wish you'd be more careful!"

William laughed gleefully, reining in. Star reared, whinnying in echo to William's defiant whoop, as she turned and charged back toward the road. He heard Hawk whinny a response and Sean hollering, "Yah!" followed by the fury of hooves. Soon, the two were galloping side by side, along the cliff road, heedless of the perilous drop only yards to their left.

They'd proceeded that way for the entire journey; William charging recklessly ahead, Sean shouting oaths and calling him names only to pass him and goad him into jumping an even more treacherous obstacle, not stopping until they'd reached the place above Aberdoir where they now stood. William's resolve melted, looking down toward the manor house; its gleaming turrets cast a long and foreboding shadow over the town. He gave serious consideration to Sean's suggestion that he wait on the hill but soon dismissed it from his mind. He was not the timid child who left this place four years earlier. He'd learned his own strength and worth, and was damned if he'd let his pompous, overbearing, snake of a brother make him believe he was worthless ever again.

"Come on." William shook the reins. "Race to the edge of town, then?"

"Aye," Sean replied, his mouth curling into a tight-lipped grin. "Well done, lad," he said quietly. He kicked in hard, setting Hawk charging ahead.

"Sot!" William laughed, kicking Star into a gallop. His momentary trepidation about riding into Aberdoir lessened with the knowledge that Sean was proud of him, even if he'd not said so in so many words.

Sean reached the edge of town first, bringing Hawk to a halt in a cloud of dust. William joined him before the cloud had settled, raising a cloud of his own.

"You cheated, Sir Sean!" he chided, laughing.

Sean laughed and bowed his head, placing a penitent hand on his chest. "My lord, I beg your pardon! I am only performing my duty as your humble tutor, seeking only to *enhance* your own horse mastery by demonstrating the superiority of my own."

"Oh, pig slop! You just like to win." William held his stomach, laughing, with his back conspicuously turned to the shadow of the manor house.

Sean waited for the dust to clear, and when William had yet to turn around, he asked, "Are you coming the whole way?"

William turned and looked up the high street to the gates of Aberdoir Hall. A sentry stood at attention, the gate behind him barred as always. "I'll wager the gate to the tower of London is more inviting looking than that one," he quipped, though there was no smile on his face.

"You're probably right." Sean agreed, nudging Hawk into a stroll.

William did the same, the two proceeding at a leisurely pace up the lane. He glanced at a few of the carts, then his eyes turned back to the manor, only paces ahead.

Before they reached the sentry, Sean leaned toward William and gestured toward his hands. "Relax."

William glanced down at his hands, realizing he was squeezing the reins so hard that his knuckles had gone white. He let go of the reins, rubbing his palms on the fabric of his trews as if merely clearing the dust of the road from his hands.

"Relax? I'm fine. Ready to go?"

Sean seemed unconvinced. "There's a tavern on that lane. Why don't you go on back, get us a table and wait for me. I won't be long."

"I'm going with you," William said hotly, then took a breath, when Sean recoiled. "I'm fine, my friend. We're delivering a letter. What could possibly happen?"

"Aye... you're right."

When they reached the gate, Sean withdrew the letter from his tunic, checked the seal, then looked to the sullen-faced sentry. "I've a letter from the duke, Lord Edward in Stonehaven."

"I'll take it," the sentry replied, reaching.

Sean placed it back in his tunic, glaring. "I'm to deliver it to Lord Aberdoir personally. Open the gate." Sean could be quite intimidating when he chose to be. His hand rested lazily on the hilt of his sword and his eyes never blinked as the guard hesitated. "Now, if you please."

The guard looked up to William, narrowing his eyes, ignoring Sean. "I know you." His eyes suddenly went wide, and he grinned. "Master Will? Is that you, lad?"

William looked closely, as the guard lifted his helmet to reveal his face. "Hello, Cletus," he replied, smiling. "How are you?"

"Me? Oh same old... " The guard reached his hand toward William, passing Sean without so much as an acknowledging glance.

William saw Sean's fingers tighten around the hilt of his sword. "It's alright, Sean." he assured him quickly, accepting Cletus' hand. "This is Cletus Gallagher, I've told you of him." He squeezed Cletus' hand before letting it go. "I spent a night or two as a guest in his hut. Very welcome nights those were, my friend."

Sean relaxed and extended his hand toward the sentry. "Forgive my impatience before, sir."

Cletus shook Sean's hand amicably, then took a step back. "Fully understandable, sir. It is unfortunate that Aberdoir is not famous for its civility." He gave a quick grin to William.

"No apologies needed." Sean smiled. "But the fact remains that I have a letter I must deliver in person to the earl of Aberdoir."

"Oh, aye," Cletus replied, opening the gate for Sean and William. As they moved past, he muttered under his breath, "Heads up, lad. He's home."

William nodded his understanding and drew in a long breath. "I know."

They trotted up the long cobbled walkway toward the house, passing the stable yard along the way. William noted the horses were all flawlessly groomed, their coats curried and glossy in the sunlight, their manes brushed smooth as a Spring maiden's. The stables were spotless, the mangers filled with the best of the summer apples and oats so that the horses would be content and flourish. The groomsman was leading a magnificent roan from the barn to the training ring.

"Beautiful beast," William said. His jaw tightened, as he caught sight of the dilapidated grooms-hut and the deplorable, worn-out boots the man wore, knowing it was the best the man could afford in Thomas' employ. "So well cared for don't you agree...?"

"Easy, lad." Sean cautioned.

William gave a quick wave to the groomsman as they passed but the man didn't seem to recognize him and did not respond.

Just as well; I've no want to stay and socialize.

When they reached the house, Sean dismounted and tethered Hawk to a post. William remained on his horse. Sean lifted a heavy brass knocker and pounded, then stepped back to wait for the door to open. "Coming, Will?"

William shook his head. Sean offered no opinion or rebuke for William's hesitance to follow him into the house, for which William was grateful.

A moment later, the heavy door creaked open and a silver haired gentleman wearing the formal dress of a chamberlain stepped into the threshold. "Yes?" he inquired, then caught site of William sitting on his horse, ten paces from the door. The man gave a quick glance over his shoulder, then stepped out onto the stairs pulling the massive door closed behind him. "Not today! You've no idea... " He hurried past Sean as if he were invisible and dashed to William, his hand to his mouth. "Is it you?"

"What the-" Sean grumbled, following behind the man. "Sir?"

William replied to the old man, quietly. "Yes, it's me. Hello, Chase."

"Another friend?" Sean growled. "Shall I never deliver this damned thing?"

"Peace, Sean," William said quickly, then turned back to Chase, who was nervously worrying the hem of his tunic between his fingers. "Is something wrong?"

"You cannot be here, today of all days—" A crash, followed by an angry shout came from within the house just beyond the door. Chase wheeled at the sound, then motioned to the hedges that lined the walk. "Behind there! Quickly!" he said, disappearing through a gap in the hedge.

William led Star through the narrow gap where Chase had gone. Sean grabbed Hawk's reins, following the two. "What's happening?" Sean asked quietly.

"Oh, what is *ever* happening," Chase replied, distressed. "The lord of the manor is in a pique of anger over a deal gone wrong and I'm afraid he's taking it out on the staff."

"Typical," William grumbled, dismounting.

"Yes. He's particularly angry with my daughter, Annlise, and I'm dreadfully worried about her. She's not his favorite at the moment, I'm afraid."

"Favorite?" Sean asked, flinching as a small stool suddenly crashed through a nearby window. "The sot has favorites among the servants? What sort of favorites?"

William impatiently pulled Sean into the hedge. "What kind do you think, lunk; *favorites*!"

Sean's face flushed as he finally understood. "Oh."

"Oh, dear, Henry's ottoman," Chase moaned. "I shall never get the mud out of the velvet. He shall blame Annlise for the stain," he muttered.

William could see Chase's concern was not really about the ottoman. "Why is my brother angry with her?" he asked quickly, pulling on Chase's clothing to get the man's full attention. A wild panic welled up in him. "She didn't slap Bryndah, did she?"

"No!" cried Chase. "No, thank the Blessed Mother; this has naught to do with Lady Bryndah."

William relaxed and released the man's clothing. "What then? Did she refuse him?"

"No. Annlise has been quite fortunate that he has, for his own reasons, decreed that her virtue was of some value."

Chase explained, ducking a little lower under the bushes. "It is more complicated. You see, she has insulted and defied him by refusing to wed as he bid her to."

"What?" William asked, confused. "What cares he how the servants pair? Has he taken to arranging marriages amongst the groomsmen and house staff?"

"Down!" Sean yelled suddenly, shoving William out of the path of flying window debris, this one caused by a bronze bust of old King Alfred. Shards of shattered window pane rained down, littering the grass.

Star reared, loosing a startled whinny. William looked up at the window and saw the shadow of a man, arm raised, ready to hurl another object through the ruined mullions of the grand window of the drawing room.

"It's not safe here." He grabbed Star's reins, mounting quickly. "Give me your hand," he said to Chase, then hauled the man up onto his horse. "Hold on."

William charged across the fussy lawn, Star's hooves leaving deep divots in the perfectly manicured green. He would not have given the grass a second thought in Stonehaven but glancing at the sod being tossed, he felt a familiar pang of dread, realizing Thomas would surely blame the innocent grounds keeper for the damage. He turned abruptly, leading his horse to the cobblestones, Sean following. The hooves clattered along the path and William hoped Thomas was still yelling at whomever and would not hear them.

"Where are we going?" Chase asked, his arms tight around William's waste.

William rounded the back of the horse barn and brought Star to an abrupt halt. "Here," he said, and dismounted, glancing back toward the house. The only part of it visible from where he stood was the back wall of the south wing, where he knew only one small window looked out over this part of estate. He was certain no one would be in that particular room— the room that used to be his own quarters. He helped Chase dismount, just as Sean rounded the corner.

"All clear?" William asked, knowing instantly that Sean had hung back deliberately, making sure they had not been seen.

Sean nodded and dismounted, leading Hawk as he joined William and Chase. "What are you doing, Will? I've still got this blasted letter to—"

"Hang the letter!" William shouted. "You're not going to deliver it right now. Unless you fancy carrying your head home on your lap." William raised a hand to forestall an argument. "Trust me! I've seen rages like this before, Sean, and be clear on this: you are not going into that house, do you understand?"

Sean stood staring, a grin slowly spreading on his face, he bowed deeply. "Aye, my lord." When he stood straight, the grin was completely gone.

To William's astonishment, he realized Sean's bow had not been in jest. Sean had responded as he had been trained; to respond to an order from... William felt his face flush at the notion that just occurred to him— the uncomfortable truth that he and Sean were not on the equal standing he always considered them to be. William was the favored adopted son of the duke of Stonehaven and Sean, simply a sentry within his guard. In the absence of Lord Edward— William suddenly realized— Sean was in service to him and even more astonishing, Sean seemed to accept this as a matter of course. The thought of his good friend being in service to him was not an altogether comfortable one for William but he would sort that out after they had left Aberdoir. His primary concern for the moment was to get far away as quickly as possible and to keep Sean from inadvertently landing himself on Thomas' famous 'watch' list. Accidents tended to happen to those who Thomas had chosen to 'watch'.

William turned to Chase and asked, "Where is your daughter now?"

"Last I saw her, she was in the scullery, crying," Chase replied.

"Why?" Sean asked.

"Because Thomas refused to release her from her betrothal." Chase sighed. "Oh, it's so complicated."

"I still fail to understand why Thomas is bargaining marriages amongst the staff," William said. "Who was she to promised to?"

Chase scowled. "A dreadful man who has maneuvered his way into the affections of some very powerful people, here and in England. His name is Tearlach, Adrian Tearlach. An up and comer with a ruthless ambition. Lord Thomas has been most eager to win his loyalties as he sees a relationship with him to be potentially very lucrative."

"How does your daughter play in this?" Sean asked. "Surely a man that ambitious would be wooing the daughter of a nobleman – no offence to you, sir."

"Oh, none taken, lad. I quite agree. It mystifies me as well. But on a couple of visits, Annlise was in attendance with Lady Bryndah and Tearlach simply took a liking to her. He fancied her and actually asked my lord Thomas if he could have her. Naturally, the request was not refused. Uh, not by Lord Thomas and Lady Bryndah, that is."

"The sot." William spat.

"I take it your daughter refused?" Sean queried.

"On the contrary," Chase said. "At first, that is. "You see, during those first visits when Annlise had caught Tearlach's eye, he had also caught hers. There was a mutual flirtation, I suppose. Then Lord Thomas approached her, encouraging her to win Tearlach's affection, even offering to provide her a modest dowry of twenty gold pieces. Annlise was beside herself with joy, thanking him, kissing his ring; it was disgusting."

William scowled at the thought of anyone kissing Thomas' ring, or any other part of him for that matter. "So, what changed?"

"Adrian Tearlach did," Chase said quietly. "Once they were properly betrothed, the marriage contract signed; his true nature began to show. He'd come to call, drunk, demanding her attention. 'Training' he called it, for when they were wed, proclaiming that a wife of Adrian Tearlach would be well trained to suit him or she would be cast to the street in disgrace."

William shook his head. "Sounds like just the sort of wretch that my brother would consider a friend. The bastard."

"So what caused this row today, sir?" Sean asked, his lips drawn tight. He seemed to be as disgusted as William was at hearing Chase's account.

"Tearlach is due for a call. Annlise told Lord Thomas she would not see him, under any circumstances. He is furious and told her he'd be sure to allow Tearlach free access to search her out. Annlise stood her ground and yelled at him. He took it as a slap in the face; you see? She's so like her sister Rebecca was... "

William's eyes went wide, in understanding. He placed his hand on the elderly man's arm, and looked at him closely. "Not this time, Quentin, he'll not harm her, I swear it. You leave it to Sean and I. We'll get her away from here; won't we, Sean."

"Uh... oh, aye... sure. " When Sean saw the tears brimming in the old man's eyes, he clasped his first to his chest and answered in firm voice, "You have my word, sir. We'll see her away."

"Bless you, Master Will, and you... I'm sorry, I don't know your name."

"Forgive me." William half laughed. "Quentin Chase, this is my companion, Sir Sean Wilbrun. Sean, Quentin... he used to be my grandfather."

"Pleased to meet you, Sir—"

"Grandfather?" Sean asked, interrupting the introductions.

Chase chuckled. "Grandfather in affection only. When Master William lived here, he spent a good deal of time in my eldest daughter, Rebecca's, care and we became quite good friends; aye?"

"Aye." William smiled in agreement.

He had long ago told Sean the story of his favorite nurse and how she'd come to a rather brutal end, having stood up to Lady Bryndah on his behalf. He could see that understanding in Sean's face and knew he would not have to explain to him why he had just volunteered to rescue Annlise from Aberdoir. He could see Sean was already working a plan.

"Well, one thing is certain, Will; you need to stay out of sight. We can't let the sot know you're anywhere near Aberdoir," Sean began. "The only ones who know you're here are Chase, here, and the fellow at the gate – can he be trusted?"

"Cletus? Absolutely." Chase assured him.

William nodded his agreement.

"Good," Sean said. "We need to leave the estate with as few

witnesses as possible. Quentin, you're to go back to the house, and—"

"Leave? But what about Annlise?" William asked. "We're taking her with us, Sean, there is no way I'll be leaving—"

"I'm getting there, lunk; be quiet!" Sean snapped.

William grinned and shut his mouth. *Equals again, aye?*

"That's better." Sean nodded sharply. "Quentin, you're to go back to the house and get your daughter ready to travel as quickly as possible. Tell her to slip out as quietly as she can and come to us. Will and I will be in the tavern on the lane, the one with the hawk—"

"The Hawk and Hound!" Quentin interjected, excitedly.

"Aye, that one." Sean confirmed. "We'll be waiting for her. We'll have the horses tethered out behind the building and then we'll slip out that way. Clear?"

"Aye, thank you, Sir Sean."

"Will? Any questions?"

"No, it's a good plan," William replied, then looked to Quentin. "We'll stay in the tavern for as long as it takes for her to join us. We'll even hire lodging for the night if we must, to secure the deception. But I swear, we shall not leave Aberdoir without her."

"Bless you."

William nodded, then mounted his horse. Sean did the same and the two galloped back through the gate, waving to Cletus as they passed but not stopping to talk. They headed straight to the Hawk and Hound. William went in first while Sean led the horses through a narrow alley and around to the back. A moment later, the two were seated at a table near the window, pints of strong barley ale before them as they waited for Annlise

Chase.

An hour and three pints later, William and Sean still sat at the table by the tavern window, staring at the passersby as they trundled about the market. Just outside the window, a fellow in harlequin dress called out to the shoppers about the marvelously carved toys he was selling.

"Good day, m'lady," he called, bowing so deeply as to touch his nose to the ground, then bouncing up spring-like, producing an oversized paper corsage as if from mid air. "A pretty flower for a pretty lady, who I'm sure has pretty wee children who would love to play pretty games with these pretty toys... "

The ladies gave half a glance to the cart, then one of them pointed out a bolt of shimmering green silk another merchant was displaying and they hurried away from the toy man. William saw the harlequin's shoulders slouch at the ladies departure but within a heartbeat, he'd sprung to another potential customer, bowing and repeating his pretty little speech. This customer, too, walked by without acknowledging the toys. William watched him with a growing admiration for the fellow's persistence in the face of constant rejection. He looked up over his pint to see Sean was also watching the harlequin.

"How much do you suppose that painted horse costs?" Sean asked, pointing with his mug.

"Hmm?" William asked, drawing a sip.

"That horse. The red one."

"Don't know," William replied. "A couple of coppers, I suppose."

Sean nodded, reaching for the pouch he wore on his belt, feeling through the material. The serving lass came by just then and cleared her throat to gain their attention. Sean emptied the pouch into his hand— a single coin— and glanced again out the window. He palmed the coin for a moment and was about to toss it onto the lass' tray when William called for another round. Sean raised his brow in question.

William grinned. "Don't worry, I brought my stipend. The pints are on me."

There again was that uncomfortable realization that Sean and he really did come from an unequal standing. Sean made a decent allowance as part of Edward's guard but, by his own choosing since his father had passed away, Sean gave most of his earnings to his mother. The little he kept for himself,— more often than not— he'd spend on little gifts for his wee brother, Duncan, who was not quite four years old. William, on the other hand, received a generous stipend each month to do with as he pleased without worry. He'd always been careful not to flaunt it before Sean, aware of his friend's pride in providing for himself and his family, but there were times— like this one— where he wondered if Sean resented his station in life.

"Here, lass," William said, tossing a coin onto her serving tray. She smiled for half a breath, before sauntering away.

"I can cover the next round," Sean said, flipping his last coin to William.

William sighed, not wanting to offend his friend by refusing, but wanting to help nonetheless. "I don't think I can hold another round," he said, laughing. "I'm already feeling lightheaded." He tossed the coin back to Sean. "Unless you wish to see me quite potted."

Sean grinned, dropping the coin back into his pouch. "Well, we can't be pulling off a proper rescue if you're potted now, can we?"

"Absolutely not," William agreed laughing, pleased with himself for finding a graceful way for Sean to keep his money. William suspected that the coin would soon be in the harlequin's pocket covering the cost of one brightly painted wooden horse for Duncan.

"The carving is rough, though," Sean said, still looking at the cart of trinkets. "You've done better work than that when you're half potted."

William laughed. "I've never done any carving while potted and I have all ten fingers to prove it." He took a closer look at the wares on the cart. The carving was quite good to William's eye and he reasoned Sean was simply talking himself out of wanting to buy it. "But thank you for the compliment. I should like to try animals like that. I've made so many bracelets I'm bored with them."

It was Sean's turn to laugh. "Is it that you've grown bored? Or run out of lassies to give them to? I believe you've adorned the wrist of every lass in Stonehaven."

"Well I cannae very well wear them m'self, can I?"

"And for all those bracelets given, what have you gotten in return? Hmm?"

William grinned and sipped his ale. "Friends."

"Uh huh, I should have so many *friends*." Sean turned his attention back to the window. "Do you think she'll be here soon?"

Before William could answer, a commotion in the street took his attention. A young woman with strawberry hair was darting between the carts, looking over her shoulder as she ran. The harlequin purposely leapt out in front of her causing a glorious collision. A crowd gathered around, laughing and pointing as the harlequin moaned in exaggerated pain, clutching at the woman's hand as he struggled to his feet.

"Let go!" she cried, looking frantically over her shoulder.

"Oh, my love! Why must you leave?" The harlequin warbled, feeding on the laughter his performance was bringing.

"Come on!" William said suddenly, jumping to his feet. "That's her." He ran for the door, Sean at his heels.

The crowd was thick and William had to shove his way through. "Let me through... please, excuse me... please... "

"Let go of me!" she cried out again, only to be answered by a trembling oath of love and more laughter.

Sean tried to push a man aside and was rudely tripped by an elderly woman's walking stick.

"Mind ye manners!" she cackled, poking him in the backside.

William heard Sean swear an oath he usually reserved for when he fell during a joust. He turned to see Sean, red-faced, glaring angrily at the old woman.

"Sean! This way!" He waved over the heads of the people standing around him.

Sean looked up, waved, and pushed the woman aside— gently, by all means, but enough that she dropped her stick and landed bottom first onto a wheel barrow full of silks.

Annlise was still trying to extricate herself from the harlequin when William spotted two other men forcing their way through the crowd on horseback, coming from the opposite direction. One, he recognized immediately as his brother; the other, a stern looking man with fire in his eyes whom he assumed was Adrian Tearlach.

He glanced over his shoulder to see Sean right behind. He

pointed out the men and saw Sean nod his understanding. "Get her and get out of here! I'll keep them busy!"

"Where will we meet?" Sean called, moving toward the harlequin.

"Head into the forest! Mark the trees as a signal – just go!" William called, then dove into the crowd, burrowing through a tangle of skirts and stockings. He wormed his way under a table, then scrambled to the back of the harlequin's cart.

"Let me go!" Annlise yelled, her voice strained and panicked.

"Unhand that woman, you blackguard!" a man yelled suddenly.

William looked up to see Sean posturing before the harlequin.

"There!" Thomas yelled.

William found his moment, pushing the cart with all his might into his brother's path, overturning the colorful faire onto the street.

"Oh no!" the harlequin wailed, releasing Annlise to scramble about to retrieve his toys.

"Go!" William called, waving to Sean.

Sean nodded and scooped a startled looking Annlise onto his shoulder, then charged back through the crowd and into the tavern.

"Stop them!" William heard Thomas shouting.

Adrian dismounted and promptly tripped on one of the spilled toys, falling to his knees. The crowd burst into a new round of laughter that abruptly turned to shrieks when Adrian angrily brandished his sword and began swinging. William pushed himself against the side of the tavern to avoid being trampled as panic-stricken marketers stampeded away from the lane. In a moment, the only people left in the lane were William, his brother, Adrian Tearlach, and the harlequin who lay face down on the cobbled street amid a growing puddle of crimson.

Adrian sheathed his sword, spinning on his heel looking all around. William crouched as far into the shadows as possible to avoid being seen.

"Where did she go?" Adrian growled, wheeling on Thomas and knotting his fingers into the hem of the earl's cloak, yanking at him.

The horse reared, startled, and Thomas slid from the saddle, landing hard on his knees. Adrian grabbed him by the cloak again, hauling him to his feet, planting his face inches from startled earl.

"Where? You told me you could control her!"

Thomas stammered for a moment struggling, his face going white. William had never seen his brother intimidated by anyone. This Adrian Tearlach must be fearsome indeed, if even Thomas showed fear in his presence.

"I... I didn't see... she vanished into the crowd!" Thomas stammered.

Adrian grunted an unintelligible reply, releasing Thomas' cloak by shoving him to the ground. Thomas slowly got to his feet, keeping a wary eye on Adrian.

"You have my guard at your disposal; they'll find her, I swear it."

Adrian glared at Thomas, his nostrils wrinkled in a snarl under oddly golden eyes. "You are useless to me, Fylbrigge. I shall find her myself!"

Thomas glared back for a moment, then spun on his heel

and remounted his horse, his cape flailing in a grand flutter as he galloped back up the lane toward the gates to Aberdoir Hall.

William stood silent, his back pressed hard against the outside wall of the tavern. Adrian stormed toward the tavern door, then stopped suddenly on the step and turned to look directly at William. "You! How long have you been there?"

William pointed innocently to his chest and shrugged his shoulders.

"Yes, you!" Adrian took a step forward, his golden eyes narrowing. "I saw you watching; where did the wench go?"

William looked over his shoulder, feigning confusion, then shrugged again. "Who d'ye mean, what wench be ye lookin' for?" he asked, affecting the course dialect of the common people. He hoped Adrian would take him for a peasant and wouldn't notice his fine linen shirt and his shining leather boots. "Be lot o' wenches 'round this part o' town, ye know. How'm I t' know which wench ye be lookin' for?"

Adrian grabbed William's collar and pushed him against the wall. "You know the one, boy! Do not trifle with me or your body shall litter the cobbles alongside that fool behind me!" He motioned with a quick flick of his head to the harlequin, still lying face down on the street. "Tell me which way she went!"

Before William could answer, a woman screamed from inside the tavern. "I said, put me down, you filthy cad!"

Her cries were answered by a thud and a man's groaning as if he'd been punched in the stomach. "I'm trying to help you, woman!"

William tried not to react to the scream or Sean's groan of assistance but, for an instant, his eyes betrayed him and he glanced toward the door.

Adrian was quick to react, his golden eyes flashing as the grin spread on his face. "In there, are they? 'Tis a lucky day for you, lad. You get to keep your blood." He gave William one more shove against the wall, then released him and stalked into the tavern.

William caught his breath quickly and quietly slipped into the tavern behind Adrian. The place was empty of patrons, the tables overturned, mugs and plates scattered about the floor. There was no sign of Sean and Annlise and for the moment, the place had gone completely silent. The tavern keeper and serving maid were huddled together by a door as Adrian stormed over to them.

"Where?" he bellowed, brandishing his sword.

The inn keeper raised a shaking finger, pointing to the door. As he did, there came another round of arguing from the back room, punctuated by the sound of crashing pottery and more defiant shouts followed by impatient groans. To William's dismay, it sounded as though the lass was getting the better of Sean, inadvertently pummeling her would-be rescuer with kitchen utensils.

Adrian heard the skirmish and moved to push the inn keeper away from the door. William picked up a pewter mug from the floor and hurled it across the room, hitting Adrian neatly in the back of the head. Adrian cursed and wheeled around just as William threw a second mug, this one hitting him square in the face. He dropped his sword and staggered forward clutching at his bleeding nose. He looked through his fingers at William, the odd golden eyes wide and focused as he lunged for his sword. William picked up a stool and hurled that at Adrian as the arguing continued in the next room.

"Go, dammit!" William hollered through the door as Adrian deflected the stool and retrieved his sword.

"You bloody foolish boy! " Adrian snarled as he lunged toward William, the woman he'd been seeking now seemingly forgotten.

There were no more mugs or stools within his reach as Adrian began his swing. Thinking quickly, William dove, curling himself into ball, literally bowling the incensed Adrian to the floor and causing his head to crash against the thick wooden leg of one of the overturned tables. As Adrian lay dazed and moaning, William scrambled past the terrified inn keeper and maid, tossing them his money pouch.

"For damages!" he explained as he ran through the door to the back room.

He ducked just in time to avoid a piece of flying crockery that crashed to the door, just where his head had been. "Annlise! It's us!" he yelled, scurrying across the room on hands and knees, to where Sean sat covering his head with his arms fending off flying pottery. Another pot crashed above them before she stopped short, her face suddenly bursting into an unexpected smile.

"Will?" She dropped the ladle she'd grabbed and ran to him, dropping to her knees on the floor next to him. She flung her arms around his head and hugged him. "Where have you been? Father told me to look for you! But this – this oaf has been in my way!"

"That's gratitude!" Sean grumbled, getting to his feet. "Risk my neck for a lady and she calls me an oaf! Really, Will, are you certain this is the lass we're supposed to be helping?"

Annlise's eyes went wide, and she drew her hand to her

mouth. "Oh, dear! You mean... you really are... ?"

"He's with me," William said simply. "I take it your father did not mention Sean."

"No, there was little time, he only told me t' look for you – Oh, my! I'm – I'm terribly sorry! Here, let me help you up!"

She tugged on Sean's arm. He raised his hand and motioned her to step back as he got to his feet on his own.

The inn keeper stuck his head through the door and whispered frantically, "The sot is waking up! Get ye out now!"

"Bloody hell!" William spat and jumped to his feet. "Sean, take Annlise and head for the forest."

"All of us go together!" Sean insisted.

"I'll be right behind you! Mark the trees like we planned," William said as, he pushed Sean and Annlise toward the door. "Go!"

"But—" Sean began as the door slammed in his face.

William turned just in time to see Adrian Tearlach stagger through the swinging door.

"You!" Tearlach raised his sword menacingly and slowly crossed the room.

"Uh, yes, me," William stammered, grabbing an iron skillet off the wall. He gave a quick glance out of the little window on the door and noted with relief that Sean and Annlise had fled on Hawk. Only Star was left tethered to the post.

Adrian raised his sword and stormed across the room. William hurled the skillet, knocking the sword from Adrian's hand and hurried out the door. Star tossed her mane and stamped her hooves excitedly when she saw him coming.

"Easy girl," he said, fumbling with the reins. He cursed Sean for not being more careful when he'd tethered Star, as the reins were knotted into a hopeless tangle around the hitching post. He had barely gotten the reins free of the post when Adrian slammed open the tavern's back door so hard, that it slammed back into the jamb behind him in an explosion of shattered wood.

William leapt onto Star and kicked in sharply before he'd even had time to secure his feet properly in the stirrups. Star reared, as he clung to her mane to keep from being thrown.

"Yah!" he shouted. The mare charged out of the alley while William miraculously righted himself in the saddle. A quick glance over his shoulder and he saw Adrian dash back into the tavern. *He's going for his horse on the other side!* "Run, Star... come on, girl. Go!" he urged, charging through the narrow alley between the shops, his eyes fixed on the open road at the end of the lane that ran parallel with the market street.

William reasoned that Sean would have gone through the narrow street and back up the hill toward the forest. A thin veil of dust lingered at the end of the alley that William assumed had been caused by Hawk galloping away. *Good, he made a clean break. All I have to do is catch up. I made it! Well done, Fylbrigge!*

His self congratulations ended abruptly when he heard a thunderous echo of hooves on cobbles. The alley was not cobbled and Star's hooves pounded relatively quietly in the dust. It had to be Adrian on the large black charger he'd ridden into the market, charging up the parallel street bent on blocking William's exit from the alley.

"Damn!" He reined in hard and turned Star on her back hooves, charging back toward the tavern. The echoes of Adrian's horse continued away toward the open road. *Good, keep going.* When he'd gotten back to the tavern, the inn keeper was standing by the door, waving a rag in the air. William pulled Star to a halt and the man hurried over.

"You have to get out of town!" the man wailed.

"That's what I'm trying to do!" William answered, breathlessly, looking back over his shoulder. He went to kick, to continue down the alley, when the inn keeper grabbed the reins. "What are you—?"

"There!" came a shout from the end of the alley where William had wanted to go. Suddenly four horsemen appeared, blocking the way.

William whirled, and saw Adrian charging toward him from the other end where he'd just come. There was no place to go.

Star reared and the inn keeper pulled her down. "This way!" he shouted, and to William's surprise, pulled him horse and all, through the small back door of the tavern. The inn keeper hurried across the room and opened the door into the tavern, where the serving lass was standing by the front door, looking one way then the other out on the lane.

"Safe!" she cried, and waved William toward the door, Star's hooves clattering on the wooden floorboards. "Run straight across and keep going!"

"Straight?" William asked, then caught site of the shop across the lane, and the portly man in a bloodstained apron waving to the serving lass. "Thank you!" he shouted, ducking, as Star raced out of the tavern door, and right toward the door of the butcher shop.

"Go!" The butcher cried, holding the door open. "Right through the back!"

William emerged into another dirty alley, where he stopped

for a moment to listen. Adrian and his men had made it to the cobbles of the market lane. If they'd seen him go through the tavern, it wouldn't take long for them to assume he'd gone through another building. *Can't stay here.* He kicked in and raced through the alley toward the open road. He kept his eyes on the end of the lane and let the clatter of the other horses fall behind him. *At least Sean's got a good head start. Good. Now all I have to do is find him.*

William cleared the end of the alley and loosed a whoop of victory that Star answered as she charged toward the forest road. *If I can get to the woods before them...* He looked over his shoulder to see Adrian and his four men emerging from the cobbled street. William had a good lead on them but he would never make it to the forest before they caught up to him. He looked again and they had gained on him. He crouched low on the saddle, allowing Star to run as fast as she could. There was no place to go but into the forest or over the cliff to his right and into the sea. Either choice could lead to disaster at this speed but the cliffs would be suicide, so he kept onward to the forest.

He raced to the thickest of the trees, dodging branches and clinging low on Star's back, trusting her to place each hoof safely, his heart pounding loudly in his ears. Oddly, he wasn't feeling frightened as he reasoned he should be, but invigorated. There he was, William Fylbrigge, the timid cast off of Aberdoir Hall, being chased by a ruthless murderer and four other horsemen— one he suspected was his own brother— who would surely hang him or run him through if they caught him.

And he was having the time of his life.

Chapter 7

"**H**OLD ON TIGHT, lass!" Sean warned. He kicked Hawk into a swift gallop away from the tavern and toward the end of the alley, Annlise on the saddle behind him with her arms locked around his waist. He hated the idea of leaving William behind to fend off Adrian alone but he'd given his word he would see this woman to safety and he was determined to keep it— even if she did seem less than grateful for the help.

"I'm truly sorry," she shouted above the noise of Hawk's racing hooves. "I had no idea. I was lookin' for Will and dinnae have a kennin' who you be."

"Never mind that now," Sean called back impatiently, more interested in getting clear of the alley than in making small-talk. "We need to get out of this place before the whole of the Aberdoir guard is set on us."

He didn't like the thought of being ambushed in the alley where there would be no place to run, but he wasn't particularly fond of the idea of running out into the open road where they'd be easily spotted either. He knew little about the people of Aberdoir and had no sense of how loyal they were to the earl and his cronies. And he did not wish to linger in town to find out. Sean knew how quickly news could spread in a small shire and he was sure several people had seen him carry Annlise, kicking and screaming, into the tavern. It occurred to him that should they recognize him racing away from town with her on his horse, it could be mistaken as an abduction.

"They won't see us," she said, as though she'd read his mind. "Just head for the road!"

"Won't see us? 'Tis broad daylight!" Sean called over his shoulder. The road was quickly approaching and the closer they got, the tighter the knot in his stomach— not for fear of ambush but because William had yet to come out of the tavern.

"Don't worry! They won't see us.Trust me!"

"Where's Will?" Sean growled, looking over his shoulder. He gave a moment's thought to reining in and turning back for his friend, when he saw movement near the tavern. Even from that distance, Sean recognized William's white shirt and his black hair. Satisfied that his friend was on his way, Sean kicked in harder and focused on the open road.

"He's behind us," he hollered to Annlise, when they'd cleared the alley. "Hold tight!" He crouched low on Hawk's back. "Yah!"

Hawk ran like the wind, faster than Sean could ever remember, across the open road, raising a cloud behind them. He was half grateful for the cloud as it concealed their identity and left a ready trail for William to follow. But it also made it easy for them to be spotted by Adrian Tearlach and his ilk as well.

"Go for the grass! Don't worry, they won't see us!" Annlise called again. "Trust me!"

"Trust? How did—"

There was no time to wonder how Annlise had read his thoughts about the dust when he heard the distant clatter of hooves on cobbles— Will had company. "Hold on," he cautioned, then turned Hawk abruptly away from the dusty road toward an open meadow. Hawk leapt over a hedge and a low wooden fence as if he'd grown wings, then thundered across the meadow, keeping true to his course toward the forest. Sean looked back again, the cloud still hung in the air above the road but there was no concealing cloud behind them on the grass.

He glanced back toward the town, now far behind them, and to his relief, he saw William emerging from an alley to the open road. "There he is!" he shouted, relieved, but only for a heartbeat as he saw the five horseman who were rapidly closing in on his friend. He looked forward, the forest was an easy sprint now and he'd be able to gain the trees, set Annlise down, then run back to help William.

"Stop!" Annlise cried, before they'd reached forest. "Stop here!"

"What? Are you daft? We're in the wide open!" Sean hollered and kept charging.

"Stop!" Annlise reached around his waist for the rein and yanked as hard as she could.

Hawk loosed a furious whinny and reared, wildly kicking his front hooves in mid-air and sending both riders onto the sod. Sean landed hard on his right hand. It snapped beneath the weight of his body as he hit the ground and his vision went black for a moment.

"What in God's name did you do that for!" Sean bellowed, clutching at his wrist. He winced at the sudden spears of pain that shot up his arm, a splinter of white bone showing through a gash in flesh. "Bloody hell!" he growled as he tried but failed to form a fist with his damaged hand.

Annlise gasped, recovering the breath that had been knocked out of her from the fall. She moved to him, and reached for his hand. "Let me look, I can help—"

"No!" He recoiled, drawing his arm close to his chest. "You've been enough help!"

"But I can heal—"

"Stay back!" he snapped, then looked around for Hawk. The horse had wandered to a patch of alfalfa and was peacefully grazing, seemingly unperturbed by the abrupt end to his race. Sean looked back toward the road, and discovered that from his spot on the ground, he could not see it. He lay at the bottom of a grassy hollow surrounded by a hillock which blocked his view. He released his breath and settled in the grass, cradling his arm.

Grudgingly, he admitted to himself that she'd halted them in a perfect place in the open air, where they'd be able to lie low in the tall grass but still be able to hear if anyone approached. Had he raced on toward the forest, they would have been in plain sight at the top of the rise. Even more startling, Sean realized as he looked toward where he had been headed, there was a group of men clad in the brown woolen robes of clerics mulling about at the forest's edge, one of them as tall and broad as a brown bear.

"Is that who I think it is?" he asked.

Annlise looked toward the huge cleric, her nose wrinkled as though the very sight of him smelled foul. "Joseph." she spat. "I'd rather cuddle a hedgehog than set eyes on that bloke. How are ye knowin' o' that one?"

"Will," Sean muttered, grinding his teeth. "He described him right; said he looked like a bear with the face of pig. I'm glad we didn't run into— Will!"

There came the sudden sound of hooves on the road.

"Will—" Sean turned and started to crawl up to the top of the hillock. "He'll run right to them! We need to warn—" The pain in his wrist stole his breath and he knew then he'd broken more than just his hand. He groaned against the pain and attempted to crawl up the hill again.

"No!" Annlise hissed suddenly, then pulled him back down into the grass. "They be only gathering berries and wild grapes I suspect. They winnae take notice of us if you stay down. Aye, 'twould not be good for Will to meet with the bastard, but you mus' trust me!"

Before Sean could argue, Annlise stood straight up and ran to the top of the hillock, in full view of the world and God Almighty. "Annlise! Down!"

"Shh!" She glared at him to silence him. "Trust me!" she said again, then turned her face suddenly to the sun. She placed the palm of her right hand flat against her sternum, the left she turned skyward. Star's hoof beats were getting closer but so were the others.

Sean could hear the men shouting for Will to halt and their horses snorting with the strain of the furious galloping. Sean desperately wanted to cry out to get William's attention but he'd draw the attention of not only the clerics in the forest, but the very man he'd promised to take Annlise away from as well. And there she was, standing bold and bright for all to see. *What foolishness is this! She'll have them on us—*

Annlise threw her head back and opened her mouth and let out a resounding song-like wail. The hooves thundered closer now, only slightly muffled, and Sean could tell that William had left the road for the meadow, his pursuers close behind. They were drawing closer and yet, Annlise stood still as a stone, lifting her strange, bell-like song to the sky. Her voice grew louder with each second and, for one terrifying moment, Sean wondered if she had betrayed them, deliberately calling them out to the clerics and the angry horseman.

When he could no longer stand being blinded by the walls of the hollow, Sean crawled up to the rim, doing his best to ignore the pain in his arm. He lay flat on his stomach, looking over the edge. To his horror, he saw William charging directly toward them with Adrian on his heels and reaching for his blade. Amongst the four men behind Adrian, Sean recognized the black-bearded man in the fluttering black cape as William's brother, Thomas. Oh, this just keeps getting better, he thought, his heart sinking.

"Annlise! Get down!" he yelled.

She did not respond to him, her song ringing all around him now, as if the grass and rocks had joined the chant.

William raced closer, on a straight course to the hillock. Adrian chased behind with his sword raised, the other four moving into flanking positions. Closer and closer they came, until they were so close that Sean swore he could feel Star's breath on his face. Still, Annlise did not move, her song reverberating all around.

"Will! I'm here!" he called to his friend.

William charged faster, Star's hooves now in a direct path with Sean's head. He flattened himself against the ground, fully expecting to be trampled.

Star was a mere arm's length away when Sean heard William's voice yelling, "Jump!" Star leapt into flight, passing over Sean's head, landing easily on the far side of the hollow.

What he witnessed then, Sean would never fully understand. Just as William touched down, Annlise cut off her song leaving only waning echoes behind. She held her rigid pose as right in front of her, Adrian, Thomas and the other riders suddenly reined to a halt. They uttered surprised curses, looking to each other and to the field beyond. Not one of them took any notice of the woman standing before them, her face and arm still turned skyward.

"Where did he go?" Adrian grumbled, sheathing his sword.

The horsemen looked to each other with startled faces. "Did you see?" one asked, as another made the sign of the cross. "He vanished!"

"You saw for yourself!"

"Into the mists!"

"'Tis sorcery!"

Sorcery? What be this? Sean looked behind and could see William quite clearly galloping away toward the forest. *He's right before them! Can't they see him?*

"That's ridiculous!" Thomas spat. "'Tis simply a trick. It must be. We'll... find him."

"You find him!" another of the riders growled, crossing himself as the other had. "That be a devil, that is! I will not be chasin' after a devil. You can keep the bounty!"

He reined in and turned his horse back toward the road. The other three followed, leaving Thomas and Adrian standing alone, only a yard away from Annlise and Sean. Yet miraculously, they took no notice of the pair.

"Devil, pah!" Adrian spat. "'Tis a glare from the sun, nothing more! Come on!"

Thomas hesitated. "I think I'll go back."

"What?" Adrian sneered. "You, Thomas? I'm surprised that you, of all people, would believe such superstitious drivel."

"Perhaps I do, Adrian," Thomas retorted, hotly. "But perhaps it is better if we let him go. For now. We've run him out of

Aberdoir. That should suffice."

"The boy insulted me! Attacked me! His accomplice stole my bride out from under your very nose. And you think it best to simply banish him from Aberdoir? Really, Thomas, don't tell me you've gone soft."

"Soft?" Thomas scoffed. "Hardly. I am simply looking out for my own best interest." He hesitated, stroking his beard. "I did not get a look at his face but I am near certain I know that boy. And if he be who I suspect he is, trust me, we shall both be richer men for letting him go— for now. Of course, I cannot stop you from doing as you wish."

The bastard. Sean thought, wishing his sword arm was not broken. So Thomas did recognize him. *How noble of you, to call the dogs off ye own brother... Let Adrian do your dirty work like you let that bastard cleric do it afore him!* Sean turned to see William approaching the forest's edge, where the clerics were all still gathered. Then, to Sean's further astonishment, he watched William gallop into the woods, right past Joseph and into the shadows; neither seeming to have taken notice of the other. He shot a look up to Annlise, who still had not moved. *What is she?*

"There is still the matter of my bride," Adrian was saying.

"Oh, yes," Thomas sighed. "I'm dreadfully sorry the wench chose to flee but I warned you she could not be trusted. The low-born never can be, you know."

Adrian snorted a laugh. "So true. But I do have my pride to guard. I shall find them. Go on back if you choose but I think I shall keep looking."

"For the mere thrill of the hunt?" Thomas asked, grinning.

"And to reclaim the twenty gold pieces you gave her for a dowry."

They turned their horses and trotted back to the road, then waved to each other as Thomas headed back toward Aberdoir and Adrian to the forest. When they had both disappeared, Annlise dropped to her knees.

"Lass!" Sean put his good arm around her and held her. "Annlise? Please, say something."

She blinked her eyes dreamily, then smiled at him.

Sean stared dumfounded, trying to think of something to say. If he understood what he'd just seen, Annlise had somehow managed to hide them in plain sight and make it seem as if William had vanished into the non-existent mist of a perfectly clear afternoon.

"Lass? What did you do?"

She did not answer, only looked at him deeply, unblinking, and for the first time he noticed that her eyes were as blue as the sky shining at him. He stared into those eyes, unable to look away, as if she held him captive by her will alone. He felt a shudder in the center of his stomach— a mixture of confusion, excitement and fear— as he tried to close his eyes and found he could not. And he found that he truly did not want to. Since the first moment he'd seen her in the melee of the market street, this was the first true look he had gotten of her face – and her eyes, those wondrously blue eyes, set deep and wide within a porcelain face, beneath a cascade of strawberry curls. *What spell is this... ? How is it I've just now seen her... Sean, get hold o' yeself, lad, this be no time to fall smitten...*

She shifted her position, keeping her unblinking eyes on him. He had the vague sense that he was walking before he felt the gentle swaying of the horse beneath him. He wondered dully when, and how, he'd remounted, though all he could see were Annlise's eyes. The world began to dim.

"Lass?" he whispered.

She raised her hand and gently caressed his eyelids. She uttered a one word command that he found impossible to disobey.

"Sleep."

Chapter 8

WILLIAM VEERED OFF the road where he saw the dust cloud end, assuming that was the way Sean had gone. He took a quick look over his shoulder and kicked in harder. Adrian was closing fast, as were the other riders. There was no sign of Sean and Annlise ahead of him that he could see, save for the fresh divots in the grass made by galloping hooves.

"Halt!" Adrian yelled from behind him, now so close that his shadow was visible on the ground, reaching for his sword.

William crouched low on Star's back, his eyes fixed on a dip in the meadow. From the periphery of his vision, he saw the other riders moving along side and he knew it was only a matter of seconds before they would be on him.

"Jump!" he yelled, as he reached the hillock. Star launched with an eager whinny, sailing over the dip as if she'd suddenly borne wings, landing gracefully on the far side. William dared not risk another look behind; he could tell the others had fallen back. Encouraged, he urged Star ever faster until at last, he reached the shelter of the forest. Star slowed on her own as they crossed into the shadows, balking when he tried to lead her to his left.

"What is it?" he asked. He reined her under control, then turned. He was startled when he saw the movement of something large from the corner of his eye. "A bear?" He looked but saw nothing. "Come on, this way – what is the matter with you?" he scolded.

But Star refused to proceed in the direction he wanted her

to go. She stamped her hooves and shook her mane with an indignant snort. William looked around again; peering through the trees, back down to the meadow.

"They've stopped! They're just standing there," he said, as though Star would understand him. He watched, amazed and confused, as the party of horseman suddenly disbanded. It was then he recognized one of the riders as Thomas. "I knew it," he grumbled.

Star suddenly balked again, backing away from something William couldn't see. "Easy, girl." He held her steady until he noticed an odd rustling in a nearby bush and heard the snapping of a twig.

"Who's there?" he called.

When no answer came, he indulged Star and let her turn away from the sound. He glanced again, through the trees, and saw Thomas and Adrian part company, with Adrian heading toward the forest road.

"Go!"

He kicked in, allowing Star to take her own course around the phantom in the bush. When they were clear, he led her into the thicker part of the forest, staying as far from the road as he could. He'd lie low in the shadows to give Adrian time to give up or get lost, before looking for the marks Sean would have made to mark his trail.

"We'll catch up soon, Star. They cannae be very far ahead."

Chapter 9

"SEAN? WAKE UP, son."

"Hmm?"

"Seany!"

Sean opened his eyes at the sound of the voice that called him. He sat up slowly, looking all around, though all he could see was darkness. "Where are you?"

"Right here," the voice answered casually, as the darkness was suddenly banished by a bright spear of campfire. Sean stared, stunned, to see his father, now two years dead, sitting across from him and smiling as he broke small pieces of wood and fed them to the campfire.

"Papa? Is that you?"

Arthur chuckled, and broke another piece of wood. "'Course it is. Dinnae you believe what your eyes tell you, lad?"

Sean nodded, absently. "But—"

"Good. Come on, sit up. Daylight's wastin' and you have work to do."

"Work... what?"

"I raised you to always finish what you start, dinnae I? If nothing else but a name, at least I give a sense of duty, aye? That much I gave you, for certain."

Sean pinched his eyes closed then blinked hard, expecting the specter of his father to vanish, but when he opened his eyes Arthur was still sitting there, patiently feeding sticks to the fire.

"Dinnae I, son? Dinnae I raise you t' finish what you start? Have you forgotten that?"

"Well, aye you did, but... I don't understand, Papa. What haven't I finished?"

Arthur reached to his belt, withdrew a small dirk and tossed it toward Sean. It landed handle up in the ground at his feet. Sean looked up, confused.

"You best take that, and finish what you started," Arthur said, then broke more wood in his hands. Sean noticed the wood he was breaking was brightly painted— like the painted horses he'd wanted to buy for Duncan from the harlequin before the trouble broke loose in Aberdoir. "He'd rather have you home wi' him than some piece o' painted wood anyhow, you know."

"Duncan?"

"Is a sorry thing he'll be missin' you, all because you didn't finish what you started... "

"Papa? I don't understand; what are you saying? What haven't I finished?"

Arthur looked up and smiled sadly. "He's counting on you, Sean. Help him find you. He's counting on you... "

Sean stared as his father's face began to fade in the firelight. "No! Papa, wait! I don't understand. Who's counting on me? What have I forgotten?"

Before he faded, the face seemed to shift, and Sean could see an oddly familiar face of a black haired man with mischievous green eyes. "I'm counting on you... help me find you... mark the trail, Sean," he said, as the face changed again, becoming younger until Sean recognized him completely. "I cannae find you!"

"Will!" Sean bolted upright, pushing off the ground with his good hand.

"Sean? Are you well?" a woman was saying.

He looked around, confused to find he'd been lying on the forest floor. Hawk nickered quietly, on the opposite side of a campfire as Annlise knelt next to him, helping him to sit up. "Easy now, t'were just a dream you were havin."

He was aware of a dull throbbing at the side of his head and when he reached up with his right hand to feel for a lump he froze, staring at the wrapping around his hand. He squeezed his fingers into a ball, and opened them again easily. He turned to Annlise, completely confounded. "It doesn't hurt."

"Ah, good then," she said, smiling as she reached to her belt and withdrew a small knife. "I can cut the binding off then?"

Sean grabbed the knife from her hand and stared at it; it was identical to the one his father had tossed to him in the odd dream he'd had. "Finish what you started?"

"Aye, I were about t' do jus' that, but I'll be needin' this," she said, cautiously retrieving the knife from his hand. "I'm just needin' to cut the bindin'," she explained, holding his hand steady while she slipped the knife under the wrapping. It fell away easily, the only evidence of it ever being injured, a slight bruise and the red ghost of the wrapping. She examined his hand, front and back, then turned her attention to the side of his head, pushing his hair behind his ear. "Ah, that's good then. Nothing t'scar, jus' a scratch here and a bit o' bruise." She smiled, satisfied. "I were fearin' there were trouble inside for all the sleepin' you done."

"Sleeping? How long have I been sleeping?" He asked scanning the sky. It was hard to judge the position of the sun through the forest, but it seemed like it should be mid-afternoon.

"Been a full night, an half a day… "

"A full night! Gads! Will must be frantic!" He rose to his feet quickly and nearly fell over as a rush of purple clouded his vision. Annlise held on to him until the sensation passed, then helped him to sit down on a nearby log.

"Sit ye here for a rest."

"The trail!" He groaned, and his father's admonition came rushing back to him, *finish what you started, he's on you to help him find you...* The message was suddenly clear to him. There was no mistake what he was to do with the dirk. "I was to mark the trees so he could find us if we got separated. How far have we gone? Have you seen him? I need to mark the trees—"

"Sean, Sean. Shh, settle, 'tis well, I swear it," she told him, as a mother would speak to a frightened child. "I heard him tell you t' mark the trees when he sent us out o' the tavern."

"You did?" Sean asked, hope coming back to him.

"Aye, 'course I'm nae certain this be the proper mark you two make, but—" She picked up a piece of fire wood and made a small flap in the bark and bent it forward. "This is the mark I've been makin'. Be it the one?"

"Aye, lass, that be it, exactly." Sean marveled at the sample she'd shown him, the same mark he and Will had used in countless games of mock treasure hunts. William liked to play at 'find-me' games, and had devised a set of 'codes' that Sean had assumed were known only between the two of them— until now. "Did you play at the games as children?" he asked, still amazed at the accuracy of the mark. "Is that how you knew Will's mark?"

"Aye, I've seen the mark afore, when he were a lad at Aberdoir, you see." Annlise half-smiled, and looked away. "But it weren't a game to him, then," she said quietly.

Sean nodded in understanding, remembering some of what William had told him of his prior life at Aberdoir Hall; about the times he'd hidden out with the servants, away from his brother and foster mother. But there was still something troubling him, and the line between Annlise's brows showed that she felt it too— something obvious they'd both overlooked. Then, as if reading each other's thoughts, they looked up to each other and Sean said, "So where is he? You say it's been a night and a day; surely he should have seen the marks by now. How far apart did you make them?"

"Twenty paces, or so."

"Aye, good. And you've made them at the same height each time?"

"Aye, every one." Her brow furrowed even deeper, her face suddenly weary and ashen. "Blessed Mother grant he's not run afoul with Adrian." She buried her face in her hands and began to sob. "I'll never forgive m'self."

Sean's stomach tightened; the same thought had crossed his mind. *I shouldn't have let him come along. He doesn't even have a sword! I knew we should have stayed together... if only she'd come to the tavern sooner... this is all her fault!* A sudden rush of anger toward her swept over him, and he clinched his jaw tight to prevent himself from speaking crossly to her. Annlise wiped her face and looked up at him, and at seeing her eyes red-rimmed and weary, her face drawn, his anger melted away. *Done is done, Will's resourceful...* "He'll find us, don't worry." He surprised himself by wanting to reach out to draw her close to him to comfort her, but before he could persuade his hand to move, she drew a long breath and calmed herself.

"Aye, the Lady grant you be right." She stood and crossed the little campsite to where Hawk was tethered. "'Tis a fine horse, tha' one," she said, as if a change of subject was in order. "Good t' know the best horses are nae all in Aberdoir servin' pompous fops like Adrian Tearlach an' Thomas Fylbrigge." She said each name through clamped teeth.

"Aye," Sean agreed, glancing toward Hawk, then back to Annlise. "His name is Hawk." He went to stand up, using the log as support with his right hand, when a ghost of a twinge shot up his arm. It wasn't painful by any means, but it did remind him of the fall he'd taken the day before. "Annlise?"

"Aye?" she replied almost shyly.

"My wrist, I'm certain it was broken. But now... " He flexed his fingers open and closed, holding his arm out to show her, and to convince himself at the same time that his hand was working properly. "There is barely a bruise. And my head, nary a lump where I struck the ground." The anger started welling up again, with the notion that he'd so easily been lulled by her beauty, that he'd allowed himself to be mislead. "How long has it really been?"

She took a step forward, her eyes widening in surprise at his sudden change of tone. "A day. I swear that's all it's been."

"Bones do not mend in a day!" he argued, storming past her toward Hawk.

"And riders do not vanish in plain sight!" she countered, the shyness gone, replaced by a cool defiant edge.

Sean froze, remembering only then what he had seen the day before, how William had suddenly seemed invisible to the riders chasing him, how they'd failed to see himself and Annlise even though she was standing right before them. She was staring at him now, and it was as if her strange blue eyes could penetrate his mind and see his thoughts.

"Aye, Sir Sean, you be rememberin' now, aye? You remember what I done for you, and you be wonderin' how I done it? You be wonderin'... what I be?" She took a step forward, her back straight and proud, her voice confident, even with the threat of tears forming on her eyelids.

Sean opened his mouth to deny the accusation then closed it, gaping at her mutely, realizing she had read his thoughts again. She moved forward toward him, and he instinctively raised a hand to hold her back, his thumb planted between his first two fingers— a superstitious sign to ward off evil— and the words shot from his mouth before he could stop them. "You be a witch? Stay there!"

She glanced at his hand, and her defiant mask dissolved into a look of sudden fear. "I mean you no harm, cannae you see that? Please dinnae tell me I misplaced m' trust in you, Sir Sean. I were certain, you bein' a friend to Will, that you would be una'standin' in the Olde Ways."

He lowered his hand, immediately ashamed of himself. For the second time he found himself lost in the blueness of her eyes, and the tears shining on her lashes tugged at something inside him. *Oh, Sean, you sot. This is no time to muddle ye head with this folly. But look at her; there be no evil there, she's so beautiful.* He shook his head, forcing himself to look away, to clear his thinking. "Lass, forgive me. It... You've just taken me by surprise, you see. Surely you can understand the position I'm in here. Will is counting on me, and it's my duty to—"

"Duty?" she gasped, a look of imminent flight about her. "You plan to turn me in then? I'm not a witch! Not like they say! I follow the old religion is all. Has Will gone so pious in his years at Stonehaven that now, for his sake, it be your duty to hunt—"

"No!" he hurried to her, holding her shoulders before she could run. "You misunderstand me. I'm no witch hunter. I assure you, you've not misplaced your trust in me. What I was trying to say, is that Will is counting on me to see you safely out of Aberdoir, and it is my duty to protect him as well."

"You made the sign 'gainst evil wi' your hand," she sniffled. "You think me an evil witch?"

He sighed, his face flushing. "That was just a foolish habit engrained in me by my upbringing." He half grinned and added, "Will would have flayed me alive if he'd seen me do that."

"He would?"

"Aye. He would."

"Then..." She hesitated for a moment, then said, quietly, "He's not abandoned his faith."

"Faith? I don't think he's abandoned his faith." Annlise's eyes brightened when he said that. But then he continued, "In fact he studies the Canon like a monk. Even the bishop at Stonehaven Abbey cannae spout out scripture, chapter and verse, as quickly as Will." He stopped when he saw the tears on her cheeks, and it dawned on him she was not referring to the 'Christian' faith. *The Old Religion? Will? No, surely he'd have told me...* His eyes went wide, and he took an involuntary step backwards. "Wait. You're telling me... that Will... William Fylbrigge is a—?"

"I'm tellin' you naught!" she answered quickly, then turned away, busying herself by gathering the few belongings she'd brought with her in bundled pack. "You can believe what you will about what we... what I am. But 'tis his business to tell you what he wishes for himself, is not for me."

Sean rushed to her, taking hold of her arm to turn her to look at him. "Annlise, I'm sorry. I don't know what I'm believing and what I'm not. What faith Will or you follow is not for me to judge or approve. It's all just a bit of a surprise to me is all. He sits every Sunday, proper as can be, with Edward at chapel. He's never mentioned anything to me about Ways or the old religion. He seems too level headed to believe in nonsense like spells and magic." His words sounded suddenly foolish to his own ear. Until that moment, he never believed in anything he couldn't see or touch, and yet, there was no denying that there was something magical about Annlise. "What I do know about him is that he is a good man, whatever faith he follows, and I trust him."

"And me?" she asked quietly, holding his gaze with her mysterious eyes. "Do you trust me, as well, Sir Sean?"

"Aye, lass, I do," he answered, his own voice sounding oddly far away from himself, as he looked into her eyes. The fear left her face, replaced with gratitude, and something more. "I do," he said again, in a whisper, and drew her closer to himself. He felt his head tip, and his neck arch toward her, as if his body had gained a will of its own. He did not fight the urge as his arms slipped from her shoulders to her waist and he felt her arms find their way to his back. Her face turned upward, her neck stretching to meet him, her eyes half closed, as he brought his lips to hers.

They had barely touched when they heard nickering in the woods, and the sound of snapping twigs. "Someone's coming," she said, pulling away, her face aglow with crimson. "Maybe it's Will." He made half an effort to hold on to her but she ducked quickly, twirling out from under his arm. Sean felt the color raise in his own face, but dismissed it quickly. Annlise dashed quietly to a large tree at the edge of their campsite and craned her neck to look around it. Sean crept up quietly behind her to get a look for himself.

"Can you see?" he asked quietly.

"There is a rider; I cannae tell if it's Will."

"I know a way." He cupped his hands around his mouth, and made a bird-like whistle, then waited a moment, and made the call again. "If that's Will, he'll answer me likewise." But the only answer that came was the stamping of hooves in leaves and the snort of a horse, eager to run again.

The rider was close enough now that Sean could hear him speaking to the horse. "Easy, Damon."

Annlise let out a small gasp, "Adrian!"

Sean pulled her away from the tree, back toward Hawk. "Come on." Without preamble, he lifted her onto Hawk's back then mounted quickly behind her. Sean knew as soon as he kicked in, that the sound of Hawk's galloping hooves would give them away, so he moved him slowly toward a concealing thicket of evergreens.

"Here," Annlise whispered.

Sean reined in, halting Hawk within the mottled shadows of the evergreen. Annlise placed her palm to her sternum as she had the day before, and mumbled something in the old language under her breath just as Adrian appeared on the path they'd just left. He was an imposing sight, everything about him black as night, from the hooded cloak, gloves and boots he wore, to the magnificent black horse he called Damon.

Sean's heart leapt to his throat as Adrian tossed the cape aside, revealing the crest that emblazoned the breastplate he wore— the crest of the elite band of mercenaries known as 'hunters', their primary prey: supposed witches. No wonder she's terrified of the sot... Sean reached for the hilt of his sword, withdrawing it carefully, silently, as Adrian drew closer. Annlise touched his hand gently, and shook her head, a warning for him to stay still.

"Well, what have we here?" Adrian muttered to himself, his interest drawn to the smoldering remains of their campfire. He dismounted, and picked up the small branch on which Annlise had demonstrated the mark she'd been making on their journey. "Look here, Damon," he chuckled, as if the horse were truly interested. "Our illusive friends have been this way." He kicked the ashes with his foot, disturbing the smallest of embers. "And recently, too." He mounted quickly, and looked about, scrutinizing each tree trunk that framed the circle of the camp. "Which way, now?" he muttered to himself.

Sean grinned, watching the hunter grow frustrated in his search, thankful that Annlise had not had time to make a signal mark when they'd left the camp.

After a moment, Adrian picked a seemingly random direction— theirs— and approached still muttering to himself, "Fools, do you think you can hide forever? No one takes what is mine! I'll find you and when I do, you, my beloved, will have much to answer for!"

Annlise stiffened her shoulders, her hand fast on her sternum. Sean held his breath, and even Hawk seemed to freeze in place, as Adrian galloped toward them— then onward beyond them, never knowing he'd come within an arm-span of his quarry.

When the way was clear, Sean led Hawk back to their

campsite, and doubled back, following the marks Annlise had made. If William had been close by, there was a danger that he'd follow the path right to the camp, and possibly run into Adrian. Sean hoped they would not have to travel far before they came across any sign of William, but it was getting dark again and soon they'd have to find another place to spend the night.

After at least four leagues and still no trace of William, Sean allowed himself the small hope that, having shaken Adrian off his trail, William had wisely headed on back to Stonehaven. He gave thought to turning toward Drumoak himself now, thinking it wiser than wandering the wilderness. He imagined William, sitting in the tavern and laughing with the lads, taking odds on when Sean would finally show up. He imagined Edward too, greeting him with a reproachful scowl for having led William into danger, that would turn to welcome when all would turn out well. But the truth of it was that a greater and growing fear nagged on him, that his friend had gotten himself turned around or hurt in the forest. Or worse, that he lay slain by Adrian's sword somewhere in the thicket, never to be found. If that happened, not only would he never be able to forgive himself, but there would be terrible, perhaps lethal, punishment to face from Lord Edward for having failed in his duty to protect his favored foster son.

Sean kept his fears to himself, only offering occasional assurances to Annlise that he was sure William was just up ahead. With only an hour or so left of daylight, it became apparent they would have to seek shelter for a second night. Sean sidled up to one of the trees Annlise had marked and drew out the dirk from his belt. He pulled the flap of bark down further, and carved a divot resembling a compass into the wood, then made a second mark in the shape of an 'X'. "I hope he understands this one. We've not used it for a long time," Sean explained.

"What is it?" she asked, watching through weary eyes.

"Change of course; if he sees this, he'll know we've gone in a different direction."

"We're going to the north then? Where you made the x?"

"No," he answered quietly, scanning the sky for the direction of the setting sun. "We're going west. And we'll not be marking our way."

"West? But why did you mark the north? How is he t' know?"

"X is the mark for home. He'll head for Stonehaven." He pulled in the reins and headed off toward the west. *I just hope he remembers that.*

Chapter 10

WILLIAM SLID OFF his saddle with a dejected sigh. He'd been searching for any sign of Sean and Annlise since he'd left Aberdoir the day before but had yet to find a single scrap of evidence that his friends were still anywhere within this damned eternal forest. At one point, near sunset yesterday, he'd spied a slice in a tree trunk, the signal he and Sean had always used in their games. Elated after hours of searching, he'd raced to the tree for a closer look, and was disappointed to find he'd been mistaken. The bark was drawn down, to be sure, but the wood beneath showed signs of weathering far too old to have been made by Sean. Two other times, he'd been certain he'd picked up the trail but had been forced to turn from the path upon hearing another horseman nearby.

Adrian had dogged him relentlessly into the night, twice surprising him by crossing the path in front of him rather than behind. It was as if the sot had anticipated his direction, forcing William to abandon his search for Sean's marks in his effort to stay out of sight. What had started out as an adventure to him— a mere game of cat and mouse— had taken an ominous turn when, at one point, Adrian had paused on a moonlit path. William had gotten a good look at the silver hunter's crest that shone in the moonlight and realized, for the first time, how deadly this opponent truly was. It had been a long night and it wasn't until dawn that it seemed he'd at last shaken Adrian from his heels. But it was also clear that he was hopelessly lost and more than a little tired and hungry.

"Any ideas, Star?" he asked the horse as he surveyed his surroundings.

Star responded with a weary nicker, then thrust her muzzle into the soft duff covering of the forest floor, chomping at leaves and ferns.

William half smiled, feeling somewhat jealous that the horse had found some breakfast. His own stomach grumbled in protest for being left empty and his thoughts began to wander. His mind conjured images of Elinor's magnificent skillet laden with salted pork strips, the bannock cakes rising in the stone oven. He closed his eyes and drew in a long breath and for a moment, swore that the aroma of the bacon in the imagined skillet was wafting under his nose, causing his stomach to grumble again. But when the aroma lingered, he opened his eyes and saw a tiny cottage at the edge of the clearing, a trail of smoke rising from the chimney.

His legs and back were aching from sitting so long in the saddle but the pins and needles coursing through him were tolerable. He led Star toward the cottage.

"Let's hope the folks are kind, aye, girl? I could do with a lie down in the barn for a few hours, if they will allow it."

Star snorted a reply, her head drooping.

"Aye, I know it. You be as weary as I am but I think 'tis safe to stop here." As he was about to knock on the door, he heard voices inside— grumpy and uninviting voices.

"I'm doin' m' best; I've but two hands, you know!" A woman was saying, accompanied by the clanging of what sounded like a metal spoon against a cauldron.

"The fire's goin' out—" an elderly sounding man remarked in

a wheezy, rasping voice.

"I can see that!"

"So why d' ye not stoke it? I'm cold!"

"Because, you... " she replied, interjecting a string of curses William had never heard a woman use, culminating in a shriek of, "– the bloody wood box is empty, again!"

William, his hand frozen in mid-knock, glanced to his left. He noted an old axe sticking out of a stump and a pile of wood in various stages of chopping lying scattered around. Clearly, there was a good amount of wood to sustain a cook fire and take the chill off a late September morning. If they didn't spend their time arguing, the box would be full, he thought, stepping away from the door.

"Come on, Star, we'll nap in the forest, and leave these folks to themselves—"

The door flew open suddenly and the woman appeared on the stoop. "Who are you?" she demanded.

William nearly stumbled in surprise as he whirled on his heel. "Uh... good morn, mistress," he said, with a quick bow. "Forgive me, I was just passing by." He flashed a quick smile and turned to lead Star back toward the forest.

He'd taken only two steps when he felt the touch on his sleeve, and the woman's voice saying, "No; wait, please." Her tone changed completely.

William turned hesitantly to face her, catching his breath unexpectedly as he got his first look at her. She was far from the old crone he'd expected to see. Her face was young, unlined by any signs of age, her hair unburdened by gray, pulled back under her caul. Instead of an angry scowl, she wore an apologetic sort of smile.

"I'm sorry, sir, that was terribly rude of me. You startled me, you see; I wasn't expecting anyone to be there when I opened the door. So few pass this far into the woods."

William stood, his mouth half open, staring stupidly.

"Have you lost your way?" she asked him, kindly.

"Oh, uh, aye. I'm afraid I have." He shook his head, banishing the astonishment from his face. He glanced past her shoulder, looking for the shrewish old woman he'd heard yelling through the cottage door but saw none. *The old man is her father then?*

His confusion must have shone, for she laughed a little, her face flushing. "I take it you heard our bit of a row, aye?"

"Are you," he began, peering over her shoulder again. "Are you all right in there?" He leaned forward, lowering his voice. "He's not a danger to you, I hope. Is he your father perhaps?"

"Oh my, no!" She burst into a trill of giggles, pulling her hand to her mouth, blushing. "That's Caleb. He be my husband."

"Husband?" William knew his astonishment looked foolish but he couldn't help it. From the sound of the man's voice, William guessed him to be at least in his sixties and this lass before him could not be more than twenty. *Well you were wrong about her, too.* "Forgive me lass. I'm afraid it is I who is being rude, now." He straightened his back, then bowed formally. "A thousand pardons."

She chuckled lightly, tapping his back. "Please, there is no need. Come now, you say you've lost your way? What be ye name, lad?"

He hesitated for a moment, an odd paranoia about sharing his name suddenly coming over him. "I am called Will, m' lady."

She nodded and smiled, and to William's relief, did not press him for his family name. "I'm pleased t' know you, Will. You may call me Martha. Now, where is it you be headed?"

"Martha, then. I was on my way to Stonehaven." *It's safe enough to tell her that, I suppose. A lot of folks live in Stonehaven after all...* "But I seem to have gotten myself turned around in the woods, I'm afraid." At that moment, he caught again the aroma of something cooking within the cabin and his stomach betrayed him with a loud gurgle.

Martha chuckled behind a tight-lipped smile. "You've been turned around for a while by the sounds of it, aye?"

William blushed but smiled. "Aye, since mid-day yesterday. I've ridden through the night. I was wondering if I could trouble you to rest in your barn for a few hours." He reached for his money pouch, remembering only then he'd given the last of his stipend to the tavern keeper in Aberdoir. He looked around apologetically, catching sight of the rusted axe and the woeful pile of wood. "I'm afraid I've no gold to offer for your hospitality but I'd be more than happy to fill your wood box, if you like."

She looked up started, then shook her head in understanding. "Oh, dear. You heard that did you?"

"Aye, I could nae help but hear you arguing with your fa— husband," he corrected himself. He craned his neck looking into the cottage to catch a glimpse of the old man, who he only then realized had become oddly silent. For a half a heartbeat, remembering the shouting he'd encountered, William wondered if this now pleasant-mannered young woman had clocked the old man on the head with a skillet or something before she'd opened the door. *Maybe it's best just to go on into the woods after all...*

"I'm sure you must think the worst of us, then," she offered, with another little giggle, a nervous habit the lass seemed to have. "You have not found us at our best. Caleb and I only argue in the mornings. It's our way, you see. Neither of us mean the other ill."

William smiled, still not sure what to make of this odd couple.

She wiped her hands on her apron hurriedly, and motioned him to the door. "Oh, come on, then. Let me show you. Come on in, please. We've more than enough bacon to share. You be our guest this morning, Will."

William took a hesitant step forward but the aroma was too wonderful to turn from. Before he had a chance to think better of it, he had followed Martha into the little cottage. Inside was dark and very warm and William was surprised to see that the fire was burning quite nicely despite the professed lack of firewood. William's stomach grumbled again, but his heart sank. The skillet rested on the grate with only two meager slabs of bacon sizzling in grease. It seemed barely enough to feed the two of them, let alone a guest and he would not feel good about depriving either of them of a breakfast. But his stomach gurgled again and he decided to be polite and accept just a bite. The furnishings were sparse; a trestle table, two benches, a pallet covered in straw that he assumed served as a bed. One corner was dominated by a large loom threaded in coarse wools, a half finished blanket on its frame, but no sign of more wool in which to finish it. The last remaining piece of furniture was a tall-backed chair with sturdy arms that was positioned with its back to the door. William could see the man's elbows on the armrests and heard a faint and rasping snore coming from the chair.

Martha stepped around to the front of the chair and spoke

in a gentle tone. "Caleb? Wake up, m' darlin'; we've a guest."

"Hmm?" Caleb yawned. "A guest?" His voice was dry, and it sounded as though every breath was a struggle for him.

"Aye, a traveler passin' on his way to Stonehaven," Martha explained, then motioned for William to come around to the front of the chair. "Come around, lad, and meet Caleb."

William walked around, his hand ready to extend in greeting. "I'm pleased to meet... "

He froze, his hand extended, his greeting still on his tongue, stunned at the sight of Caleb sitting small and frail in the chair. His legs, bound in strips of linen, were twisted at an impossible angle at his knees. It was obvious the man was lamed, which explained why he had not offered to help with the wood. But it wasn't the frailness of the body, or the lameness of the legs or even the gnarled and twisted birdlike hand that Caleb extended in greeting that had shaken William to his core. It was the youth of his face and the brightness of his eyes that despite his physical malady had an air of quiet dignity about them.

William forced the shock from his face and gently accepted Caleb's hand in greeting. "I'm pleased to meet you, sir. My name is Will."

"Welcome, Will. Sit," Caleb replied in his weak rasp of a voice, motioning to the pallet.

William lowered himself slowly, making an effort not to stare at the man in the chair.

Martha busied herself with the skillet, amicably divvying up the meager amount of bacon into three servings. "You must be hungered aft' ridin' all night," she said, pushing the strips onto three plates.

William's stomach had stopped rebelling as he looked upon

Caleb's fragile frame, discovering he was suddenly not feeling hungry at all anymore when Martha brought the plate to him. He accepted it politely but held it on his lap while Martha positioned Caleb's plate on his lap for him.

"Thank you, sweeting," he muttered to his wife, with an affectionate smile.

She beamed at him, then retrieved her own plate, and settled on the bench next to her husband's chair.

"Are ye not hungry?" Caleb asked, when William had yet to eat.

William nibbled a morsel, then placed the rest down, staring into his plate, not quite knowing what to say to his hosts.

"Ye curious, aye?"

William looked up, startled, "Hmm? I'm sorry, what?"

Caleb grinned. "You be wondering how we come to have such a fine side o' bacon for breakfast."

"Caleb, don't tease," Martha admonished with a lilt of her nervous giggle. "You know 'tis not the bacon he's wonderin' on."

William felt the blush rising to his face and was thankful for the dimness of the cottage. "'Tis fine bacon. Thank you," he said awkwardly.

"Not many cross our threshold these days," Caleb said, conversationally between nibbles. Even the act of chewing seemed to be a chore for him. "You mus' have an adventuresome streak in you."

"I suppose I do." William chuckled lightly, but found it difficult to look Caleb in the eye for more than a few seconds. "But your cottage is far from the road. I'm sure if you were closer to the highway, you would have all manner of guests."

As soon as his words left his mouth, he knew he sounded

daft but he did not want to sound rude or ungrateful for their hospitality by saying what he knew to be the grim truth. Even if they lived in the center of Stonehaven proper, they would be sore pressed for visitors— cripples were a bad omen and people tended to avoid them at all cost. William looked up to see Caleb looking to his plate, a weary smile on his lips, as he shook his head.

"We're not forty paces off Edin Road," Caleb said. "Many pass us each day going hither and yon, fore and frae Aberdoir or Stonehaven... "

"Forty paces?" William blurted. "That's impossible."

Martha looked up, startled.

Caleb merely grinned, and continued eating his bacon. "You callin' me a liar in m'own home?" he asked, with a hint of amusement.

"Oh... no, sir, forgive me... but forty paces? Surely I'd have come across it in my travels. I'm certain I saw no road... "

"You come to us from ahind?" Martha ventured.

William thought for a moment, then felt a complete fool. "Of course. I did indeed."

"Well, there you are then," Caleb chuckled. "Had you kept goin' you'd have seen the road and you'd be nigh on ye way t' Stonehaven, instead o' enjoying this grand feast of bacon."

William wasn't sure if there was a tone of sarcasm in Caleb's words, insinuating that only the most weary and hungry would dare share breakfast with the decrepit little cripple in the chair. William forced his voice to be light, saying, "I thank you for your hospitality—"

"But you've got to get back on the road now," Caleb finished for him.

William opened his mouth to deny Caleb's assumption but could not find the words. The man was right, after all, William did want to get out and continue looking for Sean. *If Sean's got any sense at all in him, he'll have turned for home by now... yes, I'm sure he has.*

"Actually, sir, I do need to continue on," William began. "You see I've been separated from my traveling companion and I'm sure he'll be looking for me back in Stonehaven." He stood and extended his hand to Caleb. "I truly do thank you, for your hospitality. I truly would like to stay and visit but they'll miss me by now."

Caleb's bony fingers closed around William's hand in a surprisingly firm grip. "Dinnae forget to cross yeself as you leave, lest you carry the ill with you."

"Caleb, please," Martha whispered.

William drew a long breath, staving off the crimson he felt rising to his face. *I'm no closer to finding Sean now than if I wait an hour; Stonehaven isn't moving. He shared his breakfast, the least I can do is show some gratitude.* William grasped Caleb's hand firmly, as though he were any able-bodied man he knew, and he saw Caleb's eyes widen for a moment, his lip curl in surprise. "The breakfast was excellent, as well as the company. And truth be told, it was a long night for me. If it be no trouble, sir, I could do with a short rest before I go on."

Caleb nodded, and motioned to the pallet, his enigmatic smile still fixed on his lips. "You're welcome to rest. There is no more bacon to offer," he said with a quiet dignity, no apology in his tone.

"I require no more, thank you." William sat down again, his attention turning toward the corner where the unfinished blanket languished on the loom, then to the wood box that was barren of any more firewood. "But I would like to repay your hospitality before I go."

"Oh I couldn't think of it," Martha protested.

William noted her glancing toward his belt— where his money pouch should be.

"'Tis good of you to sit and visit," she said in clear disappointment, averting her glance, a slight blush on her face.

William reached for his belt, then turned his hands palms up. "I'm sorry I've no money with me but I would be happy to refill your wood box."

Martha's face brightened, belying her protest. "Oh, it would be too much t' make you chop—"

William raised his hand, forestalling her ersatz protestations. "I insist. I shan't leave your cottage until the box is filled."

"'Tis kind of you," she replied through her little nervous giggle, giving a quick glance to Caleb, before taking his plate.

"Aye, 'tis kind," Caleb agreed, the sarcasm gone from his tone. "And I'll not turn down the offer."

William relaxed. "I wish there was something more I could do."

Caleb's smile vanished, his gaze now intent. "There is."

William felt a sudden twinge of apprehension. "Aye?"

"You can sit and indulge me in a spot of sport," Caleb replied, the grin coming back.

"As you wish. What sort of sport?"

"As you see, my days are quite dull and long, with naught to do but count the trees outside my window. My body is of little use to me; but my mind is still quick, or so I like to believe."

William nodded, his curiosity now piqued. "I can see that it is."

"Then, indulge me," Caleb grinned, and sat back, tenting his fingers under his chin.

"Indulge you?"

Caleb only grinned wider, then began a visual survey of William from his toes to his head, scrutinizing each detail about him, his eyes coming to rest on the billows of his sleeves.

"You say you be frae Stonehaven?" Caleb asked.

Martha's back went suddenly stiff.

William looked from one to the other, before allowing himself to answer, "Aye, Stonehaven is my home."

Caleb leaned forward slightly. "You be one of the gentry there, are you nae, lad?"

"Caleb!" Martha blurted. "Please—"

"Hush, woman. You are. You be a member of Lord Edward's house. A close member."

William stared, taken aback. He had always been rather proud of his relationship with Lord Edward but somehow Caleb's surprising assertions and Martha's startled reaction made him feel oddly self conscious. "How did you know this, sir?"

Caleb chuckled and reached a bony hand toward William's arm and began to tug at his sleeves, worrying the fabric between his fingers. "'Tis finely loomed, this is. Cambric I'd say. And your boots," he continued, pointing toward William's dust-covered but still impressive leather boots, "show no sign of wear such would be those of a common laborer. And in the clasp on ye belt be the mark of the house of Stonehaven."

William smiled in spite of his trepidation. "Well done." Finding no good reason to remain coy, he replied, "You do indeed have a quick mind and eye, Caleb. Yes, it is cambric, dirty as it be at the moment. And yes, I am a member of Lord Edward's house." He stood and bowed formally, "I am William Fylbrigge. Lord Edward is my foster father."

"Fylbrigge!" Martha gasped, her eyes going wide. "Ye not kin to that devil in Aberdoir, are you lad?"

William straightened quickly. *I knew I should have kept that to myself*. "I am," he answered quietly.

She made an incredulous snort, her hands flying to her hips. "And here I give you breakfast. I think you best be getting on now. I can fill m' own wood box, thank you. The last thing I wish is to be beholdin' to a Fylbrigge for anything."

"No, please, I mean you no ill—"

"Hah! 'Tis the same thing the sod o' the manor told us afore he sent the writ— Caleb, what've you brought upon us now?"

"Martha, my darlin'," Caleb called, as loudly as his raspy voice would allow. She stopped suddenly, her hand flying to her temples, her breaths coming in short sobs.

William backed away slightly, moving stealthily toward the door while Caleb cooed calming platitudes to his wife. He was nearly out the door when Caleb called to him, "Are you going so soon?"

William turned to face Caleb. "Aye, sir. I've no wish to upset ye lady."

"No, please." Martha sniffed, blowing her nose into her handkerchief. "Forgive me, please. That was completely unforgivable. Please dinnae think ill o' me, Mr. Fylbrigge—"

"Lass, please, I'm simply Will. Forget I ever told you my name. I assure you, my name is the only thing I share with my brother at Fylbrigge manor."

She looked up to him then, and wiped her eyes. Caleb gave her hand a squeeze, and smiled his patient smile. "There, you see? 'Tis naught to worry on with this lad," he assured her quietly.

"Aye, husband, I see," she agreed, then smiled reluctantly.

"Now, the lad has offered to fill our box for us. I say we accept his kind offer and let him be on his way." Caleb looked toward William. "That is, if the offer still holds."

William bowed his head slightly and answered, "It does. I should be glad to."

Martha wiped her eyes again, then kissed her husband gently on the forehead, before showing William to the door. "I shan't be long," she said over her shoulder, then turned to William. "This way."

"Good day to you, Caleb," William said with a bow, then paused, adding, "I should like to visit again sometime, if that would be all right."

Caleb tipped his head in reply. "I would like it if you did... William Fylbrigge." He yawned, and closed his eyes, astonishingly dropping off to sleep as William watched.

He lingered only for a moment, watching Caleb's steady breathing, until he heard the thump from the axe behind him. Martha had begun a second swing but before she could bring the axe down, William held up his hand.

"I believe that be *my* job, m' lady."

She made her nervous giggle again, and handed him the axe.

Though still tired from his long night, something inside him urged him to do more than a fair job for Caleb and Martha, he wanted to do more than they expected of him. A quarter-hour later, he had split enough logs to not only fill the wood box for one day but for at least three. He also wanted to take Star and race all the way back to Stonehaven and place an order with the local butcher for a ham to be sent. He wanted the tailors to know there was a talented weaver here in the woods who may be able to take in work should they need help. He wanted to do anything to reach out and make life easier for the couple if for no other reason than to put Martha's fears to rest about his family connections— and because it seemed right.

He tossed the last bit of wood onto the pile, then stuck the axe into the block. "There," he said, mopping his brow with his sleeve as Martha stood near, leaning in her doorway with her arms folded. She'd stood there watching him the whole time he'd been chopping.

"Thank you kindly, Will," she said. "'Tis more than you needed to do, you know."

"I dinnae mind," he replied with a shrug, taking a seat on the corner of the block. As soon as he rested the axe, he realized how weary he was truly feeling. He planted his palms on his knees and dropped his head for a moment, attempting to conceal a yawn. But when he looked up, she was standing before him, holding a tin dipper from the rain barrel. He accepted it without comment, sipped, and handed it back. "Thank you." He wiped his palms on his leggings, and stood, stifling a second yawn. Forty paces to the road? A third yawn escaped him before he could stop it, and he felt a gentle hand on his shoulder, pushing him back down to sit.

"You cannae be thinkin' of goin' now? Rest ye some, Will. 'Tis why you stopped here in the first place, aye?"

"Aye, 'tis, lass, but I'm feeling well enough to continue."

She looked at him skeptically, and he knew that he couldn't

deny the fact that he was exhausted. But the more he thought on Sean and Annlise, the more anxious he was to get back on the road. And the sooner he got to Stonehaven, the sooner he could send something back to Caleb and Martha— though he would not say that to her.

"You say the road back to Stonehaven be that way?"

She sighed in quiet disappointment. "Aye. It be no more than a half a day's ride. Surely you have time to rest, just a little."

It sounded tempting. He glanced toward the side of the house where Star was tethered. He noted that Martha had provided her with a pail of clear water. Star was munching on a stack of grass stalks. His stomach gurgled at the sight.

"Will?" Martha nudged his shoulder. "Did you hear me?"

He jumped, tearing his gaze from his horse. "Oh, aye, lass. Forgive me." He stood again. "I do appreciate ye offer but I really must be going on." Thinking quickly, he added, "I've a feeling my companion may be just ahead on the road here."

As if in answer, the distant sounds of hooves came from the direction of the road.

"That could be him." She smiled, seeming to be unconvinced. "Well, I'll not keep any man longer than he wishes. You are welcome to stay or leave as it pleases you."

He let the comment go unchallenged and went to Star, giving a gentle pat to her mane. She responded with a snort and a bob of her head, seemingly unperturbed at being disturbed from her snack. William allowed her to dip her muzzle in the water pail, then led her back to where Martha stood.

"Was nice of you to chat with Caleb, like you done. For that, I'm grateful. You best be goin'. You'll miss your friend," she commented.

"It was my pleasure," William said, taking her hand and bowing over it. Her face turned crimson and she turned away. The hoof falls reached them again, louder this time. "It sounds as though that rider is approaching from the north, so it probably is not Sean, but aye, I should be going."

"Bloody hell!" Martha suddenly gasped.

William looked up confused at what he could have possibly said to offend her. Then he saw what she did, and he bit his tongue from swearing an even viler oath.

"'Tis a black rider! What poor sot be he tracking?" she hissed.

"Adrian!" William blurted, instantly recognizing the devil who'd dogged him all night. "Damn! I must go!"

Martha spun on her heal. "You?"

"I'm afraid so," William answered, mounting quickly and drawing up the reins.

Her eyes went wide. "Go!" she yelled. She slapped Star's hind quarters. "And dinnae look back!"

William didn't argue, though he wished he had more time to thank her. He kicked in hard and set Star at a gallop toward the road.

"Not that way!" Martha yelled, "you'll run right to him!"

"Trust me!" William yelled over his shoulder.

Pieces of Caleb's puzzle started coming together in his mind. *She knows of the hunters, and she fears them. He's young... but lame... that trick, he called a sport could almost rightly be called magic. 'Twas no accident that lamed him, 'twas the witch trials.* He kicked in and charged forward until he could see Adrian clearly on the path before him. Then he reined in hard, causing Star to rear and whinny. Adrian looked up instantly and reached for his sword. William turned Star and dashed into the woods.

Knowing Adrian would follow, he crossed the road and charged easterly, away from Caleb's cottage.

He raced hard and fast, his former fatigue banished with a rush of adrenalin.

"Yah!" Adrian's voice rang through the forest as he kicked his steed into a gallop.

"Go, Star!" William urged.

Star seemed to take on wings. The brief rest she'd had seemed to have done her a world of good and William mentally thanked his hosts. He crouched low in the saddle as Star flew through the forest, nimbly avoiding the obstacles of branches and fallen logs. Behind him, he could hear the furious pounding of Adrian's horse as he gained ground. William tried to keep his bearings as he led Star on the frenzied zigzag chase but soon realized he'd gotten himself lost yet again. He had a vague sense that he'd left Caleb and Martha to the south but he'd turned around so often that he feared he may be running back toward them. A glance over his shoulder and he could see Adrian closing the space, his horse running full out.

"I have you!" the hunter cried out, close enough to hear the sound of the sword leaving the sheath.

"Go, Star!" He kicked in again, crouching even lower on the saddle. He'd come to a clearing, a dark strip in the middle that to his horror, William realized was the wide end of the chasm he'd jumped with Sean. There was no time to veer away and he hoped Star could jump as easily as she had the day before. But that had been after only a moment's gallop and William could sense she was growing tired.

"Ha!" came the yell behind him. William knew he had only two choices— bring Star to a halt and risk fighting Adrian without a sword, or push on and hope she would clear the jump.

Before he could weigh the options, the chasm was upon them, and Star was suddenly airborne. William looked down with a surreal fascination as he passed over the chasm and the roaring river that flowed fifty feet below him. Star's hooves touched lightly on the other side. William glanced behind and nearly fainted in relief to see that Adrian had not risked the jump and was pacing angrily on his horse waving a fist in the air. It won't take long for him to find the narrow part of the ravine....

"Go, Star. We'll rest when we reach the thicket, go!"

A moment later, he veered away from the path and back into the untamed forest. He pulled Star to a slow canter, then to a halt. He sat perfectly still, nearly holding his breath, listening for the sound of Adrian's horse. When all was quiet for several moments, he relaxed.

"Turned around again, Star," he sighed, leaning against a tree in frustration. Something sticking out of the tree caught on his sleeve and he turned to knock away the twig he assumed it to be. He stopped, overjoyed at what he'd been leaning against—a freshly sliced piece of bark, folded down, the wood beneath still white and fresh. Sean!

"Star, I found him!"

Star snorted, and began nibbling on a fern.

"If he followed our usual pattern, then another tree should be marked... there! Finally! We've found them, Star."

He remounted quickly, with a renewed sense of hope, following the familiar trail of markings, each slice just as they had always made them. His thoughts now focused only on following the trail and reuniting with Sean. His morning with

Caleb and Martha in their little cottage was pushed nearly completely from his mind.

Unknown to William, Adrian had long since crossed the ravine and had also discovered the markings on the trees.

Chapter 11

THEY TRAVELED WESTWARD following the path of a meandering stream, until the last spears of daylight filtering through the trees turned soft and the orange clouds of sunset faded to a rose colored glow. They stopped when they came across the dilapidated remains of an old and long abandoned earthen barn. The barn door hung askew from rusted hinges. A gaping hole in the roof offered convenient access for nesting for wild sparrows and starlings. One wall leaned precariously inward, causing a low dip in what remained of the hay loft. The entire back wall was blackened with ancient soot, a scar left over from some long past calamity that had apparently claimed the farm house that once stood aside it. Only the remains of a stone hearth and the outline of the foundation provided any evidence that a house had ever existed there at all.

Sean pulled in the reins and slid from the saddle quietly, searching for any signs of human life. Annlise remained on Hawk, her hand resting at the base of her throat, her eyes half closed. The waning glow of the sunset fell softly on her face and, for a moment, he could not help but admire the perfect smoothness of her features. She turned slightly and opened her eyes and smiled when she noticed him looking at her. He returned the smile and reached a hand to help her dismount.

"'Tis safe to rest here, then?" she asked.

"As far as I can tell," he replied. "All is quiet."

She accepted his hand as he led her toward the old barn.

"I've looked all around, there be no sign of traveler nor farmer. Perhaps an owl or two may roost here but other than that, we are quite alone." He led Hawk into the barn, tethering the rein to an old post.

Annlise stroked the horse's muzzle while Sean loosened the saddle and removed the pack.

"Shouldn't he be kept ready?" she asked, quietly.

Sean hesitated for a moment, then removed the saddle. "Probably," he admitted. "But he's been saddled for near two days now. He's needing the rest."

An old leather bucket dangled from a rusted hook near the rotting door. Sean picked it up, and put his fist to the bottom, testing the stoutness of the leather. To his satisfaction it held firm. "I'll get some water from the stream for Hawk. I'll only be a moment."

He looked around, squinting into the darkness of the old barn. "Looks like there's still some hay in the crib there; you can take the blanket and lie there if you wish. "

Annlise glanced over her shoulder toward the old crib, pulling her shawl tightly around her shoulders. "And where shall you rest... sir?" Her head tilted in such a way that her hair fell over one shoulder, a provocative curl to her lip.

He stood silent, unsure of the tone in her voice. "I... shall be standing watch," he answered, then turned quickly, heading toward the stream.

When he reached the water, he knelt and splashed his face. The water felt incredibly refreshing and he lingered for a moment, mulling over the events of the day, trying to force himself to concentrate on what he thought to be of immediate importance. *Will is surely back to Stonehaven by now. He'll explain to Edward what has delayed me, explain why the letter wasn't delivered. All will be well; Will has a way with Edward. He'll explain. After all, Will told me to watch after her, keep her safe... keep her...* He splashed his face again as his thoughts strayed farther away from William and Edward and letters to be delivered, and closer to the lass who lay resting in the rotting barn behind him.

A gentle wind wafted around him, rustling the trees as he walked back to the barn. The sun had given way to night but the full moon had risen early, bathing the old barn in a silver glow. Hawk nickered quietly before drinking the water Sean offered from the leather bucket. When he'd drunk his fill, Sean hung the bucket back on the hook and sat quietly in the doorway, listening to the sounds around him; the sway of the trees, the moaning of the old beams in the wind. *There's no one out there; it's quiet as a tomb.* He yawned and leaned back against a post, watching the stars twinkle into view.

A soft hand touched his shoulder. "'Tis a beautiful night."

"Hmm?" He turned, slightly startled. He hadn't heard her approach but he couldn't stop the smile from finding his face. "I thought you were sleeping."

"I tried," she replied. "But the breeze called me." She took a deep breath and turned her face toward the moon. "There be naught like the smell of the wind on a warm September eve."

He rose and stood behind her, breathing in what he thought was the smell of heather on the wind, but soon realized the sweet scent was coming from Annlise. She stood very still, looking up to the sky. He found his feet began to move, as if of their own accord until he was standing nearly against her, his hand resting gently on her shoulder. He brushed the side of her neck and she responded with an inviting tilt of her head.

"You must be weary, Sir Sean," she said coyly. "Are you sure you dinnae care to... " She turned and looked up to him, her magical eyes catching the moonlight. "Care to... rest?"

Before he knew what he was doing, he cupped her cheeks with his hands and answered her with a kiss. She responded with a soft moan, her hands finding the small of his back. He kissed her again, his fingers dancing through the soft curls of her hair as he pulled her closer and kissed her more deeply. She pulled away suddenly, and he had a moment of panic that he'd overstepped.

"Forgive me, lass."

She only stared, her expression changing with each breath until he saw the tear glistening on her lashes. "You... you must think me wanton... wicked."

He felt the blush rise to his face. He hadn't thought of anything other than how beautiful she was and the strange ache that was growing in him to be close to her. He shook his head, struggling to find the words that would explain what he was feeling. "I... no, lass. I... "

"I've not given my gift to any man." She looked up to him from under her bangs. "It was what made me... attractive to—" She turned suddenly burying her face in her hands, and began to weep quietly. "Adrian wanted a virgin bride; that is what was promised him."

Sean placed his hand on her shoulder again, relieved that she did not flinch at his touch. "You've no need to explain, Annlise. Shh, lass. I'll not be taking advantage of you. Truth is... uh, I've not... ."

"No?" A shy giggle escaped her. She spun on her heel suddenly, flinging her arms around him. "I thought there were no good men left in the whole of Scotland. Thank the Blessed Mother I was wrong."

"Lass?"

She looked up to him, then pulled his head forward, kissing him hard and deep, tangling her fingers in his hair.

"'Tis not taking advantage... if the gift is freely given."

He responded eagerly, pulling her closer, then it was he who pulled away. "Are you certain?"

She responded by stroking his cheek with one hand while the other meandered to the buckle that held his scabbard to his belt, her eyes never leaving his. In one easy motion, the clasp was released, the belt unfastened, the blade slid to the floor, and the front of his tunic hung open bearing his chest to the cool night air.

"I'm certain," she whispered, placing a soft kiss on the divot in the center of his chest.

He turned her face to him with a gentle caress beneath her chin and kissed her again. He lifted her off her feet and carried her to the blanket that had been spread among the hay in the old crib.

They gave themselves freely and unashamed, reveling in the joys of untried bodies until exhausted, they fell into a deep, contented sleep. They lie tangled in each other's arms, neither of them aware of anything but the warmth of the other's body. They heard nothing but each other's heartbeats and the soft creaking of the timbers. Neither heard the breaking of branches or the rush of hooves that was fast approaching the barn.

* * *

"Two days!" Adrian growled, as he allowed the horse a brief rest to drink from the stream. He scooped a palm full of water for himself, then splashed his face and neck. "Two days wasted!" he grumbled to the horse. "The wench should have been grateful to wed. I would have taken her away from servitude to that fop in Aberdoir and given her a household of her own to command. Servants of her own— and security. And all I asked in return was an obedient wife, a well cooked meal, and a fair bed companion when I wish— and if I wish it before the wedding, then so much the better. But she had the audacity to flaunt her *virtue*, to refuse me and run away!" He yanked down the reins, turning the horse to look at him, as if the beast had offered an argument. "I tell you this, Damon; Adrian Tearlach is *never* refused! *No one* runs away from me!"

Damon snorted and bobbed his head. Adrian sniffed a humorless chuckle and released the reins, allowing the horse to drink his fill.

"I must be a fool, traipsing through this confounded forest, leaping at shadows and following false trails." He picked up a twig, idly turning it in his hands, squinting into the darkening forest. "I know they came this way; I saw the fire. Annlise, my darling, I know you're out here - somewhere." He snapped the twig. "You and your *accomplices*. I'll find you. And you will not run from me again."

He stood and mounted, impatiently turning the horse from the stream, backtracking to the last marked tree he had passed. This mark was slightly different than the others, marked with an 'x' under the flap.

"I wonder which of them made this. The wench, the thief or the… rabbit," he chuckled at his jest, thinking of the young man he'd been tracking since entering the woods. "He's led me on a merry chase, hasn't he, Damon? Thinks he's clever, doubling back, leaping ravines." His chuckle turned dark. "I've managed to find him often enough; I'll find him again and the fool shall lead me right to her. I just need to be patient."

He thought of the young man who Annlise had ridden off with, twisting the leather reins in his fist. "And he shall rue the day he dared to steal what belongs to me; whoever he is, he shall pay. Both of them! And as for our rabbit, I would skin him alive just for the sport of it, if not for Thomas' want that I leave him... for now." The thought darkened his mood even further.

He examined the mark on the tree again, and looked back to the direction from where he'd been before. "'Tis definitely a different mark; what would it mean? A change in direction perhaps? A secret message?" Behind him, the path was growing dark, though he could still see some of the trail markings showing white in the gloaming. The trail had been leading him steadily to the north west, toward Bannenvale, but if he were to turn in the direction this new mark seemed to indicate, he would eventually come to Stonehaven. *Would they go there? Perhaps... What does this mark truly mean?* He squinted into the half light, toward the northwest, but found no more marks. The way toward Stonehaven was also unmarked. He sat silently, in a quandary of which way to go, when he heard the twigs snapping and the snort of a horse in the forest behind him.

He listened silently. The horse was walking slowly, as if stopping every so often, its rider murmuring quiet commands. "That way, Star, there's a stream; we can stop for now."

Adrian grinned to himself. *And there you are right on time, my little rabbit. I must have gotten ahead of you after all.* He eased his horse into the shadows to wait.

"That's it, drink up," William urged, as Star plunged her muzzle into the stream. He remained in the saddle, fearful that if he dismounted, he'd be tempted to sink into a soft mound of forest ferns and fall asleep. He stifled a yawn and stretched his arms above his head. "That water does look refreshing."

Star shook her mane and slurped noisily.

"You wretched temptress, you've convinced me," he laughed and gave in, sliding off the saddle. "I suppose I can afford a quick splash and a moment's rest."

He knelt and drank, being sure to listen carefully to the forest sounds around him. Too often during the course of the day, he'd believed he'd finally shaken Adrian from his trail only to turn to see his shadow on his heels again. William was beginning to believe the man had an uncanny ability to read his mind. Even when he had deliberately doubled back, and crossed his own trail to obscure Star's hoof tracks, Adrian had found him. At one point, William decided to lead Star to travel within the stream so as to leave no tracks at all. He had followed it for as long as he could, keeping the shore and Sean's trail always within sight until the trickle turned into a torrent, the stream giving way to the Annlee River. He was certain Adrian could not have possibly predicted his trail—he had no idea, himself, where he was bound— but after miles of walking in water and hours of solitude, William emerged from the stream only to see Adrian's shadowy form charging toward him once again.

He'd only barely managed to elude the hunter that last time. If it hadn't been for Star's nimble leap over another gorge, the bank crumbling after she'd galloped away, preventing Adrian from following, he would surely have caught up with him.

He took a mouthful of water and splashed his face and hair, the cold water reviving him. When Star had drunk her fill, he mounted and sat quietly listening. Satisfied with the silence, he urged her forward toward the direction he expected to find the next marked tree.

"There it is. Whoa, Star." The 'X' under the flap was a less than welcome sight. "He's telling me to go home. The sot. Send me home, while he's off adventuring! And just how on Mother's earth does he expect me to find the road from here?"

He loosed a frustrated sigh and spun the horse, scanning the trees in all directions. There were no more signs and he'd been turned around so many times during the course of the day, that he had no idea if Stonehaven was to the north or south, or across the sea. *Ok, Will, no time to panic. Just think for a moment. If I were Sean, which direction would I choose? That way? No, too much meadow. He'd go for cover. South? No, that's where I've just come...* He turned again until he faced the darkest, thickest part of the forest that was too dark even to see if there was a path. *That's the way. Right through the dark; good cover, and difficult to follow.*

He kicked in, turning Star towards the dark, when she balked, nearly rearing.

"Whoa, Star, easy. Come on; go."

It was then he saw the faint glint of steel in the shadow, and heard the scrape of a blade leaving a scabbard. Star reared with a frantic whinny as a black-clad hand reached from the darkness, grasping the bridle, preventing William from retreating. His hand instinctually went to his hip and he cursed himself— not for the first time on this unexpected adventure— for leaving

Stonehaven without a sword. All he could put his hand on was the small knife that he carried as a matter of habit— designed for carving trinkets, not for fighting, but it was better than nothing.

The blade appeared from the darkness first, gleaming silver in the moonlight, its point aiming at him as the rider emerged from the shadows, the dreaded silver crest of the king's hunters shining as brightly as the blade. His hood was drawn back and as his horse drew up alongside, all William could discern of the man's face were his oddly golden eyes and a row of shining teeth smiling luridly from the shadowed face. William raised his knife and lunged toward the hand that held Star's bridle. With little effort, the hunter swung the tip of the sword, grazing William's palm and flicking the knife out of his hand.

"What's your hurry, lad?" the hunter asked, in a low unnervingly calm voice. "I think it's time we got to know each other." He yanked the bridle sharply, causing Star to stomp and toss her mane. "I am Adrian Tearlach, and you are... inconsequential."

"Let her go!" William growled, holding tightly to the reins. He was barely aware of the stinging in his palm or the blood that was falling from the cut.

The blade flashed again as the hunter swung, slicing the rein from William's grasp. Before he could react the sword flashed again, coming to rest on the fabric of William's tunic at the center of his chest.

"You've cost me a lot of precious time, boy. Time better spent on more *lucrative* quarry than you!"

William forced himself not to react in haste to his situation. "Time? Is that all you're interested in? Time? What could that possibly cost—"

"Silence!" The blade flicked upward, coming to rest at William's throat.

William closed his mouth.

"That's better. Frightened? I swear I can hear your heart racing like a rabbit caught in a snare." The hunter grinned. "Well fear not, my little rabbit, you shall keep your pelt for now, so long as you do as I say."

"And what would that be?" William asked, trying to sound unconcerned.

"Lead me. I grow weary of the maze of this forest."

"Lead you? Where?"

"To *her*, fool! You know where your accomplice has sequestered my bride and you will lead me to them!"

"I have no idea what you mean," William replied, quietly. "I have no accomplice. Who are you referring to, sir?"

The blade dipped suddenly, slashing open the front of William's tunic, barely avoiding his flesh, before coming to rest again against the divot beneath his throat.

"Do not dare insult me, boy! I saw you in the square. I saw you call to the dog who carried the ungrateful wench away! I followed you out of Aberdoir and into these damned woods. You're following his trail— that much is clear— and you will now lead me."

"I don't know where they went."

"I don't believe you."

"It's true, I've lost my way just as you have."

"Then you truly are an inconsequential rabbit." Adrian drew closer, his ferret-like grin growing wider.

William felt the cold touch of the blade under his chin. He

held his breath and braced himself for a strike when he sensed a slight hesitation in Adrian's threat.

"No, you may keep your flesh, my young friend. There must be something of value to your hide for Lord Thomas to be interested in your well being; what would that be? Could you possibly be the younger brother he's spoken of? Yes, the resemblance is plausible."

William considered identifying himself, then thought better of it. He did not relish the prospect of becoming Tearlach's hostage to elicit ransom from his brother. It would be too easy for Thomas to refuse to pay and rejoice when Adrian murdered him. Perhaps that was Thomas' plan all along.

He looked Adrian in the eye and replied calmly, "You are mistaken, sir. I've never met him."

"Do not think me a fool, boy!" Adrian growled, pressing the blade closer to the flesh. "You may be valuable to me after all. If you are the brother I've heard tell of, then you are indeed more use to me in your flesh."

As the two stared at each other in silence, William's mind raced, searching for a way out of the predicament he was in. *Think Fylbrigge! What did Sean teach me about disarming? Use my weapon; I don't have a weapon!* The staring continued, Adrian leering, as though he were savoring the fear William knew he was showing. Moments lingered as they held their frozen tableau, the forest growing silent with the dying of the breeze.

It was then he heard the soft nickering of a horse to the not too distant north, beyond the thicket. *Hawk! Sean!* Involuntarily, William looked quickly toward the source of the sound, inadvertently betraying his thought. Adrian sneered and turned his head slightly to the sound, his grin shining like the teeth of a demon in the moonlight. He lowered his blade and released the bridle. But before William had a chance to take a breath of relief, Adrian whirled and brought the hilt of the sword crashing against the side of his head.

He fell from Star, dazed. While he lay on the ground, watching the shadowed rider gallop away, the forest began to fade into black silence. He had no sense of time passing as he lay there but it seemed only a heartbeat had passed when Star nudged him with her muzzle and he opened his eyes. It was then he heard the frantic whinny of furious horses, and the sound of a woman's scream coming from the direction that Adrian had just gone.

Sean lay dreaming, lulled by the gentle swaying of the trees and the kiss of the warm night wind. Aside him, Annlise turned quietly, nestling her back neatly against his stomach, their knees spooned in a perfect match. His left arm fell naturally over her waist, her head finding the perfect pillow in the muscles of his right arm. The warmth of her body and the delicate flowery scent of her hair found their way to his dream, transporting him from the musty pile of hay to the freshness of a summer meadow. There she stood, washed in the sunshine and smiling, calling to him to follow her.

His dream feet followed, unencumbered by his physical being. He saw her from above, laughing and running, her gown flowing behind her in the wind as he felt himself rise effortlessly on the breeze. She turned her face up to him, her magnificent eyes sparkling with tears of laughter. Waving to him, she clapped her hands as he whirled higher into the sky. He'd never felt so free, so content, as he swooped and swirled for her delight. His only want in life at that moment, that she never turn those eyes from him.

Again he rose, turning lazy circles in the sky, watching his own shadow dance eagle-like on the grass around her. It was then she raised her arms and called to him, "Sean! Come to me!" He swirled again, enjoying the game for a moment longer. "Sean, come to me," she called again. He made one more turn before another shadow darkened the ground around her. The shadow grew larger, taking a definite shape— a rider - wild and angry, sword grasped in its outstretched arm. Still she stood looking up to him, unaware of the threat behind her. The rider hurled his sword. Sean opened his mouth to call to her in warning but all that issued was a piercing screech of pain, as he plummeted earthward.

"Sean!" Annlise screamed.

Sean opened his eyes gasping at the sudden pain in his gut. Before he had a chance to see what was happening, a second kick sent him flailing to his back.

"Adrian, no! Leave him alone!" Annlise cried, flinging herself at their assailant, clawing at the black fabric that billowed around him.

"Back, wench!" The attacker growled, tossing her aside as though she were no more than a child's poppet made of flaxen scraps and wool.

Sean groped at his side, instinctively reaching for the hilt of his sword and cursing himself as he remembered it falling to the barn floor before he carried Annlise to the hay. A steel clad boot came down on his wrist, pinning it to the floor. A half-breath later, a second boot was planted on his chest and the point of a blade rested at his throat. Sean walked his gaze up the long blade to the hand that held it, to the silver crest that shown in the moonlight and finally to the attacker's face— his eyes wide, teeth bared within a snarling grin.

"I believe you have something that belongs to me," Adrian said, in a calm but threatening tone.

Sean kept his eyes fixed on his attacker, his mind racing for a way to gain the advantage though knowing what he needed was a miracle. He was living his worst nightmare; weaponless, trapped in the one position he'd never been able to recover from— flat on his back with a blade to his throat.

"I've nothing of yours," Sean said, clenching his teeth.

"I think you do," Adrian growled, then drew the sword in a graceful arc over Sean's head and held it two-fisted, poised above his throat. "I am justified to take your hands off at the elbows for thievery alone." He raised the sword higher. "But a far worse crime has been committed in this barn tonight and for that, I am justified in ending your miserable existence!"

"What crime?" Sean asked, struggling to draw breath under the weight of the man standing on his chest. His heart pounded wildly echoing through his skull and he could feel his face reddening.

Somewhere in the shadows, he could hear Annlise sobbing as she crept low along the wall and he prayed she had the presence of mind to flee while Adrian's attention was on him. He could hear Hawk struggling against the tether, snorting and stamping his feet at the intruder, and a second horse— Sean assumed was Adrian's— shuffling and whinnying in response, the two horses feeding each other's agitation. *Annlise, take Hawk! Please God, let her get out...*

"There has been no crime!" Sean argued, hoping to hold

Adrian's attention.

"Don't insult me, dog! The blood about your loins tells the entire lurid tale. You've taken what was mine! Thief!" Adrian screeched, crazily. "Now you will pay!"

The blade raised, pre-strike. The horses responded wildly until the barn echoed. Sean braced himself, waiting for the blade to fall.

Then the ground began to tremble, followed by the thundering of hooves and the splintering of wood and Adrian loosed a furious scream. There came the thud of a body being thrown to the ground as the weight fell away from Sean's chest and arm. He turned his head in time to roll to his side and avoid being trampled by the tangle of hooves. A moment later, all was silent. He lay cradling the wrist he feared had been broken again— eyes closed, forcing his breath to come slowly.

A hand touched him gently on the shoulder. "Sean? Are you well?"

He opened his eyes, disbelieving and grinned. "You're late, Fearless," was all he said at seeing William crouching next him— brandishing in one hand, the most formidable looking branch he'd ever seen and he laughed despite the pain in his ribs from Adrian's boot. "Only you would enter a battle armed with a stick."

"Perhaps it's time I acquire a proper blade?" William replied with a grin, tossing the branch aside. He scooped up a pair of doe-skin leggings from the hay and dropped them next to Sean as he approached. "And it would seem to me, I'm not *too* late." He chuckled nervously, then cleared his throat and politely turned his head, allowing Sean a modicum of dignity to cover himself.

Sean felt his face flush; there would be a tale to tell he knew, but it would wait. He glanced around, seeking out Annlise, hoping for her sake— and William's— that she'd had a chance to pull her kirtle on and reclaim her apron. He was relieved to see her standing nearby, properly dressed and wringing her hands as she looked over the heap on the floor that was Adrian Tearlach. He lay sprawled face down in a pile of ancient dung. The sword that had nearly ended Sean's life had been wrenched from its owner and lay harmlessly amongst the muck.

"There's a blade for you to acquire," Sean said in half-jest.

"No, not that one. It belongs to a madman. It's probably cursed," William replied quietly, no jest in his voice at all.

Sean silently agreed.

After a moment, William asked, "Are you well?"

"Aye." Sean assured him. He made a quick check of his ribs; they were bruised but didn't seem to be broken. He flexed his hand carefully, relieved that the wrist was not broken as he feared but merely a little twisted and bruised. All would heal soon enough.

"Thank God, you arrived when you—" he began, then paused, noticing the jagged slice on the front of William's tunic and the darkened mark on the side of his face. *He's been fighting.* "Why are you here?"

"What?" William asked startled.

"You should be back in Stonehaven," Sean answered angrily. "Didn't you see the mark? You were supposed to head for home! Instead you're out challenging hunters?"

"Sean!" Annlise gasped, wringing her hands in her apron. "He jus' saved ye—"

"What were you thinking?" Sean went on, ignoring her. "No

armor, no cloak—"

"But... I just saved—"

"You don't even have a sword!"

William only stared for a moment, then stood and retrieved Adrian's sword from the dung. "There. Now I have one. Satisfied?"

"You be reckless and unprepared! You could have been killed!"

After a long, silent stare, William approached. In a low tone he said, "It was not me who lay unarmed and naked while knowing the hunter was stalking."

Sean sighed and shook his head, feeling like an ass. "Will, you dinnae want *that* blade; you be right, 'tis likely cursed."

"It's better than a branch and at the least I shall be prepared for the ride home."

A low moan came from the heap of hay where Adrian had fallen.

"He's coming 'round," William said, turning his back and walking toward the hunter.

"Will..." Sean began, then let it go when William turned his attention to Adrian.

Annlise had heard the moan as well and was already kneeling beside Adrian, examining the gash on his forehead left by William's branch. "He'll not be wakin' for a while. Would serve this black hearted beast right for you t' run him through wi' his own blade!" she muttered under his breath.

"I would be justified," William agreed, looking down at the sword in his hand. "But that would make me no better than the beast, would it?" He glanced over his shoulder toward Sean, then tossed the blade to the far side of the barn.

Sean only nodded his agreement.

Annlise looked up at William, then grinned. She flung her arms around his neck. "Will... Thank the Blessed Mother you rode in when you done; you saved him, you saved us both. Thank you"

"Was my honor." William replied, embracing her briefly. "Are you hurt?"

She shook her head, forcing a smile. "I'm fine and well. Dinnae worry on me." Sean walked unsteadily to join his friends, still favoring the wrist Adrian had stood on. "Here, let me look at that," Annlise reached for his arm gently, then confirmed what he already knew. "It is well, Sean. The bones are sound, only bruised."

"I trust you, lass," Sean replied quietly, then closed his fist slowly, to prove to himself that the wrist had not been broken.

"What should we do with this sot?" William asked, poking at Adrian with his toe.

"Leave him—" Annlise began.

"No!" Sean said. "Wake him up."

William looked up, startled. "Are you daft?"

"You know I'm not! Tie him up first if it makes you feel better, then wake the bastard up," Sean snarled. "There's some rope on the wall there."

"Easy, Sean," William said calmly, though Sean could sense the tenseness in his voice.

"I'll get it," Annlise said, then hurried to bring the rope to William.

"Tie him hard," Sean told him, "then take Annlise and the horses and wait for me outside."

"What? No, I'm not about to leave you again—"

"Just do it!" Sean yelled, leaving no room for argument.

"Aye, sir," William answered under his breath, then made quick work of tightly tying Adrian's hands and ankles. Without glancing at Sean he led Annlise away, taking Star's reins on his way out. Annlise retrieved Hawk and followed William out of the barn.

Sean knelt next to Adrian and shook the hunter's face. "Wake up."

Adrian moaned, his eyes slowly opening. When Sean was satisfied that the hunter was conscious enough to understand what he was saying, he leaned in close. "You care nothing for her. Why this?"

Adrian struggled against the bonds then relaxed, a rancid grin crossing his face. "To hunt; to kill. Give in to the thrill sometime and you'll understand."

Sean placed his knee on Adrian's chest, leaning to look him in the eye. "I'll never understand your kind."

"Oh, I think you understand perfectly. You want to kill me right now. Don't you? We are the same, you and I."

Sean's good hand grabbed and curled around Adrian's throat. Adrian's grin broadened. It took every ounce of self control Sean possessed to keep from strangling the sot.

"Go ahead. Give in to the beast, boy. Kill me! For if you don't— mark my words, the day will come that I shall surely kill you, all of you!"

Sean released Adrian's throat and leaned down close. "Perhaps you will, but not today. Remember that. Today, I let you breathe." He stood and stalked across the barn, pausing in the doorway where Will and Annlise were listening silently. He turned back to Adrian. "I leave you to your fate. If it be God's will you leave this barn before you starve to death, then so be it. But I leave you still breathing. There is no blood on my hands."

"You have not seen the last of me!" Adrian grunted, struggling to free himself. "This isn't over, Annlise!"

She stopped and turned, her eyes flashing, ready to holler back. Sean grabbed her upper arm and shook his head. "Don't." He signaled to William, and the three headed into the woods as Adrian's threats echoed around them.

"No one crosses Adrian Tearlach! Fear me, rabbit! I shall find you too!"

Chapter 12

SEAN TOOK THE lead in leaving the barn with Annlise seated on Hawk behind him, her arms wrapped tightly around his waist. He set a brisk pace, keeping the waning moonlight to his left to find the north toward Stonehaven. Twice, William called for a halt, certain they had gone afoul. Both times, Sean had merely glared at him and said in a curt tone, "I know the way." After that William thought it wise to simply follow and trust. After all, Sean had traveled these woods a few times more than he had. They traveled in silence until the dawn, Sean keeping his eyes fixed dead ahead, Annlise glancing back to William occasionally with a non-convincing smile of assurance that they were safely on the right road. William kept alert for signs that Adrian had managed to escape the barn and find them yet again.

Thoughts of Adrian and his threats echoed in William's head as they traveled, the hunter's strange golden eyes burning into his memory. *He is no threat now. He doesn't know for certain who I am and so what if he does; 'tis not like he can march into Drumoak after me.*

"'Tis a serious foe you've earned, Will."

William looked to Annlise. "Hmm? You be hearing my thoughts, lass?" William asked, only half jesting.

"I dinnae need to hear them when you wear ye worry on ye face, plain for the world to see," she said quietly. "Ye right to worry. Adrian Tearlach is not one t' cross. I'm fearin' I brung a curse down on you... both."

Sean's shoulders tensed, but he said nothing. Annlise turned her gaze away from William, watching the path over Sean's shoulder.

William brought Star alongside Hawk, matching his pace. "We left the sod well behind us in the barn. I should think we have seen the last of him; aye, Sean? We showed him we are not to be trifled with, dinnae we? Took him down well an' easy an left him trussed up right good back there. He'll think twice afore making good on his threat."

"Are you seeking to convince me or yourself?" Sean chuckled, though no smile accompanied the laugh.

Annlise cast her gaze down. "You dinnae know what the sod be capable of doin'."

William had a sudden recollection of Martha and Caleb, living all but ruined in their little cottage in the woods. "I have an idea on it, Annlise. He's a hunter. I saw the crest."

"Aye, a hunter. Then you know the threat he be t' folk like us who be—"

William shot her a warning glance and a quick shake of his head and a gesture toward Sean. Annlise sighed and nodded her understanding.

"What folk would that be?" Sean asked, not looking back.

"Common folk," she said quietly. "Anyone weaker than he. And you dare nae be speaking against him or he be findin' reason t' bring a charge o' heresy down on you tha' fast." She snapped her fingers. "I were a blind fool for a long time not to see... not to see what he were doing."

"On what authority does he have the right to bring down charges?" Sean asked.

"The crest he wears gi' him the right... or so he says. Is none willin' t' argue. I'm fearin' he'll be calling charges on you two."

"Not likely. I am no heretic and neither is Will. And you? You are in our protection. I shan't worry on him."

"What else has been happening in Aberdoir, lass?" William asked quietly.

"Ye brother be ruling us hard, Will. He has no soul, I swear." She glanced down, spoke quietly as if to herself. "People been disappearin' only t' appear again a' the stakes, though there be no public trials. He would assure us the magistrates have tried and found the poor souls guilty of witchcraft... but I know it jus' be on Adrian's word alone that the fires are lit."

William listened, his thoughts meandering to his childhood and the horrible nightmare memories of the fire that burned in the center of Aberdoir when he was six— the one that claimed Rebecca.

"Some were arrested for no other reason than jus' speaking up against the hunters," Annlise continued. "They be brung to the gaol and tortured terrible. An' Lord Thomas is careful to keep his own hands clean... callin' on the priests, then goin' t' the altar for absolution. An' Adrian is right careful too and is certain that some— nae many— survive to live as an example of what it costs t' speak ye mind against—" Her voice caught and she shook her head, falling silent.

"Caleb," William whispered.

Annlise looked up. "You know of Caleb? The weaver?"

William nodded.

"Be he well?" she asked. "Tell me he be well, please."

After a pause, he found the words to answer. "He's alive, aye. He and Martha have a cottage halfway on the Edin Road. I came across them while looking for you and Sean."

"Were terrible what they done to him," she whispered. "Because of that dragon."

"Bryndah?" William turned quickly. "She did that?"

Annlise nodded, not looking at him. "She ordered draperies to be made for the dining hall and did not like the fabric. She refused to pay. He argued and threatened to take her before a magistrate. That was his undoing."

"She filed a counter charge of heresy?"

"Aye, claimed the fabric had satanic images woven into it – can you believe it? Poor sot were taken right away t' the gaol. He were already sore mangled afore he ever come t' trial."

William shook his head. "They did not even have a verdict before they did that to him?"

"Och, no. Confessions are less trouble and save the cost of trial, you see. But he held his ground. In the end, the charge was dismissed f'r lack of evidence," she chuckled.

William looked at her, confused at her chuckle.

"Bryndah, in a fit of anger, had burned the fabric, thus destroying the *evidence*. The magistrate, Mother bless him, not only dismissed the charge but ordered Bryndah to pay for the curtains!"

"So Caleb at least was not left penniless," William said, trying to find a glimmer of hope in the story.

"The fee for one set o' curtains dinnae last long, Will. And there were no more orders comin' for more."

"But why? I've seen the work. It's brilliant."

Annlise's eyes glazed, and a hard scowl crossed her forehead. "Because half the town would nae do business with him for fear of bringing down the wrath of Lady Bryndah. And the other half feared being cursed by comin' in contact wi' a cripple."

William sighed. "Foolish superstitions. He's a good man, even I can tell that."

"Aye," Annlise agreed. "But that is why he and Martha left town. I'm glad to know they're still alive at least. I've wondered how they were."

William reached to take Annlise's hand but she turned away.

Sean shook Hawk's reins, quickening the pace. William fell back in line behind and made no further attempt at conversation.

After another hour before the thicket gave way to a familiar meadow and William began to recognize his surroundings. I'll be damned. He did know the way.

"What is this place?" Annlise asked, looking across the grassy meadow, the first rays of dawn beginning to paint the sky.

The light caught on a stone, standing like a sentry in the center of the meadow. Directly to the north two small cairns marked an overgrown gateway, beyond that the hill dropped away out of sight. Her eyes fixed on the standing stone, her hand rising naturally to rest on her sternum.

"Odin," she whispered.

William nodded, but remained quiet. He had no desire to explain to Sean how he knew the ancient names. It was a circle built eons before in honor of the gods of the old faith; the faith he followed secretly with Elinor's teachings. The stone crosses, with the circles at the crossing points that marked the four compass points of the circle, had been placed long before any Roman had set foot in Scotland bringing Christianity with them. But the crosses had been placed so long ago that most folks had forgotten the old way and assumed them to be Christian in nature. Those who knew their true heritage did not speak of it freely for fear of persecution. A small stone kirk had been built at the east point, sheltering a well that once honored Brighid, the Blessed Mother. Now however, the effigy of Brighid had been replaced by a statue of the Virgin Mary. William knew the history; but he knew enough to keep his knowledge to himself.

Sean knew the place as something quite different. To him, it was the place he'd been baptized, took the Sacraments, and more importantly, the place where his father's funeral and burial had been. It was the last place William would want to have Sean discover the only secret he kept from his friend.

"'Tis the cemetery, lass," William replied quietly, sending a glance toward Sean, hoping Annlise would understand that he did not wish to discuss the old ways just then.

She looked at him sadly. "Aye, so 'tis. Will? D' ye still follow—?"

He shook his head quickly once. She did not finish her question.

Sean spoke quietly, the first words he'd said in hours. "We can afford a rest. Stonehaven is just over the hill." He dismounted and held a hand up to Annlise. "There is a well near the kirk. The horses could do with a drink."

"Not from that well," she declared. "'Tis a blessed well."

Sean looked up, surprised. "Excuse me?"

"Uh, I'm sure Mother Mary will not mind, Annlise." William interjected quickly.

"Mary? William Fylbrigge!" Her hands went to her hips. "D' ye nae see the mark on that well?"

"What mark?" Sean asked, looking toward the well. "The trinity?"

"The trisk—" Annlise began.

"Trinity! Aye, I see it," William finished for her. "Plain as plain is, yes. Come on I'll give you a tour of the kirk. Sean, you've not been to your father's cairn for a while. Why dinnae you go pay ye respect; I'll get the horses watered."

"Will—"

"No trouble, really! Come on, Annlise."

"Not to that well!"

"Then, just come to keep me company while I get a drink!" William pulled her toward him, whispering between closed teeth, "I know the mark is for Brighid, just come, aye?"

"Lass," Sean began. "Go on with him. He's right. M'father is lyin' there on the hill. I think I'd like the moment." He gave a curious look to William. "Perhaps, sometime later, you can tell me what that mark is, if it not be a sign of the trinity." He crossed himself, then turned and walked away toward the graves.

William watched him for a moment then turned toward the well, leading the horses by their reins.

"Will?"

"Aye?"

"You're nae t' water the horses from there, are you?"

He stopped and turned to her. "Annlise, it is a well. It is water. Do you think Star and Hawk be the first horses to drink from it?"

"But 'tis sacred! Have ye nae respect?"

"Have ye nae sense!?"

"What?"

"He doesn't know, Annlise. And I would like it to remain such."

A flush crossed her face. "Ye believe he'd cross ye?"

"No!"

"Then why d' ye fear him? You have nae trouble leavin' me to him, and you know right well what I be."

"I trust him with my life."

He led the horses to the shallow well, a small pool of water fed by a natural fountain. To please Annlise and his own conscience, he did not allow the horses to lower their muzzles into the pool. Instead, he dipped his hat into the water for Star to drink from, then for Hawk. She watched silently, seemingly placated by his compromise.

"So why do you fear him?" she asked after a time.

"I dinnae," he answered. "I fear for him should he ever know. I'll not have his blood on my hands too, Annlise."

"What blood be on ye hands?"

He turned away without answering, kneeling by the pool, motioning her to join him. "I've no gold for the well to offer the Blessed Mother."

She knelt beside him and took his hand. "Then, ye heart will do. Jus' as Rebecca taught you. 'Tis her blood you be claimin', aye?"

He nodded, then turned his face toward the water.

She gave his hand a squeeze. "You were but a wee lad of six, Will. Were naught anything you done that sent her to the stake and naught you could do to save her. Aft' all this time, you still be blaming yourself?"

"Perhaps," he replied, without looking at her, "I should have spoken out."

"You were six! No one would have given you half a listen. You know children have no voice in Aberdoir. Especially when they be tellin' a truth the master does nae want to hear." She paused for a moment, then added quietly, "You were nae the only child who knew the truth. D' ye nae blame me as well?"

He looked at her quickly. "No, of course not."

"I dinnae know why not. I knew Rebecca dinnae use magic to help you get away from Bryndah and so did Richard—"

A sudden ire rose in him. "Don't talk to me about Richard!"

She sat back, eyes wide. "He was your friend."

William stood and turned away. "I thought that for a long time. I was wrong."

"I think it be you who is wrong. He would do anything for you."

He wheeled on her. "He did nothing for me, Annlise. Nothing but lead me from one punishment to the next. He would break a plate, I would be blamed. He would say nothing while I was whipped for it. He would lead me into places we did not belong, then abandon me when we were discovered. How can you say he would do anything for me when he let me stay tied to that post—"

He closed his eyes and drew a long breath. His anger toward Richard had nothing to do with Annlise, and he was ashamed with himself for railing. "Forgive me."

"There is nothing to forgive. You own your anger. I'll not deny you have reason to keep it. But..."

"But?" He looked her in the eye.

"I know the lad, too. I've looked after him since you left, Will." She gave him a half-smile. "He misses you."

"I'm surprised he even remembers me," he muttered.

"Of course he does. He's even mentioned how glad he is for you, for bein' free of Fylbrigge Manor."

"Glad for me?" William said, stunned. "He would spare a thought for me, even now?"

"Aye," she said quietly, placing her hand gently on his sleeve. "Can you nae spare a kind thought for him? I know you remember the worst days more clearly but I recall many a time the two of you spent laughin' and enjoyin' each other's company. D' ye never think on those times?"

"Sometimes," he admitted. "All right. For the sake of those times, I will spare a prayer. Peace be to Richard." He crossed himself dutifully, with a nod to the Madonna, then turned and gestured toward the well. "Would you lead the blessing? I'd like to hear it again in the old way."

Annlise smiled shyly, then began to sing in the old language. William felt a small lump rise in his throat at the sound of her song, one that Rebecca had taught him to sing as a child. Her Gaelic rang clear, echoing through the tiny chapel. The vestige of Mother Mary, placed centuries before by the Christian monks, gazed down patiently, her stone face smiling sweetly as Annlise's song to Mother Brighid echoed around her.

Before he realized it, he had joined the song, lifting his own voice in harmony, forming the Gaelic as naturally as Annlise had. He sang freely, allowing himself to be wrapped in the tones, unconcerned with any who would hear. The song washed over him, through him, taking with it his fears of Adrian and the pain of the memories his trip to Aberdoir had stirred. It cleansed him and eased his mind and when the echoes had waned, he felt the first true peace he'd felt in a very long time. When he opened his eyes, the horses had wandered to the grassy meadow and Annlise was gone.

* * *

"Are you well, lad?"

William got to his feet slowly, his knees stiff from kneeling. The little kirk seemed darker than it should and the sun too low in the sky— it could not have been more than a quarter hour since he and Annlise had sung their hymn to the Blessed Mother – or so he believed. He turned to see Sean standing in the arched entry, the afternoon sun haloed around his darkened silhouette but Annlise was nowhere to be seen.

Sean stepped fully into the chapel, crossing himself before the tiny stone altar as he approached. "Will? I dinnae wish to interrupt if you be prayin', but you've been here the better part of the day."

"Praying? Oh. Aye." He glanced at the sun again. "Well, if the truth should be told, I was nae praying."

Sean chuckled. "Do I look like a priest? Save your confession. Sleeping, aye?"

William nodded, affecting an embarrassed smile. "You winnae tell Father Dunkirk I been sleeping in here. I will be doing penance for a month."

"Two. But just think how clean the cathedral stairs shall be when ye done scrubbing." Sean laughed, motioning toward the archway. "Now, if you would give me a moment."

"Dinnae sleep too long, mate." William headed for the door. "Or you'll be right beside me scrubbing—" he began, then silenced himself seeing that Sean had taken his place on the kneeler, quietly resting his forehead on folded hands. William left his friend to his privacy.

He crossed the meadow toward the horses. Watching them graze on the sweet grass made him suddenly aware of the ache in his belly. Thoughts of Drumoak and the fine dinner that surely awaited him began to push aside concerns about Sean finding out his secret commitment to Brighid and the old religion, or that Annlise would somehow reveal it to the world. *No, she knows the consequences too well to truly be a worry on that score.* His stomach growled and he turned his thoughts back to the kitchen in Drumoak, where he imagined Elinor's glorious stew kettle bubbling away and the loaves of fresh bread cooling on the rack. *Annlise is going to like her... I hope.*

He looked about and realized Annlise was not with the horses as he had hoped. "Annlise?" he called, his only answer the echo of his own voice. He looked toward the forest, then toward the road to Stonehaven, then toward the east, where he saw her standing with her back toward him looking over the cliffs to the sea beyond. "Annlise!" He began to run toward her, then stopped as she turned and raised her palm to him in a signal to stop. "What is it?" Annlise placed her palm to her sternum and turned her face to the sun. *She's hiding!*

Just then, he was startled by the sudden clamor of hooves and the rattle of carriage wheels approaching from out of the wooded road. Two mounted escorts dressed in the familiar colors of Drumoak led the procession, their horses keeping an unhurried but steady pace. Behind them, pulled by a team of four of Edward's proud stallions, was the formal coach the duke reserved for his personal use.

"Bloody hell," William muttered under his breath, suddenly aware of the condition of his clothing and the not-so-pleasant aroma emanating from his tattered shirt. Edward prided himself in cleanliness; it was one of the few things he demanded of William at all times. He glanced back toward the cliff where he knew Annlise was standing though he could not see her. *I will have to ask her to teach me that charm.* He gave a thought to ducking into the nearby bushes, hoping he had yet to be spotted but the hope was quickly dashed when one of the escorts waved and pointed him out to his companion. William gave a half-hearted wave of recognition and forced a welcoming smile to his face, then walked to meet the party.

"Halt!" The escort on the left called, bringing the procession to a stop. He leaned over the pommel of his saddle and grinned down at William. "Well if my eyes are not deceiving me, I believe we have found Edward's prodigal fosterling. What say you, Simon? Be it Will or be it—" He looked slowly from William's dusty boots to his tattered shirt. "– a beggar who is lost and seeking alms?"

Simon trotted his horse around William, also looking him up and down. "My guess is beggar, Ewan." He pulled in close to William, leaning as Ewan had done and took an exaggerated sniff of the air. "Ah, but now, wait a moment. That smell – aye, 'tis Will Fylbrigge for certain. He be the only lad in the highlands who can wear the scent of horse dung and make it attractive, aye?" He laughed and dismounted.

"Very funny, Simon." William chuckled. "I'm glad to see you lads."

"Jesting aside, Will, we are glad to see you, too," Simon said, the smile running away from his face for a moment. "Edward is ready to send the dogs and every horseman in Stonehaven out to find you. If not for this lot we're escorting to the castle, we would be out with them. You have some things to answer for, lad."

"Is something wrong? Why have we stopped?" a woman's voice called from the carriage.

William's empty stomach lurched at the sound of her voice. "I take it that Lord Edward is not with you?"

"Nae," Simon answered, rolling his eyes toward the carriage, putting his nose in the air. "We have the honor of escorting none other than Herself of Aberdoir in for a visit."

William swallowed. "Lady Bryndah?"

"That be she." Ewan leaned over the pommel again, whispering, "If it were not for Lady Mehlyndia bein' wi' her, and the fact tha' good horses are hard t' come by, I'd run the bloody carriage over yon cliff for the tongue lashin' we been taking."

"Lady Mehlyndia is with—"

The carriage door slammed open, exposing the silk-slippered foot that had kicked it. "Will one of you dunderheads answer me now! Why have we stopped?!"

"Ah! 'Tis the love call of the bonnie flower of the highlands; that would be for you, Ewan."

"Me? I have not earned the grand rank of dunderhead, lad. Last I were kenning, I were still a lowly codpiece. I must achieve hedge-swine and miscreant before I make it to dunderhead."

The voluminous silk skirt made an appearance from the carriage, before the whole woman emerged. "Why have we stopped?" she demanded again. "Who are you talking to?"

William stepped quickly to the opposite side of the carriage, signaling with a vertical finger to his lips to Ewan.

"No one of any consequence, m' lady. A beggar 'tis all." Ewan gave a quick wink to William. "Shall I kick him to the mud for you?"

"Dinnae over do it, sot." William muttered under his breath, as he crouched near the front wheel, peeking through the spokes. When he caught full sight of the woman clad in silk, an old but familiar tremor had found its way to the pit of his stomach. He'd never told Simon or Ewan anything about his life before Drumoak, or his feelings about Lady Bryndah, and preferred not to have to explain it to them now. He backed away planning to skirt around the back and into the kirk until another voice spoke from inside the carriage.

"William? Is that you?"

He jumped, whirling on his heel. "Lady Mehlyndia!" He felt the blood rush to his face, as it usually did when Edward's youngest daughter was near. "Uh... aye, 'tis me."

She giggled behind her hand. "What have you been about? You are quite filthy."

He brushed at his tunic and sleeves while making an awkward bow, which only made Mehlyndia giggle louder.

"Sister! Look who—"

"Shh!" William waved his hands frantically. He looked over his shoulder quickly to see if Mehlyndia had caught Bryndah's attention. Bryndah was still berating Simon and Ewan with a venomous tongue lashing, spewing oaths that William thought could embarrass a merchant man.

"What?" Mehlyndia whispered, still threatening giggles. "Why must I shh?"

"Please, m' lady... uh, I am not rightly presentable... you see, to be presented... "

"'Tis only Bryndah, William. She's delivering me home from our holiday." She brought her hand to her mouth, a sudden light of understanding flashing across her eyes. "Oh, dear. You have been with us at Drumoak so long now that I sometimes forget you were fostered by her. You wish not to let your foster mother see you in such... as that."

"Aye, that's—"

"You'll want a chance to clean up from whatever adventure you've been about, I'm sure."

"Aye, that's—"

"But William, it's been a good long time since she's seen you and, just a moment ago, she told me how she misses you so and was asking how you are faring at Drumoak; you are so like a son to her, you know. I am certain a smudge of road dirt will not turn her from you."

William blinked, surprised at Mehlyndia's words, then remembered that she had been kept as unaware as Simon and Ewan about Bryndah's true nature and what he'd endured while in her fosterage. He knew far too well Lady Bryndah's talent for affecting a sweet, disarming demeanor when it suited her. She did it so well that even Edward had been fooled. Even with the scars on his back, it had taken William a good long time to convince the duke that his ill-treatment at Aberdoir was not due to Thomas alone. Mehlyndia had been sheltered from the truth about Bryndah by both William and Edward, and had always adored her older sister. Edward had long nurtured that relationship, perhaps hoping some of Mehlyndia's genuine sweetness would infect his eldest daughter as well. William thought it best not to change that perception at the moment, though he still wished to excuse himself.

"Uh, aye, that is exactly correct, m' lady. I should like to clean up. Please, do not betray my presence just now. I should not like to upset her; my, uh, adventures always worried her, you see, and I find no good cause to let my, uh, dear foster mother see that I've been about yet another."

Mehlyndia smiled her sweet smile. "You are so thoughtful.

I shall not betray you. After all, she has already had quite an upset. Something dreadful happened at Fylbrigge Hall a few days ago, you see."

"Dreadful?" William tensed.

"Yes." She leaned out the window and lowered her voice as if to impart some bit of gossip. "Her waiting lady was abducted by rogues in the market! Poor Bryndah has been beside herself with worry and Lord Thomas has even issued warrants and rewards for the capture of the scoundrels and the lass' safe return."

"Warrants? Blessed Mother!" he blurted, then covered, "Uh, mother... the rogues left her be, aye?" *Thomas sent the hunter! Bloody hell.*

"Oh, dear sweet William, you need not fear. Bryndah was quite safe. I see you do still care for her."

"Uh... aye, I suppose. Does the snake... uh, that is, does Lord Thomas have any notion who the culprits may be?"

She nodded knowingly. "I believe he does, though he would not say. But I can tell you that they will not be long on the run. Thomas has dispatched a squad of his best men and he has offered a bounty of twenty crowns for their heads."

"Twenty cro—!"

"The lady's own betrothed is leading the search. He was devastated, I am told, and has vowed to find her and slay the scoundrels with his own sword." She expressed a wistful sigh. "Is that not the most romantic thing you have ever heard?"

William absently brought his hand to his throat. "Romantic... absolutely. Except for the scoundrels, of course." He swallowed hard. "Well then, I believe the lady has enough on her mind without me adding to her worries."

"... and your skin for shoe leather if you dare insult me with such twaddle again!"

"Go quickly, then." Mehlyndia giggled. "She's coming."

Bryndah climbed back into the carriage and put her head out the window next to Mehlyndia. "Is that creature bothering you, sister?"

William bowed lowly, concealing his face with his hair. "Beggin' y' pardon, mistress. I were jus' off t' find me way t' Stone'aven. Dinnae mean nae 'arm in delayin' ye. Were only 'opin' for ye touch o' charity."

"Charity! Not likely. Go and let us proceed in peace, before I have you arrested and tossed in prison for blocking the road! Filthy beggar."

He heard Mehlyndia's stifled giggle. "Sister, Father has told me to always have a farthing for alms. It brings good luck."

"Let him earn an honest wage – oh very well. If you must."

Mehlyndia tossed a farthing to the ground near William's feet. "That should buy you a bath, sir. Good day."

"Aye m' lady; thank ye, m' lady... "

The window panel slammed shut and the carriage moved forward before William dared look up. When he did, he saw an amused looking Sean standing in the door of the kirk.

"A whole farthing? I hope Edward offers a bigger dowry than that for you. I say you are worth at least a shilling."

"Sean! Did you hear that?" William ran toward his friend. "Twenty crowns! The bastard has offered twenty crowns!"

"Aye, I heard," Sean said, his jaw going tight. "Come on. We need to get to Drumoak." He waved toward Annlise, who was now running from her spot near the cliff. Sean set a quick pace to meet her.

"That is more gold than I have ever seen him willing to part with. Is keeping Adrian for an ally that important?" William asked.

"He cares nothing about Adrian, Will, nor Annlise. 'Tis blood money."

William pulled Sean's arm to a halt and turned him to face himself. "What are you saying?"

Sean looked William in the eye, his lips closed into a tight thin line. William understood then, without Sean having to answer.

"He knew it was me?"

"Aye."

"But, in the woods, Adrian had the chance and he held back. Why did he not do the deed then?"

"He was told not to. I heard Thomas tell him not to until he could have a chance to think. My guess is that by offering a bounty, that it could be claimed you were brought down by mistake."

"Leaving his hands clean."

"Exactly. Adrian was set a-chase before the bounty was offered. I saw that with my own eyes. Obviously he did not know about it."

William thought for a moment, retracing his encounter with Adrian in his mind. "You're right, Sean. Thomas dinnae tell him who I am. He said he did not know why he was to spare me but it would more than likely be worth it to him if he did."

"There you are, then. Thomas knows full well it was you but he would not tell anyone. He has the hunters looking for someone anonymous."

Annlise joined them, catching her breath. "Is everything well?"

"No," William grumbled, then explained the situation to Annlise.

"Well then. There be only one thing to do," she said, a resolute nod of her head. "We go straight away to Lord Edward and we tell him the whole bloody truth! And I go back to Aberdoir."

"What?" William shouted. "After all we've been through to bring you out?"

"Lass, no," Sean protested. "What possible good will that do?"

Annlise mounted Hawk with a sigh. "You men be thick in the skull. I should think it be obvious. You tell Edward what's been done. He will go to Thomas and tell him 'twere all a misunderstandin' and t' recall the bounty. Thomas cannae very well tell the duke he knew it were Will all along now, can he?"

William and Sean looked at each other.

"She's bloody brilliant," William admitted.

"Aye," Sean agreed, then turned to Annlise. "But why must you go back to Aberdoir? You winnae be safe there, lass."

Annlise grinned. "Oh, I think I shall. I know the truth you see."

Sean's shoulders sank as he gave up the protest. "Well if naught else, you have proven you can take care of yeself. I dinnae have to like it."

Annlise reached for Sean's hand. "Nor do I."

Sean mounted behind Annlise. William mounted Star. Without further conversation, they kicked into a fast gallop toward Stonehaven.

Chapter 13

THE HUNTER CARELESSLY tossed the coin onto the tray, his eyes never venturing above the bodice of the lass who served him. Why look further north when the view to the south was so pleasing? His companion sipped at his ale, trying not to look toward the ample charms the wench possessed. Another day, he may have participated in a bit of flirtation, but not in Stonehaven— not within sight of his father-in-law's castle.

Adrian took the lass' hand and bade her to sit on his knee. She obliged with a piggish chortle that seemed to amuse him in its coarseness. Thomas was not amused. They had matters to discuss that he would rather not share with some low-born wench. He watched them over his ale, waiting for an opportunity to interrupt. He knew it was not wise to rush these things with Adrian.

"Oh now, deary, tha'll cost you more than a farthin'," she said giggling, as Adrian planted a kiss at the valley between her bosoms. Without looking up, he slid a silver coin into the crease.

"Will this do?"

"Coo, aye!"

She slid off his knee, extending her hand with a bat of her eye. Adrian looked up to her face then, actually looking at her for the first time. His grin grew wider, apparently pleased with what he saw as he placed a far too gentlemanly kiss on the wench's hand. His eyes lingered for a moment on the wooden bracelet carved with an intricate filigree vine that dangled from her wrist.

"D' ye like it?"

"Indeed," he answered seriously, examining it further. "Where shall we conclude our arrangement?"

She raised a brow toward the staircase that led to the rooms above, then sauntered in that direction.

Thomas resigned himself to waiting and settled back against the wooden chair. "I suppose this takes precedence over our business?"

Adrian swallowed the last of his pint, setting the mug down hard on the table. He grinned, looking at Thomas from under his brow. His odd golden eyes caught the red glow from the sunset coming through the window, giving them a chilling, wicked glow. "This *is* our business, my lord."

"I fail to see how."

"Do you? You surprise me. You being so shrewd in your alliances, I should think it is obvious. I am simply securing allies." He stood and straightened his tunic and belt.

"Again, I say; I fail to see what possible advantage to our business it is for you to indulge in an afternoon frolic with a whore." He signaled the innkeeper to bring him another.

"Let me ask you this. When you wish to make an alliance, do you not first seek out those who can offer you information about them?"

"And what possible information can this wench offer about my brother? You don't believe she is privy to the comings and goings of Drumoak, do you?"

The innkeeper set the mug on the table. "There ye are, sir. Anything else?"

"Privacy," Thomas snapped with a dismissive wave of the hand.

"You are singularly the most obtuse man I have ever known, Thomas," Adrian chuckled. "Look about this room and what do you see?"

"An inn. I see tables, chairs." He took a sip, looking down into his mug, then stopped. He held the mug to the light, for the first time noticing the emblem that adorned the bottom. He looked about, noticing the mark on the trays, the wall, and even emblazoned on the door. "Edward's eagle."

"Very good." Adrian applauded. "Edward, himself, may not frequent this little establishment but it is apparent by the tributes littered about, that he is a generous benefactor. Either to the inn or those who do frequent its fares."

"The guard."

"Among others. Did you happen to take notice of the bobble the wench wore at her wrist?"

"Yes," he sniffed, "I was unimpressed. Common. Carved in wood. What of it?"

Adrian laughed under his breath. "Did it not look at all familiar?"

"Enlighten me, I grow weary of your riddles."

"Did you not tell me your brother was fond of carving trinkets? One of the qualities you find so un-endearing about him is his penchant for befriending the lowborn."

Thomas grinned. "Yes indeed, so you believe that trinket may have come from him?"

"If it did, then I shall count her as a very valuable ally." He brushed his sleeves and turned toward the stair. "Either way, I shall enjoy the afternoon."

* * *

A quarter hour later Adrian returned, looking as brushed and neat as he had when he went up the stairs. The wench followed a moment later, flushed and slightly disheveled. Thomas took note of the pink welt rising on her neck. "I take it your *meeting* was successful."

"It is astounding what one can learn so quickly." Adrian gestured toward the table in the far corner. "It seems your brother is quite popular with the locals."

Thomas sniffed. "He's wealthy."

"And generous, it seems. No wonder you worry about your fortune. He is likely to spend it all on trifles."

"He is merely spending Edward's money for the moment. But you are correct in my concern. I want what is tied up in trust before he has a chance to whither it away on wenches and wine."

"A simple accident should secure that for you, I should think."

Thomas set his mug down hard, pulling Adrian toward him, looking to be certain no one could hear their conversation. "Fool. If it were that simple, he would have landed at the bottom of the well ten years ago. My father and Edward conspired long ago to ensure that no 'accident' befell him before he reached majority. Until he is twenty-one or married, Edward has complete control of his portion of the holdings. If he is dead before then, Edward keeps the lot. My only hope was he succumb to the sweats but he had an uncanny luck in never contracting so much as a sniffle!"

"Outfoxed early on, were you?"

Thomas sneered. "Cheated early on! I am the eldest son and if not for that damned provision in his will, I would be my father's *only* son." He took a swig from his mug, and looked out the window, adding under his breath, "Legitimate son, that is."

Adrian raised an interested brow. "Are there others?"

Thomas half chuckled. "My father had a fondness— not unlike your own, my friend— for trifling with the, shall we say, lesser born. One of his bastards was born within the walls of Fylbrigge Hall. With my own mother, herself round as a brood mare with him in attendance at the birth, if you can believe it!"

"She must have been a very understanding woman," Adrian chuckled.

"A fool, more like it," Thomas grumbled, shaking his head. "She had no idea who sired Rebecca's bairn."

"What became of him?"

Thomas grinned. "My wife is talented with herbs. A trifle she learned as a child. She mixed a brew— for laboring— that brought about the child's early birth. He lasted only an hour and it all appeared perfectly natural."

Adrian grinned. "And one bastard brother out of the way. Why did she not employ her talents when William was on the way?"

"She never got the opportunity," Thomas said, scowling. "She was kept away from the birth."

"Pity. But at least there is that one less obstacle to your fortune."

Thomas sat scowling, staring out the window. "I wish I could be certain."

"Another bastard?"

"Possibly," Thomas answered quietly. "Like William, my

father sprinkled trinkets about to wenches hither and yon."

"Carved wooden bracelets?" Adrian chuckled.

Thomas shook his head. "Spun silver pendants, in the shape of a knot. Rebecca wore hers blatantly. My mother never suspected... " He swallowed the last of his ale and set the mug down hard. "Back to the business at hand. By right, I should have sole inheritance of all my father's holdings. Right now Edward has full control of everything, and even what was left to me, I must spend at Edward's almighty discretion. I want to be free of him and take what is rightfully mine. I must find a way to get it before it becomes William's outright."

"There is always a way," Adrian grinned. "A man convicted can own no estate."

It was Thomas' turn to look interested. "True, what are you getting at?"

"You said Edward keeps the inheritance if your brother dies, but does the will take into account what would happen to it should he be convicted? Or, for that matter, executed?"

"Then whatever property belonged to him reverts to the crown." Thomas shook his head. "Even Edward could not touch it."

"'Tis a simple matter of filling the proper palms with gold, my friend."

"And you know which palms that would be, I assume."

Adrian sat back in his chair coolly.

A slow grin spread on Thomas' face. "I knew it was a good idea to release you from that barn."

Adrian glared, then smiled. "I owe you some thanks for that, I suppose. I never did ask how you knew to find me."

"A hunch. I found the whelp hiding there once long ago, after he'd run away. An elderly couple had taken him in believing him to be a lost urchin. I barely found it again myself."

"It seemed quite abandoned."

"And why not?" Thomas shrugged. "I had it burned."

Adrian was impressed, raising his mug in salute. He turned and called to the innkeeper. "A scroll and ink, quickly!" Adrian tossed him a couple of farthings. "Now leave us in complete privacy."

The innkeeper nodded, obliging immediately.

"Now then, we need to craft a believable accounting of the unpleasantness surrounding Annlise's departure and have it brought to Edward immediately."

Chapter 14

SEAN HOPED TO enter Drumoak quietly, and have a chance to clean up and relax before going to see the duke. But as luck would have it, Lord Edward stood at the gate when the three disheveled riders approached from the woodland road. William signaled them to hold back but it was too late. Edward saw them and gave the sentry at the gate a quiet order before disappearing into his castle.

The sentry waved a signal to Sean, then hurried to meet the three where they stood.

"'Tis Isaac Walford. He's not smiling," Sean observed. A lump formed in the pit of his stomach as he remembered the undelivered letter that was still in his tunic.

"So much for a quiet homecoming," William sighed. He forced a smile to greet the approaching sentry. "Well met, Isaac, how be you—"

"Lord Edward has been asking for you," Isaac said, interrupting William's pleasant greeting. "You're t' go directly to his study. He's not in a mood to be left waiting."

"Now?" William asked. "Should I at least clean—"

"Not you, Will. Sean. He dinnae mention you." Isaac gave a brief nod to Annlise. "Or you, miss."

"I hardly think he could mention me, sir," Annlise replied. "Though I should very much like to see him as soon as possible."

"Annlise." Sean placed his hand on her shoulder and spoke quietly, "Not yet."

"But the sooner—"

"Not yet, I said!"

Annlise closed her mouth hard, her eyes wide at the tone of his voice.

"Sean," William started, "we're all weary of the road. Isaac, perhaps it would be best that we rest and clean up before going to—"

"Beggin' ye pardon, Master William, but Lord Edward said *now* and he said *Sean*," Isaac said, matching Sean's abrupt tone, leaving no room for argument.

"But surely—"

"Will," Sean interrupted. "He called you *master*, lad. That means 'tis serious."

William nodded silently; a sudden childish flush crossed his face, an expression that Sean hadn't seen on him in a long time. Sean fixed a carefree grin on his face in an effort to lighten the mood. "Now dinnae fear, master, I am sure I will nae be quartered today – not while he's entertaining Lady Bryndah. He'll be waiting until she leaves at least."

"That is not funny—"

"Will, you take Annlise to see m' mum, aye? She'll have a clean frock and a hot bowl for her. You get settled and as soon as I be done wi' Lord Edward, I'll come fetch you."

"Are you certain' 'tis well?" Annlise asked, the same doubtful expression crossing her face as William wore.

"Aye, lass."

Sean helped her dismount, then followed Isaac back to the castle.

"Laurel!"

Laurel spun on her heel, startled, dropping the basket of

fresh flowers she was carrying when she heard Elinor's call from the end of the corridor. The flowers had been meant to brighten Lady Mehlyndia's bed chamber upon her return. Laurel guiltily scrambled to pick up the fallen petals before Elinor could see she had yet to deliver the basket.

Once again, she had lingered, distracted from her duties by her unrelenting curiosity for things that did not concern her. She thought perhaps Elinor would be forgiving once she told the older woman what she'd just learned. She could scarcely believe it herself and, as she hurried to retrieve the flowers, she realized her hands were shaking.

Elinor hurried up the corridor, her arms laden with fresh linens. "Child! Have you not brung those in yet? The lady will be here any moment and the room is as stale as a tomb."

"Any moment?" Laurel looked up, startled anew. "But I thought the lady was hours away!"

"The carriages are already here. And we have another room to prepare as well. Lady Bryndah is with her." Elinor leaned forward and lowered her voice. "Though I'd rather fluff the stable than the guest apartment for that old shrew."

Laurel swallowed a shocked giggle. "Elinor, you're wicked!"

"Wicked, perhaps; honest for certain. Come on now, we've just enough time to throw open the shutters and turn the linens." She hurried Laurel past the pillars of the grand corridor toward Mehlyndia's suite at the end.

Laurel hurried behind. Once in the room, she gave a glance down the corridor, then quickly closed the door. Elinor was already bustling about, pushing back bed curtains, and fluffing the down pillows.

"Elinor, I've news."

"Talk while helping, Laurel."

She set the basket of flowers on a table near the window, then stood staring out at the courtyard below. "Terrible news," she said quietly.

"Child, we've work to—" Elinor stopped then, apparently noticing what Laurel was watching from the window. "Ah, Master William is home, and... who is that with Sean?"

"If she be who I think she is, 'tis Lady Bryndah's waiting lady. Just as the messenger told Edward she would be with them." She shook her head, drawing her hand to her mouth. "I heard him talking to Lord Edward and did not want to believe – they could never do such a terrible thing."

Elinor placed her hand gently on the girl's shoulder. "Have you been listening outside Edward's door again?"

Laurel nodded, keeping her eyes on the returning travelers and the woman sharing Sean's saddle. "Please dinnae be angry; I promise I will never do it again—"

"Aye, until the next time," Elinor said dryly. "It has something to do with that lass?"

"Look, the sentry is already going for him. They'll be in the dock by sunset."

Elinor turned Laurel to face her, placing both hands on her shoulders. "Who will be in the dock? Child, will you please stop speaking in riddles and just tell me what you heard?"

"Will and Sean," Laurel whispered, sniffling onto her sleeve. "Edward sent for Sean because of that message. He's fierce angered, Elinor. He told Isaac he'd have heads if what was in that message was true, that Sean and Will had something to do with the abduction of that lady and a murder in Aberdoir!"

"Murder?" Elinor gaped, looking from Laurel to the courtyard and back. "What has it to do with Will and Sean?"

"I'm not certain, only that I heard Edward growling at Isaac to be sure Sean is brought to him at once upon his return, to get the truth from him. And if he be bearin' a lady with him, then to fetch him with arms if he must. And look, there she is. What have they done, Elinor?"

"It is not for us to know, Laurel." Elinor stiffened her jaw and watched the exchange between Isaac and Sean for a moment.

Laurel heaved a small sigh of relief in seeing Sean accompany Isaac calmly and without the prodding of the sentry's sword. William and the lady stood back and lingered for a moment before heading toward the barn.

Elinor pulled the curtains closed. "Hurry, we have rooms to prepare." She hurried toward the door.

"But, don't you care what happens to them? Elinor!" Laurel rushed out, barely able to keep up with Elinor's determined pace down the corridor toward the guest chamber. "We have to warn them, don't you see?"

"I'd say the time for warnings is past, Laurel."

"Elinor! Wait for me! What if Edward has learned about Will's lessons—"

Elinor stopped short, whirling on her heel. "Hush child! Are you gone daft?"

Laurel snapped her jaw closed, realizing she'd been rather loud.

Elinor pulled her quickly into the guest suite and closed the door. "You must never mention that aloud! You know full well the terrible risk I've taken with Will and you for these four years, teaching you the old ways. Too dangerous for you to be spoutin' loud enough for all of Stonehaven to hear." Elinor's stern look softened. She took the tip of her handkerchief and dabbed away a tear that had welled on Laurel's cheek. "Now then, there is no evidence that lass has anything to do with Will's lessons, right? Did you hear Edward say anything that would make you think he knew?"

Laurel blinked back further tears, and swallowed hard. "Aye." She drew her hand to her mouth and whispered, "Someone saw them vanish into mist as if by magic."

Elinor went pale for a moment. "Did Edward believe it?"

"He called it nonsense, but what if—"

Elinor exhaled. "Good, then. Let's not buy trouble, child." Elinor hurriedly tossed open the windows and only half fluffed the pillows, then pushed Laurel toward the door. "One more room to prepare, and we best be to it fast."

"Another?"

"Aye, Will's. He's home after all, aye?"

"Aye."

"Then it be my duty to put his room to order and, perhaps, draw him a good hot bath, as I'm sure he's needin' one." Elinor looked over her shoulder, then whispered, "That will give me the excuse I need to be in there a little longer and to be certain that his lesson books and potions are well out of sight. Just to be safe. Go now, see if you can catch him before he's called to see Edward to let him know about all this. Go."

"Aye," Laurel agreed. She ran from Elinor, toward a back staircase that would get her quickly from the castle to the courtyard. Hopefully she could catch a moment with William, before he 'vanished' again. *Lunk, ye not being careful! Disappearin' in plain sight! Och, I thought you had more sense than that, you silly clodheid!*

* * *

Lord Edward sat in the ornate chair before his writing table in his study, reading and re-reading a scroll bearing an official looking seal. The way his right thumb absently stroked his beard and the deep vertical furrow forming between his brows were sure signs the duke was not in good humor. Sean stood by the door, rocking from heel to toe and trying not to appear impatient while he waited for the duke to finally look up and speak. At last Edward placed the parchment aside, folded his hands casually on his lap and looked up. Sean straightened his back and stood still, setting his eyes straight ahead and not on the duke.

"I have come to hear a rather disturbing rumor, Sir Sean. Would you know anything about it?"

"M' lord?"

"It seems that an abduction has taken place at Fylbrigge Manor. Lady Bryndah's personal attendant was taken from the market place while she was on an errand with a chaperone."

Chaperone? There was no chaperone. Sean stood silent, waiting to hear the version of the story that had reached Stonehaven.

"Two men attacked her chaperone and left him dead on the cobbles, then one carried her away. The other, I'm told, slashed his way through a mob and left several patrons and shop keepers bloodied or dying. Terrible thing."

"What?" Sean risked a look.

"There is even one account of a witness who swears the two vanished into the mist without a trace - as if by magic - if one believes in such nonsense."

Sean swallowed, remembering how he'd hidden in plain

view with Annlise, how Will seemed to vanish, horse and all. "Nonsense, aye."

"My daughter is understandably concerned for the safety of her gentlewoman, given the brutality of these two rogues." Lord Edward looked up under his brow. "You would not happen to know anything about this, would you? Since you have just returned from Aberdoir, Sir Sean?"

"I... believe the details of the incident may be... exaggerated, as rumors tend to grow from town to—"

Edward slammed the flat of his hand on the table. "Do you think I am a fool?"

"No, m' lord."

Edward glared for a moment then sat back in his chair, tenting his fingers under his chin. "It shall fall to me to dispense justice should these rumors prove true. If a murder – *several* murders – have indeed happened in Aberdoir, then I shall issue warrants immediately."

"I am unaware of any deaths, m' lord," Sean replied, truthfully.

"And what of the maid? Are you unaware of her as well?"

Sean swallowed and drew a breath, not knowing how to respond. Technically, he had whisked Annlise away but it had been William's idea; indeed, it had been on William's order. He had no idea where the rumors of mass murder had derived from and he was certain Will did not kill anyone. But then, he had been in the kitchen of the tavern with Annlise while most of the melee on the street was happening.

Edward sighed and stood, his demeanor softening. "Sean, please. Tell me what happened. I know full well that you and William are involved somehow and I cannot bring myself to believe the situation is as it has come to me. But I am bound by the laws to respond to the information that I have. And given the descriptions of the men and their horses—" He picked up the parchment and traced the page with his finger, "—one wearing the livery colors of the guard of the house of Stonehaven and mounted upon a chestnut Arabian, the other finely dressed in cambric and doeskin who was seen fleeing the town on a black—" Edward set the parchment aside again. "Need I continue?"

"There was no killing, m' lord. I swear to that on my life!"

"I have reports on—"

"My lord, there was no killing! None by my hand, nor by Will's— he does not even carry a sword! Only a fool could believe him even capable—"

"Stand down!"

Sean closed his mouth and stood straight. Yelling at the duke was not the wisest course he could take. "Forgive me."

Edward leaned on his palms, his brows deepened into a sharp 'v', his usually bright blue eyes turned grey and cold. Sean had never seen such a look on the duke's face, hard and angry. The look could easily give credence to the monster tales that Bryndah had filled young William's head with about the villainous Lord Edward. For a brief moment, Sean wondered if there was not a seed of truth to the stories. If there was, would he soon be visiting the hidden dungeons of Drumoak— if they even truly existed. He held his peace and his tongue, and braced himself for the expected berating. He was not prepared for what he saw next; the slow grin forming on the duke's face.

"No sword?" Edward asked.

Sean nodded.

"Then he could not possibly be our marauding killer. Could he?"

Sean shook his head.

"And therefore, you could not possibly be the guard who carried away the maid."

Sean swallowed.

Edward waited for an answer but when there was none forthcoming, he stood and turned his back to Sean. He looked out the window toward the main entry and spoke quietly. "I have known you for the whole of your life, lad."

Sean looked up, surprised at Edward's sudden change of tone.

The duke continued to look away; talking as if to himself, almost wistfully. "I have watched you grow and thrive among the squires and wards. There is no doubt in my mind that you shall make a fine knight one day. I have seen to it that you have had the best training and same opportunities I give all of my wards; in more than one instance, I have favored you in placement where you should otherwise be ineligible."

"M' lord, I am grateful," Sean said quietly, though Edward showed no acknowledgement that he'd heard. "Why you have given me these opportunities has always been a mystery to me, given my lowly birth."

Edward turned and faced Sean, a strange half-smile forming. "Lowly birth?" He chuckled and turned back toward the window. "You are mistaken on that, lad; your father was a fine man. Many days I miss his company. But that is a conversation for another day."

Sean bowed his head at the memory of his father. "Thank you, m' lord. You honor him."

Edward was quiet for a moment, then drew a long breath. "Back to the matter at hand. Tell me, lad. Who is the lass who shared your saddle upon your return? Yes, I saw her."

Before Sean could answer, the chamber door burst open. Two men— dressed head to foot in black, their riding cloaks billowing— swept into the room. Ewan, red faced and breathless, his hand clutching his sword hurried in behind.

"My lord, I tried to stop these two—"

"I will not be kept waiting!" The first growled, then threw back his riding hood. "I shall speak to Lord Edward now and you—" He waved dismissively toward Ewan. "-shall leave!"

"Thomas," Edward growled, "it is you who shall leave and wait as I bid you to wait!"

Ewan stood his ground, his sword poised. Sean drew his as well, flanking the intruders. Thomas Fylbrigge glowered at him, his lip curling into a grin. "Have you not arrested him yet, Lord Edward?"

"No one is to be arrested, though I am sorely tempted to chain you to the ceiling! Do not test me further this day, Thomas, for you shall surely gain my displeasure." Edward raised a hand, pointing to the door. "Now go!"

Sean raised his sword, to emphasize Edward's command. Thomas stood unmoved. The man who came with him stood equally still, his face still shrouded by his riding cloak, one gloved hand clasping the hilt of his sword. It was clear neither would leave the room without confrontation.

Thomas signaled for the man to hold, then looked to Edward. "I say again, my lord, I must speak to you now."

Ewan took a step closer, then held waiting for Edward's command. Sean kept his stance, ready should the hooded man swing. The man turned slightly. Sean knew then who it was who stood shrouded by his hood, as the road-dusty silver crest became visible beneath the cape. The head turned and Sean could see the golden eyes of Adrian Tearlach peering at him, from beneath the hood.

Sean kept his voice steady, forgetting his own issue with these two men. Assuming his role as a sentry to Edward, he raised his sword. "My lord has told you to leave."

"I do not take orders from criminals, boy," Thomas growled then held up his hand in a gesture of peace, glancing toward Edward. "I see he has swayed you already."

"There was nothing to sway, Thomas. You have, yet again, brought me a fairy story that you would have me believe as truth." Edward tossed the parchment toward Thomas. "Do you think me so daft as to not see what you are about? You would have me believe it was Sean Wilbrun who is called out in this bulletin."

"Is *that* his name? Wilbrun?" Thomas asked, half grinning. "Well, my lord, Master Wilbrun has taken something that does not belong to him. I have simply come to reclaim it, and to see that justice is done to him and his accomplice – whoever he may be."

Edward leaned on his palms. "Do not test me, Thomas. You know the implications of your accusations. You know quite well who it is you are accusing."

"Do I?" Thomas grinned. "Did you hear him, Adrian? He said I know who the scoundrel is."

Adrian stood silent, staring toward Sean.

"Well then, my lord, if you know who, then I shall ask you again. Have you yet arrested him?"

"On what evidence?" Edward bellowed. "Hearsay? I have heard Wilbrun's account and it is vastly different. Unless you have more evidence— *hard* evidence— that either he or 'his accomplice' were present at this alleged abduction then I give you one last opportunity to leave here as free men, otherwise, I shall instruct my sentries to arrest the both of you!"

Thomas motioned for the hunter to step forward. "If you would."

Adrian nodded, keeping his face cloaked beneath his hood. He reached into his sash and withdrew a small leather coin pouch and tossed it on the table in front of Edward. Sean recognized it at once - it bore an embossed crest of a diving hawk and the initials 'w.f.'. Edward picked it up and looked at it closely. Sean could see that he, too, recognized the emblem and initials. The duke opened the purse and poured the contents into his hand; several silver coins, a gold crown, and a thin teardrop shaped ivory plectrum— the kind used by musicians to pluck the strings of their lutes, also bearing the initials 'w.f.'.

"Does this look familiar, my lord?" Thomas asked, his face smug. "I seem to remember that plectrum was a gift that was presented this twelfth-night past with the request that it be put to use for the entertainment of your guests. Geoffrey, the luthier, presented it on your behalf I believe. Am I correct, my lord?"

"Where did you come by this?" Edward asked, keeping his voice low.

"The pouch and its contents were hastily given to a tavern keeper as a bribe to buy his silence," Adrian answered. "The man had witnessed the affair in the street, my lord."

Edward looked up. "Explain."

"The murder of the innocent merchant and abduction of the lass." Adrian went on. "The scoundrels dragged the poor woman through his tavern! In payment for a safe escape, the accomplice pressed this into the tavern keeper's hand."

Edward cocked a skeptical brow. "Then how did you come to own it?"

"After he saw the blood and the bodies on the cobbles outside of his shop, the man had a fit of... conscience, shall we say, and wanted no part of this blood money. He gave it to me."

"You filthy liar!" Sean shouted, raising his sword to strike.

"Stand down!" Edward ordered.

"But my lord—"

"Stand down! This is not a formal hearing, no one is on trial here! I simply wish to know what transpired." Edward looked toward Adrian. "Explain the bodies on the cobbles."

"Terrible thing! Obviously the killer was crazed. The victims were slashed wickedly and without provocation, while the other made off with the woman. The street shall be stained for years."

Thomas leaned on the table, looking eye to eye at Edward. "You know what must be done, my lord. This villain must be found and dealt with, no matter who he is."

Thomas straightened his back, turned on his heel and strode to the door, beckoning Adrian to follow. "I shall take my leave, my lord. Please forgive the intrusion but I am sure you now understand the gravity of this. I trust you shall do what must be done." He left the room without further word, Adrian following close behind.

Edward motioned for Ewan to follow and to close the door behind him.

Sean stood silent, his mind racing, his heart beating loudly in his chest. *How did that snake get out of that barn? I should have killed him while I had the chance.*

"Sean," Edward tapped him, making him startle. "Peace, lad."

"It was lies, my lord. There was no killing; I am certain of it."

"I believe you."

"You do?"

"I have never known you to lie to me, so I do not expect you will begin now." Edward raised a brow for confirmation. Sean nodded. "And one more thing. Tearlach said something rather telling in his account – two things actually; did you hear them?"

"I'm not sure I know what you mean, my lord."

"The lady's chaperone has suddenly become a merchant. Now I ask you, would my daughter's first lady be chaperoned by a merchant?"

Sean shook his head. "I had missed that. And the second?"

"Did we not just discuss the fact that William had no sword?"

"Aye, sire. He's right stubborn and refuses to carry a blade at all. I've badgered him about it for ages, thinking it a foolish habit to be about without one—" Sean's eyes went wide. "Yet, Tearlach said the victims were slashed."

Edward's grin broadened. "For once, I am pleased with William's stubbornness. Well now, that settles the matter of the killings for me. There is still the matter of this, however." He picked up the plectrum, turning it thoughtfully between his fingers. "There is no mistaking this. William was there."

"But Lord Thomas did not name him out right. Why? It is clear to me he has no desire to protect Will by any means." Sean wondered aloud.

"To come right out and say it was William—" Edward chuckled under his breath. "— would be the same as asking me to put a warrant on his brother. He cannot do that outright; it is political, complicated, and pure Thomas Fylbrigge. Oh, he'll do his best to damage William's reputation for certain. And that may become troublesome when it is William's time to assume the duties that come with his birthright. I must remember to make him more visible to the people so they can know him better and draw their own opinions on which of Henry Fylbrigge's sons is more worthy of their admiration, aye?" He chuckled quietly again, turning to look out the window.

"Will always told me he thought his brother was out to destroy him. I admit I never fully believed him."

"Well, William does have a tendency to exaggerate sometimes. But alas, I fear he is correct on that count. That is why I am surprised he went to Aberdoir with you at all."

"He's not the timid lad he was, my lord," Sean said. "You would be amazed at his courage; I know I was. And though he does not carry a blade by habit, he is more than capable of wielding one."

Edward looked up, the light of inspiration coming to his face. "Is that so?"

"Why, yes. We spar often." Sean allowed a grin. "I still win, but he's very good."

Edward's brow went up, interested. "Could he hold his own against say, Ewan or Simon?"

"Absolutely. In fact he has, though neither will readily admit being bested by a nobleman." Sean laughed.

"That's it!" Edward thumbed his hand on the table suddenly, causing Sean to jump.

"My lord?"

"A tourney! What better way to present William to his future subjects. I shall call a tourney. Allow him to show off." Edward grinned, pleased with himself and the idea. "I expect that you shall compete as well, Sean. I should like to see you best the guards of Aberdoir."

Sean stood tall, pleased with Edward's vote of confidence in him. "I shall be honored, my lord."

"Good, good. That is what I shall do then. And it shall put all this unpleasantness behind us. Now then, there is just one more thing I would like you to clear up for me. Tell me about the lass, Sean."

Taken aback by the sudden change of subject, Sean drew a long breath and reluctantly relayed the story of how Chase had met them at the door and begged for them to whisk Annlise away from Aberdoir and away from the man who Thomas had promised her too. He was thorough in his account of the flight through the town, Will's diversion, and the flight into the woods. He was careful to leave out any mention of how Annlise had used what he could only call magic, to hide them in plain sight. He also left out any mention of his broken wrist being miraculously healed in one night and that he truly was guilty of stealing something precious— Annlise's virtue. *'Tis not stolen if it be freely given, is it?*

"She came of her own accord, my lord," Sean concluded, crossing his fist over his chest in a gesture of truth. "I swear it."

"Ah, I am beginning to understand. So it was not an abduction; it was more of a rescue mission?"

"Aye!"

"So you are not an abductor, you merely helped facilitate a runaway servant make clean her escape."

"Aye! Nae, nae, she… " Sean sighed. There was no argument.

Edward was right. He'd helped a runaway servant. An offence no less severe than if he had truly abducted the lady. "Aye, I suppose I did."

"Relax, son, I have no intention of running you to the dock. I do, however, need to find an excuse not to charge you. Tell me again, from the beginning. Why were you in Aberdoir to begin with?"

"I went to deliver your letter—"

"Yes? What is it?"

Sean felt his face turn hot, as he reached into his tunic and withdrew the letter he was to deliver. "In all the excitement, m' lord... I failed to... I beg your forgiveness." He handed the letter to Edward.

Edward took it slowly. Sean braced himself for another rebuke and a fresh round of yelling. But it was not yelling he heard from the duke; it was a sudden fit of laughter.

"All this trouble because I sent you to deliver this? Do you know what this is?"

"No, sire, I never looked at it. You see the seal—"

"Easy, lad, I am not accusing. It is an invitation to my daughter to come and stay for a few days when she returned with Mehlyndia."

"What? But the lady Bryndah passed us on the road! She could not know about the invitation."

"She came because of the unpleasantness. Fearing to send Mehlyndia home in the coach by herself. She came with her staff in train. Well now, I do believe everything shall iron itself out. William has every right to visit Aberdoir, does he not? After all, it is his ancestral home. So that justifies his presence there. And Annlise would have been part of Bryndah's train, so that justifies her presence here. You see?"

Sean shook his head.

"There was no abduction, you simply escorted her to Drumoak where she could rejoin her lady. There was no killing. As you have told me in truth, no crime has been committed; therefore, there is no criminal to hunt and no accomplice to charge." Edward thumped the table. "Now then, you are a mess, Sir Sean, and in need of a bath. Go wash."

"Uh... aye, my lord." Sean turned to go.

"One more thing," Edward said.

Sean paused and turned.

"Under the circumstance, I think it wise that you are not seen with the lady, Annlise. It would not do your reputation well to be seen in the company of a betrothed woman."

Sean stared for a moment, then nodded his understanding before turning to leave. Outside the chamber, he leaned against the wall and drew a long breath, realizing for the first time he'd been shaking inside.

Betrothed! Not if I have anything more to say about it.

Chapter 15

AFTER SEAN'S DEPARTURE for the castle at Isaac's insistence, William reluctantly took Annlise directly to Agnes as Sean had suggested, though something in the pit of his stomach prevented him from feeling completely comfortable about the arrangement.

"She's a pious woman, Annlise. Please keep that in mind and be discreet in what you say."

"A body would think I be still to suckling by the way you worry."

William halted, pulling Annlise to the side of the cabin before knocking on Agnes' door. "Must you be so stubborn? I am only telling you for your own good."

"I am right capable of behaving as a lady," she replied hotly. "If living with Bryndah be not enough practice for discretion, I dinnae know what be."

William had no ready argument. Instead, he turned his hands up in frustration. "Blessed Mother, guide her!"

"So mote it be." Annlise grinned and took his hand. "Honestly, I'll be fine. And you've assured it now, haven't you?"

William grinned in spite of his anxiety. "I have indeed. Now, let's get this over, aye?" He gave a quick rap on the door. "Agnes? Are you about? 'Tis Will."

After a moment, the door opened slowly. Her hand beckoned them to enter, then Agnes ushered them hurriedly through the door. She took a cautious glance left and right, before closing it quickly behind them. Her face went slightly pale at the sight of

Annlise.

"Be you from Aberdoir, miss? Are you Lady Bryndah's maid?"

"Aye, how'd you know?"

Agnes crossed herself, muttering, "Sweet Mary, preserve me."

Annlise glanced at William and he gave her his best 'I told you' look. He took hold of Agnes' hand and fighting down his own rising worry, assumed a gentleman's demeanor.

"Easy, dear lady. We mean you no distress."

Agnes gave his hand a squeeze smiling in spite of herself. "You're filthy, Master William."

He blushed, looking at his blackened hands and nails. Annlise suppressed a slight chuckle.

"Well, I tried. I'll be a nobleman some other day. So, I take it the rumors Lady Mehlyndia told me of on the road have reached here?"

"Word be out all about Stonehaven, Master William," Agnes explained, in hushed tones. "They be lookin' for her, saying she was abducted right off the high street in Aberdoir!"

"Abducted?" Annlise hissed, impatiently. "What utter nonsense! Was of m' own will, I come here!"

"Aye, I'm seeing that be the case, miss, and I dinnae doubt ye word," Agnes said. She herded Annlise and William toward the back wall of the cottage, as far from the window as she could move them. "But 'tis not me you need be convincin', is it."

"How could news have come to Stonehaven so quickly? Did the birds carry the word straight away?" William growled. He dropped himself on a wooden bench near the hearth. "Foolish notion, I know perfectly well how it traveled so fast. I take it the page from Aberdoir arrived yesterday, demanding to be shown immediately to Lord Edward with important – nay, *urgent* news from Lord Thomas. I imagine he painted quite a tale of woe and pity."

Agnes lowered her voice. "More like a tale of murder and abduction."

"Murder?" Annlise gasped. "There was no murder!"

"There was," William said quietly. "I saw it."

"What? Who?" Annlise turned to Agnes, reaching for the woman's hand. "Who do they say was murdered?"

"They say it was your escort, miss, if I'm understanding it right," Agnes answered, drawing her hand away.

"Escort? But I had no escort! Will, d' ye think it may be someone else they be lookin' for? Maybe it is not us at all!"

"No, it isn't someone else, Annlise," William replied quietly. "There was a murder. It was the man in the motley hat selling toys in the market who was killed. Adrian cut him in half where he stood. But it seems that my brother has chosen to paint a different story and has elevated the poor man from fool to escort. And I'm sure there will be none in Aberdoir who are likely to contradict him."

"Adrian... killed the harlequin?"

"The man dared place his hand on you. Does it surprise you that Adrian would take offence?" William asked.

"I suppose it should not, but... aye, it does," she said quietly, then turned her face quickly.

"Surprised that he killed? Or that he cared?"

Annlise brushed her cheek quickly, then turned back to face him. A strange half smile crossed her face. "'Tis foolish to think it were for caring for me."

"Aye, it be foolish! Next, you'll be saying it was romantic!"

"What?"

"'Tis what Lady Mehlyndia thought too." He mocked Mehlyndia's high voice. "'Isn't that the most romantic thing you've ever heard? He's off hunting the rogues who stole his lady love!' Gaah!" He wheeled to face her. "Is that it?"

"Will, no—"

"You saw what he almost did to Sean and still you think this is some romantic game? Och!" He threw his hands in the air turning away.

"William Fylbrigge, you are such an ass!"

William spun on his heel. "An ass? Annlise, I have seen with my own eyes what the man is capable of doing. I have just spent two days lost in the bloody Black Forest keeping out of his way, and was nearly run through so you and Sean could have a toss in the hay—"

"You and Sean?" Agnes gasped, crossing herself. "Have you eloped?"

Annlise turned scarlet, her eyes going wide. "No! I have only just met him." She glared at William, growling under her breath. "We are still quite unfamiliar to each other!"

William felt instantly ashamed that he'd betrayed her private moment— and Sean's— to, of all people, Sean's mother. And after warning Annlise to be discreet, here he'd just lost control himself. Agnes was still pious enough to consider it a sin for Sean to take a woman out of marriage— though William could only assume that Annlise would not have been his first or only. And he knew Annlise had just told an outright lie to Agnes— he had seen the blood on their loins— but he held his tongue. It was not, after all, his secret to betray.

"Well, thank the Lord for that!" Agnes said. "Nothing against you, lass, but a scandal is the last thing Sean needs upon him right now. He is coming up in rank within Lord Edward's guard."

"I'm sure his rank is in no jeopardy because of Annlise, Agnes," William assured her. "I am not so optimistic for my own, however. I'm certain 'tis my name that Thomas will demand that Lord Edward put on the warrants."

Agnes placed her hand on his shoulder. "I've not heard of any warrants being put out. And Elinor says tha' Lord Edward has been sequestered in his study since the page left him. I can tell ye, he is none too pleased that the gossip has already started."

William patted her hand upon his shoulder. "Thank you. I trust you."

"Good." She risked a peek through the shutter. "None be lookin'. Seems the gossips have not seen you come in here."

"I was careful coming in," William said, standing. "I know I am asking much of you, but if you could let her stay here until I've had an opportunity to speak to Lord Edward myself and smooth this whole thing over, I should be eternally grateful. Please?"

Agnes twisted her apron in her hand for a moment, and turned away. "Am I likely to refuse you, Master William? You bein' the lord's foster son?"

William spoke quietly, "I would never use my relationship to Lord Edward to make demands of you. I ask as friend in need. Nothing more. Of course you are free to refuse, good lady."

Agnes turned to look him in the eye, a sort of strange, sad smile crept onto her face. She looked at him oddly and for a moment, William thought she would turn him down. She surprised him by placing her palm gently against his cheek.

"So like your father," she said quietly. She withdrew her

hand from his face and placed it on her own, failing to conceal the crimson that had crept onto her cheeks. She turned quickly and busied herself by gathering a basket and the bonnet she wore in the garden. "You may stay and be welcome, miss. There be a basin and pitcher of water in the back room there. I expect you'll be wanting to wash the dust from ye hair and face. There be fresh linen in the cupboard. I will bring some supper when I come back from the castle."

Annlise stood, nodding politely. William could see she shared his relief. "Thank you, ma'am. I promise I shall not be trouble. And 'tis only until Sir Sean comes to fetch me—"

"Sean? No, lass, no." Agnes' eyes went wide, her hand reaching for Annlise's forearm, grasping it tightly. "I beg you, please leave him out of this trouble. Please! They will surely think he is the one who killed that man if they see you— and with all those vicious black caped riders about town!"

"What riders?" William turned Agnes to face him. "Black riders?"

"Aye. They came on the heels of the page."

"Why didn't you tell me this sooner?"

"I only now remembered—"

"Hunters." Annlise said simply, turning toward the window. "They did not waste time."

"Aye, my brother is right efficient." William hissed. "I should have realized he would have sent them out well ahead of his coming to Edward. They don't wait for orders to strike once they've been sent to hunt. They'll have descriptions and a bounty all ready."

"Master William, the men they described—" Agnes pulled a crumpled piece of parchment from her pocket and handed it to

William. "These be up all about Stonehaven."

William took the parchment and read slowly, shaking his head. "They waste no time in posting the placards."

"It be my Sean they be lookin' for," Agnes whispered. Her eyes welled up, but she kept her voice steady. "My son is not a murderer. But the gossip is starting and you know how rumors grow in this town. They'll have him guilty and hanged without trial if they see her with him. Trust me, you dinnae want to be on the wrong end of the rumor vine in this town, Master William."

William and Annlise looked at each other, the same thought seemingly crossing both minds at the same time. Even though he was fairly certain there was more decency in the good people of Stonehaven than to turn on one of their favorite sons— as Sean had become, after rising from stable hand to sentry— William knew, it was too much to ask of Agnes for Annlise to stay with her now.

Annlise stood and gathered her riding cloak. "I shall go. I would not like to bring trouble to your hearth, mum."

"Lass, I wish you no ill, I beg you understand."

"Where will you go?" William asked, strategically stepping between Annlise and the door.

"There must be an inn or tavern about town. No one will know who I be."

"What about the hunters?" William asked. "Surely they will know who you are or suspect you to be. A young woman, new to town? Traveling alone?"

"Well if they ask, then I shall tell them that I be here of my own free will! I can tell them the truth that I left with you and Sean of my own accord."

Agnes let out a small gasp.

"Then I shall not use his name – nor yours, Will, if it keep you both out of m' trouble."

"But the hunters—"

"Hang them! Have I nae lived in their shadow long enough to know how to stay out of their way? 'Tis something our kind knows how to do very well—"

"Annlise!" William snapped, hoping Agnes did not understand what Annlise had nearly revealed.

"Your kind?" Agnes asked. She stepped closer to Annlise, looking back and forth between the young woman and William. "And what kind would that be, lass?"

"The misunderstood kind!" William answered, thinking quickly. "She serves Lady Bryndah; isn't that reason enough to be fair acquainted with knowing how to hide?"

A look of sudden understanding crossed Agnes' face. "Forgive me, Master William. You have grown so since you've come, that it is easy for me to forget how you arrived. Is this why it be so important for you to help her? Because of your time with Lady Bryndah? That is your kind?"

William stood stunned for a moment. He had forgotten that Agnes was among the people who had tended his wounds when he had arrived four years ago. She, Elinor, and Laurel were the only other souls, besides Sean who knew what he had endured in his years as Bryndah's foster son.

"Aye," he answered simply. "It is what she meant by 'our kind'."

The awkward moment was broken by the sudden rapping on the door. Agnes jumped, then exhaled in relief when it was Laurel's voice they heard calling.

"Will? Are you in there?"

Agnes opened the door. "Come in, child, before all of Stonehaven knows you're here."

"I be looking for – oh, hello." Laurel gave a half curtsey to Annlise, then skirted around her quickly, running to William. "Where have you been? We've been pacing a path in the carpet worried for you." Before William could reply, she grabbed his hand and began pulling him toward the door. "Elinor has drawn a bath and your room is ready. You need to get there quick and clean up before you go in to see the duke. Och, Will, we were sure you must have been waylaid by some highwayman—"

He glanced over his shoulder to Annlise and shrugged. "I'll send for you—" he said as Laurel pulled him through the door.

"And then, Elinor heard Edward yelling at someone."

William pulled his hand free. "Who was he yelling at?"

"Well I'm not in the way of knowing every nobleman that comes, am I?" She ran a few steps ahead, then turned and beckoned him to hurry. "But I think one was your brother. I saw him leaving a moment ago."

"Thomas is here?"

"Aye, so is the dragon; I was just obliged to tidy the guest suite. I haven't seen her yet, though, but I'm sure she's with Lady Mehlyndia. I just hope I don't have to make up another room for that other fellow who was with Thomas. I dinnae like the look of that one, his face shrouded up under that hood and all. He looks right devilish—"

"What man?" William grabbed her hand, spinning her around to stop. "Did you see his face?"

"No, I just told you, it was shrouded."

"Did he wear a crest? On his tunic, a silver cross?"

Laurel's eyes went wide in sudden understanding. "A hunter? That man is a hunter?"

"Aye," he answered, looking up and down the street. It was then he noticed the placards like the one Agnes had shown him nailed to nearly every door and post. "Come on, let's get in before anyone sees me."

"Now you be worried about being seen!" Laurel clucked her tongue. "You were nae worried when they seen you disappear!"

William stopped again, spinning Laurel. "What? What do you mean? I never disappeared."

"That man—" Laurel's hand flew to her mouth. "Blessed Mother, what if it was him who saw it! Will, you must be more careful! Are you wantin' to be roasted alive?"

"What are you talking about?"

For the first time, Laurel stopped moving. She looked somehow older and William felt a trepidation stir in his stomach waiting for what she would tell him.

"Roasting is nothing to jest about." He forced a smile. "What have you heard?"

Laurel shook her head. "They be saying someone saw you disappear— as if into the mist."

His jaw dropped. "What? That's impossible!"

"The charm is in Elinor's book, Will. Do you swear that you never used it?"

"How can you ask?"

"Swear it!"

William placed his right fist to his chest, mimicking the gesture of loyalty the sentries made before the duke. "I swear. 'Tis a baseless rumor." He reached for her hand. "It wasn't me."

"Well, it surely wasn't Sean. Then it must have been—"

He put his hand to her lips. "Not here."

She nodded, turned and ran toward the castle.

He followed Laurel at a run to the kitchen entrance of the castle. He knew there was no chance that he would meet either his brother or sister-in-law in the kitchen or on the back stairs. They were far too proper and proud to even know where the kitchen was located. Elinor was just entering when they got there.

"There you are! Thank the Blessed Mother!"

"Has Father sent for me?"

"Not yet, lamb." She ushered him toward the back stairs. "You've time to go and bathe and dress. You'll be expected to dine with him."

"A last supper?" he said, only half jesting.

Elinor chuckled. "You should have more faith in Edward than that. Go wash."

"Is Sean with Edward?" He paused on the stair and turned to face Elinor. "Or is he headed for the gaol?"

Elinor stepped close and spoke quietly, reassuringly. "The last I knew he was in speaking with Edward. Thomas and his man come and gone but Sean is still there. I take it as a good sign that Thomas looked sour when he was leaving. Means he dinnae get his way about something."

William felt the first signs of relief. Elinor had a way of knowing and this was the first hopeful thing he'd heard since returning to Stonehaven. "Thank you. Would you... if you can manage it, send Sean my way as soon as possible. If Edward allows him leave, that is."

"Straight away, lamb." Elinor smiled, her blue eyes sparkling. William could not resist embracing her with a squeeze.

"Thank you."

"Och, lad, you smell of a dung heap. Go wash."

He released her, chuckling, then hurried the back way up to his room to do as he was told. He got a whiff of himself as he ran and decided Elinor had been kind in her assessment of his aroma. His smell could be easily remedied with a bath. He was fairly confident that Sean's rank would be safe and Edward would be fair. The only thing on his mind, as he made his way to his suite, was the puzzle of why someone would have said he vanished into the mist.

"A tourney?" William stopped midway through pulling his shirt from over his head, preparing for the bath that had been drawn for him.

Sean grinned and, folding his hands across his chest, leaned back against William's chamber door. "Aye, that's what he said. He sees it as a way to put you forward. Pit you against the rogues of Aberdoir, no doubt."

"You must be jesting! Me? Against the guards?"

"Och, no! Would be of equal rank, lad." Sean raised his brow knowingly. "You'd be matched against a nobleman."

"Thomas?! Is Edward daft? I'm no match for him—"

"You are too! And if you want my opinion, I say it be a right fine idea."

"Do you, now?" William scoffed, tossing the shirt to the floor. "And what be the gain for Edward when I am pummeled into the gravel on the very first set? You know bloody well I cannae handle a lance."

Sean laughed out loud. "Well, no one can accuse you of being a braggart. Take heart, Will. The armor should prevent most of the lance from running you through."

"I'm pleased my imminent demise amuses you so."

William dropped his backside onto the edge of his bed and began yanking off his road-dusty boots. The left proved to be stubborn. Sean was still chuckling, seemingly not aware that William's alarm at the thought of participating in his first tourney was genuine. He gave a hard yank and at last extricated the boot from his foot and threw it hard to the floor, turning sharply toward Sean at the same time.

"Quiet, Sean! Has Edward made you heir to my belongings? He has, hasn't he! Well let me put you straight, Sean Wilbrun! If you keep laughing, I shall strike you from my will and you will stay in the barracks, rusting in your ancient armor!" he growled, his own voice sounding foreign in his ears.

Sean silenced himself, dumbstruck, slowly straightening his back, assuming a more formal posture. "Forgive me, my lord. I seem to have forgotten my place. 'Twas only a jest."

William felt the blood rise to his face. A gulf seemed to open up between him and his friend. He glanced down, not wanting to meet Sean's glare. Only then did he realize he was standing in only his undergarments. He found that he could not contain his own laughter.

"Some nobleman I shall be, aye? The great Lord Naked of Stonehaven."

Sean's posture relaxed much to William's relief, though he said nothing.

"Sean, please—" William sighed and threw his hands up, then let them drop by his sides. "I am weary from the road, dirty as a sow, and have more aches than I can express. I've concealed a fugitive bride only to be told she's supposed to be here, endured

Laurel's badgering for the details of my battle to the death with that hunter, and been sent to my chamber like a bairn to bathe. God only knows what retribution Edward has in mind for me for whatever the crime I have supposedly committed—" He drew a breath. "And here I stand berating my dearest friend in naught but my knickers. Please forgive my rudeness."

Sean did his best to suppress the grin. "If I do, will you reinstate me in your will? I rather fancy the doeskin trews."

"They're yours," William chuckled.

The door opened suddenly, bumping Sean in the back. Before he could protest, Laurel poked her head through.

"Sean! There you are. I was waiting by Edward's chamber, how did you manage to get past – Will, haven't you bathed yet?"

William scrambled to retrieve his shirt, modestly holding it in front of himself.

"He's getting there," Sean replied calmly, seeming to enjoy William's awkward moment. "He could use another kettle of hot water. That water has sat there for a while and is likely cold."

William was lowering himself into the bath quickly, holding the shirt protectively. To his dismay, Laurel hurried to the tub, heedless of his embarrassment, and dipped her hand into the water.

"Oh aye, that's gone right tepid. You'll catch your death if you sit too long there – I'll fetch another kettle. Is there anything else you need?"

"Laurel!" He slapped at her hand, splashing her a little. "A bit of privacy would be nice."

She rolled her eyes, her hands going to her hips. "'Tis not like the sight of you is anything special. I'm only trying to do my job."

"I thought your job was waiting on Mehlyndia." He splashed again.

"She's had her bath," Laurel replied, matter-of-fact. "Besides, she's entertaining her sister and is not in need of my service." She sat herself down on the edge of the bed and began picking at a bowl of fruit that Elinor had provided. She found an apple she liked and took a bite.

William glanced to Sean for support. Sean was laughing under his breath and William could see he was enjoying Laurel's distraction far too much to hope that his dignity would be rescued any time soon.

"Would you two please leave me some privacy!"

Sean bowed from the waist, rolling his wrist from head to toe. "As you wish, my lord." He stood straight and extended his hand toward Laurel. "Come on, lass."

She took his hand and hopped off the bed, still chewing on the apple. "Aye, I'm going. I have another room to prepare anyway. Sean, your lady friend is going to be in the castle after all. Agnes is putting the west-end suite in order right now." She informed him, with an impish wink. "It's right handy to the back stairs."

Sean's face went pale, all trace of amusement gone in an instant. He wheeled on Laurel. "In the castle? In God's name why?" He turned, stalking toward the tub. "I thought you brought her to my mother."

"I... I did!"

"Tearlach is in the castle!" Sean flared, not hearing. "Why didn't you do as I asked, just this once?"

"Sean!" Laurel put a hand on Sean's arm. "Will did; why are you yelling?"

He pulled away, quickly storming toward William. "Do you think he will leave her in peace if he sees her here?"

"Sean—" Laurel pulled on his arm again. "You are not listening—"

He spun to face her. "The man is dangerous! Do you not understand that? Did you see the crest he wears? Do you know what it means to someone like her?"

Her eyes went wide and she looked quickly to Will. He was equally surprised that Sean knew the danger the hunters presented to people like her. Did that mean Sean knew her secret— and his own?

"How do you mean?" she asked carefully. "What does the crest mean?"

"It means he acts as he wishes with the blessing of the crown. He takes what he wishes, and what he wishes is to have Annlise— and she has little choice but to go with him as he bids." A look of sudden distress replaced the anger and he turned his back to both Laurel and William.

William exhaled, relieved that Sean did not seem to associate the true danger the witch-hunters posed to people like her – or like himself.

"Sean," William began quietly, "I did bring her to your mother. But when we heard news... she did not wish to bring any danger to your mother. You know she has her own mind. She will do as she will. Besides, you said Edward thinks it best she simply rejoin Bryndah's train."

Sean nodded and drew a breath before he turned around. "She doesn't love him," he said simply. "All Tearlach wants is a prize, not a bride. She deserves so much better."

Laurel gasped, bringing her hand to her mouth. "Sean—

you're in love," she whispered, taking a tentative step toward him. "Is that what this is about?"

Sean tightened his jaw, his lips drawn to a narrow line. "I will not let him hurt her." He turned and stalked toward the chamber door. "I'll stop him myself, if I must—"

"Sean, wait!" Giving no thought to his modesty— or Laurel— William jumped up from the tub to stop Sean from leaving the room.

But before Sean had a chance to open the door, it swung open and Elinor glided in wearing a cheerful smile and carrying a stack of fresh linens.

"Oh, Sean, there you are, dear. Wee Duncan is asking on you. He's in the kitchen with your mum. Laurel, that room will not make itself; go on now, hurry. Will, you're dripping on the tapestry." She set the linens down on the edge of the bed, picked up William's soiled clothing and without taking a breath, breezed past Sean. "Dinnae forget dinner with the duke." And, as quickly as she had entered, she was out of the room, closing the door behind her.

The three stood silent, looking at the now-closed door. Laurel allowed a tiny giggle to break the trance. "You're dripping."

William looked down and turned scarlet before getting quickly back into the tub.

"I'll go fetch that kettle," she said, turning toward the door. She gave Sean an affectionate pat on the back as she passed him. "Be careful," she whispered. She stood on her toes to give him a quick kiss on the cheek before she left the room.

Sean stood silently staring at the closed door with his back to William, head down. After a moment, he began to speak in a voice William had never heard from Sean.

"There are times I should like to abandon propriety and duty, and live as I choose; in service only to myself, free to love and wed. Why should life be free only to those of noble blood?"

"Is it?" William asked quietly. "Though I, too, would like it, I do not expect to be allowed to choose my bride. Edward shall more than likely decide for me and it will be for the betterment of his holdings."

"Don't you have any thoughts of who you would prefer?"

William was quiet.

Sean turned then. "What of Lady Mehlyndia?"

"He will choose for her as well, I suppose." The revelation came on him like lightning. The thought of watching Mehlyndia being sent to a far off place to wed for business reasons brought on a sudden and unexpected shudder. The revelation was not lost on Sean.

"You understand how I feel now?"

William nodded, trying to understand his own revelation.

Sean allowed a half grin. "I shouldn't worry too hard, lad. I'm fairly confident Edward has already chosen mates for the both of you."

"What do you mean?"

"Purely for business purposes, mind you – the last heir to the house of Fylbrigge would give him the entire holding. He already has half of it after all, through one daughter."

William's jaw dropped. "I never thought of that! He... you mean he would... Mehlyndia... and me?"

"The best of both worlds for you, lad. Love and money."

William felt his face flush. "I care little for the money. I am not even certain how I feel about *her*. She may have affections for McLander the goat herder, for all I am aware, and choose to run away with him."

"And if she did, then you as her chosen suitor, would have the right to go after her and force her to come back with you. McLander would have no voice in it at all."

"I would never force her!" William protested.

"You would, you're a nobleman," Sean said with a shrug. "You've the power and the money."

"I would not, sot! I do not let power and money dictate my conscience... do I?"

Sean sat on the corner of the bed, tossing William a wash cloth from the stack of linens Elinor had left. "No, lad," he said gently. "You may come from the same bolt as your brother but you are most definitely a different cut of the cloth than he is." He picked up a towel and considered it in his hand for a moment. "I, on the other hand, am woven of a courser thread entirely... and jute cannot be woven into cambric."

"Is that truly how you see yourself?"

"It is not a matter of how I see anything, Will. It is simply how it is. We're born to our lot and there we stay."

"Well then, by that thinking, you should be out mucking stalls."

"My father was raised to first groomsman!" Sean said sharply, a flush coming to his face. "I'm a sentry! Not a stable—"

William sank into the hot water to his chin, grinning.

"What is so amusing?"

William reached for the lamb's wool cloth and stood, wrapping it around his waist. "You are, Sir Made-of-Jute, who has risen from his lot quite nicely I'd say. As did your father before you."

Sean relaxed and conceded a grin. "True, he did, and so have I. But only through Edward's good graces. You're very clever, Lord Naked-of-Stonehaven, but I cannot leave here and expect to find a position guarding some other duke, or earl, or even baron. Outside of Stonehaven, I am as low born as it gets." He tossed Will a clean tunic that had been lain on the bed. "The blood in my veins is as—"

"Red as mine!" William snapped.

He pulled the tunic over his head quickly then grabbed his dirk from the bedside table. He drew a straight swift line across the palm. A thin red line of blood rose up immediately. Before Sean could blink, William had grabbed his right hand and turned it palm up.

"Should I cut your palm so you can see you are no lower born than I?"

Neither had noticed the door opening, or Laurel standing with the kettle in her hand. "Sean, I think it best you not let him cut you."

Sean jumped, yanking his hand away from Will, grazing his palm against the dirk in the process. "Damn! Wench, will you please stop sneaking up on me!" He sucked small red pearl of blood forming on his palm.

"It's red then? Your blood?" She winked as she set the kettle down on the hearth. "I see you're done but Elinor told me to bring the kettle so I've brung the kettle—"

"How long were you listening?" William asked as he hurriedly pulled up his trews.

"Long enough. Sean, you really are bleeding, let me see." She took his hand before he could protest, then winced suddenly. "What have you done to your wrist? It's all marked."

"What?" William said, moving Laurel aside, forgetting about his own bleeding palm for the moment. He looked at the wrist she had grabbed and sure enough, an ever blackening mark was beginning to show. "I didn't grab you that hard, did I?"

Sean's face went suddenly pale as he watched the mark grow. "Uh... no, Will, you didn't... Laurel, did you say Annlise was settled?"

"Yes, in the chamber aside Lady Bryndah." She pushed his sleeve up carefully exposing the entirety of his wounded arm, revealing a ghastly purple scar and traces of a greenish paste. She shot a look to William, one brow raised as if to confirm her suspicion.

William recognized the signs as well and took a step back, allowing Sean his privacy.

Sean pulled the sleeve down and gingerly dabbed a cloth onto his palm. The cut was slight and had already stopped bleeding. "I am going to make sure she... is well."

"She's fine, Sean. Let me set your wrist—"

William pulled her back "West corridor, Sean. Use the back stairs."

"But your wrist—"

Ignoring Laurel, Sean gave William a nod and hurried out of the room.

Laurel glared up at William. "What in the name of all things sacred was the meaning of that? That arm is *broken!*"

"I have eyes, Laurel, I saw it. But I swear to you, it was not broken when you walked in the room."

"What? Will, are you daft? And what was all that cutting of palms? You've both gone mad since you brung that woman—" Her eyes went wide suddenly. "Oh, no. She . . ."

"Oh, yes. Annlise healed that arm, I would wager my life on it. The traces of boneset and yarrow were still on his skin." William pulled his boots on quickly.

"She knows the Ways?"

"She's born to them, Laurel. She could probably teach Elinor a lesson or two." He raked his hair quickly with his hand and began pacing the floor. "He knew! All this time he knew and he never told me!"

"Knew?"

"That she does magic!"

Laurel took up pacing along side, matching William's steps. "There is no reason to panic."

"No?"

"No, Sean would not call her out."

"I am not worried about her! I'm worried for him! Do you know who her suitor is?"

Laurel stopped in her tracks and gasped. "The hunter."

"Aye. The hunter."

"Seems to me the danger is more for her then, if she is truly practicing the Ways. And not very good at them if you ask me," she muttered like an afterthought.

"Why do you say that?"

"Well if she healed his arm, then it should have stayed healed, shouldn't it? I know it is a difficult task and takes a lot of concentration to heal a bone but once healed, it should stay healed."

William nodded his agreement, remembering a time when Elinor had treated his ankle after he'd fallen from his horse a few years earlier. She had wrapped it in the same green paste he'd seen on Sean's wrist and helped him to sleep, singing a chant he could barely recall. He thought hard on the incident—how long had it taken him to heal, did he have any relapses? Did Elinor do anything else after the ritual? The answer seemed to come to them both at the same moment.

"Elinor stayed very close to me for a few days after I hurt my ankle."

"Aye, except for the day you escaped her eye and went out to the barn."

"And the bruising came back... that's why Annlise was adamant about coming into the castle— to be close to him."

"Oh aye, adamant she were too, nearly as bossy as her mistress about it." Laurel scowled. "What does Sean want with such a shrew as that."

"She is not a shrew," William said, taken aback.

"She is, too." she argued under her breath. "She's not good for him, Will. I feel it in my bones. She is not good for him. She's bewitched him, that's what she's done!"

"Laurel!"

"She has, that's why he's gone all daft about her!"

William took her by the shoulders and looked her in the eye. "Laurel May McCary! You of all people should know that is not how the Ways work! There are no charms that can change a man's mind or heart."

Laurel glared back. "Oh, aren't there? We are novices, you and I. She, apparently, is not. And how many times has Elinor told us not to dabble with charms that influence free will?"

William sighed and turned away. "Miss Laurel, I think your brown eyes are suddenly green as mine, that's what I think."

"What? You think I'm just jealous?"

William grinned.

"I am not jealous, William Fylbrigge. I'm only... worried, same as you. She is a danger to him, you cannae deny that."

William's grin faded. "No, I cannae. She is not as careful as she should be and that is what worries me the most. Come on, let's go get in the way and save the sot from himself."

"I thought you'd never ask."

Sean slipped through the door that the staff used for quick access to the circular stairway leading to the guest suites. He pressed his arm to his chest, trying to will down a rush of nausea that was rising from the pain in his wrist. Each step seemed to bring a new degree of pain. He stopped on the last landing, pressing his face against the cold stone wall, waiting for the wave to pass. *What in God's name is this?*

Five steps led to the door and directly across would be Annlise's room. He reached for the handle, then stopped, hearing women's voices on the other side.

"It be a lie, m' lady! I am well and fine, you can see for yeself." Annlise was saying. Sean could tell she was struggling to keep her voice calm. He knew that tone.

"But, how did you get away from the rogues?" It was Mehlyndia. "Was there a struggle? Did he run them through?"

"Let the child rest, Mehlyndia," a third voice cooed. "It is obvious she is delirious from the ordeal. She can tell us all about it after a while. Now come, dear, into your chamber and some fresh clothes."

"M' lady, please!" Annlise cried.

Bryndah? He risked a peek through the small grated opening on the door. Bryndah had a wicked grasp on Annlise's arm, pushing her toward her chamber door while presenting a concerned frown to Mehlyndia.

"Miss, please, I should like to tell you now! There were no—"

"You need your rest!" Bryndah opened the door and pushed Annlise through, closing it quickly behind her and leaving Mehlyndia standing in the corridor alone.

He pushed the door open quietly and stepped up behind her. "M' lady?"

She spun on her heel. "Sean! I did not hear you... you're hurt?"

He glanced to his hand, then shook his head. He summoned up as much of a smile as he could. "Just a twist. Nothing serious. Is she all right? The lady?"

Mehlyndia worried her handkerchief between her hands. "No. I fear the unthinkable may have happened to her and she is so distraught, she will not speak of it. 'Tis obvious she is not in her own mind."

"Unthinkable?"

Mehlyndia turned scarlet and turned away. "Bryndah told me. She... she saw the signs on her. Her skirt – oh, but 'tis not something of which I should be speaking. Bryndah shall take good care to see she gets the rest she requires and is back to sleep."

"Back? She's been sleeping then?"

"Oh yes, as soon as she arrived Bryndah made sure she went straight away. The poor thing was raving! Do you know, she actually believes that she was not abducted?" She shook her head, looking toward the door. It had become quiet on the other side. "Bryndah must have helped her sleep again. She's very good with medicinal powders." She looked closely at Sean's hand. "That does not look at all well, Sean. Perhaps I could ask

Bryndah to look at it."

"No! That is... I was on my way to find—"

"Of course," Mehlyndia said, with a sympathetic smile. "You would prefer your mum, yes, I quite understand. Agnes is just finishing in my room, if you hurry you can catch her."

Sean did his best to bow. "Thank you, my lady."

"Poor man, was it terrible?"

"My lady?"

"The battle with the rogue." She leaned close to him, looking about, and whispered. "I know your secret. I understand you wish to remain modest."

"Secret?" Sean blurted.

"That you rescued her, you and William." She beamed a smile. "In her raving, that much was clear."

"Oh, well, you see—"

"I shall be glad to tell Father. He should give you a medal!"

"No, no thank you, my lady. I've already spoken to Lord Edward. He is aware of the truth."

She sighed wistfully. "So modest."

"Sean? Is that you, son?"

"Agnes, come quickly, he's hurt his arm." Mehlyndia hurried to meet Agnes.

"'Tis naught—"

"I'll be the judge of that," Agnes scolded, gingerly taking his wrist in her hand. "Broken."

"Oh dear!" Mehlyndia gasped.

"My lady, 'tis well. Mum, it is only a twist really." Sean protested. He hated to be babied. "It doesn't even— ah!"

"Come on, down to the kitchen. My lady, your room is quite fresh now." She gave a polite curtsey.

"Thank you. Go on, mend that well for him."

"Oh, I shall." She gave Sean a stern look. "I shall be quite sure to fix anything he's put afoul."

Sean gave another listen, and look toward the door. *I can't go in as long as Bryndah's in there.* The pain in his wrist was becoming unbearable and he knew from years of experience that he could not hide his pain from his mother for long. Reluctantly, he followed her down to the kitchen, working out how he would explain how his wrist had come to be broken, while doing nothing more than watching William bathe.

William and Laurel emerged from the stairwell in time to catch a glimpse of Sean turning the far corner behind his mother. Annlise's door was still closed, though they could hear voices.

"That's Bryndah," William whispered.

"Aye, and Lady Mehlyndia." Laurel agreed. "Can you hear what they're saying?"

William got as close to the door as he dared, and strained to hear. "They're arguing, I think."

"Let me see?" Laurel crouched down by the keyhole, pressing her eye to the door. She let out a quick gasp, drawing her hand to her mouth.

"What? What is it?"

She stood quickly, motioning for him to follow her away from the door. "They're coming out!"

They raced to the far end of the corridor. William gave a quick glance over his shoulder and turned just in time to prevent a collision with Edward. "Father! Hello!"

"What's all this? William, I've been waiting for you. I was getting concerned."

"Well, here I am," he said, bowing.

"So I see." He looked over William's shoulder toward the corridor he had just run from. "Is something wrong?"

"Wrong? No, not at all."

Edward raised a brow, scrutinizing William head to foot. William looked down self consciously, suddenly uncertain if there was something about him that would get him into trouble. His clothes were fresh, his boots brushed. "What happened to your eye?"

William put his hand to his cheek, suddenly remembering the blow he'd taken from the hilt of Adrian's sword. My fault for not even checking the mirror. He could feel the sting of the bruise and the swelling on his cheek. When he pulled his hand away, he saw that the cut on his palm had started bleeding again.

"I, uh... fell off my horse. In the woods... "

Edward took hold of William's chin, looking closely at the wound. "Is there anything else damaged? I see your hand is bleeding."

"Oh no, I'm well, thank you. I cut my hand a few moments ago myself. I was careless with my carving knife."

Laurel tapped Edward on the sleeve. "He did, m'lord. I saw him."

"Well then, since you have such an indisputable corroboration in Laurel... "

She smiled, offering a little curtsey.

"Laurel, would you please excuse us. William – my suite. Now."

William gave Laurel a look that said 'help' then followed Edward to his suite.

＊ ＊ ＊

"Father, I know you must be angry—"

"Have a seat."

"Aye, sir." William took his customary seat near the window, adjacent to Edward's writing table.

Edward had his back to him, pouring some wine from the decanter he kept on a stand near the door. He seemed to be moving deliberately slowly, inspecting the decanter against the light and taking a thoughtful sip before filling the goblet. After what felt like a long while, he turned and, carrying two glasses, joined William. He placed one on the table in front of him. That was when William noticed the familiar object on the table— his money pouch.

Edward picked it up and handed it to William. "I believe this is yours."

William nodded, taking it from him and tucking it into his tunic.

"Do you know how it came to be here?"

William shook his head, silently.

Edward sat back in his chair across from William and tented his fingers on his chest— the position he always took when choosing his words carefully. William waited, knowing from experience it was not wise to guess what Edward was going to say. After what felt like an hour, Edward took a sip of his wine and leaned forward.

"I assume you have seen the posters."

"Aye, sir."

"They do not paint a flattering picture of the culprit they describe."

"No, sir."

He opened the scroll that was on the table and handed it to William. "This paints an even bleaker portrait."

William read, his face flushing with anger as he got to the bottom of the scroll. "Rubbish!" He rolled the parchment and slid it back across the table. "Father, we did not abduct anyone."

Edward grinned and sat back. "Peace, son, I know. Sean has told me his version and I am content to believe him. Annlise came of her own free will. There is no crime in that. I just thought you should see what the talk of the town may be about when you are walking about in the coming days."

William relaxed, sitting back. "The gossips, I'm sure, will have a festival with this. There is little doubt that I am the one described there."

"William, I realize I have been fairly liberal with you, allowing an abundant amount of freedom for you to go about as you please, associate with whom you wish. And quite frankly, I believe I've done right by you. You've flourished enormously in the past four years. Your talents are many, your studies most impressive. You are a most remarkable young man, all around." He stood, walking toward the window to look out.

William was pleased with the praise but the growing furrow on Edward's brow told him there was another side to this coin.

"I am grateful for everything you've done for me... sir."

Edward turned to look then, brow softening. "Relax. I am not about to cut you out. I am, however, concerned of what damage to your reputation may come from this."

"I was not aware that I had a reputation to guard, just yet."

Edward chuckled. "Lad, from the moment you arrived in Stonehaven, you have had a reputation. Favorable, I'm glad to say, and I should like it to stay that way. That is why I need to know how your money pouch came into the possession of the hunter who came to visit me."

William looked up, trying to remember how he had become parted with it in the first place. He glanced to the wine goblet on the table, then recalled. "I don't know how he got it. I gave it to the inn keeper in Aberdoir."

Edward leaned on the table, hovering over William. "There is gold in there, William. A fortune to an inn keeper. Tell me what was so important that you would give him your entire pouch?"

"I felt responsible for the damage to his establishment after the, um... fight," William said quietly. He braced for Edward's anger.

"It was not a bribe?"

"Bribe?" William looked up confused.

"To buy his silence for what was transpiring?"

"No! Father, I swear," he said, placing his fist on his chest. "When Sean ran through with Annlise, there was some damage done to some chairs and dishes. I felt it appropriate to compensate... wait, you said the hunter had it?" William growled under his breath, sitting back in his chair. His fear of Edward's retribution was now pushed aside in favor of his anger toward Adrian. "That bastard had no right to take that! It was meant for damages."

Edward relaxed and returned to his chair. "Thank you. I believe you."

"Thank you." William scowled, thinking of the poor innkeeper. Lord knows what Adrian had done to him to get that pouch. "Is the man well?"

"Which man?"

"The inn keeper. Father, it is only right that he is compensated—"

"Peace, son. I shall see that his establishment is put to right." He clapped his hands, rubbing the palms, a gesture William also recognized meaning the matter was now closed. "Now then, on to more pleasant matters."

"Sean told me you want to hold a tournament."

"Ah, good, then you know. I believe it will be just the thing to sway the gossip vine away from this unseemly business to more festive matters. Don't you?"

William shook his head, unable to stifle a chuckle. "Father, I never realized you were so worried about the town gossip."

Edward grew serious. "Of course I am. They are my people. I am responsible for their well being, their lives, their establishments. If they are discontent, I am discontent. And though that may sound altruistic, I assure you it is completely selfish."

"Selfish? I think it is what puts you above many of your colleagues."

Edward smiled, accepting the compliment. "I appreciate you saying that but selfish, it is. I take concern so that I know what I am up against. I cannot go blithely through life ignoring the ill winds that pass through here. I must keep them content so they do not turn on me."

"Stonehaven would never turn on you, Father. They are good people—"

"They would turn in a heartbeat if they felt their interests were served better by some other duke. It is politics, William, you will learn this. Reputation is paramount. Which is why I am adamant that yours be clean and well respected. So think on this, how do you wish to be seen by the people?"

William thought for a moment. The people in Aberdoir lived in fear of the hard hand that ruled there. There were no festivals, no players coming through, no Christmas balls or harvest fairs, as was the custom in Stonehaven. He had given very little thought to his own reputation. "I wish to be liked, of course. But, I should like to be a good man."

Edward beamed. "You are on your way, lad. We shall start with the inn keeper in Aberdoir. It seems to me the damage you feel responsible for was not of your making. But still, it is quite telling that you are so worried about it. You have a good heart, son, and that is what I should like to be known most about you. I should like you to be able to step away from the specter of your brother's reputation."

"I should like that, as well. I am quite weary of people wincing upon hearing I am a Fylbrigge." He stood suddenly, remembering how Martha and Caleb had recoiled from him. "Father, there is someone else I mean to help."

"Aye?"

"A weaver. I met him while traveling. He and his wife live in a small cottage not far off the Edin Road. They offered me a moment of respite. I was without my money pouch and could not repay their kindness." He considered for a moment how much to tell Edward about Caleb and his condition, since it was Bryndah who had caused the man so much pain.

"What is it, son?"

"He had an unfortunate circumstance and was arrested by the hunters."

Edward sat back, listening. "Go on."

"He was accused and tortured, Father. Before there was even a trial, he was tortured. Badly." He felt a lump growing in his throat remembering the man. "He is young, only in his twenties, yet he is frail and withered as an old man. That is how it left him, Father."

"It is unfortunate that anyone should be punished, but a crime is a crime—"

"He was innocent!"

"But you said he was tortured. Innocents are not tortured, William. Not before a trial."

"He was, Father. It is because confessions are less costly than trials! He did not confess, so he was sent to trial." William leaned in as Edward had over him. "The magistrate found him innocent, Father, and he was set free. Free to live crippled and lamed for a crime he did not commit." He stood and turned toward the window. Across the town the tower of the gaol loomed over the streets, casting an ugly shadow over the houses. "Are you as aware of what goes on in the gaol as you are with the town, Father?"

"Of course I am. It is part of my tenant, after all." Edward stood and joined William at the window. "I assure you no one leaves Stonehaven gaol in the condition you describe. Only the guilty are punished."

William looked at him, incredulous. "You don't believe me?"

"I believe you are an idealist and there is no crime in that, son. But, I assume, you have heard only one side to his story."

"No, Father, I—"

"I find it commendable and exactly what I would expect from you, to care for the poor and the lamed." He gave William a pat on the back and pulled the window closed, just as the sun was setting behind the tower. "You say he is a weaver?"

"Yes."

"Elinor has been after me for some time to update the draperies in the guest suite. I shall give her leave to arrange for your friend—"

"Caleb."

"Caleb, to provide them. See to it that he has the funds and provisions necessary."

William smiled. "Thank you, Father."

"If I am pleased, then he shall have future work to do for me."

"Do you believe me, then, of his innocence?"

"Son, if he is free, then it is in the past and inconsequential. I am a man who looks forward, not back." He led William toward the door. "And, at the moment, I am going to look forward to a nap."

William offered no argument, relieved that the meeting had come to an end. "Sleep well." He turned before leaving. "Thank you."

It was not the outcome he had hoped for Caleb, though he had to admit that steady work and compensation would please Martha far more than charity. William was content in knowing that he had kept his word to her and help was on the way. But a stone was growing in the pit of his stomach at Edward's refusal to accept that Caleb had been tortured without cause. *Well then, it shall be my mission to make him see.*

"I fell from my horse. Simple, careless accident."

Agnes looked up from under her caul, her lips pursed in disbelief as she bound strips of hot linen around Sean's damaged wrist. "And I'm to believe you've been walking about this way for three days and no one since you been back has thought to mention that you may be needin some help?"

"I did not want to trouble them. It really has not hurt— OWW!"

He flushed, trying not to look his mother in the eye. He felt foolish, sitting on the stool and being mended by his mother. Like the many times when he was a child, he ran schemes through his head to try to explain away the injury so she would not find out what he had been up to. He tried to remember if he had ever been successful in convincing her. *Honest, Mum, I wasn't jumping from the loft, the wind blew me off... No, Mum, I wasn't playing too close to the wagon, the wheel broke free and ran over my foot all on its own...*

She always knew.

"Stop your fussing and sit still. Honestly, what were you thinking, lad? Knocking about for days like this, you'll be lucky if you dinnae end up lame. Never seen the like—"

She prattled on, all the while expertly wrapping and dressing the arm. Sean surrendered any hope of argument and submitted to her ministrations without protest. He was half amused at the notion that given all the training he'd had in matters of survival— should he be captured in battle— of how to remain true to his liege even under the most diabolical of tortures. If he were ever to be captured by his mother, the secrets of the kingdom would be lost at once.

At last she finished and stepped away, tossing a few remaining shreds of linen into the bin. "There, how's that feel now?"

He hated to admit that it was a relief to have it bound. "Have you ever considered becoming an inquisitor? I think you'd be right good at it." He saw no smile on her face. "It was a jest,

Mum. It's feels much better. Thank you."

"You keep that bound with the poultice on it for a few days and it should be fine. Lucky it were clean and not in the wee bones or I would have sent for the surgeon." She turned away quickly, busying herself by sweeping bits of linen. Her anger had given way to maternal worry. "I still may if it doesn't look better in a week."

"The surgeon is expensive, Mum, and he won't be necessary."

Sean flexed his fingers to demonstrate. She acknowledged it with a nod, offering no further suggestion of the surgeon, much to Sean's pleasure. The last time a surgeon was called, it was to relieve Arthur of the terrible swelling that came about just before he died. Sean remembered how the bloodletting only hastened his father's demise. He had little use for surgeons after that, far more preferring the administrations of his mother or Elinor.

"Well, it will mend then but mind you tell me if you want me to summon him."

"Mum, if I never see a surgeon for the rest of my life it shall be too often!" He said it more sharply than he intended, not realizing until then how strongly he felt on the matter. Once he started, he was bound to finish his thought. "He did nothing for Papa but make his dying more difficult than it otherwise would have been. It put you in debt for nearly two years and for what? He's still gone! Promise me you will never, ever, call a surgeon on my behalf."

Agnes stood shaking her head. "And what if he could save your life? Would you have me let you die?"

"Aye, for all the good a surgeon would do. After all, the cost of a cairn on the hillside would be a good lot less."

Sean was instantly ashamed that he'd gone too far.

"Stop it!" Her voice caught "Do you think I dinnae think about such a cairn every time you go off with Galan, or somewhere Edward may send you? D' ye not think I've worried about it since the day Edward pinned tha' badge t' ye brat an give ye tha' rank? I see it in m' sleep, Seany. Every time I close m' eyes, I see you ridin' off wi' ye sword swingin' and the arrows flyin'— and when you go away f'r three days and come home with... with... with warrants and placards lookin' f'r you... " She buried her face in her hands and turned away.

Sean felt his heart sink to his knees. It was the first time since Arthur's death that he'd seen his mother cry. That she was crying for him made him feel lower than dirt. "So you've seen the posters?"

She nodded, blowing her nose into her handkerchief. "Will assures me they all be lies and naught will come of it. You're not bound for getting arrested. Aye?"

He put his good arm around her and pulled her close to himself, speaking quietly. "Nae, mum. 'Tis well. Edward is a very smart man. He's nae believin' the lies that be on the posters. I've already been up to see him, and I told him the truth about it all and he believes me." He gave her a squeeze.

Agnes caught her breath, then looked up to him, a new wrinkle coming to her brow. "You've been to see him?"

"Aye."

"And he never asked about your wrist?"

Sean had no answer other than a noncommittal shrug of his shoulder. How could he explain to her that when he'd spoken to Edward, his wrist had been whole and well, that the break he'd suffered three days earlier had already been healed. How could he even explain to himself? And why wasn't it still healed? He glanced down to his palm and the faint trace of blood left from the scrape of William's dirk. The break had returned almost at the same instant this cut had happened. He wondered if it had somehow broken the magic— if that's what it truly was— that had healed him.

His thoughts went to Annlise, now presumably sleeping in her chamber under Bryndah's watchful eye, and to the stain on her skirt that had worried Mehlyndia so. His stomach sank. There *will be more than my wrist to answer for.*

Annlise opened her eyes slowly. The room had gone dark and only the faintest glow shown through the window. She sat up, dismayed to realize she'd slept the day away. Looking about, the room was unfamiliar but quite grand. The bed dressings were rich and soft, the pillows overstuffed with down. A flash of panic seized her. *Is this the master's bed? Oh Sweet Brighid, what am I doing here?* She looked quickly to her side, praying she was alone in the bed. She exhaled in relief, finding no sleeping stranger beside her.

Her head swirled as she fumbled about the side table, searching for a flint and candle.

"Here, let me."

She gasped as the candle was lit and the form of a woman came into view. She looked familiar, though Annlise was not certain who she could be. She lit another candle, then the oil lamp. The glow from the flame cast a warm circle of orange on her face. She smiled sweetly, taking a seat near the bed.

"Are you feeling better?" she asked, reaching for a pitcher and pouring some water to into a goblet, then offering it to

Annlise.

Annlise accepted the goblet automatically, and took a sip. "I... have a thorn of a headache. Miss— Mehlyndia? I'm sorry, miss, I dinna recognize ye; my head seems terrible muddled." She took a sip from the goblet, then stopped. "What be in here? 'Tis bitter."

"A powder."

Annlise sniffed at the goblet, trying to discern the ingredients. "What sort of powder, miss?"

Mehlyndia tugged nervously at her bodice. Even in the candle light, Annlise could see a blush rise on her face. "Lady Bryndah prepared it for you. She is ever so worried for you."

"Bryndah?"

Annlise gasped, placing the cup down quickly. She knew only too well of Bryndah's skills with powders and potions. She mixed them often for Lord Thomas; sleeping potions being her specialty. Thomas was prone to fits of insomnia and Bryndah's mixes were quite effective. But she was also devious and would slip the powder into his evening cordial when she wished him to sleep especially soundly. But sleeping powder was not the only mixture Annlise had known Bryndah to concoct. She had on at least three occasions prepared a mixture for herself after returning from holiday away from her husband. The pennyroyal she'd prepared was unmistakable in its purpose— it brought about the end of an unintended pregnancy.

"I am feeling better miss, thank you. I dinnae think I need this."

"Please, you must." Mehlyndia insisted, placing the cup back in Annlise's hand. "Bryndah will be quite disappointed that I did not keep my word and care for you as she wished me to."

"But I am fine. I dinnae need it; please, miss." A shard of

pain shot through her head; the sort that comes from waking too quickly. Why would Bryndah insist that her sister push a goblet of pennyroyal on her? She struggled, trying to remember the day's events. Her head fogged and she drew her hand to her forehead.

"There you see? You are still ill."

"No, I am only weary. Please, miss, why cannae I recall – where is this place?"

Mehlyndia stood and fluffed a pillow behind Annlise. "Bryndah was right. She warned me that you would be distraught from the trauma. 'Tis why she mixed the jimsonweed for you to sleep."

"She gi' me – no, no, miss, I cannae be f'getting."

Another wave swept over her. Mehlyndia pushed gently on her shoulders and she lay down without protest. Recent memories were slipping. Annlise closed her eyes, trying to remember why she was at Drumoak, why she wanted desperately to run from the room to find... Sean. *Sweet Mother, where is Sean?* Her eyes started to blink. Fighting was pointless, she knew, but as she drifted, she thought hard on his face, the sound of his voice and the way he felt against her. There was more that was fading, something urgent that she tried to pull from the mist of her mind, that she needed to attend to but could not reach.

She forced open her eyes to see that the morning sun was just beginning to show through the window. Mehlyndia had gone and in her place was her sister Bryndah, watching her. Behind her, barely visible in the shadows, stood Lord Thomas and his hooded companion— dressed head to foot in black, save for the silver crest upon his chest.

Part III

1604

Chapter 16

1 November 1604

SEAN SPENT A fitful night, unable to relax and clear the clutter of the past few weeks. Each time he closed his eyes, his mind would fill with images of Annlise. A collage of changing scenes played over and over as he tried to make sense of it all. She had come with them freely, of that he was absolutely certain— even if her first reaction was to hurl crockery at him. When they had come together in the abandoned barn— against his better instinct— he'd surrendered to his passions but only *after* she'd encouraged him and consented. *You cannae take what be freely given.*

In the half light of early dawn, he gave in to his insomnia, stepping quietly from his cot so not to wake his little brother. Duncan, nearly four now, had taken to crawling in to sleep with Sean, especially now that the November winds had stripped the trees of the leaves, making them cast long finger-like shadows on moonlit walls.

He dressed silently, without lighting a candle. The moon was nearly full and still bright even though the rose colored clouds were beginning to show in the eastern sky. *I wonder if she sees the same clouds.* He caught himself, angry that she had slipped tenderly into his thoughts yet again. *'Tis she you should be angry with, you bloody sot. Risk life and limb and what have you to show for it?* He flexed his fingers. "Still bloody lame."

"Hmm?" Duncan rubbed his eyes. "Seany? It still dark."

"Shh, lad." Sean sat on the edge of the bed, drawing the blanket up to Duncan's chin. "Go back to sleep, aye? The wind is gone and there are no more trees scratchin' at the shutters."

The lad yawned, stretching his little face into a comical mask. "You chase them 'way?"

"Aye, every one of them."

"No more mons'ers?"

"Not a single monster. Sean chased them all the way back to the faeries. Now, back to sleep, lad." He brushed his fingers gently across Duncan's brow and eye lids until the lad closed his eyes. "And when you wake, it will be the day you've been waiting for."

"To'nament day," Duncan said dreamily. "Mum says will be tumblers an' poppets."

"Oh, aye. You like poppets?"

"Mmhmm." Duncan yawned again, then cuddled under the blanket and closed his eyes.

Sean waited a moment, listening to the soft breathing to be sure the tot had gone back to sleep, before he crossed the room to his chest of drawers. He quietly pulled open the top drawer, fumbling around until his hand closed around the small leather bundle he had tucked away there. He untied the leather thong that kept it closed and opened the bundle on the top of the dresser. The entirety of his savings spilled out— four silver shillings and a thistle crown— just enough to cover the entry fee for the tournament and perhaps buy a wooden poppet for Duncan. If he won any of the contests, he would more than earn this much back and he would put it back in the drawer. Perhaps he would even win enough to pay off the last of what his mother owed to the surgeon.

He fished his hand back into the drawer until he found another small pouch, one he rarely took from its hiding place. He opened it carefully, pouring the contents into his palm. The trinket was small, probably not worth much, but silver was silver. He held the pendant by the delicate chain, holding it up to the light of the rising sun just beginning to stream through his window. It had been a gift to him upon his Christening. Though his mother was always vague about its origins, she had impressed upon him that he should keep it safe and one day, perhaps he would present it to someone special. He watched it spin on the end of the chain, the delicately woven strands of knotted silver sparkling in the light, before carefully placing it back into the little pouch. *No, Duncan, I'm sorry, but this will not be traded for a poppet today.*

The thought of the poppet brought back another invading memory of Annlise— arguing with the toy vendor in Aberdoir who had unwittingly aided in her escape from Fylbrigge Manor. *I should have given up right there. It would have saved me all this grief.*

The sun peeked over the trees in the valley, casting its long shadows across the landscape. Sean took note— and said a brief prayer of thanks— that there was no red in the early morning sky and the few clouds that veiled the sky were wispy horsetails. The autumn had been kind this year, belying the threat of snow that always loomed in November skies.

He swallowed down some of the bread he'd taken from Agnes' pantry and headed out of the cottage to the barn. His left wrist was still a problem and, as if to mock the hope the glorious sky brought him, the simple act of brushing away bread crumbs from his tunic sent a sudden spasm all the way to his shoulder. He growled, more of anger than pain, and stopped to tighten the ties on the leather vambrace that was now a fixture on his left wrist. He flexed his fingers and to his relief the pain was greatly subdued by the tight laces on the brace.

"You're up early."

Sean whirled, startled to find Laurel standing behind him. "Laurel! Gads, lass. Where did you come from?"

"I was born here. I thought you knew that." She plucked a basket from the wall, chuckling. "Eggs," she explained.

"Are the chickens even awake?" he asked, unable to resist a chuckle himself.

"No. But then, that just makes it easier." She paused suddenly, feeling into the pocket of her apron. "Oh bother."

"What is it?"

"Lucy."

"Lucy?"

"Aye, I promised Duncan I would bring her for him and I forgot her back in m' room. She's a little old now, as far as mice go, but he's right gentle with her. She doesn't try to run up his sleeves or naught," she prattled on about the little mouse.

As usual, Sean barely kept up with her rapid narrative that seemed to change direction every third sentence or so. He was content to follow her about, glad for her company. He hadn't realized until then how little of Laurel he'd seen in the past month.

"So after we turn the rooms, I'll have enough time to change. But I still don't know. Do you think blue is too grand?" She stopped, hands on hips. "Sean Wilbrun, are you even listening?"

"Hmm? Oh, aye. Of course."

"So, what do you think? Is it too grand?"

He blushed, covering a smile.

"I knew it." she sighed and fell quiet, the trace of a rare frown crossing her face.

"Laurel, I'm sorry. I have had other things on my mind. Now, what about blue is too grand?"

"The gown. Lady Mehlyndia has given me one of the gowns she no longer wears to wear to the tournament. It's blue and so grand. She said I should look like a lady." She looked down at her stained linen apron covering her flaxen kirtle. "I've never worn... and look at my hands, all rough and my nails broken." She sat down on a hay bale and looked away. "Even dressed in spun gold, I would never look like a lady."

Sean sat down next to her, and with his good hand, took hold of hers. "Spun gold would look dull next to your smile."

She looked at him as though he'd slapped her. "Why must you always tease?"

"I was nae teasing. I thought I was paying a compliment." He stood and walked toward the stall where Hawk was housed. "I seem to have a talent for saying the wrong thing to a lass. I was raised to be an honest man. But when I am honest, I am called a tease... or worse."

"Sean, I just didn't expect what you said." She stood next to him, watching Hawk swaying on his feet as he slept. "And I should scratch the eyes out of any woman who would dare call you anything worse than a tease. Do you really think I'll look like a lady?"

He placed his right fist to his heart and bowed. "I do, my lady."

For a moment he feared she would think he was merely playing at their old game of damsel and knight. So he stood, making a point to keep his face serious. He relaxed when she smiled with a faint blush.

"So... who called you something worse than tease?"

Sean simply looked at her, then walked away toward the training ring behind the barn. "I need to exercise before the tournament." He hoped she would understand and ask no further. Laurel had a way of getting him to say far more than he intended but to her credit, he could trust her not to repeat any of it. Annlise was not a subject he cared to share with her though. Annlise was not a subject he wanted to share with anyone.

"Well, it looks like you won't have to exercise alone," she said as they approached the ring.

"Hmm?" Sean looked ahead, then stopped, laughing quietly to see William dressed in leather armor, engaged in a dramatic battle with a sparring dummy.

"Sweet Minerva's wig!" Laurel gasped. "I had no idea he could move so... "

"Gracefully?" Sean finished for her.

She nodded, watching William go through his courses, seemingly mesmerized by the sight. "I knew he had been training with Galan but I never really took notice. He makes the sword dance as if it were a part of his arm."

Sean watched with her for a moment, allowing himself a bit of pride, knowing Galan could not take all the credit for William's prowess with a sword. "If I told you a wee secret, would you think me boasting?"

Her face brightened. "No! Tell me. I can keep secrets."

"I know, that's why I'll tell you. Galan did nae teach him that particular move."

Her eyes went wide. "You?"

"If you had come to watch more often, you would have seen." He chuckled. "It's not *all* slashing and maiming."

Just then William took a leap, whirling in mid air, bringing the heel of his boot against the head of the dummy and sending it rolling from the ring. In the same elegant movement, the sword arced full circle in what would surely be a fatal blow to an enemy in battle.

"Well, maybe some of it is slashing and maiming."

Laurel cheered when William stopped for a moment. He looked up and smiled, bowing regally from the waist.

"Well done, lad!" Sean called as he jogged over to join William in the middle of the ring.

"Are you daft? I nearly broke my leg." William looked at the now headless dummy and grinned. "But it looks like our friend here fared a tad worse, aye?"

Sean scooped up the head— a burlap sack stuffed with sod and straw— and handed it to William. "For your mantel."

William laughed, setting it back on the body. "Much better."

Laurel stepped up close to the dummy, looking up at the head. It had been set to represent a man of about six feet and it towered over Laurel, making her seem as small as a child. "He's so big! Who's head was it that you saw, Will?"

"What do you mean?"

"I saw how you attacked it. I could never attack a burlap sack that savagely without laughing, unless I was imagining it to be someone I dinnae like."

"I was thinking the same thing, Will." Sean admitted, comparing the height of the dummy to William. "The size is right. Laurel, I think our Will has just decapitated his brother."

She gasped in mock shock. "How plead you to such a charge, sir?"

"Absolutely guilty." William grinned, sheathing his sword. "I'd say it is a perfect likeness, wouldn't you?"

She wrinkled her nose and closed one eye. "I think you're daft. It is far better looking than he is."

"'Tis my turn. Stand back you two," Sean said.

He drew his sword. William and Laurel stood aside, watching from a hay bale near the side of the ring.

"Who are you going to slash and maim?" Laurel called.

"For me to know," Sean answered, taking a defensive stance. "Watch and learn."

He held the sword firmly with his right hand, balancing with the left. He stared at the dummy, having no trouble deciding who's face he would conjure in his mind to strike at. He could even see the golden eyes and the black cape fluttering in the wind.

"You have taken what is mine, dog!"

Sean snarled, remembering the threats in the abandoned barn and the defiant grin on the hunter's face as he was escorting Annlise to the coach that took her back to Aberdoir. The memory made the illusion clear and he executed his leaping attack, bringing his heel hard against the dummy's head, sending it farther than William had. The sword came down with a flash, severing the dummy's arm at the shoulder and almost before it hit the ground, he had whirled and thrust the point into the stomach and up, effectively disemboweling the thing.

He removed the sword and stepped back.

William and Laurel sat staring. Laurel's eyes were wide, her hand drawn up to her mouth. There was nothing playful in her expression. She stood and slowly walked toward the fallen head. "This is not a game for you, is it?"

Sean shook his head.

William picked up the head and carried it back to the dummy. "No hunter is worth losing your soul over, Sean. Remember that when the contests begin."

Laurel gasped. "That hunter is going to be here?"

"Most likely." Sean admitted. "Of course, he won't oblige me by standing still like our friend here. It shall be harder to cut him in half."

"Sean— don't," William cautioned, gesturing toward Laurel. Her eyes were still wide and brimming with tears. Sean had never seen such a look on her.

"He's going to kill you," she said, sobbing.

"Not today, lass. 'Tis only games," Sean said, forcing a smile. He relaxed his stance and let the anger drain away. There was no sense in frightening Laurel. "We will not even be allowed to use real weapons."

She looked up, hopeful. "True?"

William tapped her on the shoulder, drawing her attention to a cart near the edge of the ring. "See there? Those are the weapons for the mock battle. All wood, lass. We might get a few nasty splinters but we should end the day with all our limbs in place."

"Wood? But you can still crack a skull—"

"Helmets," William said, tapping his head. "And armor head to toe. It is about skill and style today. Not killing."

"What about the jousting? I've watched you, Will. As wonderful as you are with your sword and kicks, you're a disaster with a lance."

William sighed. "Aye, I cannae argue. That is why I am not going to take part in that event."

Sean raised a brow. "This whole tournament is for your advancement. Edward is certainly not expecting you to win every event but he was bloody well clear that he wanted you to participate in them all. How are you not going to take part?"

William grinned. "I'm going to fall in the qualifying round. Simple as that."

"Fall?" Sean nearly shouted. "Deliberately?"

"Aye."

"'Tis a full armored joust!"

"How else am I to bow out gracefully?"

Sean shook his head, dropping an arm around William's shoulder. "M' lord, I must ask. Have you ever fallen from your horse in full armor?"

William thought for a moment. "Well, no, but I suspect it works the same way as without armor; I fall and land on the ground."

"Will, falling while wearing five stones worth of armor is not nearly the same. You're likely to break something."

"I hadn't thought of that," William admitted. "I suppose Edward wouldn't be pleased for me to dent up the brand new suit he's had made for me."

"New armor?" Sean's mind wandered to his own ancient armor, realizing how worn and dingy it would look next to the rest of the guard, and William in particular.

William nodded. "I hate it. It's dreadful and difficult to see out of or even move properly."

"It always is the first time. You will get used to wearing it."

"If I have my way, I shall never don it again after today." A sly grin crept to his face. "Though it did make Thomas growl. It may be worth wearing simply to make him jealous."

Sean laughed then. "So he's seen it?"

"Aye, Edward made a point of ordering it from Thomas' own armourer. Well, actually my father's armourer."

"I saw it too, Sean. It's on a stand in the great hall," Laurel said. "It looks very heavy."

"That's yours? I thought it was Edward's. Very impressive, lad."

William's face flushed. "Very difficult to put on."

Sean laughed. "That's what the squires are there for. Even I shall have help getting into my own."

"You shall both be like real knights today." Laurel sighed. "Not a game any more, is it."

"And you shall be a lady," Sean reminded her gently, wiping a stray tear that lingered on her cheek. "'Twould be my honor to carry your token."

She sniffled. "You're teasing again. Wouldn't you rather carry a token for her?" She gestured toward the road.

Sean turned in time to see the caravans had begun to arrive in town. He recognized the first coach as the one Annlise had ridden away in. His heart both leapt and sank at the thought that she may be in the stands today. He watched the coach make its way down the long approach toward the castle, followed by Thomas' entire entourage of grooms and man servants. Bryndah's ladies followed behind. Sean scanned each face with a mix of both hope and dread but he did not find her. When the train had passed, he turned back to speak to Laurel. He was dismayed to see she had walked away and was nearly back to the castle. He hadn't realized he'd stared so long.

"Laurel! Wait! What about your token?"

She did not turn to look but lifted her skirt and ran into the castle.

"Will?"

"Aye?"

"Do you understand the least bit about women?"

"No."

The day started early for Edward as well. A nagging uneasiness had deprived him of a restful night. The day he had planned, admittedly, was a gamble— bringing the rival dukes with their entourages together under the auspice of a friendly tournament. He had been cagy in his planning, sending invitations to Lothian, Kylkannon, and Aberdoir, each carefully worded so as none would realize the other would be present.

Edward had always enjoyed a stable, if not guarded, relationship with Ogham of Lothian and Woodhall of Kylkannon. Edward held a geographical advantage - controlling key ports in the North and access to the large rivers - that Lothian and Kylkannon relied on for trade purposes. Kylkannon and Lothian held strategic positions in the highlands that provided protection from the south. Each rival depended upon cordial relations— if Kylkannon allowed an invasion from the south, Edward would simply retaliate by enforcing a blockade against them from the north. If Lothian opened a border, it would mean war with Kylkannon, which would result in Edward choosing sides— likely with Kylkannon. Edward had the biggest resource of soldiers and a fleet of ships at his disposal, so neither Lothian or Kylkannon were likely to jump lightly into battle. Edward made certain to always include the rival dukes in his convocations, as a gesture of goodwill and to reinforce his superiority of strength. In return for their loyalty, he provided to their coffers handsomely.

The wild hare in the mix was Aberdoir. Thomas would ally with whomever offered him more power than the other. Aberdoir also had good access to ports and could easily open a way around any of Edward's embargoes from the north. If he courted Woodhall and Ogham too dearly, the three together would indeed be a formidable force against all that Edward possessed.

But Thomas lacked the one thing he needed to be an actual threat— a good reputation. In his early days, while Henry was still alive and in charge of that tenant, Thomas had managed to alienate Woodhall, Lothian, and a few lesser earls by double dealing one against the other in a matter of horse sales. He was young and eager to earn the best prices for the thoroughbreds and thought he was being clever in selling the same horses to two different dukes. Henry had nearly come to ruin over the deal. Thomas had accepted an advance payment for four fine Arabian blacks he promised to deliver to Lothian personally. He had to travel through Kylkannon to get there and saw nothing wrong in selling the same four horses to Woodhall. He had accepted payment in gold and trade of four of Woodhall's nags that were a near identical match— save for their advanced age. He did not count on Ogham recognizing the team as Woodhall's; Ogham had sold the same team only a year before.

Henry placated Ogham by giving him the pick of his stable, as his gift. Ogham chose the four finest that Henry had promised to Edward, who, in turn, had promised to deliver them as a coronation gift to James VI upon his ascension at Elizabeth's death. Edward had finally solved the issue by buying the horses from Ogham at twice the price Henry would have asked and providing Ogham with horses from his own stable.

Thomas was never asked to make deals again. Neither Woodhall nor Ogham had any use for him as an ally. So long as Edward kept the routes open and offered protection, there was no need to rattle their swords against Thomas.

Edward pondered all this as he dressed in the half light of dawn. Thomas' new alliance with the king's hunter troubled him greatly. It was not that Edward objected to the man's occupation but that a little reconnaissance mission— by Ewan and Simon— to both Lothian and Kylkannon had revealed a very troubling fact. Tearlach had dealings with both. Edward reasoned that Thomas' eagerness in courting the hunter's alliance was his way of forging a bridge to the Ogham and Woodhall.

Edward had a delicate balance to keep. He needed to keep a rein on Thomas but at the same time, he needed to offer his son-in-law a lucrative incentive to buy his loyalties. He had toyed with the idea of naming Thomas as his heir, purely for political reasons. Let Thomas know he was in line, groom him, give him a handsome stipend and perhaps he would even prove a valuable asset. Thomas was already aware of the large inheritance that awaited him, only five years away when William turned twenty-one. But he also knew William stood to inherit a good sum of that, though he did not know just how much; Edward had been cagy in keeping that a secret, though he now pondered the wisdom of that decision. Perhaps all he needed to do was reveal to Thomas that his own inheritance was nearly four times that of what William was to receive. Both brothers would be wealthy beyond the imagining of most men.

Adrian Tearlach was not someone with whom Edward chose to associate, but the hunter was also a man whom he did not want for an enemy. The decision he'd made over the lass Sean and William had brought back from Aberdoir had been a difficult one. She had clearly not wanted to marry the man and Edward was always loath to force any woman to marry against her will. But if it meant keeping peace and avoiding the scandal that would surely come to Drumoak should she be allowed to stay, then he would use his authority to enforce the betrothal.

After an early morning meeting with all involved, it became apparent to Edward that Annlise had a spark of her own. Though she was clearly dismayed at the notion of returning to Aberdoir, she showed an undeniable look of relief in knowing that as part of the bargain to send her back, Thomas would drop all warrants he'd issued against the 'rogues'. Sean would face no charge of abetting a runaway and William would not be considered a suspect in the killing of an unknown merchant—who Edward was not even certain truly existed.

Adrian, to his credit, agreed not to accuse her of adultery for what had obviously occurred during her flight from Aberdoir. No names were mentioned nor did Edward want them. The identity of her 'attacker' was never disclosed, though Edward had no doubt who she was protecting. He had made a few bargains that morning, one with Annlise; in return for her continued silence on the man's identity, Edward would offer his protection should anyone retaliate for her flight. Annlise agreed but only after she was assured that Sean would face no threat of dismissal or demotion. Edward agreed.

Thomas reluctantly admitted that he had never actually

seen William kill anyone on the street in Aberdoir. In return for dropping the warrants, Edward agreed not to place any sanctions against Aberdoir. Tearlach agreed not to seek retaliation against any member of Edward's household only after Edward agreed to ensure that Annlise would return to Aberdoir. All went away placated, if not happy.

The worst part of the unholy bargain was the pang of conscience Edward suffered when he thought of Sean, who had been kept ignorant of all the dealings. It was obvious the lad cared greatly for the lady, but he was young and there were many maids in and about Stonehaven to choose. His heart would mend in time.

The sun was well over the horizon when Edward had finished dressing and stood on his balcony watching the approaching caravan. Aberdoir arrived first, as he expected. Good. There would be time for him to sit with Thomas privately, to reiterate the terms of his bargain— in the event Thomas became 'forgetful.'

Laurel hurried into the kitchen, dropping the basket on a work bench quickly as she dashed through the room. "Elinor? Elinor, where are you? I need—"

She pushed the door that led to the pantry and nearly collided with Elinor as she was coming through. "Child! What is all the bother? Did you get the eggs?"

"Hmm? Oh aye, they're on the bench. Elinor, I need something very special. It's important and I dinnae think it be again' the rules. If I make an offering t' the Blessed Lord and Lady, I think it would be allowed just this one time and it will not be for harm—"

Elinor grabbed hold of Laurel's arm with one hand, covering her mouth with the other. "Slow down, child! What are you prattlin' on with now? What offerin' are you talking about?"

Laurel took a long deep breath. "A charm."

Elinor's brow rose. "What sort of charm?"

"Nothing harmful, I swear it on m' mother's grave."

"Your mother isn't dead."

"If she were – please, Elinor."

Elinor looked around the kitchen to make certain they were alone, then ushered Laurel quickly through the pantry to the staircase that led to her chamber. When they arrived, Elinor closed the door quickly behind them.

"Now, tell me *slowly* – what you need the charm for and for who."

Laurel chewed on her lip for a moment, suddenly shy about what she was going to say. "You promise you winnae think me daft?"

"Laurel," Elinor sighed. "I already know you are daft, I dinnae need to think it further." She smiled kindly, leading Laurel to the bench that held her book and herbal elements. "Now tell me. 'Tis best to be honest and I need to know all your motives for wanting a charm before I prepare anything. You know how I feel about dabblin' in such things."

"Aye, Elinor. It is not something to be done lightly or for ill reasons."

"Because—?"

"Because, the Blessed Lord and Lady do not offer their gifts for free or for harm," Laurel said, dutifully reciting the *golden rule* that Elinor had lectured on many times during their studies.

"Good. Now, tell me what you need."

"It's for Will. To help him in the tournament."

Elinor's brow shot up again. "I cannae make a charm to help him win, Laurel. Cheating is definitely against the rules."

"No, no! This is not for cheating. I dinnae give a half a copper whether he wins."

Elinor gave her another skeptical look. "Do you fancy him, child? You know I cannae make that sort of charm for you either."

Laurel felt her face turn hot. *Fancy him? Will?* A quick flash of memories from their adventures together along the sea and lessons learned and studied secretly together. Laurel could not deny that she always enjoyed her times alone with him. She swallowed hard.

"Child," Elinor sighed. "I should have seen this coming. You know there can be nothing between the two of you. He's gentry, lass, and—"

"I know, I know." She waved her hands impatiently. "I am not asking for a love charm!"

"Well, then?"

"He's expected to ride in the joust," she said simply.

"Oh, merciful Mother of all, no wonder you asked." Elinor reached for her book with one hand, flipping open a small wooden chest with the other. "Say no more."

"You've seen him practice too?"

"Aye. He's a disaster. I thought Edward would let him decline that event."

"Sean said the entire tournament was meant for Will's advancement. It's all politics, you know. He's going to be run through like a pig on a spit, all because Edward wants to show him off!"

"I dinnae think it be that dire, lass" Elinor flipped through the pages of her book, running her finger down column after column of minutely written script. "Ah! This may do. You shall have to hand him something of yours. Something personal."

"A token!" Laurel said excited. "He could carry a token from me, aye?"

"That is, if he'll accept it."

"Why wouldn't he?"

Elinor gave her a side glance. "Politics, dear. I'm sure he'll be carrying a token for Lady Mehlyndia." Laurel frowned. "But you can always try. Do you have a ribbon or string or something that can tie?"

Laurel looked about her person, hoping to find inspiration, coming to the drawstring at the collar of her chemise. She untied it and pulled it through, handing it to Elinor. "How about this?"

Elinor's eyes lit up. "Wonderful! In fact, it is perfect. He can use it as the draw in his own shirt. Now, let's get busy, we've not a lot of time."

"Aye, I know. The caravans are already arriving."

"Then we work fast, aye?"

Elinor's hands were a blur, pulling herbs and oils, and all the while muttering her secret prayers under her breath. She lit a small candle under a warming pan and dropped in her elements, crushing them with the pestle.

"Now, dip your string into the mix and repeat the prayer with me. Mean it with all your heart and soul, and when we're finished, you must make your offering. Do you have one?"

Laurel glanced over to the window where the little box that housed her beloved little Lucy rested. "I am going to give Lucy to Duncan. He loves her. I was going to let him look after her for today but I am willing to let him keep her. Do you think that will be enough?"

Elinor smiled, a sparkle forming on her eyelid. "Yes, child. It's truly a sacrifice, and comes from ye heart. The prayer."

They recited together:

In the name of the Lady and the Lord,
I ask your favor fall on he,
Who bears this token blessed by thee,
As thine own love doth bless this charm
Let nothing earthborn cause him harm.

"Well, now, 'tis the will of the Blessed Mother an' Father if they'll keep him in his saddle." Elinor wrapped the string around her hand and tucked it carefully into her pocket. "Before you utter another word to anyone else and before you do another thing, you take Lucy to Duncan."

Laurel nodded. She understood the rule. She could do nothing for herself at all until her offering was complete. She couldn't even ask Elinor if Will would know about the string. She had to trust that the charm would be successful and that Will would be wearing it when he faced off on the first qualifying match of the joust.

She gathered Lucy and held the little mouse in her hand, stroking the velvet fur of her tiny ears. Lucy sat on her haunches, looking up to Laurel with her little inky eyes, waiting for the customary crumb she would always offer. Laurel had a bread crumb and Lucy took it, munching contentedly in Laurel's palm. *Duncan will take good care of you.* She put the mouse back in her box and, with only a nod to Elinor, headed down the dark stairs.

She ran across the kitchen yard to the path that led to the Wilbrun's cottage, barely able to see through the tears forming in her eyes. She had trouble deciding what the tears were for; the loss of her little pet, the comfort she felt knowing William would have a protective charm to wear, or the confusion she felt over Sean's infatuation with that woman from Aberdoir. *Will may be gentry and I understand he could not wear the token, but Sean...*

Stonehaven came to life quickly once the caravans had all entered the town. Edward had declared the day a holiday and the streets were adorned with colorful banners and flags. The shops were closed but merchants had carts with colorful tarps above them lining the street. Ladies dressed in their best gowns and workmen shed their dusty tunics for their best garments.

Edward had burdened Geoffrey McGuiness with the task of organizing musicians and street players to entertain and amuse the children. Tumblers and jugglers, puppet masters and mummers were organized by Geoffrey's near military precision. Each one was instructed on where and when they would perform, and were under strict orders to smile and be cordial. Geoffrey had been given a generous budget to dispense wages as he deemed appropriate, guaranteeing a fine performance would be given by all.

The keeping of the roster for the tournament was assigned to Galan Berra. It was his responsibility to ensure that all participants were qualified and fit enough to compete. In more formal tournaments, only the gentry would be allowed to compete, however Edward wanted to give the opportunity to his guardsmen as well. Any member of the guards who wished to compete need only pay a half-shilling entry fee, demonstrate their fitness, and possess proof of their affiliation with the duke they would represent. This last bit was waved for the Stonehaven guards as Galan knew them all and needed no proof of their affiliation. From the others, a written letter was required. Fortunately, this requirement was included in the invitations and none were turned away for lack of affiliation.

By mid-morning, the roster was full; each household well represented by equal numbers of gentry and guards in each event. Edward was adamant that no sequestering of rank take place, giving everyone equal status on the gaming field. This had ruffled a few feathers – particularly Ogham, who thought it near heresy that he might be matched against a simple sentry in the grand joust. Some had requested that two champions would emerge at the end – one from the gentry, and one from the 'low born', as Woodhall had put it – but Edward insisted on it being a one winner competition, the prize being the same, whether won by a nobleman or a member of the guard.

The prize would be announced at the beginning of the game. Edward had chosen not to compete, claiming an onset of gout he was minding. He would sit in the best seat and watch. He would also choose winners should a tie in points occur.

Inside the castle a bustle of activity was happening in each wing, where the visitors were dressing or freshening. A table laden with pastries and fruits, meats and fine cheese had been laid out and the great hall became a sea of colorful gowns and feathered hats as the guests mulled about eating and chatting.

William, muddy and sweaty from his morning exercise, slipped through the kitchen door and up the back steps to avoid meeting anyone. He mused that if any had seen him, he could easily be mistaken for the pig keeper, given his filthy clothes. He approached his door, just as Elinor was leaving. She turned with a start when she saw him, then laughed.

"'Tis a good thing I have ye bath ready, aye? I was jus' leavin' you to it. Your fresh clothes are laid out f'r you, dear." She led him back into the room to point out the array on the bed.

"You're far too good to me, Elinor," he said, bowing regally.

"I'll leave you in peace then. But hurry, Edward will be wanting you to walk about with him."

"Aye, I will, thank you." He glanced at the bed. "More new clothes?"

"Oh, aye. The shirt be a gift from me and Laurel. I hope you don't mind or think it forward, but this is your first tournament and we wished you to have something of us... to wear you see."

William smiled, holding up the shirt. "I shall consider it a token, my lady."

"Good, now I must hurry. I've got m' own bath and dressin' to do!"

"Tell Laurel thank you." he called, but she had already disappeared through the door.

Left alone, he quickly shed the muddy leggings and tunic he'd worn in the ring. It seemed silly that he should clean up only to get filthy during the competitions. But he had to admit there were few things in life that settled his nerves and helped clear his mind better than a good hot bath. He sank into the water, brooding over what the day may bring. He had no worries where it came to sword play. He was eager in fact to have a chance to prove his skills in front of the lads— Ewan and Simon in particular, who gave no mercy in their taunts of how too much lace and velvet made for bad swordsmen. The joust was another thing. He wished there was some honorable way to get out of that particular event. *I'll be skewered, plain and simple... that's it, Will, you're done in.* He wished he had the luxury of just sitting until his fingers were wrinkled and the water was cold but he knew he had to hurry and only lingered long enough to get clean.

He dried off quickly, then surveyed the garments Elinor had lain out for him. He groaned inwardly at the ornately embroidered doublet and ridiculously colored pantaloons. He wished for the millionth time that he did not have to dress as noblemen— the style was far too English for his taste. He would rather don a kilt and brat like the guardsmen wore in warmer weather, or the comfortable doeskin trews he wore when he was free to knock about as he chose. The one item he was glad of was the simple linen shirt he would wear under the doublet. *Thank you, Elinor and Laurel!* He pulled the shirt over his head, pausing at the odd scent of rosemary emanating off the fabric.

The scent was stronger than a regular laundering would have left it, but not unpleasant, and it gave him a sudden inspiration. He hurried to his dresser and pulled open the drawer, withdrawing a leather bound bundle. *Well now, we'll see if I've learned anything in four years.*

He carefully opened the bundle, freeing the leather bound journal inside— the book he'd been keeping since Elinor first presented it to him upon his arrival at Drumoak. He thumbed through the early pages quickly. There was not much there of use, just a few daily diary entries and an occasional drawing. He paused at one page, smiling to himself at the coarsely drawn map he'd made of the catacombs under the castle; it had been done one day when he, Sean, and Laurel had had a particularly enjoyable adventure in the caves. He turned a few more pages until he found what he was looking for— a charm to bolster his self confidence.

The page the charm was written on was separate from the rest of the book, and for good reason— he had taken it from Elinor's massive tome. The words were a simple prayer for strength and guidance from the Blessed Mother and Father. *It should be recited from the heart while anointing oneself with a few drops of oil of chicory. I could use this to keep myself from being run through what would be the harm?*

A small tremor stirred in his stomach as he pondered the charm. He had the oil, the words, and the desire. He would find an offering. It was within Elinor's adamant rules that no charm ever be used to cause harm. But the worm in his middle grew more persistent and he knew what the cause was – guilt. He'd taken the page from Elinor's book back when he was desperate to overcome his night frights, memories of Aberdoir and the monk who had beaten him. He had never used the charm, knowing he was not strong enough in his talents at the time, but he was quite certain he could make it work now.

And it was the confidence in himself that he could perform the charm successfully that made him return the page to his book and put it all away. *I don't need it yet. Someday, perhaps. Not now.* He would make it through the joust, for better or worse, on his own.

Just before he closed the drawer, there came a knock on his chamber door. Instinctively, he pushed the drawer in quickly and turned the key to lock it before he answered. No one, other than Elinor and Laurel, knew of the existence of his book and he meant to keep it that way. Even if it was Sean— as he assumed was the one knocking— he preferred to keep this one thing to himself. The knock came again, louder this time.

"Patience, Sean, I'm coming."

He pulled open the door but it was not Sean who stood knocking. William was not prepared to see the face that greeted him.

"Hello, Will," Richard Fylbrigge said, quietly. "May I come in?"

William nodded, stunned, stepping aside and gesturing for Richard to enter. Some inner instinct he barely knew was there, told him to keep the door open.

Richard smiled shyly, his eyes cast slightly away from looking into William's. He looked about the room, lingering on a collection of wooden horses that lined the mantel over the fireplace. "These are beautifully done," he said, admiring the detail on one of the models. "Who made these?"

"I did," William answered, watching Richard carefully, being sure to keep the way between himself and the door clear should he decide to run. *What a foolish notion,* he scolded himself.

"You?" Richard smiled, nodding. "I might have known. You were clever with a carving knife as a child. Do you remember the poppets you carved from the apples?"

"What do you want, Richard?" William surprised himself with the coldness of his own voice.

Richard looked up sharply, seemingly as stunned with the tone as William had been. He stepped away from the wooden horses, assuming a more formal stance. "It has been a long time since I've seen you. I simply wished to see how you do."

"I do fine," William answered curtly.

Richard shifted his weight between his feet, ostensibly looking for something to say as an uneasy silence fell between them. William had been so preoccupied with a growing trepidation about the joust— and the probability that he may face Thomas as an opponent— that he'd not considered the likelihood that Richard would be on hand to represent Aberdoir. But of course, it was only natural that his nephew would attend the event. After all, Edward was Richard's grandfather and he had every right in the world to participate.

"I should go," Richard said finally, moving toward the door.

Inexplicably, William stepped between Richard and the door, raising his palm in a signal of truce. "No, please." He forced as cordial a smile as he could manage. "You're right. It has been a long time."

"Nearly five years," Richard said casually, looking again toward the menagerie of wooden horses. He went to pick up one in particular, stopping first to look toward William. "May I?"

William nodded.

Richard took the largest of the models in hand. William was not surprised this was the one that had caught his eye; it was meant to be a representation of a large war horse.

"You know," Richard began tentatively, turning the horse over in his hands. "Father never did break that horse. Lucifer... you remember the one, I'm sure."

"How could I forget," William replied dryly, reaching for the horse. He placed it back on the mantel, positioning it carefully among its smaller siblings. "I remember everything about that horse." He turned to look Richard in the eye. "I remember everything about the day I last saw him... and you."

Richard looked up with an uncomfortable expression that told William that his nephew also remembered the last time they'd seen Lucifer. It was the day they'd stolen away from their lessons in the abbey into the barn and Richard had betrayed his hiding place to Brother Joseph— and his whip. His right hand found its way to his left wrist and he began absently messaging the faded scars that still striped his skin.

"Do you?" Richard asked, his eyes fixed squarely on William's hands.

"Do I?"

"Truly remember that day?"

"Well enough that I would rather not conjure up the memory of it again."

"You blame me, I know. Will, I did not come here to confront—"

"Then why are you here?"

"I told you, it has been a long while and I only wished to see you. To see if Drumoak has been kind to you."

William felt the blood rising to his face. He knew he wasn't being fair. Richard was making an effort to be sociable and cordial. The least he could do was to be polite, but just the sight of the young man brought back every black memory of Aberdoir he carried with him. He tried, as Annlise had suggested, to remember the good times he'd had with Richard. No matter how he tried the memory that burned above the rest, was watching his nephew— his best friend, who he had trusted beyond all others— betray his hiding place to Brother Joseph knowing he would be beaten for running away from his lessons. No matter how he tried, he could not push the memory down far enough to allow him to be cordial with Richard just yet.

"As you can see, Drumoak has been very kind." He stepped away from the door, a silent signal to Richard that he was now invited to leave.

Richard understood and stepped toward the door without further conversation. However, he was stopped before he could leave by the sudden appearance of a vision in silk brocade.

"Richard!" Mehlyndia squealed, reaching for Richard's hand. "What a grand surprise. I'm so glad you're here. I'm eager to watch you in the tournament." She looked up quickly to William, seemingly oblivious to the scowl he knew his face was wearing. "How nice for you two to have a chance to visit again." Before either lad could interrupt her, she was rushing into the room and throwing the curtains wide, flooding the room with light. "There, much better. Wait until you see who else I've brought to visit."

William turned toward the door with a sudden panic. *Oh Blessed Mother please do not let it be her sister.* He steeled his breath as he caught the first glimpse of the blue taffeta skirt as it appeared in his door. For a flash of a moment, he calculated the distance from his window to the ground and if he could possibly leap without doing himself much damage.

He kept his eyes fixed only on the skirt as she stood in the doorway, trying to find his courage to look up to her face. He moved his eyes up slowly, confused that Bryndah was somehow a lot shorter than he remembered her. When he finally drew up the courage to look at her face, his eyes went wide in wonder at the lovely lass who filled the doorway.

"You look as though you do not know me," Laurel said shyly.

"I'm certain I do not, my lady," William said. He bowed,

reaching for her hand and planting a courtly kiss upon the back of it.

"Ahem," Richard coughed quietly.

Mehlyndia hurried to stand between Richard and William, to make a proper introduction. "Richard Fylbrigge, I should like to present Miss Laurel May McCary." She nodded an encouragement to Laurel, who flushed as she offered her hand to Richard.

"I am honored," Richard said, then bowed and kissed her hand as William had.

William's jaw dropped in sudden revulsion at the sight. He had to check himself from snatching Laurel's hand away before the lout's lips could touch it.

"Richard, Laurel is in need of an escort. As my first lady for the day, she shall sit with me in the high booth."

Richard smiled an alarmingly charming smile. William was even more alarmed at Laurel's coy smile and the way she fluttered her long lashes in return.

"I should be honored to escort the lady. But alas, I cannot sit with you as I will be participating in the games," Richard replied smoothly. "Perhaps the lady would allow me to carry her token?"

Laurel glanced toward Mehlyndia, as if for instructions. Mehlyndia made a half wink, making a secret sort of circular motion with her finger near her bodice. Laurel seemed to understand the coded message as she produced a length of ribbon, as if by magic from her bodice.

"Will this do?" she asked, handing the ribbon to Richard.

Richard accepted the ribbon with a bow. "Thank you, my lady."

William stood back, dumbfounded. Had this scene been premeditated? Were the ladies only play acting? He looked toward Mehlyndia for some sort of signal that this sickening charade was about to end but she only stood, smiling and watching.

Richard offered his elbow. Laurel looked again to Mehlyndia for guidance. Mehlyndia coyly demonstrated the proper placement of fingertips upon her elbow. Laurel placed her dainty fingers as if it were the most natural thing on earth for her to be escorted by a nobleman's son to a gala event.

William stood aghast as the pair vanished down the corridor. Mehlyndia giggled behind him, reminding him he was not alone.

"What, in the name of all things holy, was the meaning of that?"

"Don't you think she looks lovely?" Mehlyndia replied, extremely proud of herself.

"Well, aye, she does... very. But... Melly, what are you thinking? Laurel is... I mean, she's not... and Richard is definitely not—"

"Oh, William, you're such a fuddle sometimes," she sighed. "Today, she is a lady. She is Lady Laurel, my first waiting lady. I should think you would be happy for her to have a day she can step out of her dreary little kirtle and spend the day almost like a princess."

"Dreary?" William spun on his heal. "There is nothing dreary about Laurel and I do not think it is right for you to be playing with her this way."

"Playing?" Mehlyndia's smile melted. "I am not playing. I'll have you know that she asked me to introduce her to Richard."

"She doesn't even know him!"

"Of course not, silly, that's why she wanted to meet him."

"But—"

"And I believe they make a fine bonny sight."

"But . . ."

He raised his hands, then dropped them by his side. There was no point in arguing with Melly once she set her mind to something. He had come to understand long ago that she existed in a reality all her own. After all, she regarded Bryndah as an angel of light so it wasn't a far stretch to understand how she could consider Richard and Laurel together as a *bonny sight.*

"Melly, what of her heart?"

"Perhaps Richard shall court her."

William shook his head, flabbergasted. Mehlyndia of all people, should know that Richard was an unreachable match for Laurel. Why was she playing at this cruel game? "But Richard is gentry!"

"William Fylbrigge, I am surprised with you! How many times have you chided me for making distinctions of rank."

He had no answer. She had him dead to right on that one.

"And besides," she began slyly, leaning toward him. "If it works as a wake up to that silly sentry, Sean to what is right before him that he cannot seem to see, then all the better."

The light came to him, then. "You mean to tell me that this is simply a charade to make Sean take notice of her?"

She smiled quite smugly.

He allowed himself to relax in the hope that Laurel was truly only playing at this little game and in spite of himself, he had to admire the plan. It was no secret to William that Laurel fancied

Sean and had done her best to catch his eye, while he seemed quite oblivious to her. Reluctantly, he admitted to himself that Laurel would be a far safer and logical mate for Sean than Annlise ever could be. Just the thought of deciding such things for Sean made him feel like he'd just betrayed his best friend by endorsing an *arranged* pairing for him— even if he would have no idea it was being done.

"Melly?"

"Aye?"

"Are we pompous?"

"Aye, I suppose, just a bit." She chuckled. "Father would say it is a hazard that goes with the blood. We did not choose our birth. We were just fortunate."

"But does being born to the right blood give us the right to arrange other peoples' lives?"

She tilted her head, looking at him curiously. "Of course," she said simply, then moved toward the door.

William offered his elbow as was expected and the two headed down toward the great hall, for the pre-tournament feast that was waiting, though William was suddenly bereft of his appetite.

The hall was full by the time William and Mehlyndia descended the grand staircase. Every seat, bench, corner and nook was occupied by someone in fine clothing. Ladies in voluminous gowns blockaded the way to the buffet. William mused that were he to ever invade a castle, he would simply hide his army beneath a sea of farthingales. He noted that the wider the skirt, the higher the rank of the lady it adorned— and the more ridiculous it looked to his eye. Ambrose Woodhall's wife, the Countess of Kylkannon, seemed to have donned a pair of banquet tables on her hips, supporting a skirt so wide that she had to turn sideways to enter through the large double doors.

"How foolish," he muttered under his breath.

"What is?" Mehlyndia asked, cordially waving to people as they mingled through the hall.

"Lady Woodhall," William whispered, gesturing with his chin in the countess' direction. "Do you suppose she's hiding a lover under that skirt?"

Mehlyndia gasped, then giggled. "William, that is a positively scandalous thing to say. Of course, she is not."

William snickered, amused by the mischievous blush on Mehlyndia's face. "You're probably right. He would be too crowded by the herd of goats and the water ox hiding there already."

Mehlyndia buried her face behind her handkerchief, her face turning bright red as she tried to stifle her laughing.

"And see Lady Drunbalk? I believe there is a pavilion bereft of its canopy."

"Actually two." A voice much deeper than Mehlyndia's replied. William turned with a start to see Edward had joined him unawares. "You have a devious wit, my boy. Perhaps this is not quite the place to use it."

William felt his face turn hot. Mehlyndia was standing with her back to her father, close to tears with stifled laughter. Ever the lady, she would never allow herself a good belly laugh in public. William cleared his throat and tapped her on the back. She turned and made a funny little squeak of surprise when she saw Edward.

"Father! I was just... looking for you." She stammered,

smoothing her skirt.

Edward extended his arm for her and she placed her hand up into the crook of his elbow, obediently. He gave her hand an affectionate pat. "You look lovely, my dear." He raised a brow, giving William a stern and unmistakable warning as he led Mehlyndia toward the group of wide-dressed ladies.

"Goats?"

William spun on his heel, prepared to apologize to whomever was now confronting him. He nearly swooned in relief to see a grinning Sean standing before him. "Aye, McLander has finally found a suitable stable for his flock."

"Lunk," Sean laughed, then gestured for William to follow him as he hurried to a quiet corner behind a pillar.

William hurried, curious by the urgency in Sean's look. "What is it?" he asked in a whisper.

Sean surprised William by suddenly seizing him by his doublet and nearly pulling him off his feet and pressing him against the pillar. William held his breath, half expecting to be struck in the face and wondering what he could have possibly done to cause Sean to attack him.

Instead of a strike, Sean made an unexpected plea. "Will, I need help. I've ne'er asked anything of you in all your time here and ne'er once have I even considered using our friendship as a way to climb the ladder to higher greatness. I'll do anything you want, I swear on my father's cairn."

William stared bug-eyed, barely able to catch his breath as Sean held him tight against the pillar. "Just let go and I'll give you anything you want."

Sean realized what he was doing and a look of utter distress crossed his face as he relaxed his grip. "Och, Will, I'm sorry."

"Easy, Sean. Tell me what's happened. Has someone threatened you?"

Sean blinked, momentarily confused. "No."

"Is Agnes well? Has something happened to Duncan?"

"No, something worse." Sean drew a weary breath and stepped away, looking toward the stairs. "Can we go upstairs, please?"

"Of course." William looked over his shoulders and hurried his friend up the stairs. He scanned the faces quickly to see if anyone was taking notice. Once out of the view of the crowd, William naturally turned toward his own chamber, then stopped, surprised as Sean hurried in the opposite direction— toward the west end guest suite. "Where are you—"

"Shh!" Sean waved him to follow right to the door across from the service staircase. He stepped quietly to the door, looking around cautiously, then knocked quietly on the door. Three short wraps, a pause, then two. The door opened quickly and Sean pulled William with him into the chamber, closing the door quickly behind them and throwing the bar to lock it.

Annlise was in Sean's arms in a heartbeat, the two embracing so hard that William feared Sean would break her ribs if he wasn't careful. He stood back, not quite knowing which way to look or why he had been bidden to follow— unless Sean merely needed him as camouflage should anyone see him in this particular hallway. *All he had to do was ask, why all the dramatics in the great hall?* A sudden notion crossed his mind, and a wave of panic with it.

"You're not planning to run away, are you? Today? From here?" He blurted, stepping up to the pair. "It would be suicide!"

Neither seemed to hear him. Annlise buried her head on

Sean's chest, weeping as he held her stroking her hair, cooing in a way William never thought Sean was capable.

"Shh, sweet lass. It will be well, I promise. All will be well."

"How can it be?" she sobbed.

"Because I'm with you now."

"You should hate me for leaving you without even a word of thanks for all you done. Without even as much as saying farewell. I wanted so much to stay. You know that, aye?"

He tightened his embrace, dropping his face to the top of her head. "I could not hate you even if I wanted to. And truth be told, I did want to."

William heard movement on the other side of the door and signaled for them to be quiet. The voices passed on to one of the other suites. He relaxed and turned to his friends. "This meeting is dangerous."

"Aye and I will nae put you in trouble. You must go on back." She sniffled into her handkerchief.

Sean took her hand and kissed it, then pressed it against his cheek. "We could flee through the catacombs," he whispered. "I spirited you away once, I can do it again. We'll go far into the highlands where even the barons dinnae care to go."

She shook her head sadly. "And what of your family? Your wee brother will be missing you fierce. And what of your mum, who loves you more dear than I think you even know?"

Sean shook his head, turning away. "They will be all right," he said in such a way that even William could tell he did not believe his own words.

"Adrian would not give a half a thought before taking revenge on them," she said quietly.

Sean turned to William with a pleading, yet resigned

expression. "I'm sorry I dragged you up here, lad. I guess you cannae help us after all."

"I will do anything I can, but," William began, taking a step away from the door, "I must agree with Annlise that if you flee together, Adrian may well come after your family."

Sean nodded, resigned, reaching for her hand. "You're certain? It is not... a mistake?"

She drew a staggering breath and squeezed his hand. "I'm certain."

"Certain?" William ventured.

Annlise stood straight and composed herself before looking at William. "I cannot see Sean again, Will. I'm certain it is for the better for everyone."

Sean stepped away, not arguing, though his face contorted as he held his tongue.

"I only seen him now to explain why I had to leave as I did. It was his life in the bargain you see? Please understand, aye?"

William nodded, not quite knowing how to respond. The morning certainly was turning out to be far more complicated than he had expected.

"If you could be so kind, Will, could you please wait outside the door, to give me a moment with Annlise?"

"Of course." William turned to open the door.

"And Will?" Sean called.

"Aye?"

"When I come to join you, none of this will have taken place."

A look crossed Sean's eyes that William had never seen but he was not inclined to argue.

"Aye," William promised, placing his fist to his chest before he slipped out the door, closing it behind him.

Chapter 17

A T THE HEIGHT OF the sun, on that spectacular and unseasonably warm November afternoon, all of Stonehaven gathered at the tournament ring. Venders pushing carts laden with colorful goods lined the outer perimeter. Tumblers and jugglers darted about, delighting the young and old with their gravity defying tricks.

Edward had insisted that every member of his household, from the chamberlain to the groundskeepers, be dressed as fine as any gentry for this special day. Orders had been placed with all the tailors and seamstresses for garments to be made. Edward granted enough funds to provide the clothing to those with lesser means and presented the attire as gifts. On William's encouragement, the fabric used to adorn the pavilion and banners was ordered from Caleb, the unfortunately lamed weaver. Edward had been so impressed with the quality of the banners, that new orders and advanced payments were made to Caleb for the making of new draperies for the grand hall.

So grandly dressed were all the workers, that it was difficult for anyone who was unfamiliar with Stonehaven to know who was gentry and who was common folk.

Little Duncan squealed, clapping his hands as one of the jugglers tossed wooden clubs about. "Do it again!" he cried, when the juggler stopped to take a wee rest.

"Duncan, you must let the poor man catch his breath," Agnes told him gently. "The fellow has been kind enough to perform his tricks over and over for you." She blushed, reaching into the silk pouch tied at her wrist and pulling out two copper coins.

"I thank you kindly, my lady," the juggler said with a slight bow of his head. "But today we are on wage, so it is my pleasure to perform on command for the young master."

Duncan grinned, puffing out his little chest to show off the new tunic and hose he sported for the special day. "Do it again!" he cheered, as the juggler made dizzying patterns with his clubs.

Just then, the trumpeter blared a fanfare, announcing the tournament was about to begin.

"Come on, sweeting, we dinnae want to miss the procession!" Agnes said, taking Duncan's hand.

"But I want to watch," Duncan whined.

"But you'll miss Seany," she coaxed. "And he's not seen you all dressed up. 'Twill be fun to see if he can recognize you, aye?"

Duncan giggled and clapped his hands at that. "Thank you, jugg'er man," he said politely, waving as Agnes led him to the stands.

They climbed the narrow scaffold stairs at the side of the pavilion and stepped onto the covered platform.

"Now you must be on your best behavior, lad," Agnes reminded him. "Remember, Lord Edward is being special nice by letting us sit in the grand seats."

"I be good," Duncan insisted. "I be a big boy now, Mum."

She held fast to his hand, taking a seat in the back row from the rail, behind Mehlyndia and Laurel. Duncan fidgeted about, trying to peek through the big skirts, but to no avail. To his dismay, another lady in a big dress stepped onto the pavilion, and blocked even the smallest view of the ring. "Mum, I cannae see! Ladies all be too big!"

The newcomer turned, with haughty glare. "What a rude

little whelp!"

Duncan's eyes went wide as he shrank behind his mother's skirt.

The woman's expression changed instantly as she surveyed the rose colored gown Agnes was wearing. The sneer turned to a pleasant smile by the time the woman looked her in the eye. She extended an elegantly decorated hand, with extraordinarily long nails. "I do not believe we have been introduced. I am Lady Bryndah Fylbrigge, of Aberdoir. You must be Lady... Wesley, is it?"

Laurel peeked over her shoulder, nudging Mehlyndia. Mehlyndia turned to see who it was Bryndah was addressing. She held her finger to her mouth with a wink, encouraging Agnes to play along.

Agnes lightly tapped Bryndah's hand with all the pomposity of any noble woman. Her head slightly tilted back, she looked down her nose surveying Bryndah head to foot as though to judge her worthiness for conversation.

Bryndah flushed, then gestured toward Duncan. "Please forgive my shortness. With all the masquerading going on today, it is difficult to know who is and is not the right sort."

Agnes arched her brow. "Indeed. I should not want my son cavorting with the wrong sort." She mimicked the pompous accent of a Londoner, perfectly camouflaging her customary burr.

Bryndah's smile widened at Agnes' obvious breeding. "But, of course, the boy should come sit to the front where he shall be better able to see." She gestured to an empty seat at the end of the front row. "My son, Richard, shall not be using the seat as he will be competing. I insist the child take the seat. That is, of course if the Lady McCary does not mind?"

Laurel gave a wink to Duncan. "I would be pleased," Laurel replied, carrying on the charade by mimicking Agnes' performance. "The duke shall be pleased of your pleasure, as well."

"But what about Mum? She has to still look over the fat dresses."

Bryndah's eyes flared and she checked it immediately, turning the scowl to sweetness. "What a perfectly delightful little one. I insist. You must take my seat, Lady Wesley, so you can better see."

Mehlyndia seemed barely able to hold back her laughter.

Agnes nodded regally and stepped forward. "Thank you, I believe I shall. You are most gracious."

Bryndah flushed but moved aside, obviously annoyed that Agnes would take her up on her offer.

When all were seated, Mehlyndia leaned close to Agnes and whispered. "Your secret is safe with me Lady... Wesley."

Agnes bit her lip trying not to laugh out loud. "Who is Lady Wesley, anyway?"

"The countess of Kent. She sent her regrets weeks ago," Mehlyndia told her, fluffing up her fan. "Besides, you look stunning and every bit as proper as a countess."

Agnes blushed, smiling. She felt like a countess.

There were four remaining seats in the grand stand and Agnes wondered who else would be joining them. She knew that Lord Edward would certainly be occupying the throne-like seat in the middle and that Elinor was due any moment to take a seat, most likely behind Laurel and next to Bryndah. That left two on the opposite side of Edward. Her wonders were soon answered when an elderly gentleman arrived, escorting the young woman Agnes knew immediately. She turned her face, not wishing for Annlise to give her identity away to Bryndah just yet.

"Oh, yes." Bryndah groaned under her breath, leaning close up behind Agnes. "You see? Father has made it so just anyone can mingle."

Agnes leaned back, as if she were interested in listening. "Oh? And who is this?"

"My husband's man servant, Chase. Thomas keeps him on merely for sentimental reasons... and of course, because Father insisted. I would have sacked him long ago if not for Father meddling in all our affairs."

"How dreadful for you," Agnes mocked, shaking her head. "And the lady?"

"My first waiting lady, Annlise. His daughter actually."

"And do you keep her for sentiment as well?"

Bryndah chuckled under her breath, quite unexpectedly. "To tell the truth? I enjoy her company. I'm rather fond of her actually."

Agnes looked at Bryndah in surprise. "Really?"

"A shock, I know. I am well aware of my reputation as a shrew, Lady Wesley. But even a shrew has at least *one* friend." Bryndah stood and waved toward Annlise. "I see you've made it, are you feeling better?"

"Aye, thank you, m' lady. The flatbread and honey were quite right."

Annlise smiled but Agnes noted her eyes were rather puffy and red-rimmed. But it was the shining silver knot-shaped pendent that dangled from the young woman's neck that made Agnes draw a quick breath. *Flat bread and honey?* Agnes felt an odd sinking in her stomach, her mind recalling the tell-tale blood stain in Annlise's skirt that was the talk of the castle after she'd departed last month.

"I knew it would, dear," Bryndah replied, sweetly. "Lady Wesley, I'd like you to meet my lady, Annlise Chase."

Agnes braced for discovery, as she turned toward Annlise. Annlise's eyes widened slightly in recognition. Agnes winked, hoping the lass would understand.

Annlise bowed her head, grinning. "I am honored, Lady Wesley."

"Are you feeling ill?" Agnes inquired in her Londoner accent, her eyes falling helplessly upon the silver pendant.

Annlise placed her hand over the little silver trinket as her smile melted and her face flushed. She turned her head quickly. "Not anymore. I had a spell a bit ago but it has passed now."

It was all Agnes needed to confirm her suspicion. "Good," she said, forcing a smile.

Annlise caught her eye and held the look for a moment before she turned away to see to her father. Agnes wondered if Chase knew he was going to soon be a grandfather. She turned back in her seat, trying to force the realization out of her mind.

Duncan fidgeted happily in the seat next to Laurel, swinging his feet in mid air beneath the bench. He looked over his shoulder to Bryndah and asked loudly, "Did you know I have a mouse?"

"Shh," Laurel warned, a finger to her mouth.

"But I do!" Duncan said. "Her name is Lucy. You wanna see, lady?"

He reached into the pocket of his tunic. Laurel gasped and placed her hand over his to stop him but he was quick and determined. He held up the wiggling creature by the tail right in front of Bryndah's face.

"See?"

Bryndah screeched and stood quickly. "Get it away!"

Duncan snatched up the mouse, protectively hiding her back into his pocket. He cried out, frightened by Bryndah's screeching, and scooted under the bench to hide.

"Is it gone? Kill the little beast!" Bryndah cried, brushing her skirt with her hands as though an army of mice were attacking.

"Bryndah! Sister, dear! Please, calm yourself," Mehlyndia cooed, taking hold of Bryndah's hands. "It is but one wee mouse and the lad has placed her safe away."

Bryndah took a breath, then looked toward Duncan, then to Agnes. She affected a false smile. "Forgive, me. Please. I... have never cared for... animals."

"Indeed!" Agnes sneered, with the perfect arch of her brow. "Duncan, darling, please keep Lucy away from Lady Bryndah. It is not safe—"

"Thank you," Bryndah began.

"—for the mouse." Agnes finished. She turned slowly and resumed her seat. It was all she could do to keep from laughing. She was grateful that her back was to Bryndah and the woman would not see her face turn red from the suppressed laughter.

"The gates!" Duncan cried, pointing as the grand gate opened for the processional of competitors.

The first to appear was Lord Edward, astride his favorite stallion, Gallant. Bedecked in grand regalia, he looked like the king entering the ring. Edward waved and approached center, where Gallant folded a front leg and bowed to the grand stand. The crowd applauded. He circled the ring once at a trot, acknowledging the spectators and visiting guests with a wave or a bow as necessary. When he approached the grand stand, he blew kisses to his daughters and winked at Agnes and Laurel. Elinor had finally arrived and was just taking a seat next to Bryndah. Edward paused and offered her a grand smile, gesturing to the ribbon on his sleeve.

Elinor beamed, bowing in reply.

Bryndah turned to see who it was that had joined her and for whom Edward borne a token. Her eyes went wide in near shock when she recognized Elinor. Elinor batted her eyes at Bryndah and reached to give her hand a squeeze.

"Nice to see you, ducks," Elinor said, then turned her attention back to Edward.

Edward grinned, then kicked into a gallop to circle the ring in grand style. As he approached the gate, he signaled the trumpeter and, with a grand fanfare, the gate swung wide, revealing the parade of competitors on horseback.

The horses nickered and scuffed, eager to be away from the crowded confines of the gathering pen. Star snorted, tossing her mane in anticipation for William's command. He leaned down onto her neck as far as his armor would allow and cooed, "Easy, girl. It won't be long."

"I wish it would be done and over," Sean mumbled under his breath, his eyes fixed on the back of one of the riders for Aberdoir. "The air is foul and near impossible to breathe suddenly."

"Keep your head, lad," William cautioned. "This is supposed to be only a mock battle."

"Mock," Sean scoffed. "Don't worry, Will. I'm not likely

to take any heads with a wooden sword." He paused, then muttered, "Though 1 may just drive it through my own heart and be done with it."

William looked up, surprised. "You cannae mean that."

"No, 1 suppose 1 dinnae." Sean shook his head. "Though it may be less painful than watching her go back to Aberdoir yet again."

"That is what's been decided then? You will accept that?"

Sean nodded and said no more. Hawk stamped and snorted, commiserating with Star in his eagerness to run. Sean stroked the stallion's mane, easing him into line.

"Gate's open," Galan said, signaling to his guards to line up. Then, giving a nod to William, he took his place to his left.. "We'll be yours to lead, lad, are you ready?"

"No but 1 suppose 1 shall be expected to do it anyway," William said with a laugh.

As hosts, the team representing the house of Stonehaven would be the last to enter the ring. William would be the only nobleman for Stonehaven, since Edward had declined to participate. He would also be the youngest and least experienced of the group. He hadn't asked for any special considerations but as the time drew closer for the event, he was secretly grateful that Galan was taking a protective place to his left and Sean to his right. Ewan, Simon, and Isaac would also run interference but only if William was in danger of serious injury. William had resented the attention initially but after seeing the might presented by the other houses, he was content to accept all the help there was to be had.

The first team to enter the ring was from Kylkannon. Lord Ambrose Woodhall, himself— dressed in a glimmering silver armor adorned with a feathered helm— led his team around the circle, greeting and waving as Edward had done. His team was impressive; his nephew, Vigo of Inverness, was the obvious champion in his team. Vigo was massive on his saddle, his armor spiked at the elbows and helm. He was no stranger to battle, as proven by the ghastly crooked nose and gashed brow which gave him the nickname 'Vigo the Ugly.' William hoped of all competitors, Vigo would not be the one he would face in a joust.

Kylkannon was followed by Lothian. Ogham, in the front, astride a massive war horse that could have been the twin to Lucifer. The hooves of the horse thundered above the sound of any other. Ogham's team was nearly the opposite of Stonehaven's as it was comprised almost entirely of nobleman and only one guard, Angus McLeary. William had never heard of this man but Sean bristled at the sight of him— the two had been rivals in games held a year ago amongst only the guards. Sean had been the clear winner of the caber until Angus threw his tree perfectly, three times in a row.

After Lothian finished their greeting parade, it was Aberdoir to go next. No surprise to William, Thomas' team was small and elite. The only sentry to ride was Cletus, who had been asked to participate only to appease Edward's edict that the games be open to all comers. Cletus hung back near the back of the team, walking his horse backward to come along side Sean for a moment before his time to ride.

Being certain he was unseen, Cletus leaned toward Sean and whispered. "You best watch him, mate. And yeself. There's something afoot wi' the' blackguard in the front."

Sean looked toward the front to see who Cletus was referring to. "Tearlach."

"Aye. He's not here for the glory of Aberdoir." Cletus took his place with his team, before any noticed he'd moved.

"No surprise there, aye?" William whispered.

"No," Sean replied, his eyes fixed squarely on Adrian's back. "Keep your eyes open, Will. I'll watch your back."

"And I yours."

Sean half smiled. "Fair enough."

Another member of the Aberdoir team shuffled back and William was surprised to see it was Richard, Laurel's ribbon tied prominently to his arm. William expected him to merely nod in greeting, simply to affirm his presence in the team or such. What he was not prepared for was for Richard to take a place beside him, as if he were part of the Stonehaven team.

Sean sent a curious glance to Will, gesturing toward Richard.

"I think you are in the wrong parade, Richard," William said casually, not looking his nephew in the eye.

"Actually, I am not," Richard said simply. "This is my parade."

"Excuse me?" William asked.

"Oh don't worry, Will, you'll still be the only nobleman to ride for Stonehaven, if that was your concern."

"It was not. What do you mean, this is your parade?"

"I tried to tell you earlier but you were not inclined to... accept an audience at the time."

"Ahem," Sean interrupted, making his protective presence obvious. "Your team is riding out momentarily, I think you should take your place."

"This is my team."

"Richard, I do not know what this is about but this is not the time for puzzles."

The Aberdoir team began to move. Richard hung back only momentarily. "You'll soon know," he said, flipping his visor down and following the team. He did not keep up however, riding somewhat behind the rest. One could consider him either the last of Aberdoir or the first of Stonehaven, by the position he took.

"Who is that?" Sean asked.

William glared at Richard's back. "No one. He used to be my brother," he said, then flipped his own visor down and lifted his hand to signal his team to ride out.

As soon as the way was clear, William kicked in and set Star at a quick trot out into the ring. The crowd burst into immediate cheers. He smiled and waved to the people in the stands, many of them he recognized as friends from about town. The ladies from the Thorn and Thistle waved ribbons calling for him to wear them. William blushed and merely smiled, hoping Edward had not noticed his familiarity with the tavern ladies. As Edward had done, he moved to the middle and both he and Star bowed to the grand stand. Edward stood by his seat, having taken it after his introductory ride and bowed in return. William trotted toward the stand as was planned, to accept his token from Mehlyndia, thus announcing who he would be championing for this day.

She leaned over the rail, holding a length of blue silk. He took it, with a bow of his head, and tucked it into his breastplate. He then turned and signaled the trumpeters as the remainder of the team road out.

As Sean approached the grand stand, he raised the visor on his helm and scanned the seats. When he saw Annlise in the grand stand only two seats away from his mother, he reined in and paused. William feared for a moment that Annlise would offer Sean a token to carry and that he would be fool enough to accept it, thus ensuring Adrian's temper would fall full onto his friend. But Annlise only nodded, placing her hand on her throat and offered only a sad sort of smile. Sean sidled up toward Laurel and held out his hand, smiling. "I believe you promised me your token, my lady."

William saw Mehlyndia hide a smug smile behind her fan as Laurel blushed and explained coyly, "I'm sorry, I have already given my token to someone."

Sean withdrew his hand, stunned, as she pointed toward Richard who was still maintaining an ambivalent position somewhere between the Stonehaven and Aberdoir teams. He looked back to her confused. "Him? But... "

Laurel sent a pleading glance to William. He did his best to avoid giving her any guidance, having grave reservations in the little plot she and Melly had devised. This was not the time to be playing on Sean's emotions. Laurel seemed to sense this as well and mercifully, pulled a ribbon from her hair and handed it to Sean.

With obvious relief, Sean kissed Laurel's hand and wound the ribbon around his fist. He then pulled a miniature wooden sword from his boot— one William had carved at his request— and presented it to Duncan, who accepted it wide eyed.

"Now, you be careful with that, lad. I'll show you how to use it later."

The crowd responded with cheers as Duncan proudly held up his prize.

The rest of the team accepted their various tokens and soon, they trotted together toward the center to join the rest of the competitors.

Edward stood and waved the crowd to silence. Speaking in a booming voice, amplified with the help of a large cone fashioned from sheep skin he announced the order of competition, paying compliments here and there to the rivals and building up anticipation for the main event, the mock battle.

The first event was to be the full armored joust. Paired matches rode against each other, the winner of each pair moving to the next round, until only two riders were left. At the end, the team whose rider had earned the most points would then melee against the team who came second. The third and fourth placed teams would be retired from the competition.

The teams drew lots for the order of competition. Aberdoir would go first and would face the team from Lothian.

William and Sean stood with their team mates against the rail of the waiting pen.

"This should be interesting," Sean whispered, watching Angus posture while preparing for his run against Cletus. "I hate to admit I'm hoping Aberdoir wins this round, but it doesn't seem likely with that pairing."

"Do not discount Cletus, Sean," William said. "I've witnessed him with a lance. Of course, I was only a lad at the time and he is older now and Angus, admittedly bigger... and why is it you want Aberdoir to win anyway?"

"Why do you think?" Sean said, spitting into the dirt, his eyes fixed squarely on Adrian as he mounted for his run.

"Because you do not want to ride against Angus?" William ventured, knowing that was far from the true reason.

"I'm not worried about Angus. He's big but he's dull and he has no grace in the saddle."

"I'm worried about him," William muttered.

Sean shook his head, allowing the first real smile he'd made since the games began. "You may be smaller but remember what I told you, agility and talent are far more valuable in the saddle than girth and raw strength."

"I'll remember that when I hit the ground."

"Oh! He's down!" Simon cheered as Angus of Lothian toppled in a heap. "That's two pints you owe me, Ewan."

"The meet is nae done." Ewan cautioned. "Lothian is nae out of it yet."

"You're daft, man, look who is up next!" Simon laughed, pointing toward the wooden plaque that held the names of the competitors. "Ogham is no match for Fylbrigge."

William raised a brow. "Thomas is next?"

"Pay attention, lad; aye. He's riding again' Ogham," Ewan said. "And I have a pint that says Ogham will break two lances on him and send him flying from the saddle. What say you, Will?"

William remembered a time long ago where he watched his older brother in a joust. If nothing else, Thomas was well at home on a horse and he did not lose easily. Ogham was impressively larger than Thomas but, as Sean had just reminded him size is not always an advantage.

"I'll take your wager. Thomas will win this meet."

"Fool's wager on your part, Ewan," Simon scoffed. "I'm with Will on this. Sean?"

Sean nodded his agreement with Simon and William.

Thomas took his place at the end of the ramp. As the squire handed him the lance, he waved toward the grandstand where his wife was seated. Bryndah did not even notice as she seemed engaged in conversation with, of all people, Sean's mother. William nudged Sean and pointed this out to him but he was more interested in watching the two horsemen prepare for their meet.

"Take note, lad," Sean said, pointing toward the ring. "Ogham's wide armor gets in the way of him holding the lance properly. Thomas' has a smooth, straight line. That is your advantage as well."

The flag was dropped and the two raced toward each other. Sean was dead right about the positioning of the lances. Thomas held his like an arrow, as Ogham's drifted far off his line. Thomas' lance struck Ogham's shield dead center, splintering the tip in a hail of wood. Aberdoir's team erupted in cheers.

Simon cheered, slapping Ewan on the back. "That's four!"

"You see?" Sean said.

William nodded. He was not entirely pleased to have won this particular wager, as it looked more and more likely that Stonehaven would ride against Aberdoir in the final meet. Aberdoir was going to be difficult to beat. Even Richard had made easy work of breaking his lances neatly against his opponent. Lothian had not won a single round and now, only Adrian was left to ride against Ogham's nephew, Rodney. When Rodney mounted, William noted the crest that flashed in the sunlight on his breast plate.

"Now, that is interesting," Sean noted. He had seen it too. "Hunter against hunter."

"I hope they skewer each other through the hearts," William growled.

"No chance of that, lad."

"Why not?"

"They would first need to have hearts in order to skewer them," Sean said with a shrug.

William watched closely, trying to see any weakness in Adrian's approach. To his dismay, it was flawless and deadly accurate. His lance broke easily against Rodney's shield. Rodney lost his balance at the end of the ramp and toppled off the horse, adding more points to Aberdoir's impressive score.

"That does it," Sean said, reaching for his helmet. "We'll make quick work against Kylkannon and then we ride against that lot."

William's stomach turned. He was not as confident as Sean that Kylkannon would be such an easy victory. Kylkannon had Vigo, who had never lost.

"Mount up, lad," Galan said, tapping William on the back. "Time to draw lots for the order of competition."

"So soon?" William muttered, reaching for his helmet.

Galan laughed, rousing his team mates into a cheer with a warrior's whoop. The crowd in the stands began to cheer as Stonehaven's order of meet was placed on the plaque. William had drawn the last lot, so he would ride last, only prolonging the agony of his wait to be done with the whole of it.

They waited to see who each would ride against and to his dismay and total horror, William groaned as he watched Vigo's name slide into the slot opposite his own.

"Tough draw, Will," Isaac said, as he readied for the first run.

William nodded. "Godspeed, Isaac."

Isaac raised a thumb in response as he flipped his visor down and took his place for the first run, facing Ambrose Woodhall.

William looked toward the stands, again seeing the curious pairing of Bryndah and Agnes. As Woodhall took his place,

Mehlyndia inexplicably encouraged Agnes to continue her masquerade by standing to wave to the rival duke, Bryndah right beside her.

"What is the meaning of that?" William wondered aloud.

Sean looked, and gaped at the site. "I have no idea. My own mother, cheering against us? Laurel seems quite amused by it all."

"So does Melly." William noted. "Women play the strangest games."

"Absolutely."

The flag dropped and Isaac charged. He held his position perfectly. Galan nodded his approval. Woodhall's lance was impressively straight as well but just as contact was made, both lances broke against the other rider's shield.

"Damn," Sean groaned. "That will cost us a point."

"We can make it up." Simon assured him. "Remember, you're riding against their weakest rider."

"Aye, Drunbalk the Daft!" Sean laughed.

"Make quick work of him, lad."

Sean grinned. "No trouble, mate."

Sean mounted and held his hand out for his lance. He looked toward the stands, saluting his duke and bowing to Laurel. Duncan stood up on the bench, clapping his hands and waving to his big brother, his little sword tied into a loop at his belt with one of Laurel's blue ribbons. Sean gave a small wave to Duncan as he lowered the visor on his helmet.

He took his position. Agnes covered her eyes with her fan when the flag was lowered and he charged; his position, as Isaac's had been, was true and straight. It was evident Galan had trained them all equally well. Hawk thundered down the ramp and when the lances met, Sean struck true center of Drunbalk's shield not only shattering the lance but sending his opponent crashing to the ground, reclaiming the lost point and earning two to spare.

The crowd erupted in cheers. "Seany! Seany!" Duncan cheered, jumping up and down next to Laurel who was waving and jumping along. Agnes sat with her hand on her chest, smiling in relief. William noticed Annlise, too, sat in a similar posture, her hand resting on her sternum and her face turned slightly upward. It was then he remembered about Sean's wrist and realized he had not complained of pain since he had visited with her earlier in the morning.

Sean trotted back toward the waiting pen, waving to the still cheering crowd.

"Well done, Sean!" William held his hand out. Sean accepted with a hearty shake.

"He was easy."

"But you've regained our lead as well."

Sean grinned, smugly. "I know."

"How is your arm?" William asked casually. "Still bound?"

Sean's smile faded and a slight flush crossed his face. But before he had a chance to reply, the rest of the team was on him congratulating the returning hero. William had his answer. Annlise had taken care of him again. He would not press his friend further. He only hoped that at least this time, the healing would hold.

"Your turn, Will," Galan said, interrupting his thoughts. "Squire, lead him out."

"I'll do it, Galan," Sean said quickly.

Galan nodded in understanding. "Keep it straight, Will."

"Thank you."

Sean took hold of Star's reigns and led her to the ramp. The crowd erupted in new cheers when William made his appearance. Edward stood up, a clear signal to the crowd that he favored William in this event. Melly stood next to him, waving her ribbons and smiling. Laurel and Elinor had moved close to the rail, standing close to each other. Laurel looked at him, unsmiling. To his surprise, she and Elinor— in tandem— assumed the same position Annlise used, right hand resting upon the sternum. He watched them curiously for a moment until Sean called to him.

"Will, look at me."

"Hmm? Aye?"

"Your lance, lad."

"Oh... thank you. Sean, are you certain this is a good idea—"

"On my life." Sean reassured him. "Just hold onto it and ride. There is no better horse rider in this event than you. I am not saying that to puff up your kilt, it is the absolute truth. Trust Star and trust yourself. Just hold the lance and aim for the shield."

"His lance is longer—"

"They are all equal."

William gave one more fleeting glance to his family in the stand, fearing he would never see them again. Laurel and Elinor were still standing in the same position but now smiling encouragement toward him. With her free hand, Laurel gestured to her sleeve and gave him a nod. Sleeve?

"Will," Sean called again.

"Huh?"

"Lad, concentrate. Acknowledge your tokens, then put the

visor down. No more thinking."

"Oh, aye; thank you, Sean."

Sean nodded, then stepped away from the ramp. William bowed to Edward, then to Mehlyndia, displaying the ribbon he carried for her and nodded toward Elinor and Laurel, gesturing toward his unseen shirt. In so doing, he suddenly understood there was something special in the gift they had given him. "Thank you!" he called, then flipped the visor down. For better or worse, it was his turn. He no longer feared this was the last he would see of life.

His heart raced as the flag was lowered. "Go, Star!"

He kicked hard. The lance found its position easily and he gripped the hilt with all his might. Vigo gained quickly, his huge bulk coming toward him like a battering ram. William aimed the lance and steeled his jaw. Just as they met, he closed his eyes and put his trust in Star to stay true on the course.

The impact of his lance against Vigo's shield rattled every bone in his arm and, for a terrifying moment, he felt as if he would fall from the horse. Star compensated and shifted under his leaning weight, just enough that he caught his balance easily. When he opened his eyes, to his astonishment the end of his lance was in shreds, wood splinters dangling. It was Vigo who lay on his back in the dirt.

The crowd was on its feet, stamping in the wooden stands, cheering and calling with Edward leading them. Not only had William *not* died in his first joust but he had just scored the highest points given in the games all day, securing first place for Stonehaven. They would ride against Aberdoir for the glory.

✳ ✳ ✳

Laurel dabbed at her forehead with the fussy little handkerchief Mehlyndia had given her. The lace was very pretty she had to admit, but so impractical. The bone stays in the corset dug into her hips and the stiffness of the skirt prevented her from finding a comfortable position. She understood now why Will always complained when he was made to *dress properly*, as she longed to return to her own linen kirtle and chemise. Watching the men on the field, she could well imagine the misery all that armor must have been and was glad that she and Elinor had chosen to charm a comfortable shirt for William to wear under all that dreadful steel.

She leaned back and said quietly to Elinor, "Did you see? I think he knows what we've done."

"Aye, I think ye right. He seen us make the sign," Elinor said. "And he rode right well after. Now, we just pray it lasts for the rest of the day."

"Did you notice her?" Laurel gestured toward Annlise. "I bet she believes it was her charm that kept Sean on his horse."

"Shh, child." Elinor warned. "I'm sure Sean needs no such— what do you mean *her* charm? Laurel May, what have you done?"

Laurel frowned, crossing her arms over her chest. "Why is it right for Will and wrong for Sean? I just hope that he got the right one."

Elinor raised her brow, looking over her shoulder. Bryndah and Mehlyndia were happily chirping on about the state of fashion and the width of gowns or some such nonsense, and blessedly oblivious to their conversation.

"The right what?"

"I gave Richard one as well... well, it wasn't my idea, was it? Lady Mehlyndia insisted, and who am I to argue? Both rode so well in their rounds that I cannae tell who has the ribbon that I charmed."

"Laurel, child, you shall be the death of me, I swear. Did you make an offering at least?"

"Of course!"

"Well then, I suppose no harm done. Someone will be the better for it, one way or t' other." Elinor glanced toward Annlise, who sat quietly picking at the lace on her skirt. "How d' ye know what she were doing?"

"I saw her do this." She placed her hand on her sternum.

"Well, Laurel, she could have done tha' for any reason. Could it be that you jus' dinnae like the lass?"

Laurel scowled, looking away. "She's not right for him."

Elinor chuckled leaning close to Laurel's ear. "I think you're forgetting something, child."

"What?"

"Sean's not carrying *her* ribbon in his armor now, is he?"

Laurel grinned and turned back in her seat.

"Well, it appears the day shall be interesting after all," Thomas chuckled, inspecting the shine on his helm. He frowned and handed it back to the squire, pointing out a dull spot that needed further polishing. "Your task has just been made more complicated by this unexpected turn of events, my friend. You may have to do the deed personally to collect your reward."

Adrian looked up from under his raised brow. "May? I was under the impression it was assured. Win or lose at this little trifle, you will owe me my due. Was that not the bargain?"

"Of course," Thomas said quickly, leaning forward. "But neither of us expected Vigo to go down as he did. I took pains to ensure the arrangement of the meet after your assurances that Vigo would take care of—" He looked over his shoulders. "—the problem."

"Vigo has taken every champion from here to Cornwall and has never, never been thrown." Adrian stepped close to Thomas with a threatening glare. "You told me the boy had never ridden in a joust."

"No one is more shocked than I am on that count." Thomas growled. "Still, you have your task."

"Do I?" Adrian chuckled. "You are too modest, my lord. Have you not looked upon the tally board?"

"What do you mean?"

"The standings. The next round is not chosen by the drawing of lots, but by points. You, my dear friend, shall be riding against your own loving brother."

"Damn!" Thomas growled. "But it would be too obvious! I cannot *take care* of the problem in full view of Edward's entire court. He would see through any such accident immediately."

Adrian grinned. "You do have your cross to bear. Too bad for you. I, on the other hand, have landed exactly where I wish to be – riding fifth."

"Fifth? Why is that so important?" Thomas glanced at the plaque, then grinned as the names were placed for the final match. "I see. Well, good for you then. Your day shall be satisfactory after all."

Adrian chuckled. "I shouldn't count yours out completely, my lord. After all, there is still the melee to come."

Thomas grinned. "Yes."

✻ ✻ ✻

Unseen by Thomas and Adrian, a shadow slipped back from the stall where they were talking and into the Stonehaven stable.

"How?" William asked half laughing, half panicking. "How did I do that?"

"Talent, lad," Simon replied laughing. "And a good bit of dumb luck!"

"More luck than talent," William insisted.

"Face it, lad." Isaac joined in, "Like it or not, you're one of us. A common ruffian."

William smiled then. "Thank you Isaac, that is high praise to my ear."

"After Vigo, Thomas should be a merry walk in the sunshine." Simon laughed. "We'll be winning the prize, 'tis certain, and it's thanks to you and Seany here."

Sean beamed, trying desperately to look humble and failing. "No, no the credit is all his. I merely tied the score... and brought back the lead. I shall be glad to share in the spoils of victory at the Thorn and Thistle."

"We've not won yet, lads." Galan broke in, a serious scowl on his face. "We won that round yes, but remember that the competition from Kylkannon was hardly worth our time. Aberdoir will be a different story. They're not to be trusted."

"He's right." Isaac agreed. "I saw that black cloaked bloke tip his lance in his run. He nearly took off a helm."

"He would have been disqualified if he had," Ewan pointed out.

"Aye, but I dinnae think it is beneath him to do it anyway."

"It isn't. In fact, he's planning on it."

All heads turned to see who had spoken as Richard stepped out of the shadows. "Are you spying on us? You do not belong here, Richard," William said, shortly.

"I told you before, Will, that I do belong here. And perhaps after you hear what I have to say, you will believe me."

"What could you possibly—"

"Let him speak," Sean said, holding William back.

"Aye," Ewan agreed. "Who is planning on what, lad?"

Richard stepped further into the light, directly toward William. "I just heard them plotting. The outcome of the games is of no consequence to them, they care little either way. What does matter to them is that you... and you, sir," he said, nodding toward Sean, "meet with unfortunate accidents. Hazards of the games as it were." He looked directly at William. "It was no luck of the draw that you rode against Vigo, Will. He was supposed to be the solution to *the problem*."

William's eyes went wide and he felt the heat rise in his cheeks. "Well then, my brother must be especially irritated that I am still standing. Thank you for the warning, Richard. I supposed it was a little too much to ask of you to have delivered it *before* I met him on the ramp. Or is it that you had wagered against me to win?"

"No!" Richard shouted, his face turning red. "I only learned of this now. I overheard them talking. I could have kept this to myself, you know, and frankly perhaps I should have."

"Peace!" Galan said stepping between them. "Lad, I do not know who you are or why you have come but I thank you for the warning. We shall be especially vigilant. I suggest you return to your own team, before you are missed."

Richard bowed his head in response, turned to go then paused and said to Galan, "I am riding third. I believe that will be against you, sir. I look forward to a fair and well met challenge." He turned and faded back into the shadow.

"Easy, Will. Don't lose your head now," Sean said, placing a hand on William's shoulder.

"He's lying. Nothing is planned."

"Are you so sure?" Sean asked. "It seems highly likely he's telling the truth. Remember, Cletus gave us a similar warning at the beginning."

"I had forgotten that." William admitted. "But you don't know Richard as I do."

"No, but I know Tearlach all too well. And think on this – what is there for Richard to gain by betraying his father?"

William looked at Sean incredulously. "Aberdoir. My father's fortune, and—" He turned away. "–Edward's..."

"Edward's what? His trust? Affection?" Sean ventured quietly. "Is that what you fear in his presence? That he's come to take your place in Edward's eyes? After all, Richard is his grandson— his own blood."

William had no answer as he stared at Sean, stunned by his insight and ashamed with himself to realize that Sean was very likely correct. Richard was no threat to his place in Drumoak, really. Yet William felt threatened, none the less, and Sean had figured it out cleanly.

"I had not given it that much thought," William said quietly. "So you believe his warning is real?"

Sean nodded.

William glanced up to the plaque just as the names were being posted. "You're riding fifth."

"I know."

"Against Tearlach."

"I know."

"What do you intend to do?"

Sean looked at William and raised his brow, grinning. "I intend to win." He turned and headed for his horse.

The competitors entered the arena from their separate stable areas in the order of their standing, to the enthusiastic cheering from the stands. The teams from Kylkannon and Lothian, having been eliminated, had joined the crowd as spectators. In every section, from the lowest commoner to the highest nobleman, wagers were made on the outcome of this final joust.

Six pairs would ride three runs each. The best two runs of the three would be declared the winner. The objective was to strike the opponent's shield true and center, to break the end of the lance as far down the shaft as possible. Lesser points were earned for contact made without a break. Points would be lost if the lance strayed from the shield, striking a breast plate or gauntlet. Should a rider strike his opponent's helmet or horse, he would be automatically disqualified and his opponent would be declared the winner. Should a rider strike true but then fall from his horse, his opponent would earn the points.

At the end of the meet, the two high scoring riders from each team would then move onto the mock battle melee— the event most anticipated and wagered upon. Speculation was already high that Sean and Adrian would be among the combatants. William had already upset the odds by turning out the high score holder after the first joust. Vigo had earned scowls and groans from those who had wagered upon him to win and the displeasure of his team mates. When William entered the ring with his team, he was met with enthusiastic cheers from most of the spectators but boos and hisses from Kylkannon. He found it amusing and took it in the spirit of the competition, blowing kisses to Ambrose as he rode by, much to the amusement of his team mates.

"Gentlemen," Edward called through the sheepskin horn. "Mount and be ready! The winning team shall split a purse of one hundred crowns."

The lads cheered and jostled each other, grinning at the prospect of taking the prize money. But it was when Edward revealed the prize that would be awarded to the single competitor who won the most points that brought about astonished gasps of awe from the crowd— and brought a hiss of ire from Thomas. Mounted upon an ornate wooden plaque, polished to perfection and honed to a deadly sharp and sparkling edge, was the sword once carried by Henry Fylbrigge.

Thomas raced on his horse toward the grand stand. "That is a family treasure, Edward! It is promised to me!"

"I believe you are mistaken," Edward answered through the horn so that all could hear. "It was bestowed upon Henry at the pleasure of my father. Upon his death, it returned to me."

Thomas' face turned scarlet. "That is my father's sword!"

Someone in the crowd called out, "Afraid you'll lose?"

Thomas whirled on his horse, looking for who had called, when another, on the opposite side of the ring, chimed in, "He'll never win that back!"

"A crown says he'll win!"

"Two says he'll lose!"

"Three says young William will take it!"

This brought cheers from the Stonehaven side and more wagering to be called from Kylkannon. "Four that it goes to Tearlach!"

William whirled on that to see who had called that wager, suddenly taking interest in where his father's sword would go. Vigo waved to him bearing a toothless smile. "Because Fylbrigges are all losers!"

"Then why are you sitting in the stands?" William called back, earning cheers from his team mates.

"Quiet!" Edward bellowed through the horn. The crowd settled only to a lesser roar, while Edward continued. "Gentlemen. Take your places for the first heat!"

Sean had remained oddly quiet during the wagering, his eyes fixed upon the glimmering blade of Henry Fylbrigge's sword.

"You are likely to win that," William said.

Sean looked at him oddly. "I have no right to it."

"Of course you do. If you win, it shall be yours."

"How do you feel about that?"

"Better you than Vigo... or Tearlach." William looked up at the sword, then toward the Aberdoir team. "Thomas has coveted that for as long as I can remember. This will only make him more determined to win."

"You beat Vigo, lad." Sean reminded him.

"Vigo was not fighting for a birthright, as Thomas perceives that sword to be."

Simon would be the first to ride. He would face Cletus. A fair and even pairing, William observed. Both men were of equal size and talent and both ironically had been trained by Galan. Cletus had begun his career in Edward's guard and had been reassigned to Aberdoir soon after Thomas and Bryndah were wed.

The flag dropped and both men charged, the hooves

beating in near unison. The lances leveled and as if it were carefully choreographed, both met the shields, splintering in a simultaneous shower of wooden shards. The breaks were measured and equal points were determined for both sides.

A chorus of mumbling wagers rose within the crowd. Odds were moving back and fourth after the first run. The men squared for the second run. Again, a near perfect match. But upon the third run, it was Simon who had a slight edge, striking first though his lance remained intact. Cletus missed entirely and the point was then awarded to Simon, giving Stonehaven an early lead.

Simon cantered toward the stable waving, calling encouragement to Ewan as he took his place. Ewan, too, had a nearly equal match though in his third run, the lance tilted too far upward missing the shield and tipping the shoulder guard of his opponent.

The crowd groaned as the point was taken from Stonehaven and added to Aberdoir, giving them the lead. Thomas could be heard above the din, cheering loudly.

"Bloody hell." Ewan grumbled, trotting into the stable. He dismounted angrily, rattling his armor. "Sorry, mates."

"What happened?" Simon asked, taking Ewan's helmet from him. "I thought you had the bloke tied up neat and tidy."

Ewan pointed up to a cloudy sky. "Bloody sun."

Simon burst into laughter.

Sean nudged William, pointing toward the stand. "Now tell me what that is about?" Laurel was standing, waving as Richard took his place to take his runs against Galan. Sean still had her ribbon tied to his gauntlet. "She's supposed to be cheering for me."

"Well she did give him a token too, after all," William reminded him.

"I thought that was a jest!" Sean said, turning on his heel and glaring toward the stand. Laurel caught his eye and her smile melted immediately. He yanked at the blue ribbon on his arm and held it up as a reminder. "Shall I just toss this?"

"No," William said, urgently. "Be as angry as you like but keep that. If you must be angry at someone, blame Melly. I'll explain it later."

Sean tucked the ribbon back into the end of his gauntlet. His sight shifted to the other side of the grand stand for a moment, the irritation in his eyes softened and he turned away quickly. William risked a glance to where he was looking and was not surprised to see Annlise watching quietly, her hands on her lap worrying a piece of red ribbon between her fingers— the same color that Adrian was displaying on his own arm.

"No!" Simon groaned, echoed by the crowd, as Galan landed hard on his back. Richard had just doubled Aberdoir's score. He raised his shield in victory, turning toward the grand stand to offer a salute to his mother and waving his blue ribbon for Laurel.

"Well done, darling!" Bryndah called, waving. "Win your grandfather's sword for your father!"

He bowed in reply, then trotted not to Aberdoir's but to Stonehaven's stable.

"Where are you going?" Thomas called to him. Richard ignored his father, keeping his back conspicuously turned from him.

"If I win it, it shall not be for Father," he called toward Bryndah, then turned to Galan who was just arriving back to his team mates. "Well met, sir," Richard said, extending a hand.

"Indeed." Galan growled, reluctantly accepting Richard's gracious gesture. "Will," he continued, struggling to catch his breath. "You're next. You need three runs to tie the score. I'm afraid I lost too much ground for you to take the lead for us."

"Three?" William groaned. "I had hoped one humiliation would have been sufficient."

"Och, you can handle Thomas, lad," Sean said, grinning. "After all, he's only lace and velvet, and you are a ruffian."

William smiled at that, despite the knot that was growing in his stomach. The trumpet sounded. William galloped toward the stand and bowed to Lord Edward. Mehlyndia stood and waved yet another ribbon for him to take. He had to strain against his armor to reach it but he managed to keep smiling. Laurel waved but did not offer a ribbon. Instead she tugged at her sleeve as if to gesture to his own shirt. He moved the horse toward her trying not to seem too obvious, as he asked, "The shirt?"

"Aye," she said. "Good luck."

He grinned, feeling somehow more confident and amused at the notion that Elinor and Laurel had seemingly gifted him with magic undergarments.

Thomas trotted up alongside, to offer his own tribute to the duke and accept a token from his wife. She stood and leaned over the rail holding a fine silk scarf. As he kissed her hand, William saw him glance up toward Annlise, an odd look crossing his face. He gestured to Bryndah to lean to him, then whispered something to her. She turned to look at Annlise and the same startled expression crossed her face. She leaned over and said something to Annlise, with the catlike smile William had learned to distrust. Annlise's hand went to the silver necklace she wore. She flushed, whispering something back.

Bryndah, leaned back to Thomas. "She says it was her sister's. It certainly does look like the knot Rebbeca wore."

"Of course," Thomas replied, seeming satisfied.

What is that all about? William wondered.

"Gentlemen, greet please," Edward said, standing at the podium.

William turned to face his brother. Thomas flashed a falsely charming smile and removed his right glove, extending his hand. William removed his glove as well and grasped Thomas' hand, not turning his gaze away from his brother's eyes.

"May the best prevail... brother," Thomas said, closing his hand vise-like around William's.

William did not flinch and closed his own hand even tighter around his brother's.

"Indeed. Godspeed."

Thomas winced almost imperceptibly as William slowly released his grasp.

The caller cried, "Take your marks!"

William lowered his visor and galloped to the end of his ramp. The squire readied the lance for him. The visor made it impossible to see anything but his opponent at the end of the row, the crowd now invisible to him. His breathing echoed loudly within the helmet. Star stamped her hooves impatiently as he grasped the lance.

The flag went down and he held his breath as he charged. Thomas leaned on his saddle, his lance coming straight and true. William closed his eyes as he'd done when facing Vigo, hoping his luck would hold. When the lances collided, he was nearly thrown from his horse with Thomas' lance landing hard against his shield, shattering to splinters.

William managed to remain on the saddle, though he struggled to keep his balance. His own lance had missed its mark and remained miserably intact in his hand.

"Point, Aberdoir!" the caller cried.

The visor blinded him again but he was glad of it as he did not want to see the disappointment on his teammates' faces. He could see Thomas preparing his next lance, and he could see the tip of that lance did not seem as blunt as the one on the end of his own.

"Squire," William said, lifting the visor to speak with the lad.

"Aye, sir?"

"Who prepared the lances for Aberdoir?"

"They have their own squire, sir." The lad squinted, looking in Thomas' direction. "Bloody hell, I see what you mean. They're using sharps."

"Is that allowed?" William asked, startled.

"Aye but it's not very sportsman like, if you ask me. Sit tight an' I'll be right back." He waved a yellow flag, calling for a pause, then ran off to where the weapons were stored.

William glared at his brother.

Thomas lifted his visor, grinning like a snake. "Not afraid, are you?" he called, taunting. The crowd responded with a mix of cheers and hisses.

"I'm not afraid of you!" William called back just as the squire returned with a sharp lance. It was heavier and more unwieldy than the blunts but also better balanced in his grip. "Thank you, lad."

"Aim for his elbow, Will. It will put him off balance," the

squire said, with a wink.

"And keep my eyes open." William added, more to himself. He flipped down the visor and positioned the lance. The crowd quieted as the flag was dropped.

William charged, struggling to keep the lance balanced and straight. Thomas rode fast and hard. The tip of his lance looked like only a small dot and William realized only at the last moment that his brother was not aiming for his shield or even his breastplate but directly at his helmet. William was forced to take the defensive move, raising his shield just in time to deflect Thomas' lance from piercing his helmet.

The crowd erupted again in a mixture of excitement and disappointment depending on which side they sat. When he got to the end of the ramp, he lifted the visor angrily.

"Foul!" William called. "That was deliberate!"

The crowd hushed as Edward stood and glared toward Thomas.

Thomas lifted his visor and bowed apologetically toward Lord Edward. "It was not deliberate, my lord."

Edward scowled, "Point Stonehaven! Foul deduction, Aberdoir!"

The crowd cheered.

"I will have that sword, whelp!" Thomas called over the noise of the crowd. "And all else that is rightly mine!"

"Not today!" William hollered back and readied the lance, taking his mark and leaving his visor up.

"Will! Don't!" he heard Sean's voice calling. Galan as well, was calling for him to put the visor down but William was determined he would see clearly and not leave his aim to chance.

The flag was lowered and he charged, holding the lance true

and straight. Thomas came on fast, his own visor down and his lance once again aimed not at William's shield but his now unprotected head.

"Not today, you bastard." William growled to himself as he charged, unflinching toward his brother. "Blessed Mother, guide me!"

As the two met, he raised his own shield and planted the pointed tip of his lance squarely against Thomas' gilded breast plate, knocking his brother to the ground. The wooden shaft of his lance shattered nearly to the pommel. As he reached the end of the ramp, he saw that Thomas' lance had pierced through his own shield, the deadly point lodged in the metal only inches from his head.

"Point Stonehaven!" Edward called, to the delight of the home town crowd.

William raised his arm in victory as he galloped back toward his team mates.

"Well done, lad!" Galan congratulated him. "But never, *ever* raise that visor again!"

"What the bloody hell were you thinking, lunk?" Sean bellowed, running up with an angry crease in his brow.

"I couldn't see," William said simply, dismounting from the horse.

Sean shook his head, then his face lit up in laughter. "Well done."

"You're up, Sean." Ewan said, handing Sean his helmet. "Will here raised the score for us but you still need to win at least one round. Win two and that sword'll be yours, lad," he added slyly, as if trying not to allow William to hear.

Sean nodded his understanding, then mounted and readied

for his run against Adrian. He set his jaw as he trotted to the middle of the ring. Adrian met him in the middle for the customary greeting of the rivals. The two men glared, bringing the horses close to each other. The crowd hushed, seeming to sense the personal conflict that was happening between these two riders.

Annlise stood in her spot, clutching the red ribbon with one hand, the other she placed on her sternum. It was difficult to tell which man she was concentrating on, as the two were so close as to almost occupy the same space.

After a moment of heavy silence, a murmur started worming through the crowd. Wagers began to be called. Sean and Adrian held their place, neither moving to their ramps.

"You took something from me, boy." Adrian growled, his odd golden eyes stared unblinking at Sean. "But you will lose everything here."

"I took nothing," Sean growled. "And I shall not lose."

"I have already re-taken her." Adrian leered, grinning. "And she did not protest."

"You lie!" Sean growled.

"I warn you. I care nothing for this little contest. I care not if I am disqualified for running my lance through your pathetic rusted armor. She will witness it all and I shall cast her and her bastard out if she comes crying to your side— which undoubtedly she shall."

Sean moved closer, resisting the impulse to reach out and pull Adrian from his horse. "I should have killed you when I had the chance. I shall not hesitate again."

* * *

"Gentleman!" Edward bellowed. "Take your places or you shall both forfeit!"

William released the breath he hardly realized he was holding when Sean finally turned to take his place on the ramp. He looked toward Annlise who had not moved from her pose. *Charm him well, lass, if that is what you're doing.*

As the flag dropped, Annlise raised high the hand with the red ribbon.

Sean let out a war cry as he kicked in, pushing Hawk to charge, his lance straight and level. Adrian raced toward him, his lance also level though just at the moment of impact, the tip turned sharply aiming toward Sean's helmet. The crowd gasped and cheered as Sean's shield deflected the attack deftly.

When the two reached the ends of their ramps, again the crowd gasped. Before Sean had had a chance to turn, Adrian had already reared his horse and was charging back down the ramp. Sean had no time to turn and raise his lance.

"Sean! Shield!" William cried out.

Sean turned just in time to bring his lance across, sending Adrian's lance flying from his hand. The hunter raised his now empty lance hand, revealing the spiked gauntlet he wore. He swung his fist catching Sean's helmet, nearly knocking him from his horse.

Screams of 'foul' and 'cheat' rang through the crowd and Edward was on his feet.

Annlise called out the name of the Blessed Mother in the old language. William looked toward her in time to understand the charm she cast as she dropped the red ribbon and began to grind it beneath her heel.

"Remove him!" Edward called as all of Stonehaven's guards rushed the field, surrounding Adrian's horse and pulling him from the saddle.

Sean was still in his saddle, standing away from the commotion. He slowly removed his helmet, revealing a purple gash on his cheek where the spike had gone through. The helmet fell to the ground as he started to totter.

William dropped his shield and threw off his helmet and ran toward his friend as fast as his cumbersome armor would allow. He reached Sean just as he began to fall forward. He tried to catch him, panicking that the armor would make it impossible for him to prevent his friend from hitting the ground. However, Sean seemed somehow weightless as William easily guided him from the horse and gently to the gravel. It was then he knew that Sean, too, had been given help, as a tattered red ribbon fell from his gauntlet.

William glanced toward Annlise, but she had vanished in the mayhem. Even Edward had joined the fray. William sat on the ground, keeping Sean protected from the chaos until he could be carried from the field.

"Sean? Lad?"

To William's profound relief, Sean blinked and looked up at him. His eyes were slightly crossed, there was blood on the side of his face and he looked as though he'd been used as the practice dummy for the melee but beneath it all, there was a slow grin spreading.

"Sean? Are you well?"

"No," Sean said through his odd grin. "I think I'm dead."

"You're not dead," William said, wanting to laugh with relief.

"But you're looking ugly."

Edward was suddenly crouching next to William. "Is he hurt?"

"Just dazed," William said, hoping he was right.

"Sean? Do you see me?" Edward asked, examining Sean's wayward line of vision.

"All two of you, Ed .... my Ed lord... "

Edward chuckled, giving Sean a gentle tap on the cheek. "And both of us are relieved." He turned, whistling sharply and motioned for the cart to be brought. "Stay with him," he said, giving William a clap on the back.

Edward stood and turned to the crowd with a smile, thrusting both arms up, his thumbs in the air. The crowd burst into cheers and whistles as Edward made his way, smiling, back to the grand stand. Laurel had scooped Duncan up into her arms and the little lad was soon sandwiched in a group hug between Laurel, Elinor and Agnes.

Once settled on the cart, Sean managed to sit, his feet dangling off the end. Half of his face was covered in blood, drawing gasps of concern from the ladies in the crowd and hoots of admiration from the men. He raised Laurel's blue ribbon, waving it high as proof of his survival.

"Am I waving in the right direction?" he asked through his half dazed grin.

"Aye, the ladies are all waving back." William assured him.

"Is Annlise still there?"

William hesitated before he answered. "I dinnae see her, lad." He scanned the crowd, realizing that it was not only Annlise who was not to be seen but it seemed the entirety of the Aberdoir entourage had left the stand. "Edward is about to make an announcement."

"I hope I did not lose too many points."

Edward quieted the crowd. A page hurried up, whispering something urgently. Edward stood back, astonished. The page shrugged, as if in apology for bringing bad news. Curious mutters wormed through the crowd. Edward leaned low, giving the page some instructions. The lad nodded, then turned and hurried to the score keeper's platform. The man nodded and readied the board.

Edward called through the horn, "Aberdoir concedes! Points awarded to Sir Sean Wilbrun for staying on the saddle and disarming an aggressor without resorting to treachery. Stonehaven shall receive the purse! There is a tie for first place between Sean Wilbrun and William Fylbrigge. Since Aberdoir has withdrawn, I choose to close the games here. The melee will have to wait for another day." The crowd shared groans of disappointment. "But the banquet is quite another matter and shall take place later this evening as planned."

The crowd erupted again, ribbons and flowers fluttered onto the arena.

William turned to congratulate his friend on his victory and found Sean had fallen to his back, passed out on the cart with the half smile still on his face. William took hold of his wrist and held it up in salute as the cart was led off the field to the waning sounds of cheers.

Chapter 18

"**A** CHEER FOR OUR champions!" Ewan called, raising his mug. Simon, Isaac, and Galan stood, as Sean and William entered the tavern. They had finally slipped away from the formality of Edward's banquet. Sean was moving a little slowly but was still able to bow appreciatively to his friends.

"Let's see the glitters," Simon said.

"See what?" William asked, innocently, turning his pockets inside out. "I've nothing that glitters. Ah, you must mean..." He gestured toward Sean's hip.

Sean grinned and slid the spectacular sword from the scabbard on his hip, displaying the hilt over his elbow in a knightly fashion. The lads gawked, impressed at the finely honed edge and mirror like shine.

"I still cannae believe he gave it to me," Sean said, sliding the sword carefully back into the scabbard. "It should be yours, Will."

William shook his head. "No. You earned it. Wear it proudly and use it wisely."

"Did you see the look on old Thomas when Edward gave it to you?" Simon laughed drawing a long sip of his ale.

"If looks were arrows, you'd be a dead man, Sean," Ewan chimed in.

"Och, but it wasn't Sean he was givin' the evil look to," Isaac pointed out and leaned over the table, looking closely at William. "He were sending those arrows at you, lad."

"You noticed that, did you?"

"Would have thought it be Sean he'd gone after," Simon said, wiping the foam from his mouth.

"Are you jestin'?" Galan laughed. "He saw what our Seany is like when he's riled, aye? Made right quick work of that sodden hunter. You done us proud, lad," he said, slapping Sean on the shoulder, nearly knocking the ale from his hand.

"I just wish we'd caught the bastard before he disappeared. Damnedest thing I ever saw, that. You saw it too, dinnae you, Simon?"

"Aye, Ewan, I saw it. Not that I'm likely to admit it, but—" He crossed himself casually. "If I were the superstitious type, I'd say he... nah, ye'd think me daft. Or drunk."

William glanced at Sean, who was staring intently into his mug.

"But you are daft and drunk, Simon, so just tell us what you think it is you didn't see that you did," Isaac said, motioning for the serving lass to bring another pitcher.

Simon leaned over, gesturing all to crouch closely. "He were right there in front of me. I were practically on his heels. And then," he snapped his fingers, "gone. Jus' like that. Ewan, tell 'em."

Sean looked up then. "Vanished as if into the mist, did he?"

"Aye," Ewan said, his eyes wide as Simon's. "Had he not seen it too, I'd deny it to m' death. Into the mist."

"Was anyone standing near him?" Sean ask, calmly rolling his mug between his palms.

"Sean—" William began.

"Well, now tha' I think of it. That lass... uh, but she were jus' standin'— come to think of it—" Ewan sat back, scratching his head. "Did I see her? I am suddenly nae certain if I did. Did you see her, Si?"

Simon took a swig of his ale and sat back. "Now tha' you say som'in'... aye, she was there. Standing like a statue, wi' her hand like this—" He placed his hand on his chest. "I near run into her but then—" He shrugged. "I think I've had too much."

William drank his ale quietly. Sean said nothing, still looking into his mug.

Galan was the first to stand, stretching his back. "Well, lads. It's been a long, long day and tomorrow will be early. Be on time, you three," he said, pointing to Simon, Ewan and Isaac. "I'm givin' Seany a holiday. He earned it."

Sean waved, not looking up.

"Are you going after Tearlach tomorrow?" William asked.

Galan shook his head. "If it were up to me, I surely would, but Edward said no."

"What?" Sean and William said together.

Galan sat back on the bench, leaning close. "Edward says to let it go. The man is a hunter, lads. Edward's got no authority on him, no matter what the sodden bastard does."

"But he cannae just get away with what he did! He tried to kill Sean!" William growled. "You have to go after him!"

"Not without orders," Galan said with a shrug.

"I do not need orders," William said, looking Galan in the eye.

"Lad, you do not know what the hunters are about—" Simon began.

William slammed his hand on the table giving them all a start. "I know far better than anyone of you what the hunters are about!" He looked each man in the eye, speaking in a low, angry tone that surprised even himself. But he held their attention as he spoke.

"When I was six, I watched an innocent woman burn to death because someone told the hunters an unfounded lie. I see good people turn in their neighbors and friends because they feared the hunters would come for them instead. They kill indiscriminately, they hurt people for sport, and they take what they wish because people like Edward would rather hold their wealth and their tongues than speak out and tell the truth about them and bring some justice back to this world!" William stood. "*I* am not afraid!"

The lads looked at each other, none knowing what to say.

"Do you plan to rid the world of hunters, alone?" Simon asked.

"He won't have to," Sean said quietly, placing his right hand on the back of William's hand. "I'm with you, Will."

"And I," Isaac said, adding his hand to Sean's.

Ewan and Simon exchanged glances, then nodded, adding their hands to the pile. "Us too."

"Galan?" William asked.

He hesitated a moment, then placed his hand on the pile. "I'll offer this. My silence. I have no idea what you lads are discussing. Should Edward ask, I will keep it to myself."

"Thank you," William said.

"Will you see us off tomorrow?" Simon asked.

Galan shook his head. "I cannae. I have a new trainee." He shook his head, making a scoffing sort of laugh. "You'll never believe who, Will."

William sat down again, shaking his head in wonder. "Richard Fylbrigge?" he asked simply.

Galan grinned, nodding. "Himself. He's to start training for a post in Edward's guard."

"Guard?" Ewan nearly choked on his ale. "He's a nobleman!"

"Aye, well; Edward said he's mine. He'll not be getting any soft treatment, I can assure you."

Galan stood and stretched again, then waved to the lads as he made his way out of the tavern. They soon followed, leaving Sean and Will to walk back to Drumoak alone.

"What are you planning to do about Annlise?"

Sean shook his head, leaving the question unanswered. "What are you planning to do about Mehlyndia?"

"What?" William asked surprised.

"You better move quickly, lad; the suitors are lining up. I saw Vigo making eyes."

"Well, I'll just have to knock him off his horse again," William chuckled. "But I shall have to borrow that big sword to do it."

"You can't have it," Sean said, a grin sliding up one side of his face. "It's busy."

"Doin' what?"

"Knocking Richard Fylbrigge off *his* horse. Ye seen 'im makin' eyes a' Laurel. The sot."

"You're drunk, you know."

"So are you."

"Aye."

Epilogue

1607

The letter was brief and meticulous in its wording. He read it over three times, being certain not to be too bold, yet not vague in his meaning.

My dear friends,

The time has come for us to put aside our differences and come together for the greater good. Our common benefactor can no longer be trusted. As you know, he has usurped my birth right, in favor of my younger brother. I am prepared to offer my allegiance, in return for the elimination of this obstacle. Together, we shall divide the spoils amongst us.

Loyally yours,
T F de Aberdoir

Satisfied, he powdered the ink, folded the parchment and placed his ring upon the seal.

Excerpts from William's Journal

7 January 1607

We are underway and a more disorderly lot this realm has never seen. I wish Father had given us a day to sleep away the haze left from the Twelfth Night festivities before insisting we move on to Kylkannon. How he could be awake and bright in his eyes this morn is mystery. The ale was freely flowing, as was the special malt from the oak casks. Ah, the aqua vita! I am not certain that is a fitting name for it as I feel half dead, and probably look as much, judging by the sniggers the lads are sharing when they think I am not paying attention. Sots.

The weather is cold, but the snow has been late in coming this year. If our luck holds, we shall be well south of Grampian Moor before the weather turns against us. Why Edward is insisting on traveling in the winter is another mystery. He must have his reasons. I'm too cold and tired to wonder on it anymore tonight.

Simon and Ewan have the first watch. Sean and Isaac are to take second. I was excused from watch, though I intend to sit up with Sean and send Isaac to bed. It will give me an opportunity to talk. He seemed put off when Edward announced my betrothal to Mehlyndia and I would like to know his mind.

William

15 January 1607

Snow. And snow and snow!

More than a week lost while we sit stranded. Of all the places on God's good Earth, why must we be stalled in Aberdoir? The place is still a dreary, colorless hulk and cold as a crypt, even with the fire burning in the great hall. Oddly, I seem to be the only one to notice the cold.

Our 'host' has been gracious enough and Edward has wanted for nothing. It is rather amusing to watch Thomas fawn and bow, and it is obvious Edward has been toying with him in demanding that I be treated with the same regard and the sentries be given the finest chambers instead of being housed in the barracks behind the stable. On Edward's request, our 'gracious hostess' has even given up her apartment to Simon and Ewan. The room in which I spent my youth Edward has deemed too small and out of the way to be suitable for quartering, so he has housed the dogs there. Sean and I have found the guest chamber to be too confining, so Edward allowed us to take over the master's suite. I find I can scarcely conceal my glee in pissing in Thomas' fireplace. And yet, for all its dubious comfort, I shall be glad when the snow has gone and we can leave Aberdoir and move on with this tour.

I have been successful thus far in avoiding any contact with the dragon though Sean has not been so fortunate. Bryndah seems to have made sport of arranging for Annlise to be his primary servant, making it an awkward time for both of them. Sean, for his part, has been courteous, and made the attempt to engage the lass in conversation but she will have none of it. I cannot remember Annlise being so cold hearted and it makes me wonder if there is more to her aloofness than a simple disinterest in Sean. I suppose I shall keep wondering, as Sean is not interested in discussing it with me.

Alas, the sky has turned leaden again and the wind is changing. Another storm. It seems we shall be here a while longer.

I'm feeling hungry. I think I shall order a barrel of apples to be brung. For all of us.

William

23 January 1607

Sean could not take another day in closed quarters. It did not take much coaxing on his part to convince me to go out, even with this blasted storm swirling. We made it only as far as the stable but this gave us the chance to talk that I've been waiting for. It did not go as I expected.

He loves her, he's admitted that much, though I had no doubt that he did. He would have her if she would but look his way. I made the mistake of jesting that he should simply have Edward ask our host to release her to us, that she may go traveling with us. I've never before seen the look Sean gave me then and for a moment, I thought he was going to strike me, and rightly so. "She's not property to be haggled and bartered for!" he told me. It was then he told me the rest. Annlise has a son not quite three years old being raised quietly among the servants' children. Sean would not say more about the lad and the look in his eye warned me not to prod him for the answer I already suspect is true on the identity of the child's sire. I have never seen Sean so angry— or so hurt.

I tried to turn the conversation to something more pleasant and asked him formally to stand with me at my wedding. Another unexpected reaction. He turned on me and grabbed me by both shoulders and looked me hard in the eye and told me if I had any sense at all in my head I would run, long and fast and far, from Mehlyndia and women in general. "Of all the evil the devil ever sent us, Will, there be none as vile as a woman."

Well, that would explain Sean's reaction to my betrothal I suppose. I usually take his advice without hesitation but on this, I think I shall follow my own heart and look forward to my wedding just the same. Now there shall be a grand day.

William

1 February 1607

My Dearest Mehlyndia,

The snow has been falling for weeks but I am kept warm in the thought of you. How is it that I have been so blessed that you have consented so willingly to be my bride. A day does not pass that I do not have your sweet smile in my thoughts and loath the time it will take me to return to Drumoak to stand with you. But this is time well spent, my love. I am learning well from Father, and he seems well pleased with my progress. I am privy to his counsel and shall be set well when this tour has ended. Shall you still be pleased with me when I am more than a humble fosterling?

It has been a full month since last we were together but that is one less month to wait. I shall count the days like pearls on a string until the last day of August brings us together again, and forever.

My love forever,
Your William.

1 February 1607

Dear Laurel,

Nothing is going as I had hoped. We are still stranded in Aberdoir. The place still stinks but at least I have better lodging. Could you please ask Elinor to send some things to me with the next page? I have a need for some chicory. No, I will not tell you, so put that pout away. And no, I am not going to get into trouble. I promised to behave and so far, you will be pleased to know, I've not incited any violence on the part of our host— though I very nearly drove Sean to murder. Thoughts of suicide to escape the tedium of the place are also a constant worry.

I am bored to distraction, Laurel. What I would not give to have you here to keep me company and keep me from taking myself too seriously. Who would have known I would find affairs of state to be so blasted tedious. But Edward seems to think I've a head for it. Maybe I do, who knows? Still, if the truth is told, I would far prefer being back at Drumoak, exploring the crypt and raiding Elinor's pantry with you, than be sitting here pretending to be a nobleman. Thank the Blessed Mother, I have my lute to make the long nights more bearable. I've even taught the lads a few tunes. Simon and Ewan are not bad singers but Isaac and Sean... well, Edward has dubbed them 'trained monkeys'. You would enjoy it, I'm certain.

I look forward to hearing from you. I miss our arguments and games. Please do not forget to send the chicory. And my wool trews! And some of your berry tart. And whatever else you care to send.

I miss you,
Will

P.S. I take it I was right— the silver dish works better than the looking glass to see what's going on. I am being careful, so you can stop staring at me.

29 March 1607

We are at last shut of Aberdoir, though our arrival at Kylkannon was hardly what we expected. Something has stirred the water. Our reception by Lord Ambrose was less than gracious; in fact, it was almost hostile. He is demanding concessions from Edward about trade routes and taxes, things we had thought were already settled. Even more curious— two of Lord Ogham of Lothian's earls have joined ranks with Ambrose. Our allies seem to be shifting their loyalties to Lothian.

I am to meet with Drunbalk and Wesley tomorrow to begin new negotiations. Me. Father must be daft.

I shall use the chicory Laurel sent, and pray the charm is the right one. There are times I wish I could ask Sean his advice on these matters, but the last thing I can imagine asking him is which charm or chant to which Goddess would get me through the meetings. How I wish I could use Annlise's charm to just disappear again.

Annlise saw us off this morning. No one has inquired of her to name the father of her son, nor has she offered to tell. The assumption seems to be the child is a product of her abduction. This could be good for her as it released her from her betrothal without shame— the blame shall be placed on her unknown abductor.

Adrian Tearlach has been conspicuously absent from Aberdoir— not that I shed tears of grief for missing him. I only find it curious, and disconcerting. I would not have expected him to go away so completely after the way he dogged me through the woods and the threats he made to Sean. I asked Sean if he thought Adrian was gone for good. He said the beast always comes back for its prize. I can only hope he's wrong.

William

* * *

Preview

The story contiues in *My Brother's Keeper.*

Prologue

28 August 1607

"COME ON, SEAN! Move!" William Fylbrigge kicked his stallion, Cirrus, into a full gallop, praying he'd reach the meetinghouse in Kylkannen before the sentence was carried out. Close on William's heels, Sean Wilbrun raced behind, more interested in saving his friend from his own reckless crusade than in saving the woman who was about to be burned alive.

"Slow down, Will!"

"This path is too long." Without warning, William turned sharply into the thicket and straight through the untamed underbrush of the forest pushing Cirrus to his limits.

"What are you doing?" Sean yelled from behind, but turned to follow without hesitation. "Watch it!" he shouted, as William ducked just in time to avoid a low hanging branch. "You can't save her if you get yourself killed!"

Oblivious to Sean's frantic warnings, William flew through the forest, dodging jagged rocks and brambles, even leaping a treacherous gorge over a raging river far below. With only William's safety in mind, and giving no thought to his own, Sean stayed close at his companion's side, racing his own horse, Hawk, matching William's flight leap for leap. He knew if William believed there was even the smallest hope to save the woman from the death-fire, he would take it without a second thought or die trying. It was Sean's duty— no matter how foolhardy the plan— to follow William and keep him alive.

Another sharp turn and a jump through a veil of hanging moss and they were at last free of the forest. They galloped into Kylkannen shire just as the doors to the meetinghouse were flung open and a boisterous crowd spilled into the square.

"There!" William hollered, then gave one more kick and drove Cirrus full charge directly toward the meetinghouse with Hawk nose to nose beside him. William reined in hard and jumped from the saddle before Cirrus had even come to a stop. Sean halted and leapt from Hawk just as quickly, not taking time to tether the reins, the blind determination on his friend's face moving him to leave the horses to wander if they chose.

A milling crowd swarmed about a raised platform surrounded by bundles of peat and kindling. They chanted and cheered as two hooded men bound a terrified young woman to a stake in the center of the platform.

"Burn, witch, burn! Burn, witch, burn!"

"We're too late!" Sean called rushing to keep up with William.

An expression of wild glee crossed William's face. "No, we're not, Sean. The torchbearers are not there yet!" The glee turned fierce as he burst through the wooden doors of the meetinghouse to confront the woman's accuser.

"Lord Ambrose Woodhall! What right have you?" William called out, as he pushed his way through a throng of spectators, ignoring their startled gapes.

Sean steeled his nerve, and tried not to notice Lord Woodhall's horde of mercenary witch hunters standing armed and scattered throughout the crowd, their faces hidden under dark hoods. His took his position at William's back ready to pull his lord and friend out should any of the armed hunters move on them. But even if the hunters did attack, Sean knew that William Fylbrigge would never turn and flee.

"Fylbrigge, stand down!" Woodhall yelled, red-faced, clearly outraged at William's bold intrusion. "You have no voice here."

"I have voice enough to call you a liar!" William said, defiantly pushing his way past the hunters who were moving toward him, his sight set squarely on Woodhall alone. "Are you ready to condemn an innocent woman for the sake of your manly pride?"

"Manly— how dare you!" Woodhall glared, angrily. "The trial has ended. The sentence has been given. The witch confessed!"

"Under torture!" William countered. "She only confessed to stop the pain. Any fool could see that."

Woodhall narrowed his eyes, and placed his hand menacingly on the hilt of his sword. "Her crime has been proven."

"She refused your bed," William shouted, reaching for his own blade. "That is her only crime."

Several hunters began to inch toward him, their swords drawn.

Sean put his hand on his friend's shoulder and spoke in his ear. "Will, we are far outnumbered here. It may be best to leave now while we still can."

"No, Sean. She's innocent!" William answered, keeping his eyes fixed squarely on Woodhall, as his rival raised his sword. William reciprocated with his own blade. The two stood, eyes locked, waiting for the other to move.

Sean held his sword at the ready behind William. "I hope you know what you're doing," he grumbled under his breath.

"I have had more than enough of you, Fylbrigge," Woodhall growled, and took several steps forward. "It is insult enough that you have wrested my trade routes from me, you will not now call me a liar in my own estate. Be gone now, or I swear by all that is holy—"

"Holy!? There is nothing holy in what you are doing!" William would not allow him to change the subject. "Three burnings of innocent women are not enough for you, that you must seek a fourth?"

"Confessions!" Woodhall hissed.

"Coerced!" William countered.

The hunters circled in closely. Sean spun on his heel, taking a defensive back-to-back position behind William.

"I'm on your back, but we won't last long in this room," Sean whispered keeping his eyes on the hunters, while mentally planning their escape route.

"Stand ready," William told Sean, quietly.

"What would you have me do, Fylbrigge?" Woodhall raised a brow and grinned. "As I said, they all confessed. The law is the law and the prescription for her transgression is clear. I do not suffer the witch to live under my authority!" He took a step closer, now standing within striking distance.

"She's not a witch and you know it. What is your price?"

"Price?"

"Yes. What is it you want that will buy her freedom."

After a moment, Woodhall growled his demand through clenched teeth, "I want my trade routes restored!"

"Give the order to release her, and you shall have what you ask."

"Will!" Sean spoke under his breath. "You can't throw away

the treaty like that."

Woodhall narrowed his eyes and examined William's face closely. "You would cross Lord Edward of Stonehaven so easily, Fylbrigge? Will you truly risk his displeasure only days before you wed his daughter?"

"The girl is innocent. Give the order!"

"And if I do not agree to free the wench?"

"You lose. No trade routes through your county. Besides, what do you gain by allowing her to die? Pride? Your manhood vindicated? Hardly seems a logical bargain." William took a step closer, fully closing the distance between them, his unblinking eyes locked on his rival.

"What is there in this for *you*, Fylbrigge? Do you fancy her? Is she to be your last conquest before you take the vow?"

William grinned and shook his head. "Hardly. I gain nothing from this. I expect I shall lose face with Lord Edward and will most likely deal with repercussions from him. I may even be disowned. Perhaps he'll withdraw his daughter's hand from me, much to my despair. But I would risk it all to know the woman you have falsely accused will live. Send her from this shire if you wish, send her to Stonehaven or beyond if the sight of her troubles you so." William's voice grew softer, yet controlled. He had the knack for getting what he wanted by making the other man feel the victor. It was for that reason Edward trusted him to negotiate trade treaties in the first place. "Give the order to free her and reclaim your trade routes. In the bargain, take the satisfaction of knowing it will surely be my own undoing."

From outside, the sound of the chanting crowd grew louder. "Burn, witch, burn! Burn, witch, burn!"

For an instant, Woodhall looked away from William and

glanced through the open door to the gathered crowd outside. The torchbearers stood ready waiting for his order to light the death-fire. William watched Woodhall's face closely as he mulled over the proposition. The rival earl had lost control of a good deal of his county due to William's negotiations, and even Sean could feel how it must gall the man that in order to regain control of his territories, he would have to relent, yet again. However, Sean knew that William was confident that the odds on his gamble—playing on Woodhall's famous lust for power—were in his favor, and that the pompous ass was not so foolish as to throw away the opportunity before him. But, the longer Woodhall mulled his decision, the faster Sean's confidence in his advantage began to wither. *We'll never make it out of here.* But just as Sean began to believe the bluff would be called, Woodhall relaxed his stance and lowered his blade.

William stood firm, his blade still raised as the hunters surrounding him made a slight forward motion. Sean mimicked their advance, raising his blade slightly. The hunters glanced to Woodhall for orders. The earl raised his hand slowly, signaling them to stand down. They immediately fell back. William lowered his blade slightly, but Sean held his ready position, still at William's back.

"Give the order."

"I have your word?" Woodhall asked carefully, watching William's sword hand.

William reached over his shoulder without taking his eyes off Woodhall. "Sean?" Sean took a small scroll from his tunic and handed it over his shoulder to William. "You have my word. The scroll is yours." He handed it to Woodhall.

Woodhall opened the scroll. It *was* the treaty he had signed only the day before—the treaty turning his key trade routes away from his county in return for limited protection from Edward's armies. William had made the deal seem advantageous during his proposal, but when all was said and done, Woodhall had given away far more control than he had gained. He looked up over the scroll to William, grinned, and then tore it into small pieces.

From the corner of his eye, Sean watched the shreds float to the floor, his heart beginning to race with fear that he had allowed William to lead them both into certain disaster.

William did not waver. His voice to remain steady and confident. "Give the order."

Woodhall stood back on his heels, arrogantly laughing out loud. "Why? I have what I need."

"Sean?"

Sean reached into his tunic again and pulled out another scroll and handed it to William in the same manner as before. Woodhall stopped laughing as he watched the relay.

It was William's turn to be arrogant. "I'm not that naive. This is the binding treaty; the one bearing Edward's seal. Give the order, and you shall have it."

Woodhall snorted, glowering at the parchment.

William allowed himself a satisfied half-grin, knowing he had reclaimed his advantage.

Woodhall turned to the hunter closest to him. "Release her," he muttered irritably with a dismissive wave of his hand, then, scowling, he held his hand open. "May I have that scroll now?"

William watched the hunter walk past him toward the door. Not wanting to turn his back on Woodhall, he asked over his shoulder, "Sean, can you see?"

"Aye." Sean answered. William tightened his grip on his sword, holding his breath, until he heard Sean say, "She's free."

"May I?" Woodhall extended his hand higher in William's direction.

"By all means. Pleasure to do business with you." With a twist of his wrist, William handed the scroll to Woodhall, then bowed and smiled politely with a defiant glint in his eye. Sean grabbed him by the shoulder and the two fled the meetinghouse.

William looked briefly in the direction of the young woman's family as he ran past them toward the edge of town, gratified to see the relieved expressions of joy on their faces as they hurried her away from the odious pile of kindling.

It occurred to Sean, they would probably never know how she had come to be released. *Just as well,* he thought, *he doesnae need any attention about this.* He looked around quickly for the horses, relieved to see them grazing not far from the edge of the woods. *I'll just be happy to get away from here in one piece.*

They flew to the horses, each mounting with a leap into the saddles. Though no hunters followed them, they kicked into full gallop, charging back through the woods, putting as much ground between them and the town as they could before slowing the horses to walk side by side.

When they had reached the safety of the road leading away from Kylkannen, William sat back on the saddle and relaxed. "Well, I'd say that was a success. I hope the girl has sense enough to leave there. Did you see the look on Woodhall's fat face? I cannae believe we got away with that farce." He laughed, then finally turned too look at Sean. "What?"

Sean reached to his friend and swatted his shoulder with the back of his hand. "You are a madman! You could have gotten yourself killed back there! Worse yet, you could have gotten *me* killed, you lunk!" He laughed heartily, but after a moment, he caught his breath and grew quiet.

"What's wrong, Sean?"

"Aren't you worried that Edward will be angry that you annulled that treaty?"

"Not at all. He never knew I bargained for routes in Kylkannen to begin with. I did that all on my own. The treaty never *officially* existed, so how could it be annulled?"

"What about the seal?"

"You mean this one?" William flashed the signet ring he wore and smiled, completely pleased with himself. "Is it my fault Ambrose can't tell my mark from Edward's?"

"I should have known," Sean laughed, shaking his head. "I swear I spend more time worrying after you for nothing. But must you always do things the hard way?"

William cocked his head and grinned. "Absolutely."

www.ingramcontent.com/pod-product-compliance
Lightning Source LLC
Chambersburg PA
CBHW060145260626
47160CB00001B/122